Trae watched her body language. It spoke volumes, a hurt, broken, and unforgiving form. Never before had he been able to tune himself into a person as he'd done on so many occasions with Reggie. He didn't like what he saw. He caused this and knowing so didn't set well with him. He kept watching, hoping to make eye contact with her. He'd long ago disregarded the voice of the instructor and all of the advice that came with it. Reggie wouldn't so much as acknowledge anything around her.

Reggie had closed herself off from the world around her. With all his might he attempted to communicate with her, not with words, but with his soul and his heart.

Please baby, look at me. I need you. Even if she heard him she wouldn't acknowledge him.

MORE THAN A BARGAIN

ANN CLAY

Genesis Press Inc.

Indigo Love Stories

An imprint Genesis Press Publishing

Indigo Love Stories
c/o Genesis Press, Inc.
1213 Hwy 45 N, 2nd Floor
Columbus, MS 39705

ISBN 1-58571-137-3
Manufactured in the United States of America

First Edition

Visit us at www.genesis-press.com
or call at 1-888-Indigo-1

DEDICATION

In memory of my parents, Christine and Mervin Smith, and my two sisters, Linda Smith and Jessie Kennedy. You're truly missed.

ACKNOWLEDGMENTS

I thank God, for his Blessings are truly remarkable. A very special thank you to Clay, Niki, and Brian for their understanding and unwavering love, my friends Cynthia, Royce, and Greta, who continue to inspire me, and to my birthday crew, I love you ladies.

Thank you Angelique Justin for your patience and your advice. Tevis Taylor and Darlene Lee, thanks so much for burning the midnight oil to help me get here. To my critique group, you ladies are wonderful. I wish you the very best.

Thank you SORMAG, Nubian Chronicles, TimBookTu, and Genesis Press for the opportunity to share my stories.

A special thank you Claudia Owens of EVONS Foundation. And last but not least, to all readers of the heart... thank you!

CHAPTER 1

Reggie rushed from the dressing room and entered the double doors of the girls' gym. She stood at the entrance for several seconds before she eased to the center of the basketball court where twenty-two women stood chattering among themselves. She noticed that most of her competition was new freshmen and transfer students. Only eight dancers from the previous year had returned, including the squad leader, Veronica Price.

Those eight dancers smugly glared down their noses at her and some of the other women. She avoided their direct stare and instead focused her attention on the coach's directions to pull a number, and then record her name in the appropriate slot on the performance sheet.

She mumbled a silent prayer before she stuck her hand into the gold basket to retrieve a number. When she unfolded the square sheet, her heart leaped, and her pulse quickened. She drew the number "one." Reggie nervously scribbled her name in the first slot and accepted the large pin-on number from the coach, then quietly moved to the rear of the gym.

For two years her friends pestered her to try-out for the dance team. She'd always dreamed of dancing for the Tigers, and they knew this was her last chance to make the squad.

"You're a senior Reggie. You won't have another chance," they reasoned.

Now, as she gazed at the paper in her hand, she wondered if she'd made a terrible mistake. Hesitation crept into her consciousness and she felt out of place.

She surveyed her rivals as her eyes strolled from one girl to next. Reggie's classic "brick house" figure was proportionately leaner than most of theirs. Her face was bare and the hair knotted at the top of her head was real, not extensions. She had eighteen years of modern dance, contemporary jazz dance, and ballet instructions. Given her training, Reggie was more than qualified to make the team. She wasn't the glamour girl nor was she one of Veronica's cronies. So, she had two strikes against her to start with.

Veronica and 'her girls', as she called them, wore snug, revealing clothing. Reggie on the other hand wore baggy shirts, shorts, and sweats. Only during dance class did she sport the standard dancewear, and quickly covered up once she was done. She didn't like the attention she got when she was barely dressed. These women didn't seem to mind.

Over the years, she'd worked relentlessly to perfect her techniques. Not only could she out-dance every woman here, given her training and skills, she could easily coach this team. Both, her roommate, Valerie, and dance instructor, Eleanor, thought so. Their strong encouragement was the reason she was here.

"Girl, you can dance circles around those hussies. Anybody can get out there and wiggle their rump. You're only cheating yourself by not auditioning," Valerie coached her.

"That's just it, Val, I'm not trying to dance a circle around them. I would like to become a member of their team," Reggie protested.

"Child pleaassee! They're so phony, when you look up the word 'fake' in Webster's dictionary, it starts out by naming each and everyone of them," Valerie sneered.

Reggie rolled her eyes at her friend's assessment of her potential teammates. She knew that not all the girls were stuck-up or fake, and being on the dance team was a big deal. They were highly favored, and they worked extremely hard to earn their prestige.

"You're crazy, you know that?" Reggie hugged Valerie and gave her a tight squeeze.

"Don't try and suck up to me. Once you get your booty on that team, you won't have no time for me," Val teased her friend.

Reggie wasn't so sure as she stood in line with the others while they listened to more instructions from the coach. She flexed her hands in and out of tight, sweaty fists in order to erase some of the perspiration from her long palms. The butterflies in the pit of her stomach fluttered like a thousand buzzards stalking a fresh carcass.

She struggled with the paper and safety pin they were instructed to pin to the back of their tanks. Some of the girls assisted one another yet none offered to help her, and she didn't bother to ask. Not because she was a snob, but she couldn't quite warm up to any of the girls at that time. This was yet another indication that she didn't necessarily fit into this group. She took another sighing breath.

As her eyes roamed the confines of the small gymnasium, she quickly met the cheering glances of her strongest supporters, her best friend and roommate, Valerie, and their mutual friend Candice. The silent but wild clapping and cheering with animated grins pasted on their faces, elicited a smile a mile wide to the tense thin line, which formed her fully ripe, ruby lips. They seemed to know just how to make her laugh, even in the worst of circumstances. The butterflies dissipated slightly. She smiled broadly in an attempt to reward them for their support.

Her visual pursuit around the gym continued as she glimpsed a few students, family, and friends of the ladies trying-out. Most came to cheer them on, others came to gloat at the potential losers, and yet others, like most of the guys, came to gawk at the barely-dressed women. She hadn't recognized any of the observers until she noticed a small group of football players at the very top of the bleachers.

The cluster of football players huddled in what seemed jovial conversation. They eyed each contestant with peaked interest. Among them was Traekin Brooks. Upon seeing his handsome face, Reggie's heart stumbled then accelerated quickly. It pounded fiercely beneath her soft firm bosom and thumped loudly in her ears. Needless to say his presence in the gym didn't help her already jittery nerves.

The man simply took her breath away the first time she saw him. Until then, she'd only heard things about him. On her tour of the campus, her student-guide talked during the entire tour about how great he was. He was an all-star football and basketball player, he was the Class President, he did this, and he did that. The girl practically wore on her last nerve; that was until she got a glimpse of this magnificent hunk for herself. When she saw him he wore a bright gold and purple T-shirt that contrasted his olive complexion. His eyes were dark, almost black and his smile crooked to one side, revealing straight, white teeth. She fell for him the moment she laid eyes on him; however, he didn't even know she existed. Hopefully, today that would change. Mostly, she just hoped she didn't make a complete fool of herself.

Reggie took a second glance around the gymnasium, peeled away the sweatpants, and then laced up her dance shoes. Valerie and Candice gave her the thumbs up. The fact that they were there helped soothe her rattled nerves. She fidgeted with the strings on her latex tights and sighed before she closed her eyes and began to concentrate on the music.

Once Reggie allowed the vibration of the music to glide up her spine and intertwine with her soul, the smooth and expertly executed moves flowed like a quiet stream down a steep hillside. The smile plastered on her face came naturally. She'd been taught when a smile was too much, almost a sneer, and when it looked fake.

Her eyes lit at each corner as they searched the space out before her. She didn't see anything or anyone in particular; a training technique she'd learned early on. It kept her calm as well as helped her concentrate on the routine. Even though her gaze wasn't focused directly at anyone, it appeared as though she gave each of the faces in the audience an equal proportion of her attention. She'd practice this particular routine so often she could do it in her sleep. Now she performed it with little thought at all.

Traekin and four of his teammates sat at the top of the bleachers to check out the new honeys.

"Whoa, check out number fifteen," Rykard exclaimed. His comment drew their attention to a transfer student wearing the number fifteen on the back of her short, tight, red tank top. Unlike the other ladies who stretched and loosened their shapely bodies in preparation for tryouts, she stood along the wall and eyed her red acrylic nails.

"Dang, Baby got booty," Corey chimed in, referring to her thick rear-end.

"Man, where has she been hiding?" Traekin's eyes honed in on the young provocative woman with her back now turned to them. "How did I miss that," he belted, rubbing both hands together. Her outfit left nothing to the imagination.

Either she is that confident in her abilities or she doesn't care whether she makes this cut or not, he thought.

"Nah, man. You think you can have anything you want on this campus, don't you?" Rykard responded.

"Well, what can I say," Trae bragged. He watched number fifteen ease away from the wall and turn slightly, giving all eyes a full view of her profile.

This girl knows just what to do to get the attention of every guy in the room.

His dark eyes watched her every move as he contemplated if she was worth his time. Unbeknownst to his friends, and many students on campus, Traekin harbored a secret. Most of his playboy image was just that. Not even his best friend knew he was selective about his women. He'd never had problems having any woman he wanted. In fact, Trae knew he could get as much booty as he wanted; when he wanted it. What his friends didn't know was that he never slept with all of the women.

In fact, he only slept with one or two selected women. And he always wore protection, for them and himself. He didn't want or need surprises. He did, however, talk to a lot of women, always on his terms. His smooth talk won them over every time, but he never made it easy for them, which is why he believed they threw themselves at him.

The women not lucky enough to sample his exquisite lovemaking often came back in hopes of getting a piece of Traekin. Most weren't able to hold his interest long enough though. He never connected emotionally with any of them, not that he wanted to anyway. He'd planned to keep his secret because he enjoyed his perceived image.

"I heard Ms. fifteen transferred from some where upstate, Michigan I think," Corey explained.

How does he know so much? Rykard thought.

"Well hello, Ms. Michigan. I'll be your lover any day," Rykard sang.

"Man, you couldn't catch a cold if the germ blew right through you," Trae teased.

"Ah, and you're all that? What makes you think you can?" he asked.

"Hey, what can I say? I can take any one of these babes if I wanted to," Trae challenged.

"Yeah, well twenty bucks says you wouldn't get nowhere with number one," Rykard countered. His attention now centered on Reggie. He'd heard how brothers got their feelings stomped on by her snootiness.

Traekin scanned the gym floor until his eyes rested on the white tank with the number one pinned to the back of it. As he took in the long, slender figure, he remembered seeing her in his Philosophy class. Although she had a pretty face, she hadn't drawn his attention because she looked nothing like the women he favored, bountiful chest, and plenty of booty.

She'd always been covered from neck to toe; still, Traekin could tell she lacked the bumps and curves, which without a doubt turned him on. He watched her as she prepared to perform her routine. She seemed so out of place with the others. She wore baggy sweat pants and sported a form fitting tank top. Her upper body was well defined, as were the flat ripples in her stomach. Trae glanced at the women surrounding her. All the other girls, unlike Reggie, wore a similar tank and snug short shorts that revealed big muscular legs and protruding firm rumps.

His eye strayed to the girl standing next to her. Number twenty. "Ah… now that's the way I like it," he smiled and pointed to the girl sporting the number twenty.

When he glanced back at Reggie, he shook his head.

"Nah man, she's not my type," his eyes still honed on her as he watched her stretch.

"You've got that right!" Corey chimed in. "Word is she don't give up nothing to no one!"

Traekin's right brow lifted with curiosity at Corey's remark.

"That's because she's waiting on me, brothers," Traekin boasted with confidence.

"Like hell she is," Rykard countered. "Twenty bucks says you get nowhere with our little tigress." He proceeded to peel off a twenty from the small roll of bills he'd pulled from his pocket.

Traekin looked at Reggie as she eased down the gray sweat pants. She was more slender than most of his conquests but built with the same intensity. She had a rump right for the picking and beautiful, long legs.

Not too bad after all, he thought.

Traekin watched her glance around the gym. He'd never been one to back away from a challenge, and as he sat in the top bleachers, he could make out the intricate details of her beautiful face.

Not bad, he gazed appreciatively, taking in the total package.

She wouldn't be that much of a challenge. At least she was good on the eyes. It helped that he wouldn't have to pretend he was enjoying her company. He liked being around beautiful women.

"I think she's been hiding the goods, fellows. That's not bad at all," he finally said verbally. Blake and David nodded in agreement.

"Bet," Traekin, grabbed Rykard's pre-offered hand, which sealed the bet.

"Give me a couple of weeks, and I'll have her screaming my name so loudly it'll be heard clear down to New Orleans," he bragged.

"What's the matter, Bro? Don't tell me you're not as good as you say you are," Rykard teased. "Two weeks is a long time for someone with your skills."

"Hey, if she is as tough as Corey claims she is, then a brother might have to melt away that coat of armor with lot's of Trae's charm." To show how confident he was about the whole thing, Trae brushed the fingers of his right hand up and down the front of his shirt, then lifted them to his mouth and blew on them, as you would dice.

He glanced out at the dance floor one more time, just as Reggie began her routine. The smooth, flawless dance steps were executed with ease and precision. The rolling of her upper body and the swirling of her hips gave them a sneak preview of the provocative and sensual passion hidden beneath the steel coat of armor. Traekin bobbed his head up and down as a huge grin graced his handsome face. Just the thought of riding the arch of her curved body beneath his made him crazy.

"Yeah, I've got that and more," he met the smiling eyes of his teammates, after they, too, got another look at the provocative way Reggie moved to the music.

"Corey holds the money," Rykard insisted. "Come on. Bring on the green man! You're always loaded. Hell, if my old man had half your money, I'd wear dollar bills on my back," Rykard boomed. Trae glanced a second time before he pulled his billfold from his back pocket and slapped a twenty into Corey's waiting hand.

"Two weeks from today," Rykard reaffirmed.

"Two weeks it is," Trae boasted.

When Reggie finished her routine, a small roar blasted from the stands. She knew it was her friends. She struck her final pose as the music ended and waited for her cue to move. Only her smiling eyes strayed momentarily to the stands where her friends continued to applaud her performance. She moved her attention back across the glossy gym floor to the table directly in front of her. There sat three women writing fiercely across the paper in front of them. Smile still in place, Reggie's chest heaved up and down, and small amounts of perspiration gathered and trickled down her face. Finally the coach looked up at her and nodded.

"Thank you, Regina. The results will be posted outside the gym on Monday," as she picked up the scattered pieces of paper between her fingers and thumped them onto the table shifting all the sheets into a neat pile.

Reggie nodded. "Thank you," she responded before turning in the direction of the door. She skipped toward the side door, stopping momentarily to pick up her sweat pants.

Why are they waiting until Monday to post the results, she wondered. In her peripheral vision, she saw her friends climb down the bleachers and head for a door as well. She exited the side door where the next girl was waiting for her turn to audition.

Reggie walked into the dressing room with her towel clutched in front of her and her sweatpants draped around her shoulders. She turned when the booming voices of her friends reverberated through the dressing room doors.

"G-i-r-l, you were great!" they cheered in unison. They all gathered around her as they squealed their delight.

"Are you sure I did okay?" Reggie asked knowing full well she had.

"Are you kidding?" Candace asked.

"She's just trying to be modest with her fast behind," Val accused.

"Everybody coming behind will have to meet your standard, girl. No way are they going to be able to match that," Linda, her dorm friend from across the hall, added.

"So, where are we going to celebrate?" the girls asked.

"Mack's. I can taste a sweet, creamy, banana split about now," Reggie suggested. Her hand rubbed the center of her flat stomach.

"Let's do it," Val commanded.

CHAPTER 2

Traekin watched Reggie skip from the gym as he eased his 6'4" frame from the wooden bleachers.

"Hey! Where are you going?" Blake asked.

Traekin turned his attention to Reggie's retreating form. "I'm on the job. The sooner I can get this over with, the sooner I get to work on Ms. Fifteen." He slapped the hands of the men in his immediate arm reach. "See you thugs around the block," he addressed them before departing the gym.

Traekin leaned against the cinder-blocked wall with one foot propped against it. He gripped his purple and gold Tigers baseball cap in his right hand and closed his eyes. He nonchalantly listened to the chatter of the fairly high-pitched voices booming from the room on the other side of the wall directly in front of him. Only when he heard the shrilling of their voices intensify, signifying their approach, did he open his dark brown eyes and pushed himself from the wall.

Their chattering ceased almost the instant the women spotted Traekin standing in the hallway. He hid the smile threatening to spill from his lips. He knew he had a profound affect on women. If nothing else, the reaction of the group in front of him proved that. It was great for his ego. He moved toward them, his attention honed on Reggie, yet he addressed them all.

"Hello ladies." The wickedly sexy smile was almost too much for any woman to bear.

Reggie allowed Trae to openly observe her. The lump lodged in her throat made it hard to swallow. *Why did he look at me that way?* And although he'd only looked at her face, she felt naked under his intense glare. She'd not realized that the women once gathered around her had now moved away like the parting of the Red Sea. She stared intently at his handsome and smooth shaven face. The bold masculinity overpowered her.

Reggie blinked once, then once more, because his lips moved but she heard nothing he'd said. She wasn't even sure he'd said anything at all. Her senses had quit functioning the instant Trae stepped into her space. *Am I imaging this whole thing* she had to ask herself. Earlier, she'd hoped to garner his attention, but she hadn't expected such a quick response, if any at all. Reggie leaned forward as though her doing so would clear her clogged ears. She opened her mouth, yet nothing came out of it. Valerie stepped forward and jabbed her in the side with her elbow, causing Reggie to glance at her. The hard poke in her side jolted her from her stupor.

When she finally found her voice, she stammered, "Excuse me, did you say something?"

His smooth, deep voice rolled over her entire being. He stood approximately two feet away, yet his smothering presence invaded every inch of her now trembling body as though they were mere inches apart. Traekin smiled down at her. His gaze spoke volumes, raw and unnerving passion. How did he expect me to concentrate if he insists on looking at me this way, she thought.

"I was just introducing myself," he began with emphasis. "Traekin Brooks," he extended his right hand out to her.

Reggie braced herself; still, it didn't prepare her for the electrifying charge his warm hand sent through her entire body. She swallowed hard.

"Reggie," she responded shyly. She'd not given her real name. She turned and made introductions. "And this is Val, Candice, Linda, Meg, and Rose." She looked at each of her friends as she introduced them.

Traekin smiled acknowledging each of them. Ah—he loved the

affect he had on women! He focused his attention back to Reggie.

"I was hoping you would join me at Favort, in the Student Union, for a bite to eat or something." *Or something! Where in the hell did that come from? I must be losing it*, he fumed silently.

"Well, my friends and I are headed to Mack's in Favort for ice cream sundaes," she answered sweetly.

She could only imagine what thoughts ran through his mind. She could tell by the expression in his eyes that he wasn't accustomed to that kind of reaction. Every woman standing in the group turned and looked at her as if she'd suddenly grown another head.

Is she crazy? her friends thought.

She must have fallen and bumped her head. This is Traekin Brooks, in the flesh, Candice thought inwardly. Her thoughts almost spilled from her lips.

"Okay," he gestured, his free hand moved out, and touched the stray cluster of hair in her face. "Maybe after you and your friends are done, we could play a game of pool or grab a drink. How about that?" His left brow lifted, and the corners of his sweet luscious lips curved upward into one of his winning smiles.

Every woman, including Reggie, nearly passed out when he touched her hair; the tips of his thick fingers grazed her face as his hand descended down to his side. Reggie's eyes fluttered shut, allowing the simple touch to ease through her whole body. When she opened them again, she found him boldly appraising her. Reggie felt warm and tingly inside. No one had ever made her feel this way. The fact that she was already stupid crazy about the man only intensified the situation and made things worse.

Suspense hung heavy in the air as Trae and the others in the group waited for her response. He watched her sweat-covered body physically tremble. Trae remembered the distant traces of her beautiful oval face when he watched her from the gym bleachers. He'd not been quite prepared for just how overwhelmingly beautiful she was up close. The unblemished, bare face was accentuated with high cheekbones and slanted brown eyes. Dimples peeked from their hiding place each time she smiled. *Wow! She is gorgeous.* What she lacked in body, according to his standards, she made up for with her beauty. He could definitely play this game.

"What if I met you at Favort later? How about four, and we could catch a game then," he proposed.

The cool, calm appearance Reggie gave was yet another performance. In no way did her outward appearance leak the slightest notion of the turmoil raging inside of her. If this interlude didn't end quickly, she was bound to give herself away. She'd dreamt of this day, and now that it was before her, *Wow!* Traekin Brooks had noticed her. *Is this real or what?* Lost in the depths of his brown eyes, Reggie was pulled back to reality by yet another of Val's invasions. This time she cleared her throat. Her eyes strayed only briefly before she gave him her answer. "I would like that very much," she nervously smiled up at him.

"Great," he fidgeted with his hat. "I guess I'll see you then," he said, slowly backing away. "Ladies," he smiled before turning and heading in the opposite direction. All eyes watched as he turned and left them standing in the hallway. As soon as Trae was out of hearing distance, Reggie's friends all broke into screaming chatter.

"G-I-R-L, did you see how fine he is?" Meg squealed.

Reggie attempted to play it cool. The bundle of nerves in her stomach was still tied in a thousand knots. She could have won an Academy Award for this last performance.

"He is cute," she downplayed Meg's outburst.

"Cute? Cute? You call him cute? Honey, a poodle is cute. Babies are cute. Girl, you must have lost your mind. This man is not cute, he's F-I-N-E!" Meg roared.

Val looked at Meg before speaking, surprised by the otherwise very quiet woman's outburst. She brought her attention back to Reggie. "Dog is right, more like DAWG; although I wouldn't necessarily identify him as a poodle. If you asked me, Reggie might be the only smart one in this group. The man still has a reputation of being a womanizer. I'm surprised there weren't a bunch of floozies hanging on him just now," Val responded. The entire group rolled their eyes upwardly. She continued, " Oh right, he couldn't have them hanging on him if he's trying to pick up Reggie."

"You're just jealous it wasn't you he asked," Rose chimed into the conversation.

"Hell, I don't care how many women hang onto him. If it were me, I'd take my chances." Candice's hands went to her lips in a praying gesture. "He is so fine!"

"I just hope Reggie has some sense," Val addressed her comment directly at her friend.

"You guys act as though he asked me out," Reggie defended. "We're just playing a game of pool."

"Girl, you better keep that man at arms length. You're gonna get hurt if you don't," Val said with finality.

Reggie thoughtfully considered Val's warning. *We're only going to play a game of pool,* she kept telling herself.

The women engaged in jovial chatter. The moment Traekin walked in the door, all eyes went in his direction. Reggie didn't have to turn to confirm he was there. She glanced down at her watch. She'd attempted on several occasions to nonchalantly sneak a peek at her watch and at the clock over the snack bar counter. She hadn't fooled anyone, especially Val.

The triple scoop of New York Cheesecake ice cream banana split had been wasted. Her eagerness to see Trae killed any appetite she had. Normally the only thing left in the clear glass bowl was the remnants of strawberry syrup stuck to its sides. She nibbled on the plastic spoon, now caught between her front teeth, when she heard the commotion begin.

Val glanced up from her sundae and locked gazes with her very best friend. She smiled. Reggie's face lit into a soft glow before she extended her hand across the table and touched Val's sleeveless arm. She sighed, as though her next move was the hardest thing in the world to do.

"You don't have to go, you know," Val assured her.

The other ladies at the table had already turned their attention to the commotion at the entrance of the snack bar and had missed the private conversation between the two friends.

"If you want company, one of us would gladly go with you. It would be awesome to know what makes Traekin Brooks tick," she offered.

Reggie shook her head. "No. I have to do this for me. I've been crazy about this man forever,\." She smiled nervously.

"No you don't have to do this. Chalk it up as your prerogative to choose or not choose Mr. Wonderful."

"Yes, I have to do this. When will I have the chance again? Maybe, just maybe I'll be able to put this crazy crush thing to rest," she contended.

"Don't sell yourself cheap, girlfriend. There's plenty of fish out here. And some are ten times better than Traekin Brooks."

Val's eyes moved from Reggie's to the tall masculine figure now standing at their table.

"Hi," he greeted them with yet another one of his "knock 'em dead" smiles.

"Hi," Reggie looked up at his waiting eyes. She instantly sucked in her breath at their intensity. His bold appraisal was too much.

No one else at the table uttered a word. They only watched the exchange with grave curiosity.

"Ready?" he asked extending his hand out to her.

Reggie gazed at it before placing her long delicate fingers into his waiting hand. "Sure," she said pushing herself from the chair; he assisted with a slight tug.

Traekin's eyes only left hers for the split second it took to bid her friends farewell. "Later," he said to her friends.

The small trembling hand encased in his was warm and silky soft. He gave it a slight squeeze, causing Reggie to look up at him. She found there a reassuring smile creased on his face. Already, she'd caused him to break his rule to never put himself on hold for any woman. If they wanted to be with him, it was when he wanted it or not at all.

With Reggie, he'd attempted to appear flexible when he'd asked her to be with him and she put him off. He could tell she was extremely nervous. He felt compelled to not push her too far or too fast. After all, he had twenty bucks riding on her. Although the money was a meager amount, he was serious about winning, no matter what it was. He didn't want to lose the wager before he got the chance to prove he could charm anything wearing a skirt. This would be the one and only time he'd break his promise to concede to a woman's wishes, no matter what the consequences were.

As he gazed down into those mesmerizing eyes, into that beautiful face, he couldn't help but feel he could comply with anything she asked him for, anything she wanted. Her innocence he'd seen in many beautiful faces, yet none demanded what hers did this very moment. He allowed the smile on his face to reach his eyes and put her at ease. Once that was accomplished, he turned and removed it quickly, chastising himself for not being in control. He had to get his emotions in check. This was a bet, a conquest, nothing else. He intended to come out on top, the winner. And besides, he didn't give into any emotional ties to the women he'd become involved with. Traekin released her hand and allowed her to proceed through the doors before him.

They walked the few feet to the game room, which was as crowded as usual. All the tables were taken.

"We're almost done here if you'll wait a few minutes," a student addressed him directly.

"Sure. Thanks," Trae replied. He turned to Reggie standing not far from him, which was in fact too far away for his likings. He had a reputation to uphold. Most of his women were always right under him. *Here we go again!* He moved closer.

"Have you played before?" he asked stealing a view of her face from beneath his long lashes.

"I've held a stick before if that's what you're asking," Reggie smiled. She wouldn't reveal for all the tea in China that her brother, Lance, was a National Billiards Champion. She'd learned the game from the best, her brother and her father. The three tables in their basement game room afforded her the luxury to perfect her skills whenever she wanted to.

Once the table was vacated, Traekin moved in and racked the balls in the center of the green, felt tabletop. He beckoned for her as he stood next to the wooden rack holstered along the wall next to the tables.

"Come," he called to her. "Let's see if we can get you fitted."

Had Reggie been prepared, she would have had her own stick, which was now packed away in its canvas case at the bottom of her dorm room closet. She walked over to where Trae stood and stopped several inches in front of him.

"I won't bite, I promise," he coached her nearer to his hard frame. He held his hand out to her once again.

Reggie didn't hesitate and took it; she couldn't resist the call of her body's desire to feel his touch again. He pulled her into a loose embrace, and her back collided with the steel wall of his lower chest and stomach. Her body temperature soared as she eased willingly into his body.

His cologne, mixed with his heady, body scent, seeped through her nostrils. His warm hands slid up the sides of her arms, which instantly sent chills up her spine. Tiny flesh bumps covered her skin, and, suddenly, she couldn't think straight. Reggie did all she could to hang on, because control had long ago walked out of the door. She felt the urge to turn into his embrace and wrap her arms around his neck, closing out the small space between them, but didn't.

Trae pulled down a stick he thought was the right size and pulled her into him, feeling her soft body in his embrace. He'd done all he could to ignore the stirring of his groin at the delicate feel of her rump brushing against him. The heat radiating through him was unbelievably irresistible. A fruit-scent from her shampoo or conditioner still lingered in her hair. He slowly wrapped one arm around her slim waist, drawing her even closer to him. His lips brushed the side of her face as he attempted to look down at her.

"Are you okay?" he whispered. He could have asked himself the same question. He wanted desperately to crush her into his body.

Reggie bobbed her head up and down. She didn't trust her voice to speak for her.

"Here," he offered her the stick. "Let's see if this works."

Reggie closed her hand around the stick. She leaped when her hand lightly brushed his. She quickly stepped out of his embrace and took long strides to the table, putting some much-needed space between them.

Traekin watched with curiosity, and a smile threatened to burst through the serious line drawn on his face. He, too, turned away quickly to conceal his emotions. He selected a stick for himself, then strolled over to the table where Reggie stood. She glanced away as though something else had garnered her attention.

"Would you like the honors?" he asked, referring to the break.

"No. You do it, please," she returned. She couldn't quite bring herself to look directly at him.

Oh yeah! This is going to be easy, he celebrated inwardly.

CHAPTER 3

Trae instead, decided to go easy on Reggie. For some strange reason he didn't want to make her feel awkward. What was happening to him? He found himself bending every rule he'd ever set to accommodate this woman. He purposely missed a shot so that she would get a chance to hit. He soon found out that girlfriend had more than held a stick. He knew he was in trouble the moment she hit the first ball. At first all he could do was stare at her in astonishment. Each hit was done with expert precision. After each hit, she laughed at him. Of course this sparked his 'trash' talking.

"Oh, baby girl can play! Now I won't feel bad about whooping your little tail," Trae bantered.

"I don't want to brag all over campus that I beat your butt," Reggie challenged, feeling more at ease with him.

"The fight is on. Let's go," he boomed after he racked for the second game.

After six games they split the total, each winning three games and tying the match.

"You're lucky I have to be at the Sports Plex. Otherwise I'd put this little game to rest," Trae threatened.

"Frankly, I think you're chicken, Traekin Brooks," Reggie countered.

"Oh you do?" Trae walked up and pulled her into his embrace.

He longed to cover her mouth with his. Instead he placed his lips just above her brow and softly left a mark that burned straight through her entire body. Control, the right amount of control was how he won his conquests. When the time is right, his kiss would seal the victory.

There would be no looking back. He glanced into her glassy, passion-filled eyes. The time wasn't yet right.

"I'm no chicken, Ms. Reggie," he whispered in a hoarse tight voice as he looked down into her upturned face. "You can have a rematch any day."

He stepped back and allowed his hands to fall down to his sides.

He watched the delicate movement of her facial muscles as she smiled. Every ounce of his being wanted her in the worst way. He would take her here and now had it not been a public place. The private thoughts consumed him.

Reggie was lost in her thoughts as well. The skin above her eyes still burned from the kiss he'd left there. The touch of his lips left a tingling sensation, and the passion in his eyes was unmistakably clear. Everything Val had said earlier vanished like a speck of dust in the wind. She would give her heart and her body to this man without a thought or care. Pulled into his spell, her eyes roamed the lines of his stern, yet handsome, face.

"Okay. I'll hold you to it," she said so softly Traekin barely heard the words.

"You're on," he leaned down further in a gesture that suggested he might kiss her. Again, Reggie waited in stressful anticipation but was disappointed when he raised his head and said, "I'll walk you back to your dorm. Do you mind?" He found the control to not break down and kiss her until her lips were swollen.

"No, I don't mind at all," she replied.

The easy conversation fell into place as it had earlier in the game room. Traekin had made her feel at ease with light conversation. He was amazed by how much she knew about football and basketball, two of his favorite subjects. Most girls he dated didn't know the difference between the two sports, yet this lady knew that T. H. Harris, for which one of the campus auditoriums had been named, led the Tigers' football team to a 35-5 record during his career. He was truly impressed by how much she knew.

They talked about her short basketball career in high school. She had played her senior year. "I'd never considered trying out for the team until my brother baited me into it," she relayed. The pattern looked familiar when compared to her present situation. Her friends now coerced her into trying out for the dance team.

"I'll take you on any day," she challenged him to a game.

"Listen, little bit, don't go writing a check your ass can't cash," he warned.

Traekin had been All American in high school and had made incredible marks at Grambling. NBA scouts had begun watching him last year. He'd been very clear, however, that he intended to finish college, no exceptions. He flexed his arm muscles, over-exaggerated his facial expression with frowns and growled at her to make his point.

"I'll still kick your butt," she said as she punched him lightly on the upper shoulder.

"Name the day and time, chicky."

"Alright. I will," she burst into laughter.

Reggie hadn't laughed this much in a while. Trae made her all giddy inside. The walk to the dorm seemed shorter than usual. They strolled in front to the dorm entryway, and stood face to face.

"I have to go. I would love to see you again," he closed the space between them.

"I'd like that," she answered.

Reggie glanced away from his face momentarily. She couldn't handle the way he made her feel when she looked at him directly. Trae touched the side of her face with the back of his hand, bringing her attention back to his face. The passion she saw there was soon replaced with a hint of laughter, setting her at ease again. He smiled, and lit the otherwise stern masculine face.

"Let's do lunch after Philosophy class tomorrow. My appetite is always peaked after an hour with Professor Gaines," he joked.

Reggie laughed, knowing full well what he said was true. Professor Gaines was known to engage his students mentally and physically in lively discussions. She bobbed her head in response, her hearty laughter echoed in the small space between them.

"Okay. I'll see you tomorrow in class," Reggie smiled.

"Sweet dreams," he whispered, turned and strolled away.

After about three or four steps, Trae turned back to her and called, "Reggie, what is your last name?" He realized he hadn't asked, or known her full name.

"Regina Miles," she answered before she waltzed into the lobby through the automatic doors. Her brother had fashioned her with the nickname Reggie as a child. With two front teeth missing, it was hard for him to pronounce her name correctly.

"Yeah, well, *Ms. Miles*, I just might have my hands full," he shook his head. He pondered a moment 22before turning and heading back in the direction he had begun.

Reggie strolled into class ten minutes before the scheduled start time, a habit she'd started her freshmen year. She liked to sit close to the front of class without sitting directly in front of the instructor. The small auditorium filled fairly quickly. She'd hope to secure a seat for her and one possibly for Trae. She'd slept restlessly. Her thoughts simmered on him most of the night. She could hardly wait to see his sexy face again. She dreamt about being enveloped in his large strong arms. Even now, the remembrance of his scent and the warmth of his body ignited a fire within.

She was so lost in her reverie that she collided into a steel hard body that stood directly in front of her. Her body fell backwards, but arms wrapped around her lean soft body and pulled her forward. Grateful for the rescue, her eyes immediately went to the face of her roadblock and rescuer. His eyes were shockingly breathtaking.

"Whoa! Where are you headed to in such a hurry?" his baritone voice caressed her ears.

"Hi. I was driving while the mind was occupied," she apologized.

"I just might have to cite you for that, ma'am. It's a violation to walk while thinking," he kidded.

More like sleepwalking, she thought. She took in every inch of his overpowering presence. The crooked slant of his smile forced her to lick her bottom lip.

Trae hadn't missed the reaction. He watched her tongue trail across her lip. Only when she finally spoke did his eyes recapture hers.

"Please, Mr. Officer, I promise I won't do it again," she pleaded in a small voice.

The crooked smile broadened when she attempted to play innocent. He saw her as just that, very naïve. The way she carried herself, suggested that she lacked experience with men. The sensation of that fact ran straight through his red-blooded veins. Without warning his groin stirred.

"Okay, lady. I'll give you a break this time." He pointed his finger at her nose and touched the fat tip with his index finger.

The movement of people around them disappeared. Only the heated exchange between Trae and Reggie occupied their thoughts. In mere seconds they savored the passion between them. "We'd better get inside. I know you like to sit near the front," he commented.

Reggie hadn't realized Traekin knew she was alive. Yet he knew where she preferred to sit. She tucked that bit of information into the back of her mind. She would have to ponder that thought another time. Most days he ended up at the back of the auditorium because he would stroll in right before class started and was usually accompanied by two or three strays. At least that's what she called the women who hung onto him. While she liked being with Trae, there was no way she would become one of them.

Today he was early. *What's the deal with that,* she wondered? She smiled secretly. *He's come to meet me.* The thought sent a gleeful sensation coursing through her.

Okay, she beamed inwardly. *Calm down girl.*

She walked pass Trae, and he followed closely behind her. They stole glances at one another during the session. At the end of class Trae took Reggie's books from her hands. Once they got to the cafeteria, he found a table secluded enough to have a private conversation. Just as they turned to enter the cafeteria line, Veronica approached them. Her syrupy smile could have soaked a lake of pancakes. Her dancing eyes embraced Trae's handsome face with longing anticipation.

"Hi Trae," she spoke, totally ignoring Reggie. "I missed you this morning," she sneered, deliberately not saying any more than that to make it seemed as though she harbored a secret about where and why they were suppose to meet that morning.

Reggie hadn't missed that hanging sentence and knew it was intended for her. She wondered if there was a hidden message in what she said. Reggie's antennas went up quickly. When she met Veronica's eyes, they spewed hot, raw hatred. Reggie didn't flinch one inch but met her stare. She was pissed. She had no intention of letting Traekin push her in the center of some crap with his women. It wasn't happening, no way.

Veronica's little secret was soon crushed the instant Trae spoke. He knew the deal and had no plans to stand by and watch Veronica mess up his quest.

"Hi, Roni. I did my weight training a little earlier than usual this morning," he addressed her. "Roni, this is Reggie. Reggie, Roni. I'm sure you two know each other. Roni is the dance team captain," he looked from one to the other. He hadn't missed the silent catfight between the two.

"Yeah, we've met," Veronica said dryly, then quickly turned her attention back to Traekin.

"Are you about to have lunch," she beamed.

Trae extended his arm and placed his hand at the small of Reggie's back. Veronica's perfectly made face almost shattered into a thousand pieces.

"Yeah, Reggie and I are about to grab a little something before the next class," he replied.

He was very specific in his words, *Reggie and I*. No invitation was offered to join them, no permission was granted to tag along.

Veronica was livid. The upward curve of her perfect lips straightened into a tight red line. Her eyes bore all the disappointment of a lost battle. Reggie knew enough about Veronica to know she could be vindictive. *Dang! Just what I need*, she thought inwardly. She knew how important it was to not start a fight with Veronica and risk losing a spot on the team. She'd already had too many strikes against her to add yet another. If anything, she needed Veronica on her side. She had the distinct suspicion that this little incident would cost her dearly.

It was obvious Veronica thought Trae was her territory and Reggie was simply trespassing. Reggie could only hope that she wouldn't have to choose between Trae and a spot on the dance team. If her intuition was correct, Veronica planned to make her choose one or the other. Her desire to be with Traekin was as strong as her desire to dance. She glanced up at Trae. Reggie tried to make certain the conversation between him and Veronica wasn't a lover's spat. It wasn't cool, nor would she allow herself to be used as a weapon to make a lover jealous. She could do without that headache.

Trae hadn't looked at her yet, however, the hand at the base of her back gently pushed her forward.

"See you around, Roni," he smiled down at her. The rolling of her eyes skyward spoke volumes. She was pissed. As they moved forward his eyes came down to regard Reggie. Stopping, he lifted her chin and planted a soft moist kiss on her cheek. Were Veronica's eyes an automatic rifle, both Trae and Reggie would be sprawled out on the cafeteria floor.

Trae and Reggie chatted quietly over lunch. They talked about his life back in the Crescent City. Reggie loved New Orleans. She'd visited her aunt, who lived on Upperline Street, every summer. It was usually after a brief stay with her grandmother, who lived in a small town not far from the city. It had been an experience she looked forward to every year. The ride on the St. Charles streetcar, headed downtown, was her favorite thing to do. She would roam the streets of the French Quarters, watching in awe the people crowded from one end of the district to the other. That had been a long time ago. Her Aunt Alma moved to Los Angeles over six years ago. She'd only gone back twice since then, both times during the Bayou Classic with Val and a couple of their friends. They'd purposely stayed away from the Quarters. "Too many people," Val complained. They managed to find other awesome things to do in the city.

"Although I've been there a few times, I haven't really gotten the full tour," she informed him.

"Well, we'll have to fix that, now won't we," he drew his face close to Reggie's. She sucked in her breath, watching the intensity of his eyes now focused on her face.

"I'm still considered a minor you know," she reminded him.

He was also a minor. Because they were under the drinking age, it hadn't meant they weren't allowed to frequent and enjoy the establishments. Not that he drank anyway, but even if he wanted a drink, he had no problem getting one.

"You're too young to drink, besides, you shouldn't drink anyway," he countered.

She smiled, showing the deep-rooted dimples at the base of her cheeks.

"So, are you telling me you don't drink?" she queried.

"No. I don't like the stuff, quite frankly," he told her. "Besides, I have to take care of this temple," he made a gestured posture over his body.

Reggie gave him a you're full of yourself glance. She could tell he was teasing her, but there was no doubt in her mind that he really did consider his body a temple. Traekin knew he had to keep himself physically fit and healthy in order to endure the beating and bruising his body took on a regular basis.

After lunch, Trae walked Reggie to her next class.

"Want to hangout later?" he asked. "There's a new movie I want to see."

"Okay." I do have an early dance class in the morning though." Every Saturday she volunteered at the local community center, teaching under-privileged girls to dance.

"Then we can do the early show. I have to be on the field pretty early myself."

Trae handed Reggie her books. His hand moved up and touched the side of her face; his thumb strolled gracefully across her bottom lip. Her mouth parted in urgent response.

"Later," he whispered.

"Later," she repeated and watched him move down the hall.

CHAPTER 4

Reggie laughed so much that the sides of her stomach ached. The movie was packed. They arrived early, so they secured some pretty good seats and settled in for the duration of the movie. She and Trae both loved to sit through the credits, and they sat in their seats until the screen went black and the lights were raised. As the ushers moved about picking up remnants of popcorn and soda containers, Trae and Reggie picked up and discarded their leftovers before they left the theater.

The monster-sized soda Reggie had consumed was knocking at her bladder's door. "I have to go to the restroom." She pointed to the open doors.

"Okay. I'll meet you right over there." He pointed to the corner by the concession stand. Reggie nodded and entered the bathroom.

When she made her way to the agreed upon meeting spot, Reggie found Trae surrounded by three women grinning from ear to ear.

He looked up without seeing her approach. Somehow he felt her presence. His eyes firmly sought hers and the agitation clearly etched on her beautiful face wasn't missed.

"Excuse me ladies." He moved away and dismissed them all. Their eyes followed his retreating back. Traekin casually closed the space between them, meeting her before she reached the concession stand. The smile he gave would make her forgive him for almost anything.

"Are you ready?" he asked reaching for her hand. The twinge of frustration she felt earlier clearly dissipated. Reggie returned his smile. The appreciation for her forgiveness was evident. She was proving to be a very sweet lady.

Reggie allowed him to take her hand. She glanced momentarily at the three women now huddled into a cluster watching them retreat. They walked the short distance to his black Ford Explorer. With his hands lodged at her tiny waist, he helped her into the sport utility vehicle. As Trae pulled into the circle drive of Reggie's dorm, Val and two other dorm residents stood near the walkway. Val met Trae at the rear passenger side of the vehicle as she squinted her eyes into a scowl.

"Just what are you trying to do to my friend, Traekin Brooks," she hissed in a hushed tone.

Trae knew Val's intentions were purely out of concern for her roommate. For that reason, and that reason alone, he kept his cool. The smile on his face he had when he originally saw her didn't move into the mask of anger he felt. Instead, his face went blank, unreadable at first, and then stone cold.

"I have no idea what you're talking about, Valerie." He met her angry stare.

Val had no plans to stand by while he strung her friend along. She was sure he was up to no good. The women he hung with did what he wanted them to do. And although she knew Reggie, she hoped this girl hadn't fallen for his bull. She couldn't help but wonder why, all of a sudden, he was interested in Reggie.

"You know what I'm talking about, Trae. Let me warn you. If you hurt my girl, we're all gonna get together and whip your high-yellow behind." Val's finger dug into his arm for emphasis.

Trae watched the charge of emotions washing over her face; the tiny, pin-like finger jabbed the side of his arm. He smiled down at her.

"What's between Reggie and me is our business, Val," he flashed a cold stare before leaving her where she stood.

He walked up to the passenger door; his hand was about to depress the handle when the door opened.

ANN CLAY

"Is everything okay?" Reggie asked. Concern showed on her face. Her eyes strayed from his face to Val's. Anger was clearly etched on both. She'd seen them talking from the side mirror while she waited on him to open her door. She couldn't hear what they said, but knew it was a serious confrontation.

As always, a smile reached his face.

"Yes. Everything is cool," he reached for her arm and helped her out of the SUV.

Reggie glanced at Val once more. She avoided her stare and pretended to be distracted by something else. Reggie turned her attention back to Trae. His eyes bore straight through her, or so it seemed.

"What are your plans after your dance class tomorrow?" he asked.

"I don't really have any plans to speak of." She shrugged. Val instantly glance over at her and then turned away again. She didn't have anything to do. Not really. She had a test on Monday but felt she had plenty of time to study for that on Sunday.

"I plan on taking a drive to Monroe tomorrow afternoon. Would you like to join me?" Trae offered.

"What for? I mean, why are you going to Monroe?"

"I have an uncle who lives there. I'd promised that I would visit tomorrow for a few hours. I don't really want to go by myself. I can't think of anyone else I would rather take with me." He replied.

Her dimples always revealed themselves whenever her full, ripe lips parted into a smile. "I think that would be fun," she answered. "Are you sure your uncle won't mind?"

"Uncle Ted loves company. The more the merrier."

Val listened to the entire conversation, and they ignored her. She cleared her throat, garnering their attention. She dramatically moved her head in a sideward motion, summoning Reggie to come to her for a private discussion. The continuous jerking of her head made Reggie look at her for a fleeting moment, and a frown masked her beautiful face conveying her disapproval of Val's intrusion.

Trae looked down into Reggie's face, waiting for a reply. He watched in a side-glance the silent communication between her and Val. He didn't like what he saw. He had to make his move fast before Val began to influence Reggie's decisions where he was concerned. It was only after she answered his question, did he breathe a sigh of relief.

"What time are we leaving?" she finally asked.

Trae took a brief moment to examine her beautiful face. Her unbelievable beauty was shocking up close. Her oval eyes tugged at his heart.

"How about eleven o'clock?" he asked.

"I'll meet you here at eleven."

Trae briefly glanced at Val and said, "See you around, Valerie."

Val only rolled her eyes at him just like people who knew her had come to expect her to. Trae moved around the front of his vehicle, jumped into the driver's seat, and pulled away from the curve. The two women watched the car until it was out of sight.

"Do you mind telling me what that was all about, Valerie Renee Richards?" she scowled at her friend.

"I don't know what's gotten into you, girl. You know that man ain't worth the time of day. What are you thinking, Reggie? Everywhere he turns up, he's got a different woman on his arm," she said in an exasperated tone.

"We're just friends, Val," she offered. "He has been extremely nice and hasn't tried anything fresh."

"Friends my behind, girl. The boy is a dog. And nah, I guess he hasn't tried anything yet. It's only been a day and a half."

"Val, please!" Reggie begged.

"What?" Her shoulders slanted upward into a questioning gesture. "I just don't want you to get hurt," she offered her friend.

"I won't," Reggie promised.

"Well, you need to be careful, Reggie. I don't want to have to tell you I told you so."

Reggie loved her friend to death. They'd been inseparable from the moment they met. She reached for her and looped her arms into her friend's. "Come on. I've got to tell you about this movie." They strolled arm in arm through the lobby door and took the elevator up to their room.

Trae lay restlessly on top of the dark gray and burgundy comforter on his bed. He had to figure out a way to accelerate this little bet thing with Reggie. He had a reputation to uphold, and she was cutting into his action. One of the three women he ran into at the theater tonight was a honey he'd had on his list for a little while. "Kelly Presley, from Memphis, Tennessee," he said out loud.

His smile deepened at the corners of his mouth. As he continued to lie in his bed, he contemplated his dilemma with Reggie. He was constantly reminded of how comfortable and easy it was to talk to her. *Hell! I don't have trouble talking to any woman,* he conceded. Most of his other conversations were empty. With Reggie it was different. She was funny and smart. She felt good in his arms, soft and firm all at once. The scent of her cologne was light and delicate. During the movies, he'd snaked his hands through the thick wavy ponytail bound together at the back of her head. He wondered what it looked or felt like draped around her neck and shoulders.

Stolen glances of her profile gave him a real good look at her. Her beauty extended beyond the physical appearance. She was sweet, considerate, and extremely shy. She fidgeted at first, but eventually relaxed enough and allowed him to hold her hand during the movie. Still, she didn't relax enough to allow him to pull her into his embrace. Usually his women, with little or no coaching, were draped around his neck before the movie was over. It always made his next step easier.

Reggie wasn't biting. She wasn't that easy. Corey may have been correct about her. Maybe he wouldn't get anywhere with her. That is exactly why he needed to speed this thing up. He despised the thought that in the end he would have wasted two precious weeks for nothing. He had business to take care of. Trae sighed loudly before he turned over onto his stomach and buried his face into the burgundy-cased pillow. *What have I gotten myself into?* he wondered.

Trae heard the outside room door open. The door to his room facing the common living area of the two-bedroom suite had been left opened. His roommate hadn't made it in by the time he'd come in. He probably had been out getting laid. *I could have been making out with some woman too, had I been smart enough to keep my mouth closed.* It was just like him to get his own tail in a bind.

When he heard the door to Rykard's bedroom close, Trae rolled over on to his back once more. Still restless, he sighed again. He closed his eyes in an attempt to shut out the world, and, at the same time, beg his body for sleep. Slumber wasn't anywhere near. He sat on the side of the bed and slipped into a pair of running shorts. After he laced his shoes, he crept from the room and headed for the door. Upper classmen didn't have curfew, but the football squad did for the next few weeks. If caught, he could be benched for the first two games.

He was willing to take that chance. He had to do something or go crazy. He headed for the field then changed his mind. It was dark and anyone living in rural Louisiana knew it was pitch black outside when there were no lights. Instead, he took the bike trail. His stride was slow and easy at first. Once he made the circle past Reggie's dorm, he broke into a full sprint all the way back to his dorm. The gold T-shirt and black shorts stuck to his body as he made his way back to his room.

Trae eased under the lukewarm spray of the shower and stood there for several minutes, allowing the water to replenish and refresh his weary soul. After he washed the perspiration from his body, he lowered his naked body into his bed and drifted off into a fitful slumber.

Val and Reggie talked for a half-hour. Reggie's eyes glowed and her hands moved constantly to animate the details about the movie. She purposely left out the little scene after the movies with Trae and the three little wenches.

"You know, Val, we're two fine sisters. Why aren't we attached to some fine brother?" Reggie asked.

"You can't talk," Val teased. "It looks like you and Mr. All-Star are hitting it off."

"We're just friends." Reggie's entire face lit up. "He is so real. I thought he would be stuck up and boring, but he's not. He's funny and smart and he makes me feel like I'm the only person in the world when he's with me," she beamed.

"Oh-oh," Val moaned.

"What?" Reggie asked. The sheepish grin was still on her face.

"Don't tell me, you're in love, right?" Val mocked her.

"Well, I'm crazy about him, Val. You already know that," she defended.

Val stood and headed toward the door.

"Where are you going?" Reggie whined.

"To bed. Where you need to go before you say too much."

"Even if I don't say it verbally, Val, it's still in my heart and I feel it. That won't change anything... anything at all," she remarked.

"No! Just maybe your head won't forget who's in charge and will do the thinking for you," she turned and closed the door behind her.

Reggie sighed. This felt so right. Her heart said so. She curled up into a knot in the center of her bed and fell asleep.

CHAPTER 5

The girls in dance class were especially silly this morning. Everything today was funny, even the reprimand they'd received for not practicing as they had been instructed to from the previous week. Their recital was fast approaching, and because many of the benefactors of the center would be attending this year's recital, Reggie planned it to be especially unique. More featured spots were assigned than usual, and a special tribute had been planned for one guest of honor in particular, founder of the Bossier City Dance Company, Ida Mae Bush.

The thunderous rapping of the leap pole on the wooden floor did little to garner the attention of the three youngest girls in the group. They huddled into a semi-circle and giggled together. She extended the pole across the center of her waist, both hands tightly gripped it on either side of her body, and she casually strolled to the center of the classroom where the girls stood. She was curious at their unusually silly behavior.

When she reached the center, she rapped the pole on the floor again directly in front of them. It was useless. Her rapping only stirred the rest of the class into a roar of laughter. Every girl in the room rushed in and hugged her by the waist, arm, leg or whatever part of her body they could grab on to.

"What am I going to do with all of you?" she yelped.

The serious look on Reggie's face soon broke, and she joined in their silliness. Before long they all were leaping and jumping around the room as discipline was forgotten. Needless to say, no new steps were added to the routine that was planned and learned in phases for the recital in twelve weeks. Nor had they made any real progress with the steps they'd already learned from last week. The mood Reggie was in today, she wasn't the least bit concerned that curtain time was in twelve weeks nor was she worried about having everything and everyone in perfect sync by curtain time. She was confident that they would make up for their playfulness next week.

She hugged each girl at the end of class. Their parents, mostly single moms, picked them up at the door. Reggie saw each and every one of them off. She got great satisfaction from helping these girls. Many she had seen blossom into very confident and proud young ladies. Most of the girls lacked self-esteem when they first came. She attempted to mentor them as well as teach them to dance. She did her best to encourage them to do well in school. She tutored many of them with math and science, and through role-playing, found creative ways of teaching them to be proud and confident.

When she first started volunteering at the center, only a few girls were enrolled, attending the classes once or twice a month. Soon the sessions grew to weekly sessions, three of them, a half-hour-each every Saturday. Two other volunteers rotated the classes with her. The girls' eagerness to learn, their ability to pick up the routines quickly, and the smiling eyes of proud parents brought her unspeakable pleasure. No amount of money could give her greater satisfaction.

After all the girls and their parents had left, Reggie gathered her things and made certain the room was in order before she turned off the lights and closed the door. She turned the knob to make certain the lock was set. As she exited the center, she observed the almost vacant parking lot. *Where is everyone today?* she pondered. Walking over to her car, Reggie released the alarm from the black keypad in her hand, opened the driver's side door, and threw her bag into the backseat of her smoke-gray Kia. She eased the car onto the main drag and popped an Erykah Badu CD into the player. She bobbed her head to the music until she pulled into a vacant spot behind her dorm.

It wasn't until then did her restlessness return. In an hour she would be with Traekin headed for Monroe. Both hands gripped the steering wheel tightly, and she dropped her head against the wheel at the mere thought. However, her nervousness was quickly replaced with anticipation when she recalled his saucy, lopsided smile. She intended to make her mark today. With her makeover, Trae definitely had to take notice of her, more than he had before.

After a quick shower, Reggie slipped into a lavender sundress that draped over her long lean figure and fell just above her ankles; a far cry from the frumpy sweats or baggy shorts she generally wore on the weekends. Small African violets were scattered at the bottom just above a deep-purple chiffon hem. When she glanced at the clock on her desk, she realized she had two minutes before she needed to be downstairs to meet Trae.

Reggie took a few moments to add a coat of mascara to her lashes and a hint of berry lip-gloss to her lips. She then puckered them into a kissable 'o'. Smiling, she wondered what it would be like to feel Traekin's lips on hers. The fire they left on her forehead and cheek had been mere samples of what they would do to her mouth. Maybe, just maybe, today she would find out what his kisses would do to her.

Reggie walked through the common living area and rapped lightly on Val's door. She hadn't seen or heard her all morning. When she didn't get an answer, she scribbled a note and left it on the entertainment center near the stereo. As she walked through the lobby doors, Trae was propped against the front passenger side of his SUV. He immediately sprang to his feet the moment he saw Reggie approach.

"Hi," he greeted her. A smile lit his face like a hundred-watt bulb. The sight of her stirred his insides a bit.

Wow! He watched a she sauntered down the walkway. He would have moved forward to greet her, only he was temporarily stunned by her unbelievable beauty. His feet froze, rooting him in place. She wore a slim fitting sundress, which danced around her hips and curvy legs when she moved. The circular mounds of her breast shifted gracefully beneath the band V-neck line. Her feet were encased in white one-inch heel sandals; red toes peeked from the front of them. Her hair hung down the center of her back and flung backward through the humidity of the hot, Louisiana, August morning. Just last night he'd wondered what it looked like around her shoulders. It was definitely breathtaking, to say the least.

The dress was a far cry from the baggy, khaki pants and V-neck Tee she wore the previous evening. Her transformation was stunning and made her beauty even more prominent. The simplicity of her dress and makeup made her more beautiful than any woman he'd ever known. Why he hadn't noticed her before was mind-boggling. How endowed she was had been the only thing of importance to him. And now, he couldn't help but think that maybe he'd missed more than he cared to admit. He shook himself physically. It was obvious his emotions were out of control.

Trae couldn't believe how restless he was last night or how he longed the entire morning to see her again. He had to get a grip. He couldn't lose focus. He was on a quest. Yet he couldn't resist his desire to be with her. After he rationalized the whole thing during his run last night, he decided that there wasn't a thing wrong with his desire to see and be with a woman whom he obviously thought was attractive. He'd never beat himself up before because he wanted to be with a certain woman. This "*thing*" with Reggie seemed so different from the rest.

Seeing her only fueled that lack of control he seemed to be having every time he was with her or thought of her, especially in the last few hours. He had to remember she was just another pretty girl dying for a taste of his alluring attention. When it was all said and done, she would be just another notch in his belt, nothing more, nothing less. It was at that very thought that he removed the smile from his eyes and replaced it with indifference. He watched as she continued her approach. The sweet indentation in her cheeks winked at him with joyous glee.

"Hi," she whispered breathlessly.

She didn't know he would be early. It seemed, as of late he always had to wait on her, something she liked very much. The Trae she'd seen in the past had always been fashionably late as though the event, whatever it was, didn't start until he arrived. Reggie thought of him as conceited before, however, the last couple of days proved that he really was a down-to-earth guy, and she enjoyed that part of him.

As she waltzed toward Trae, her heart raced a million miles a second. His tall masculine figure loomed over everything. Even the sun seemed to be hiding behind his broad wide shoulders.

Reggie saw the eagerness in his eyes when he spotted her. Or maybe she imagined it, because in almost that very same instant the excitement dissipated. He smiled, but it didn't reach his eyes fully. It didn't matter, she consoled. She was happy. His eyes swallowed her whole, and for now his attention was on her. She couldn't have asked for more. Maybe it was the dress. She wasn't known for her fashion. Not very many people saw her dressed up. She wanted to make a good impression, and it seemed to have worked.

"I hope I didn't keep you waiting long," she sighed, attempting to catch her breath.

"No. Not at all," his dark eyes partly hidden beneath the long lashes watched her as she approached. "Are you ready?"

"Yeah," she replied looking up into his face.

Trae extended his hand, placed it at the small of her back, and gently pushed her towards the passenger's door. He opened it and instantly the cool air met Reggie as she slid into the tan leather seat with Trae's help. Stepping up on the hoist, she could have climbed in without assistance. Trae wasn't having any of that. *If anything, this was a ploy to get his hands on me and drive me crazy,* she speculated. He closed the door and moved around the front of the vehicle, providing Reggie an opportunity to watch his handsome face without his knowledge as he strolled to the driver's side. With ease, he slid into the driver's seat and glanced over at her.

She slipped the cool silver metal into the socket of the seat belt fastener. When her eyes came up to meet his, she froze. Her eyes fixated on the full swells of his lips. The motion of his tongue gliding over his bottom lip and then catching between his straight, white teeth sparked an irresistible urge to touch them with her own lips. Her lips parted. His mouth moved into a slow hypnotic smile. *There*, she consoled herself. *That's the smile I saw earlier.*

Trae pulled away from the curve toward Interstate 20.

"Did you eat?" he pulled his eyes away from the road temporarily.

"No. I didn't have time to grab anything after class. Can we stop for something?"

"Do you think you can hold out until we get to Uncle Ted's place?" he replied, as he briefly glanced over at her. "He's planned a little something out in his backyard."

Reggie almost groaned. Generally when folks in these parts said they were having a little something in the backyard, it meant an all out feast with swarms of people invited. She hadn't expected to be lured off to some stranger's house where there would be more strangers lurking at her. She hoped she wouldn't regret her decision to accompany Trae.

In the back of her mind, she wondered how many women he'd already taken there. *What if they mistake me for one of his other women? Would I be able to handle that?* She pondered the thought for a minute longer. She wasn't like any of the girls he'd dated. *So why is he taking me to meet his family?* She finally decided not to worry about it.

"Okay. I think I can do that," she smiled.

"Great," he replied.

Once they entered Monroe city limits, Reggie caught sight of a female on a corner. She gazed out of the window in wonder. For some reason the woman she spotted looked a lot like Veronica. What was she doing here and why was she standing on the street corner. *It couldn't have been her.* She didn't know how she allowed Veronica to wander into her thoughts. She didn't want her to spoil her mood.

Trae looked over at her and asked, "Something wrong?"

"No." She looked into his handsome face before leaning back into the headrest.

Trae pulled into a long driveway lined by thick trees and bushes where a canary yellow house sat far back on the property. Trae didn't stop until he circled to the back of the house. A few pickup trucks and a white Cadillac were parked along a paved driveway. Trae pulled up near the Cadillac. He turned off the engine but left the keys in the ignition. Reggie waited until he opened her door and helped her from the car.

The smooth sounds of ageless Blues greeted her ears, and the deliciously spicy aroma of a Cajun crab boil assaulted her senses, causing her mouth to water.

"Hmmm, something smells great." she rubbed her tummy.

Trae reached for her hand and led her near the open patio lined with wooden tables and benches.

"Hey, look here. My favorite nephew, yeah," they heard a boisterous voice booming from the tall canvas where three huge vats, filled with steamy spices spewing from them, sat on spitted flames.

"Boy, where you been? Come here and hug yore old uncle here," ordered the tall red man with red hair and red freckles on his nose and cheeks. Open arms extended to him, Traekin moved into his uncle's embrace. He held firm to Reggie's hand in the process pulling her along when his uncle pulled him in closer.

Uncle Ted jovially slapped him on his back. "It's about time you come and see me, yeah boy." He smiled down at his nephew. Ted stood considerably taller than Trae, and towered him by several inches. "Look what we got here. Who's this pretty lil' lady you're hanging onto." He glanced over Trae's shoulder.

"Uncle Ted, this is Regina Miles. We call her Reggie. She goes to Grambling." He extended the clutched hand to his uncle.

"Well, let me look at you, bay. Who your people? Are you from around these parts?" his heavy Creole accent was clipped and fast.

Reggie's smile extended a mile long. Already she knew she liked Uncle Ted. "I'm glad to meet you. I'm from Bossier City." She shook his hand. "Family names include Miles, Henry, Dupree, and Bougese. I also have family living in Convent and in Lafourche Parish, Thibodaux to be exact."

"Dupree, hah. I bet I know some of your people from Bossier. I travel up there quite often." The red mustache curved upward when he smiled.

"Uncle Ted is in the seafood business. Most of the packaged and fresh seafood in these parts come from his catfish and crawfish farms," Trae offered proudly.

"Wow!" she was impressed. "I love seafood. So I have you to thank, Mr. Ted."

"Please call me Ted or you can call me Uncle Ted if you like. That Mister stuff make me feel old," he joked.

"Sure, Uncle Ted," she honored him.

"Well, little lady, you're in the right place, cause I got seafood that will keep a smile on that cute little face of yours." He laughed. "Come on," he called to everyone. "The guest of honor is here. Let's eat!"

They made quick introductions with everyone. She met Trae's younger cousin, Theodore, who could have been Trae's identical twin. He was only thirteen years old and nearly as tall, only he lacked Trae's wide sturdy build. She doubted seriously that it would be long before his hormones kicked in. By looking at his dad and his cousin, he too was going to be a big man.

Everyone treated Reggie like she'd been a long-time visitor or more like family, which really put her at ease. Trae's cousin Shelly asked Reggie if she was her cousin's girlfriend.

"We're just friends." She smiled at the young lady who had just recently celebrated her sixteenth birthday. Shelly commented that Trae never brought girls to the house when he came to visit and that she must be someone special. Reggie briefly considered what she'd heard. She could only hope so. So far, she liked everything about him. He was sweet and very attentive. Based on what she'd heard about him, Trae treated her differently. She celebrated that thought quietly.

Trae watched in amazement as Reggie interacted with his family. He'd overheard Shelly tell her he hadn't invited girls to his home before. She had been correct. He rarely, if ever brought girls around his family, especially during his high school years. He never brought home the girls he dated, mostly because many of them were much older than he was.

He hadn't taken any one girl to his senior prom because he didn't want his options limited. Once the girls in his class found out his intention, a small cluster of them came alone. They all had plans to get Trae to take them home. They purposely sat at a table together and waited on a chance to dance with him. He made his rounds, dancing with each girl at least once.

He smiled inwardly as he remembered. His buddies ragged him until they saw the chicks lining up waiting on him.

"Dang! Give a brother some slack?" one of his classmates asked. "Let somebody else have a turn."

He had a pretty big ego and it had yet to be deflated. The way he figured it, women were always going to flock around him. He wasn't the least bit worried about what his cousin said to Reggie.

Reggie scooted in between the bench and table next to Trae's aunt Alice. When the men tending to the huge vats pulled up the colanders jammed packed with crabs, shrimp, corn, onions, and potatoes, her mouth watered her eyes to tears. She thought she'd died and gone to heaven. They emptied each colander on white butcher's paper spread out on the wooden tables. Everyone gathered around and dug in. Reggie fit in perfectly. She peeled and ate shrimp and crab like an old pro. When her belly was stuffed, she glanced over at Trae who was still putting them away. Her mouth was on fire, but she wouldn't eat her seafood any other way, hot!

Once everyone was stuffed, the tempo of the music changed. The youngster put on Mystikal's old jam, "Danger." Even the older folks got up and began to shake their stuff. Trae pulled Reggie up to her feet and began twirling her around. Ten straight minutes of dancing and everyone was ready for dessert. Fat planks of pralines lined a glass tray, as did chunks of homemade chocolate, lemon, and coconut cakes. Trae went for his aunt's famous sweet potato pie, while Reggie choose a chunk of the coconut cake.

They sat across from one another and enjoyed their dessert. The way things progressed, Trae didn't have time to woo Reggie all afternoon as he had planned. It would seem his little family visit hadn't quite worked out as he'd hoped. Nonetheless, he'd enjoyed himself and enjoyed Reggie's company. She was fun to be with and made it easy to be himself. He didn't have to impress her. He'd observed her sitting around the table talking trash to his uncle and his friends about the upcoming football season. They too were impressed at just how much she knew about sports. His cousin, the younger Theodore, tried to pick her up.

Trae intervened quickly. "Hey, little man, listen up. This is my girl. Go find your own." Trae playfully pushed him away.

Now, as he accepted the fork full of cake Reggie pushed into his mouth, he liked more and more of what he saw in her.

"Are you having a good time?" he asked.

With a mouth full of cake she shook her head up and down. After she swallowed the cake, she said, "I'm having a blast. Thank you for asking me."

Her smile alone was reward enough for him. The dimples danced

and winked at him again and again. Trae sliced a forkful of sweet potato pie and offered it to her. Most girls would have gawked at the offer.
She, on the other hand, opened her mouth and accepted the proffered
treat.

"Hmm, that's good," she smiled.

Trae coaxed her to join in the egg race and ball toss, however, he
couldn't get her to take a ride with him on one of his uncle's dirt bikes.
He reached over and attempted to drag her onto the back of the bike.

"Look at what I have on, Traekin. No way are you getting me on the
back of a bike," she yipped moving out of his reach.

"Oh, yeah. I forgot. Maybe next time?"

"Yeah, Creole boy. Next time."

Reggie felt so completely at home that she fell asleep lounged under
a huge shaded tree. Neither the loud chatter nor the music interrupted
the slumber that overtook her. She didn't sleep very well last night.
Visions of Traekin haunted her. When Trae returned from the bike ride,
he found her stretched out on the canvas lounger. He quietly leaned
over and kissed her on the brow. She stirred a little before slowly raising
heavy lids.

"Hi, sleepyhead. You're ruining a perfectly good party." He smiled
down at her.

"I am?" she asked groggily.

"Yeah. You're missing all the good music and outrageous lies told by
all these old folks." He chuckled.

Reggie laughed too. She scooted over on the lounger so he could sit
next to her.

His family hadn't overlooked the intimate interlude between Reggie
and Trae. Kinfolks had been watching the interactions between the two
the entire afternoon. Ted wrapped his arm around his wife's shoulder
and kissed her cheek.

"Look's like we might get ourselves a little niece-in-law, Alice girl.
What you think?" He looked into his wife's dark brown eyes.

"I think you might be right." She smiled eyeing the two on the lounger.

By the time the sun started to descend, many of their friends had begun to leave. Trae and Reggie helped his aunt and uncle put away leftovers and packed doggie bags for themselves.

"Well Unc, it's time to hit the road." Trae slapped his uncle on the back.

"Don't be a stranger. You know you're always welcome here anytime. And, young lady, that goes for you, too. You don't have to wait until Traekin brings you back either, you hear me?" He reached for and embraced Reggie to his chest.

"Okay, thanks," she said.

Trae pulled Reggie's hand into his and laced his fingers through hers. As they strolled through the lobby doors of her dorm, their eyes scanned the crowds huddled everywhere. Just about every nook and cranny of the huge lobby was occupied. Neither was ready to end the evening. Reggie longed to be kissed. She had yet to sample the sweet lips that tempted her. She wished desperately that he would hold her and kiss her passionately, but she knew that wasn't about to happen here in the open lobby.

Several pairs of eyes watched them as they stood in front of elevator. Inviting him up to the room wasn't a great idea since she hadn't discussed it with Val before leaving.

"I would invite you up, but I don't know what Val's plans are." She looked up into his handsome face. "I can call up, though," she said as an afterthought.

"No. It's okay. I have some things to catch up on." He hid the disappointment in his eyes. "I had a great time today." His eyes slowly gazed over her face.

"I had a wonderful time. Thank you so much, Trae," Reggie uttered sincerely.

"Well," he hesitated for a moment, "do you mind if I call you tomorrow?"

"I won't mind at all," she said as she reached into the small bag slung over her shoulder. She scribbled on the square yellow sheet of paper.

"I put my cell number on there as well." She looked up and caught him appraising her.

Trae's large hands closed around hers and the yellow paper. He lowered his eyes until they were focused on her lips. He contemplated his next move, to kiss her like he'd longed to do all day.

Reggie's breath caught in her throat when hands closed around hers. The rapid rise and fall of her chest became more prominent when she watched his gaze move to her mouth. She clamped her lips tightly together to suppress the whimper threatening to spill from her throat.

As if in slow motion, Trae raised her hand to his open mouth and flickered the tip of his tongue across the blunt tips of her fingers. Reggie trembled. She felt exposed to him and the guaranteed fifty or so pair of eyes now observing their interlude. He released her hand. It was still suspended in the air when he took several steps backwards.

"Sweet dreams," his raspy voice spoke just above a whisper. He turned and strolled away. There was no telling what he might have done had he stayed. Trae found it easy to show the emotions he needed to seduce Reggie. He had a problem controlling them once they were out. He battled to keep them in check. *What on earth is happening to me? Why does she have this effect on me?* He was sure to spend yet another restless night without relief.

CHAPTER 6

Reggie peeled away her sticky dress and underwear and stepped into the shower. She allowed the warm spray to drench her from head to toe. Once she was done, she padded over to her bed in a pair of cotton pajamas and climbed into bed, and hugged her knees to her chest. She had some reading to catch up on, yet she could only daydream about Trae. She pulled the syllabus from the folder pocket and glared at it for several seconds before her mind registered that the black letters were merely a blur.

She took a long sighing breath before placing the stapled sheets back into the folder. Setting the book and folder on the nightstand, Reggie left her bedroom, walked through the common living area and rapped lightly on Valerie's door.

"Val," she called.

Her hand rested on the cool knob. No answer. She wondered where Val had gone. Reggie searched the common area for a note. Ordinarily, Val left a sticky-note on the pegboard or the door. Not today.

Tired from a long yet enjoyable day, Reggie crawled back into her bed, this time she pulled the covers up and over her head. It didn't take very long to fall into a deep, wanting sleep.

When Trae pulled up to his dorm parking lot, Reggie was still on his mind. He took long deliberate steps up the stairs to the inside lobby of his dorm. There he met a smiling and barely dressed Veronica just inside the revolving doors. The smile plastered on her face would have lit up most of central Louisiana.

"Hi," she greeted him warmly.

Ah! Just what I need. A warm body, soft and pliable beneath his, to take away the ache threatening to rip the seams of his snug denim jeans was what he needed the most.

"Hey, Roni. What's up?" he addressed her casually.

"I've been waiting on you," she replied seductively. "I thought you might need a little pampering tonight."

She walked straight into the wall of his chest, her arms instantly curving around his slim waist. The cushions of her breasts brushed against him, warm and soft against his chest. She lifted up onto her toes, leaned into him, and placed her red painted lips at the base of his neck. Heat soared through his body with the simple touch and sent the blood rushing to the bulge in his pants. With controlled proficiency, he wrapped his arms around Veronica's waist and pulled her in closer. He covered her lips with firm urgency.

He allowed a small moan to escape his lips. The sound was like music to Veronica's ears. She would make him pay, however, for the little misunderstanding yesterday. Nonetheless, she was happy it would be her who shared his bed tonight. Trae broke the kiss first. He released her, then draped his arm around her shoulder and led her to his room.

They strolled down the hall to his room, stopping every few steps to lock lips. When they finally reached the door leading to the common area of his room, he once again embraced her tightly. Their kiss was passionate and filled with such urgency that they nearly crashed into the door. Instantly, his hands went down to caress her firm round buttocks. He pressed her into his rolling hips.

Trae planted juicy deliberate kisses down the center of her neck. The simple move caused her body to yield. She cried out his name shamelessly. Trae couldn't help the moans escaping from the back of his throat. His mind was totally and fully on Reggie even though he was locked in Veronica's embrace. It was Reggie he yearned for at the moment. The sweet smell of her soft firm body was all that ran through his mind.

He released one hand and placed it on the knob of the door and began to turn it. As it creaked open, he pulled Veronica's pulsating body in with his. It wasn't until he heard the clearing of throats did he break the lock he had on her mouth. The cloud of fog quickly lifted. He jerked from Veronica's embrace and gave his attention to the eyes now glued on the two of them.

He met the stares of Rykard, Corey, and another teammate, Ben Parker. Veronica didn't seem the least bit shy or embarrassed. As Trae looked down into her face, he realized that he'd only allowed Veronica to seduce him because he couldn't have his way with the one person he wanted to be with.

In a small, thankful way, he was glad the fellas were there. He had an excuse to get rid of Veronica before he did something he might regret later. For the life of him he couldn't understand what the hell was wrong with him. He'd never before had trouble being with more than one woman at a time. This certainly was the wrong damn time to get morals. He pushed Veronica away slightly.

"Hey, maybe we can do this another time," he whispered down into her ear.

The pout on her swollen kissed lips clearly stated that she wasn't happy about the interruption, nor did she like the fact that Trae hadn't asked them to leave so they could finish what they'd started. Any other time he would have.

"Can't you make them leave?" she whined.

He looked over at the three who only stared. He turned Veronica toward the door and led her out into the hallway.

"Listen, Roni, I'm sorry. How about a rain check?" he leaned down and kissed her opened mouth.

When he pulled away, Veronica's head was still tilted back, her eyelids were closed, and her mouth was partially open. He broke the spell when he offered to walk her back to the lobby. Her eyes flew up and she stared at him in disbelief.

"No, don't worry about it. I know my way back," the anger clearly etched on her face and laced deep in her voice.

Trae watched her sashay back down the hall. He waited the few seconds it took for her to disappear. He passed the back of his hand over his mouth to remove remnants of Veronica's lipstick from his lips. When he stepped back into the room, the lively discussion brewed to a louder roar.

"Damn, man," Rykard spoke first. "Two minutes earlier and you would have been face to face with Reggie's roommate. She and two of their friends just left here. They were here, I'm guessing, to check on you and Reggie. They stayed a little while, and we had a nice time, man."

The concern on Trae's face was obvious. All he needed was one stupid move to mess up his bet. This crap needed to end. He was still hell bent on winning this bet, no matter what.

"What did they want?" he asked.

"They waited for you and Reggie. I guess they thought you had planned to bring her here, you know what I mean," Corey sneered.

Trae rolled his eyes at him. His plans changed while they were at his uncle's house. He was relieved they had. Luck hadn't been with him today. Had he known Valerie was here, he would have accepted Reggie's invitation. He hadn't cared where the interlude occurred...just that it did. *So Val came here to intervene. How had she known what my plans were? Someone talked. How else could they have known I'd bring her here?*

"Looks like somebody's on to you, man," Ben added.

"Shut the hell up, Ben," Trae barked. "You couldn't get a piece if it was shoved in your face."

The other two laughed at Trae's insult. Ben huffed his way to the door, and before he walked through the door he turned and said, "Looks like you're the one not getting the piece, Player." He slammed the door.

"Dang, man. You were rough on my man." Rykard stepped around Trae.

Trae lowered his huge frame into the nearest chair. Gloom stretched across his handsome face. He peered up at his two friends.

"I think the two of you are sabotaging my stuff." He glared at them both.

"Listen." Rykard sat across from him. "Your behind was the one around here bragging about what you can do brother. You didn't expect us to help you, did you?" he asked.

"No! I sure in hell didn't expect the two of you to be against me."

"Look, man, it wouldn't have mattered. Those ladies meant business," Corey added. "You didn't stand a chance."

Trae rose from the chair and looked at them both.

"Somehow, I get the feeling they didn't just wander over here." He turned and headed for the shower.

When he flung his naked body into the bed, the cold shower had done nothing to relieve the aching throb that was guaranteed to rob him of precious sleep. After he tossed and turned for hours, Trae fell into a restless slumber. The knock at his bedroom door jarred him awake.

"Trae," Rykard called before sticking his head in the door. "Let's go, man."

Trae threw one of the pillows at the door. Rykard moved into a blocking position just as it landed against the wall near him.

"Go away, traitor," he groaned.

"Alright, man. Coach ain't gonna like the fact that you're not in the game room in the next half-hour," he reminded Trae.

When Trae walked into the game room, the staff members seated at the front behind a long table glanced up.

"Glad to see you could grace us with your presence, Brooks," the coach barked.

Trae knew better than to make any comment. Instead, he sauntered over to the nearest open chair and eased himself into it. Three hours after intensive play reviews, Trae and his teammates wandered off to the University Cafeteria for a bite to eat. He was in a sour mood this morning and everyone knew it.

"Hey, what animal climbed up his butt," one of the guys joked.

Trae threw him a dark, cold glare. The pupils in his brown eyes almost became a narrow slit. He trampled off to the opposite side of the cafeteria. When he had enough to eat, which wasn't very much, he walked back to his dorm. He'd considered going by Reggie's dorm, then quickly changed his mind. If anyone could brighten his mood it was she. The way things were headed, the chances to mess things up were pretty significant. He opted, instead, to go to his roomwhere he attempted to do the homework assignment he'd put off since Thursday. He'd managed to stay on the Dean's List even with the hectic schedule he kept. When he wasn't at football practice or in class, he was in the students' office. As Class President, he delegated some responsibilities to the other class officers.

At this rate, if he didn't buckle down with schoolwork, he would fall behind in his studies. Frustrated because he hadn't made any headway with homework, Trae picked up the phone and punched in the numbers from the yellow slip of paper. After he didn't get an answer, he hung up and dialed the number to her cell phone. He felt the sudden urge and unmistakable need to hear her voice. After the second ring he heard her chipper voice chime from the other end of the phone.

"Talk to me," she sang.

"Hi beautiful. What are you up to?"

His smooth deep voice was like music to her ears.

"Well, in about ten minutes, I'll be in the library making a mad attempt to study for an exam I have tomorrow. And you?" Reggie eagerly anticipated his reply.

She'd hoped for a call earlier. Reggie realized after mid-day she couldn't wait on Traekin to call her. She and Val went to Sunday school and then to brunch. Reggie eagerly shared the events of the previous day and how wonderful she felt about how things had progressed with Trae. Val cautioned her to be careful. She knew how easy it was to be hurt by someone like Traekin. Val also confessed that she and a few of the girls had gone to Traekin's room because she thought he would try to seduce her there. Reggie wasn't at all happy with her friend's confession, still, she understood they tried to protect her.

"Val, I love you, and I appreciate what you're trying to do. I can handle this okay. Promise me you won't do anything like that again."

The disappointment was clear, but Val understood her friend better than she understood herself.

"Okay. Don't make me tell you I told you so," she warned.

"You won't do that even if it came down to it." She smiled at her roommate.

How can Val understand how this man makes me feel? It wasn't like anything she'd experienced before. Reggie had had her share of loser boyfriends. All they wanted to do was bed her, and she wasn't having it. Something about Trae was so right. She hoped her friend would understand and be happy for her. *She just needs to get use to the idea of sharing me with the big guy*, she quietly defended her friend's action. *Once Val gets to know him better, I'm sure she'll loosen up a bit.*

"Well, I need to study myself," he confessed. "Truth be known, I've had a terrible time with this study stuff. I haven't been able to concentrate"

"How about a little support?" she asked.

Funny how she read my mind, he pondered. He knew he had to do the homework, but since he couldn't get his mind off of her, if they were together just maybe he might get in the mood to do what he had to. *Kill two birds with one stone*, he thought. She seemed to stimulate him when they were together. *Yes, I want to be with her right now*, he conceded.

"That would be great," he answered. "I'll meet you there in about fifteen minutes."

"I'll see you in a little while," she sang into the phone. "Bye."

"Bye," he offered. She'd already hung up.

Reggie placed the phone back into the side pocket of her bag. She made certain it was powered off. Nothing annoyed her more than the interruption of a ringing cell phone while in class or the library. The campus had strict rules about the use of cell phones in the library, class, and other official activities. She passed through the metal detector and looked for a secluded table. When she spotted an area off the one side of the library that would allow her to see Trae when he came through the door, she headed for an opened table. A young lady stopped her. Reggie remembered her from try-outs on Wednesday.

"Hi," she greeted in a happy hushed tone. "I'm Jerica. I was at try-outs for the dance team."

"Hi," Reggie greeted her back. "I'm Reggie." She was happy to know someone from that group was friendly.

"I'm really anxious about the list they're supposed to post tomorrow," her chipper voice was a little exaggerated.

She, too, was anxious but chose not to think about it. Besides, for the last three or four days, Traekin had consumed her thoughts entirely.

She smiled down sweetly at Jerica. "Good luck. I hope to see you on the next go round," she said sincerely.

And she hoped that she would. It would be nice to have someone sincere to relate to in the event she made the team. She didn't want to sound negative. Maybe she should have said 'when she made the team.' Everyone was confident in her ability to make this team. Why should she doubt them?

"See you around," she replied.

"See you," Reggie left to claim the table she'd spotted earlier. When she resumed her approach, the table was now occupied.

Oh well, she sighed and moved to find another spot.

Reggie had just settled in when she felt his presence. The illumination of the space he occupied hypnotized her as he stood towering over her. He leaned down, her face was upturned as she waited, and he placed a warm kiss on her nose. She was so certain he would kiss her on the mouth, that she held her breath in anticipation. She was disappointed when his mouth missed her parted lips.

"Hi." The warm minty scent of his breath washed over her like a cool summer rain. *God I can't get next to this woman like I want to*, he thought in mild frustration.

Suddenly the quest to lay her was no longer important. He hadn't understood why he'd been having such a hard time dealing with this woman until now. He had feelings for her. Now he had to determine what in the hell to do about it. Having feelings for a woman was something he'd not been accustomed to. He purposefully stayed out of this territory. *What now?* he wondered. He could play this little game until the end. Then what? He would end up with nothing. If he told her about his bet, he risked losing her.

Maybe she wouldn't find out. The chances of that happening were certainly nil. Val and her gang would skin his hide for sure. Also, if he didn't tell her and she found out, the consequences would be worse. He wouldn't only lose her as a conquest but would also risk their friendship. Right now their friendship seemed more important to him. *What happened to Mr. Debonair?* he wondered. *What will your boys think when they find out?* he agonized. *Forget the boys.* He just had to figure out when to tell her the truth. It would undoubtedly break her heart. The mere thought caused tightness in his chest.

Reggie looked at him. She couldn't believe how handsome he was.

The powerfully strong lines of his chin and jaw tempted her to reach out and stroke the long exquisite lines of his face. Without a thought, without hesitation, she gave into her temptation. Her touch was sudden. They both jumped when her soft, satiny palm made contact with his shaven, smooth jaw.

When Trae responded to her simple, but erotic touch, his mind spun out of control. He leaned in closer to her face to capture her lips, but instead moved his lips to her ear lobe. His murmur made Reggie moan with need.

"I missed you," he whispered lustfully in her ear. The hot air from his mouth sent chills down the entire length of her body. The commanding scent of his cologne and the sheer nearness of his mouth to her face enticed her.

"Trae," she whispered.

Trae found control and managed to move into the chair directly across from her. His eyes and smile were filled with unspoken desire. Several minutes passed before either spoke. Only the passion-filled air between them delivered the words they dared not say. Trae laced his fingers through hers, and he lightly squeezed her slim delicate fingers. She allowed the warmth from his hands to flow through her. Then an unexpected presence appeared from nowhere and severed their intimate moment. Reggie's eyes strayed first. Trae didn't bother to look up until he heard a high-pitched voice.

CHAPTER 7

The anger was evident in Veronica's voice. She didn't like being played. She knew Trae didn't have serious relationships with any one woman. He'd made that clear in the beginning. She didn't have cause to be angry with him for staring hazily into the eyes of another woman. He'd made it clear he belonged to no one. She was ticked, though, that just last night he'd been all over her, like white on rice.

"What are you doing here, Trae?" she snapped.

Cool, calm, and collected, Trae addressed her. "Hello, Veronica." His eyes and his words were so chilling that even Reggie knew she didn't want to be on the receiving end of this conversation. Reggie eased from her chair.

"Excuse me, I'll be right back." She looked at Trae's disapproving scowl.

She remembered she didn't take the same crap from him that other women had; Reggie stepped away from the table. His defiant stare said exactly that. Just how she got away with it, he had yet to learn. Trae returned his cold calculating glare to Veronica. She instantly regretted her comment. She knew that although they didn't have the kind of meaningful relationship she wanted, she wanted one with him. She would endur his involvement with other women. In the end he always came to her for what he needed.

Reggie pretended to occupy herself with a set of journals on the opposite side of the library. She casually glanced back at the table where Trae sat and Veronica stood. She hadn't taken a seat and Reggie didn't understand why. The conversation, although hushed, was in loud accusing tones. The expression on Veronica's face was obvious frustration. On the other hand, Trae's expression showed indifference. She only saw him nod his head a few times.

Veronica seemed to do a lot of talking. When his lips did move, it seemed Veronica's face went into a mass of total despair. As much as Reggie didn't care for this woman, her heart immediately went out to Veronica. The devastation on her face matched the broken heart pinned in her chest. Reggie took a few mental notes and decided then that she would guard her own heart dearly. She vowed to never have this done to her. A girl could never be sure.

Reggie moved to yet another area of the library. She attempted to buy the two more time to complete their conversation. She hadn't expected him to ease up behind her. Trae wrapped his arms around her tiny waist. The feel of his large hand seared through the cotton T-shirt. His head bent down and kissed her on the back of her ear. She shamelessly succumbed to his touch. Her body melted into the wall of his chest.

"We've got some studying to do, little girl," he teased.

Reggie smiled up at him. She allowed him to lead her back to their table. They both settled into a comfortable silence as they studied. Trae was content to just have her near while he completed his work. Reggie felt the same. A couple of hours into their study session, they strayed a little, conversing comfortably about the coming week. And, for the second time that day, she was reminded that the list from the try-out would be posted the next morning.

"Are you worried?" he asked.

Reggie shrugged her shoulders upward. Eventually her eyes reached his anxious face. The sincerity she saw there offered her reassurance. She took a calming breath before she responded.

"I don't know. I guess I'm a little antsy."

"Why?" he asked. "You were the best dancer there."

A shy smile slid across Reggie's face. She felt inclined to believe Trae said those things to flatter her. He seemed to read her very well and commented, "I'm not just saying so Regg. I think you're a fantastic dancer." He leaned back in the chair and observed the surprised look on her face.

She'd not missed the new pet name he'd given her. Regg! The sound, as it rolled off of his tongue, was seductive and whenever he called her name, whether it was Regina, or Reggie, or as he did moments ago, Regg, it was filled with intimacy, so full of passion. Reggie was very comfortable with her dancing abilities. She wasn't worried about her capabilities as a dancer. What did worry her, however, was the political climate. The politics of making the dance team might play a greater roll than she'd like. In the past, there had been girls well qualified for the team that didn't make it.

"I guess we'll find out tomorrow," she replied nervously.

"Why don't I go with you in the morning to check the list?"

Just great! she thought. Earlier, she had to ask herself if she could stand the disappointment of finding out she didn't make the initial cut. The thought of Trae there to witness the whole ordeal would be unimaginable. She saw the determined and supportive look on his face.

"Okay," she sighed. "If you want to."

"What time will they post the list?"

"By ten."

"Why don't we go after Philosophy class? You think you can wait that long?"

His hand extended across the table and rested on top of hers. The warmth of it soothed the raging nerves that fluttered in her stomach. Even if she didn't make the list, she was glad she'd tried out. It had brought something good to her. She wouldn't be here with Trae had she not, and this alone was more than a dream come true. Then her mind shifted for a moment, and a little voice nagged her. She looked into his handsome face and knew she had to follow her heart.

"Yeah, sure," she answered.

"I don't know about you, but I'm starved. A couple of slices of pizza would certainly curb the appetite right about now." He smiled across the table at her. In his mind he said, *Pizza won't fill the need I have to be buried deep inside of your body. I need that more than anything in the world.* His groin stirred. He rose from the chair quickly to change the direction of his thought. He shoved his books into the open bag as he watched her from beneath long, dark lashes.

"Are you game?" he asked.

Reggie stood and followed his lead. With both of their bags slung over his shoulder, Trae allowed her to precede him through the pizzeria. They enjoyed pizza and the comfortable conversation, which surfaced naturally for them both. The sour mood he'd been in earlier seemed to dissipate totally while in her presence. After pizza he followed her to her dorm parking lot. The realization that he could spend his every waking moment with her hit him hard. Trae knew then that he would have to tell her about the bet. Not tonight, he thought. He wasn't ready to taint the spectacular weekend they'd spent together. Not only that, Trae knew she had a stressful day ahead of her tomorrow if she didn't make the initial cut for the dance squad. He worried that he would break her heart, and it killed him inside.

He waited until Reggie pulled into a spot before propelling his SUV directly in front of it and shifting the gear into park. He got out, walked around, and stood at the front bumper of her car. Her backpack hung loosely by his side. When she got out she automatically met his expectant glance with the same beautiful smile. His heart rammed against his chest. The emotions he felt were so awesome he found he couldn't resist her any longer. As soon as she was within arms reach, he pulled her into a very snug embrace.

He wrapped his arms around her slim body and held her tight. Trae savored the sensation of her body meshed up against his. Her body's sweet and unconditional surrender heightened the already explosive passion raging through him. His brown eyes hid behind closed lids and his face rested comfortably on top of her head. Her slim arms wrapped around his waist and her fingers gripping the fabric of his shirt made his heart quicken. Firmly, but gently, he added pressure to the already firm grip.

Reggie was totally and utterly surprised by Trae's gesture, even though she'd yearned for it the moment she laid eyes on him at the library. The entire afternoon seemed to be charged by something she couldn't explain. His posture, his words, and his demeanor were all fueled by something she couldn't quite label. She chalked up the behavior as an apology, maybe, for Veronica's interruption and wanting to make certain she knew she had his undivided attention.

She couldn't, however, ignore the strange feeling that Trae felt differently about her than he did a few days ago. Much of it could have stemmed from her desire to be more than just another pretty face or someone to occupy his time until he got bored enough to move on to the next woman. She celebrated at the many heart-felt possibilities. She wanted his heart totally and completely. She wasn't sure that a man like Trae could give himself to any woman. Maybe that was why he strayed so often and so freely.

As she lavished in the hot blazed comforts of his arms, she opened her heart to feel something she didn't think she was capable of. She should have been afraid, knowing what she knew about his reputation. She should have remembered the scene with Veronica earlier this afternoon. She didn't really know this man, only what she'd heard and only what she'd learned over the last few days, and yet every thing he had been the past weekend was everything she wanted.

His hands had been on her the entire time at the pizzeria. The electric-filled hands stroked her hair and face, and lit her mind and body on fire. She wanted him to do more than touch her with his hands. Those thoughts made her shudder within his embrace. In response to her willingness, he held her tighter.

After a few seconds of savoring her passion, a low groan escaped from the back of his throat. His lips trailed down the length of her face until they reached the soft warm flesh of her neck. She relinquished her body to him. He dropped the book bag at his feet and moved his large hand to the round firm buttocks. Trae lifted her slightly off of her feet and squeezed her body into his, which induced her head to fall backwards. The soft cry escaped from her lips, "Trae." It made his body shutter.

Lost in the drugged and dreamy feel of their interlude, Traekin had nearly forgotten where they were. He didn't want to compromise her. Not here, not now, not ever! He found the strength needed to release the fog. He whispered hoarsely in her ear. "Baby, I'm going to pull away. Not because I want to, okay?" He slowly loosened his hold on her until his face was inches from hers.

When her eyes finally opened, he saw in them the mask of succulent and sensual cravings he knew was evident in his own eyes. They stared into the depths of each other's eyes, drinking from them the knowledge that their need for one another would go unchecked tonight. Not daring to tempt his control, Traekin kissed her brow, and slowly and completely released her. Both felt the instant loss.

Trae bent slightly and retrieved her book bag from the pavement. Before he released it into her hands he leaned over and kissed her cheek.

"I'll see you in class tomorrow," he murmured softly.

"Good night," her low husky voice and her glassy looks gave credence to how she felt.

"Sweet dreams," he heard himself saying but hadn't been certain he spoken. He'd been so caught up in the erotic glow of her eyes he wasn't sure.

Reggie stepped around him and headed for the back entrance of the dorm. She turned for one last glance. He stood with one arm stretch across the space between him and his vehicle, his hand gripped on the back of it for support. His eyes were steady on her. She smiled and returned her steps until she was through the doors. She didn't look back a second time. Trae stood in the same spot for a few minutes contemplating his plight with Reggie. What had gone wrong he wondered?

When he got to his room, Rykard was stretched out on the couch with the television remote in his hand.

"Hey, what's up?" he greeted Trae.

"Yo man, I need to talk," the seriousness in his voice was apparent.

Rykard knew something was up with Trae. He'd acted strangely the last several days. After his trip to Monroe, the ordeal with Val, and then Veronica, he started thinking his friend was well over his head. They had been friends a long time, even before they came to Grambling. Both had been in the same football league during high school and often played against one another. On occasions, they'd roomed together at state and parish football camps. From those beginnings, they fostered a great relationship and mutual respect for one another. Rykard never considered himself as big of a player as Trae, still he liked his share of women and understood where Trae came from when he dealt with women. Too many of them liked head games. He liked the feel of their bodies next to his, yet he hated the petty games.

Rykard knew what kind of woman Reggie was when he made the bet with Trae. He knew, because he'd tried talking to her roommate. She was truly his kind of woman, fine as hell, however, too straight-laced for his taste at the time. She and Reggie were very much alike. So Val's appearance at his door last night was one of shock and realization. She was the last person he expected to show up at his door. He liked her a lot. She spoke her mind. Getting to know her while she waited for her friend was more beneficial for him than her little scheme to breakup Trae and Reggie helped her. She'd come to their room in case Trae attempted to bring Reggie there to seduce her. Trae and Reggie hadn't shown up.

So you could say he knew that Trae would get nowhere with Reggie, at least in her bed. She was too classy for that. What he was anxious to find out right now was whether or not Trae planned to admit it. Right away he saw the deadpan expression on his face, and couldn't help but think that tonight was payday. It was too good to be true! Why now? Couldn't this wait until tomorrow in front of all the fellows? He wanted Trae to admit defeat in front of the boys so he couldn't down play the whole thing.

The more Rykard thought about this wager between him and his friend, the more he thought that maybe he had been unfair and had taken advantage of Trae's ignorance about Reggie. They had always been straight up with one another and loved the bantering relationship they had. This was the one time he hadn't been straight up with him.

The more he watched Trae, the more he thought that he was ready to relinquish the bet. The first ever! What he wasn't prepared for, were the words that escaped his friend's lips. NO! This couldn't be. This was Traekin Brooks, his main man. The tall cat who got all the chicks, just as he bragged about in the gym last week. Rykard bolted straight up on the couch the instant the words left Trae's lips.

"I'm in love with Reggie," the words were stated so simply and clearly.

It had only taken Trae a few minutes to reach that conclusion. He had been just as shocked as his friend who now sat with his mouth gapped. As he stood in her parking lot earlier, he couldn't fathom what in the hell was wrong with him. Every time he was with her he went completely out of his mind. He did things that, for him, were totally out of character and unheard of. He hadn't handled her the way he'd treated other women. Other women, women he'd dealt with since he was in his early teens. He didn't negotiated with women. They did things on his terms. So, to bend every rule he'd ever set drove him crazy. And this uncontrollable urge to be with her was unexplainable. *What is this?* he kept asking himself.

"What!" Rykard boomed. "Man, what are you talking about?"

"I know this sounds crazy, Ry, man! I don't know what in the hell else this could be. I started out wooing this girl, and in return, I got a dose of something I don't know what in the hell to do with." His large frame fell into the closest chair.

Rykard continued to look at him as though he'd crash-landed from Mars, alien head and all. He couldn't believe his ears. The confession alone spoke volumes. He and Trae were tight, but damn, even that kind of crap he kept to himself. What do you say to a brother who's been bitten?

"Are you sure?" Rykard asked and knew instantly that it was a stupid question to ask.

Trae looked at him in absolute despair. His hands washed over his face. He could feel the prickly evidence of his after-five shadow. His hands came together into a cup where he rested his forehead. He spoke without looking up. He didn't know if he could stand the accusation in his friend's face. It was enough to hear it in his voice.

"You win the bet man," he yielded.

How could he kick his friend down when he needed to be lifted? Somehow the bet didn't mean anything. If Trae was serious about what he said, he obviously didn't know how to deal with this. In all the time he'd known him, Trae had never given any indication that he had feelings for any of the women he'd been involved with. Rykard steered away from relationships for altogether different reasons. Women didn't understand him, how he thought, what he wanted out of life. He managed to be a player much better than survive a serious relationship. Somehow he knew he wouldn't be able to help him out.

"Have you told her?" he asked.

"What? That I love her?" he asked in returned.

"That, and the bet."

"No. No, I haven't told her either one."

"Good. Maybe it's not too late. Just back out of this thing, man. Nobody gets hurt."

"It's not that easy, man. I have feelings for this woman. I've already tried to ignore them. You've seen how I've acted over the past several days. I have to tell her about the bet. I can't let her find out from anyone else." The horror of the fact etched his face into a sour mask.

"No. You can't do that, Trae. Maybe she won't find out," Rykard attempted to instill some hope into his friend.

"If there's a crawfish left in Louisiana, Rykard, she's bound to find out." He stood and walked over to the stack of CDs on the entertainment stand and fingered a few of them before he turned to face Rykard.

"You're a player, man. I'm a player. What do I know about this foolishness of the heart?" Rykard asked as his shoulder shrugged upward and his hands extended out in the same gesture. He wouldn't admit that he might be headed down that same road. He spent a few hours with Val today. He understood the seriousness of Trae's dilemma. He liked her company as well.

Trae sighed long and hard. He rammed a hard fist on the back of the chair where he stood. He paced the small space between the chair and stereo, which only heightened his frustration. He stopped a moment; Rykard helplessly stood by and watched him.

"I'm telling her about the bet and taking my chances. I have to. I don't want to lose her friendship, even if we don't become lovers."

Rykard slipped back onto the couch. He couldn't believe his ears. Surely if Trae had been hit by the craziness of falling for a woman, nobody else was immune. His eyes shifted, and he took a long hard look at Trae. He respected this man. They'd never been at odds about anything. He had always been there when he needed support and right now Trae needed some support in return.

He eased from the couch, walked directly to him, and extended his hand.

"You know I got your back, man," he waited for Trae's response.

Trae accepted the hand and pulled him in and patted him on the back. "Thanks, man," he said relieved. "I know I can always count on you."

"So, when are you going to tell her?" he asked.

"In a couple of days. I need some time to break this to her. I can't do it any sooner than that because the list for tryouts comes out tomorrow. If she doesn't make the list, I'll wait a little. I don't want to devastate her more than I know I have to, man. I just need you to not say anything to the boys just yet."

"Don't worry about it, man. Like I said, I got your back."

When Reggie entered her room, Val was in the shower. After about ten minutes, she stuck her head in the door.

"Hey, when did you get in?" she queried.

"About ten minutes or so. What's up?" Reggie turned around fully to regard her friend.

Val sported a grin a mile long. Reggie couldn't help herself and joined in on the contagious gesture. "Well," she encouraged.

"Well. You're not the only girl in town wooing a jock," she teased.

Reggie's eyes lit up brightly. "Oh. And just who is this jock supposed to be?" she was dying to know.

"Rykard Wiggins." All of Val's front teeth were visible.

If Reggie's shocked expression wasn't apparent, her words gave Val the clue. "The Rykard Wiggins," she whooped.

Val's head bobbed up and down while she did a little dance. Reggie pulled her down on the bed.

"You little wench! When did this happen?" Reggie yelped.

"A few days ago," she boasted. The glow from her smiling face was enough to light up the entire dorm.

"Details, and don't give me no crap. I want to know everything!"

CHAPTER 8

Reggie rolled over to the edge of her bed. The silk nightcap she'd place on her head before crawling beneath the cool covers was lodged between the pillows and the fitted sheets. After she and Val talked for a few hours, she attempted to study a little more for her eight o'clock exam. The physics book and notes were scattered on the floor next to the bed. Stretching her arms over her head, she released the yawn she tried desperately to stifle.

Moments before, the alarm clock severed the wondrous dream of Trae and her on the sandy Gulf beach. It took a few minutes to find the right knob, but she finally punched the snooze button. The dream was too good to end yet, and she was just getting to the best part. Trae was about to pull her into his arms and with her hand still resting on top of the clock, she slipped back into her dream. However, eight minutes later the piercing alarm granted her no mercy. She lazily thumped the dial a last time before finally shutting it off.

As her legs hung over the sides of the bed, her toes touched the yellow text highlighter caught in the center of the opened book. A groan escaped her lips as she remembered the challenges the day would bring. She had fifty minutes to complete an exam she was sure was going to take two and a half-hours. The instructor insisted that anyone who finished his exams cheated because he never expected them to. He warned the class that his tests were meant to challenge them beyond what was traditionally expected.

"If I gave you only enough questions to answer within a timeframe, then you wouldn't have to do any more than what's on the test. Not knowing what my parameters are in this case, and giving you more questions than I know you can answer, might force you to go beyond what you think is required. You'll thank me when you take next semester's Physics class," he boasted.

Reggie didn't want to have to thank him. In fact, she was certain the next Physics course wouldn't be on her schedule. She asked herself several times why had she taken this class. It wasn't a required course for her. The thought of her physics woes were quickly pushed aside as she remembered that she would also find out if she made the list for the next level of tryouts. Reggie groaned once more. Why she put herself through these aggravations she would never know.

To Reggie's amazement, she felt pretty good about the exam. The call from Trae early that morning helped boost her confidence. She smiled throughout the entire exam. He told her he would be there with her in spirit, and he was. By the time she got to their Philosophy class, she could hardly contain her excitement.

She was earlier than usual, so she waited by the entrance of the auditorium until she saw his face above the heads moving through the halls. Her whole body lit up when his eyes met hers. They seemed to penetrate straight through her, and her breath caught in her chest as he neared. Their eyes remained locked until he was standing over her. The dimpled smile welcomed him as it did every time she laid eyes on him.

"Hi," she gasped breathlessly. She continued to gaze into his gorgeous face.

No words could explain what happened to him each time he saw her. A week ago no one could tell him that he would be this crazy about a woman without being called a liar. He would've even bet away his inheritance on it. Hell that's how he got himself in this mess in the first place. He'd been tempted to call her last night and ask her to meet him by the front curb. He intended to ease the annoying tightness in his groin by making her his until she screamed his name.

Good sense took over each time he picked up the receiver and he'd gently place it back into the cradle. He became restless after talking his feelings over with Rykard. He couldn't get Reggie out of his mind. All he could think about was the way she felt in his arms and how easily she yielded to his demand. After tussling with the tangled sheets and comforter, he sat on the side of his bed waiting for a decent hour to call her. He knew she had an early test. He wanted to wish her well and was sincere in his thoughts; however, it was the undying need to hear her voice that motivated him to call.

He gazed into her beautiful face. No wonder he was crazy out of his mind. Her slanted eyes and deep dimples did him in every time. The need to feel her immediately caused him to extend his arms out before she was within his reach. When the large tips of his fingers came in contact with her face, they continued until they gripped the back of her head, and slowly he pulled her into his embrace.

Trae looked down into her upturned face. He lowered his head and kissed the corner of her mouth. The ragged air caught between them sparked passion caused by the feathered touch of their lips. Both wanted more than the gentle touching of their mouths. Reggie's smiling face slipped into a mask of passion.

"Hi," he replied. Taking a moment to savor her touch, he stepped back and appraised her fully and completely. "How was your test?" he asked just above a whisper. His eyes were still laced with unleashed passion.

"Great," she was surprisingly able to say. "Thanks for the pep talk. It helped," she said as she gazed into his tense, dark eyes. Her chest still heaved from the recent kiss.

Profound, hungry, passion-filled eyes uttered his need for her, and when his lips parted he said, "I missed you."

The surprised look in her bright eyes warmed his heart. How could she not know what she did to him?

"I missed you," she said in a quivering voice.

Trae groaned inwardly and took a couple of steps back.

"We'd better get inside." He willed the little control he had left to pull the books from her hands and pushed her gently through the doors.

Reggie moved down the slanted aisle as she looked behind her. Her eyes strayed upward to meet his handsome face as she allowed him to push her toward an open row of seats. The twinkle in her eyes and sweet smile on her face expressed how happy she was to be with him. They moved toward the middle of the row before sitting. Professor Gaines stood before the overhead projector and adjusted the focus for the day's presentation. They stole glances at one another. Each time, their eyes made secret promises to unleash the passion standing between them.

When Reggie and Trae exited the auditorium, they stood for a moment allowing other classmates to move around them.

"Are you ready to check the list?" he asked.

"Yes." She tried hard to hide the nervousness.

Trae took her hand in his and led her toward the women's gym. When they reached the board outside of the faculty offices, a number of girls stood clustered around the board. Some cheered with small yelps. Others turned away, disappointment clearly etched on their faces. Trae could feel the slight moisture in the palm of the hand he held. Reggie attempted to sound and look brave, but he knew how nerve-racking this was for her. He squeezed her hand firmly and pulled her forward.

As they made their way to the board, Reggie's apprehension increased. She looked into Trae's face and was frightened by what she saw there. Hope. He wanted her name on the list as much as she did. What if it wasn't? Dread slipped through her soul. She didn't want to disappoint him and for that reason she had second thoughts about letting Trae tag along. Still he held her hand firmly to show support. She sighed deeply before her feet, heavy with dread, moved closer to the small crowd who anxiously scanned the list for their number.

The list, held in place by a clear plastic thumbtack, listed student numbers in numeric order. Reggie's eyes anxiously roamed the list. Trae stood so close to her that her arm rested against his mid-section. Nervously, she browsed the list before taking in a sharp breath. Her number was there! She made the list.

Trae, keen on every movement she made, could feel the sudden burst of energy in her body. A sigh of relief escaped his lips. He could tell without confirmation that she'd found her student number on the list. It wasn't confirmed until she actually looked into his waiting eyes. Her smile made his heart rejoice. The corners of his mouth creased into a smile in response. No words were exchanged. She nodded. He in turned nodded and lightly squeezed her hand.

"Let's get something to eat. This calls for a celebration," he beamed.

"I'm game," she eagerly responded.

A mixture of emotions gripped Traekin. In a way he was glad that Reggie made the list. He didn't quite know how to console her had her name not been there. Truth be known, he had mixed feelings because sooner or later he had to tell Reggie how he felt about her, and tell her about the bet. He wasn't prepared to break her heart. So, he struggled with his feelings because he didn't exactly know how to break the news to her.

Selfishly, he decided to wait until Wednesday to tell her. They would celebrate her good news for the next couple of days. She deserved that much, he thought. With his mind made up, he was determined to enjoy the moment. He didn't want to share her with anyone. Instead of going to the cafeteria for lunch, he offered to take her to a local eatery right outside the campus grounds. They found a secluded table in the back of the restaurant.

As they sat across from one another, memories of the afternoon at his uncle's house stole a part of his attention. The shrimp po-boy she munched on oozed with tender plumb shrimp surrounded by golden-crusted bread. Her tongue ran across her bottom lip to catch juices that slipped down the sides of her mouth. He leaned forward and caught the curvy end of her chin and held it between his thumb and index finger.

"Is that good?" he asked seductively.

Her mouth full, she bobbed her head up and down, her chin still caught between his fingers. Slowly, he released her face. His eyes remained on her luscious lips. He licked his own before capturing his bottom lip between his evenly white teeth. He was definitely losing it. It was hard getting her out of his system. The need to have her seemed to occupy his every thought. He successfully moved his roaming thoughts and was able to enjoy lunch.

Afternoon classes seemed to drag on. Meeting between classes for a few minutes, they planned to spend Blue Monday at Favort to celebrate Reggie's good news. He held her hand as they made their way into the club. The dim lights glowed, and the blaring sounds of reggae music spewed from the speakers at the DJ stand. As usual, the place was packed. Once they found a spot next to the crowded bar, Trae leaned over the counter and ordered two ginger ales.

Reggie rested comfortably against the wall of Trae's chest, his arm securely wrapped around her tiny waist. They watched the sultry, esoteric movements of the dancers swaying from side to side. The sassy rhythm of the music seduced them, prompting them to rock their rear-ends up and down to the beat. She and Trae were not unaffected. They swayed in sync to the music until it was replaced with a slow ballad.

Trae took the glass from her hand, set both of their drinks on the bar, and led her to the dance floor. He didn't ask her for the dance. He was so accustomed to getting what he wanted without asking. He realized that he'd broken that mold with Reggie. An afterthought, when they reached the floor, he whispered in her ear, "I hope you don't mind. I should have asked first."

"It's okay. I would love to dance."

They fell into step, their bodies receptive and magnetized into singular motion as though they'd practice it for a long time. Reggie fitted snuggly in the center of his body. Her head was just below the top of his shoulder. The first song turned into a second, and then a third. Reggie wrapped her arms around his back, just beneath his arms. With her eyes closed, she drank from the warm scent of his body.

The swaying was hypnotic and soothing, and when the song ended, neither wanted to stop. They continued to sway a few more seconds before he looked down into her face. Dancers around them had already changed their rhythm to keep up with the now funky pulsating beat.

"I don't think this dance goes with that song," he yelled over the music.

Reggie reluctantly unwound her arms from around his waist and began to move to the music. Before long the slow steps were replaced with a fast bebop. When the song finally ended, they were both winded as they moved off the dance floor. Trae ordered another round of ginger ales and guided Reggie to a less crowded part of the club.

On the far side of the room, eyes reaping of hate watched them move through the crowded club. An eerie feeling made Reggie turn, and she wasn't sure why until she met Veronica's cold, calculating glare.

Trae's eyes followed hers. When he caught a glimpse of who had caught Reggie's attention, he nodded to acknowledge Veronica. The vicious stare was quickly replaced with an overly zealous sneer, as though Reggie had only imagined that Veronica's previous stare had been laced with dynamite. He held up his glass to her in some kind of salute. The fingers of his other hand were still intertwined with hers.

For God's sake, Veronica. You could certainly be Satan's daughter, she admonished inwardly. *You're not fooling anybody, girlfriend.* With that thought in mind, Reggie sneered back at her. She didn't like playing games, especially with Veronica.

Trae chose not to sit, for selfish reasons of course, and leaned on the bar which circled the club. By standing, he was able to pull Reggie close into his embrace. He fought for control every time her soft torso leaned into his body. A couple of hours passed by the time they finished the last dance and Trae led Reggie from the club. He helped her into the passenger side of his SUV. When he pulled into the circular driveway of her dorm, he put the car in park but left the engine running. He reached behind him and pulled from the back seat a small box and handed it to her.

"This is for you. A little something I hope you will accept." He laid the box in her opened hands.

"Trae," she exclaimed. "What's the occasion?"

Trae ran his hand down the small portions of hair covering the sides of her face.

"No special reason." His eyes locked with hers across the semi-dark space between them.

"Thank you," she offered quietly.

"Go on. Open it."

When Reggie opened the box she found a half-heart charm with her name engraved on it. One hand went to her mouth, her eyes grew large, and the dimples in her cheeks lit as she attempted to hide her smile.

"It's gorgeous." She looked appreciatively at him.

"I noticed your charm bracelet and wanted to let you know how special you are." He fingered the other half of the charm dangling from his gold key ring beneath the steering wheel. "Always," was engraved on his charm.

Reggie leaned in. Her eyes were focused on Trae's luscious mouth. Unlike before, he didn't deny her the sweet, tender, parted lips. She touched them with trembling fingers first, and then replaced them with her tender lips. Touching them lightly at first, then with grave urgency, she sealed and savored his lips. Her tongue flicked back and forth, tasting and enjoying his sweet delicious lips.

Trae held on to the steering wheel with one hand and the headrest of her seat with the other. The agonizing torture of Reggie's kiss was more than he'd bargain for. To give her time to explore his mouth without censure, he firmly gripped the leather until he was ready to take control of the kiss. He allowed her to explore the depths of his mouth freely before taking the lead. With expert precision, he eased his tongue into her parted lips, commanding her mouth to open completely. There was no mistaking the moan from the back of her throat.

He effortlessly moved his hand downward and snaked his fingers through the hair at the nape of her head. She surrendered shamelessly to his call. Their breathing was hot and raspy, and the world around them went black. The swelling of his shaft propelled him to pull her into his lap. He fought with the metal buckle as he released the seat belt holding her in the seat. Once it slid across her lap, Trae pulled her into his hard frame and proceeded to use his honed skills to unmercifully assault every living nerve in her body. The charm clasped between her fingers fell into her lap, her arms extended around his thick neck.

Totally immersed in the rapture of his sensuous mouth on hers, Reggie lost control of her body and mind. She hadn't cared that they sat in the front of her dorm necking like savage beasts. She would have given up every inch of her virgin body to him without a second thought. It was Trae who broke the hold he had on her body and her mind. Slowly, he eased her away and placed her back into the passenger seat.

His hands were still on her waist. The touch of his fingers seared her flesh through the silk blouse. It took them a few minutes to resume normal breathing, and when he was finally able to speak, he broke the dizzy silence between them. "It's late," he managed in a rough strange voice.

Reggie slowly opened her eyes, revealing the passion she couldn't control. She could barely make out the outline of his face. She was still under his hypnotic spell. Trae knew one of them had to be strong and he felt obligated to be that anchor. His sudden urge to be her protector kept him from doing things he wouldn't have given a second thought to had she been someone else.

"Are you okay?" he asked. He moved his hands from her waist and captured her face between them.

Reggie desperately tried to break through the dense, passionate fog. "Yes," she finally whispered.

He kissed her sweetly on the lips, then pulled away. "I'll walk you to the elevator." He turned off the ignition before easing from the driver's side.

Reggie had straightened her clothing and hair by the time he made it around to her door. When he opened it, she allowed him to help her down from the SUV. She then turned to retrieve the charm now caught in the middle tray between the two seats. She placed it back in the box. Trae stood close behind her until she turned and was ready to move. They strolled through the doors hand in hand. Only a few couples nestled together on the couches and love seats in the opened areas that occupied the large lobby. He released her hand the moment they walked up to the elevator.

"I'll see you tomorrow," Trae said softly. A hint of passion was still lodged in the dark eyes.

Reggie watched him intensely. Everything in her heart wanted to forget common sense and allow Trae to fill her with the passion she saw in his eyes.

He must have read her thoughts, because he pulled her into his embrace and held there. "Don't worry, sweetheart. When the time is right I will love you with all of my heart," he confessed.

Every fiber in her body faltered. Had he not been holding her she would have fallen. He held her tighter.

"Oh Reggie," he moaned down into her ear. "What are you doing to me?"

How could she tell him she'd fallen madly in love with him, even before they'd formerly met? How could she not sound like an idiot, revealing her entire soul to him? Telling him she would go to the ends of the earth with him would sound a bit irrational, especially since she'd known him for only a short time. Her heart was convinced that all was right between them.

Ready to take the leap, she opened her mouth to confess her feelings, but that chance was quickly taken when he covered her mouth and just as quickly stepped away and turned to leave. When he looked back, he stopped long enough to regard her before he exited through the double doors. It happened so fast that Reggie wasn't sure he had kissed her. The warmth of his body was now lost, and she felt abandoned.

CHAPTER 9

Trae drove around for an hour before heading to Monroe. It was late, still he knew the back door to his uncle's house was often left unlocked. He eased the SUV into the empty space next to his uncle's Cadillac. The soft glow of the cabinet lamp offered enough light to make it through the kitchen without bumping into anything. Just when he began to climb the stairs, he noticed light creeping from beneath the heavy oak door to his uncle's study.

Trae moved down the stairs and tapped lightly on the door. He waited for a response before entering the large room with floor-to-ceiling bookshelves, which were on at least two of the four walls of the room.

"Hey, Unc, why are you up so late?"

"Trae," Ted's tired and wearied voice flooded across the space between them. The weariness alone caused Trae's some alarm. He saw the dark circles under his light-brown eyes. The freckles on his face were more prominent than usual against the ashen complexion.

"Is everything okay, son?" He watched Trae enter the room.

"I guess I should ask you the same question, Unc. Is there something I can do?"

Theodore shook his head. "No, son. Everything's fine. I just got some paperwork that I waited until the last minute to do. Now I'm burning the midnight oil trying to get it done."

"My offer still stands. Can I help you get any of it done?"

"Nah, I'm fine. You still haven't answered my question. What brings you out at such a late hour, boy? Not that I'm not happy to see you. You're more than welcome here anytime you like. This is your home, too, you know?"

"Thanks. I just got kind of restless on campus. Thought I would crash here for the night and head back early in the morning."

"Want to talk about it?"

Theodore was the spitting image of his father. Trae's ninety-year-old grandfather was the center of their family. Trae's father, Larry, the baby of seven siblings, didn't inherit the red hair or freckles, as did his other brothers. Uncle Ted was the oldest and garnered as much attention as his grandfather. He was well respected by his younger siblings, and he looked out for them, even today. He pretty much treated his niece and nephews as he did his own kids. No one was treated any different from the other.

The kids love his playful banter. He teased them, spoiled them, and fussed at them with equal opportunity. It was known that he playfully and secretly told all the kids, "Now you know you're my favorite. Don't tell you sister or brother or cousin, cause they might get jealous." All the kids knew he did this and loved the attention he gave them.

Trae stood in the center of the doorframe, his head almost touching the top of it. He casually leaned on the open frame as he spoke with his uncle. He felt comfortable talking with him about anything. They had that kind of relationship.

Trae seemed surprised by his uncle's approval of Reggie. It would seem everyone had been taken by her. Trae hadn't thought his feelings for Reggie were so transparent. He hadn't known how strongly he felt for her until the night they embraced in the dorm parking lot. What he felt for her was so overpowering; even he couldn't explain his actions tonight. Yet, his uncle pointed out to him his strong attraction to her was warranted. After all, Reggie was smart, attractive, and had reciprocal feelings for him. Trae seemed to be a different person Saturday. Everyone noted the change.

Uncle Ted advised, "You'll never know until you cross that

bridge whether or not the two of you were meant for each other. You sometimes have to take chances to get what you want, and if this was meant to be, then it will happen. If it don't happen now, then it will when the time is right."

Trae contemplated his words for a few minutes before spilling the beans. He had nothing to lose at this point. He told his uncle about the wager with his friends. He'd somehow hoped that he would advise him not to tell her. His words were simple and as sharp as the twenty-inch blade he used to fillet fish. "She'll never respect you or trust you again if you don't tell her, Traekin."

There it was; open like an exposed wound. Trae sulked for yet another few minutes and bobbed his head up and down. He knew his uncle was right. He'd thought so, still he needed the affirmation he'd just gotten.

"I will," Trae assured him. "I have to."

After talking for thirty or so minutes, Trae pushed his long tired body between the cool sheets and dozed off. It wasn't until light came streaming from the lace curtains did he sit straight up in the queen-size bed. He glanced at the clock on the television set and let loose an explicit yelp.

"Oh shit!"

He threw aside the covers, jolted into the adjoining bathroom, and turned the knob of the shower. Without waiting for the water to reach the right temperature, Trae eased his body under the fierce spray and quickly cleansed himself. As he dressed he could hear footsteps going down the stairs. It had to be his aunt. No one else would be up at this time of morning.

He knew there was no way to make it back to the campus and on the field before practice began. He groaned inwardly. He definitely didn't need the coach on his butt. With no time for self-pity, Trae dressed quickly and bolted down the stairs.

"Trae," his aunt held her hand to her heart. "You startled me, boy. What on earth are you doing here? When did you get here? Do you want some breakfast?"

"Sorry, T. I didn't mean to scare you. I'm late, so I'll have to pass on breakfast." His response only answered one of her three questions. He knew he didn't have time to give an adequate explanation for his unplanned visit. He walked over and pecked her on the cheek before exiting through the back door.

Trae evaded law enforcement as he raced down the two-lane highway. He merged in and out of lanes at an exceptionally high speed. In Louisiana, anything over twenty-miles-per-hour of the speed limit is an automatic arrest. Had the police been anywhere in sight, he would have, with certainty, been taken to jail. The Louisiana State Police didn't play. As he eased through the parking lot of the stadium, he was thankful that none had been around.

Even though he escaped the jaws of the State Police, he knew for sure that his luck had run out. He knew that coach was going to send him to hell and back before it was all said and done. Not only was he late, but on top of that, he'd broken curfew and left campus. He raced through the long corridor and swiftly eased through the open doors of the locker room. Most of the players were making their way out to the field. Rykard slowed as he heard some of their teammates address him, however, he was too late to warn him. The coach was on him, loud and thunderously barking into Trae's face. Too late to help his friend, Rykard turned and headed to the field. He would have to wait until after practice, maybe even as late as the evening, before finding out why Trae hadn't made it back to the dorm last night.

As soon as the instructor dismissed class, Reggie hurried to the side bench to gather up her belongings. She was overly anxious to see Trae. The anticipation of his lips on hers made her insides scalding hot. The morning seemed to drag on forever. Every moment was consumed with the thought of being enveloped in his long, strong, muscular arms. The sensation of his hands gliding down the sides of her arms and back sent thunderous bolts of fire up her spine.

Her mind, focused on the smothering passion she saw in his eyes last night, blocked out everything around her. She'd been so lost in her thoughts that Reggie didn't hear the instructor call her. The hurried task of jamming her stuff in to her bag only ceased when Eleanor closed her hand around Reggie's wrist.

"Reggie." Eleanor's hand moved around the small of her arm. "Is everything okay?" she asked, concern was etched in her warm brown eyes.

Reggie was alarmed by the intrusion into her thoughts and physically jumped when the warm hand made contact with her arm. She did her best to hide her irritation at the unwanted interruption of her thoughts. She was in a hurry. Her desire to see Trae was so strong that even dance class was a distraction this morning.

She worked harder than usual to move in unison with the group. The pace was all wrong for her mood. Because the steps were routine, she didn't have to think twice to execute them in the right sequence. However, at times, the frustration was clearly written on her pretty face. Besides, she could have skipped class but decided that dance had always served as a release. She couldn't see Trae until after class anyway.

"I'm fine," Reggie stuttered. "Really, I'm okay."

"I noticed how distracted you were during class."

"Just a little distracted." Reggie smiled hoping to end the conversation so that she could head out. "Nothing to worry about, honestly."

"Okay. Don't forget we're meeting here at six to work on your routine."

Reggie hadn't forgotten. At the moment it wasn't a priority. In fact, it was so low on her list of priorities that she'd considered not going. If Trae wanted to be with her tonight, she planned to call and cancel the scheduled practice. She bobbed her head up and down and continued to stuff her things into her bag.

"I'll be here at six sharp." Reggie took a few seconds to look up and acknowledge the woman who had become her dance mentor. She smiled sweetly at her. "I'm cool," she reassured her again.

"Good. Have a good day."

Breathing a sigh of relief, Reggie hurried down the hall to the lobby. Her eyes anxiously scanned the confines of the open spacious area. After the third search, she still didn't see him. She walked to the doors and glanced out of the paned opening, her eyes searching the hundreds of faces standing and walking about. When she didn't see Trae's face among them, Reggie moved back to the inner portion of the lobby and lowered her sweatpants bottom in the nearest chair.

After sitting and pacing for fifteen minutes, she grabbed her backpack and headed back toward an empty dance room. She dropped her bag and then kneeled to retrieve a CD from one of its side pockets. As the music filtered through the room, she inched out of the gray sweats. Just as she began to transition from one step to the next in her dance routine, she felt hands encircle her waist. She could tell it was him even before she turned.

She turned completely in his embrace, and without words or hesitation, Trae pulled her tight into the circle of his arms as his head lowered until his lips just barely touched hers. He watched her from beneath partially closed lids. Her smooth skin glowed, her eyes fluttered closed, and her mouth parted as she waited for him.

He didn't tarry long. His mouth covered hers, and a soulful moan slipped between them. Heat soared through his body at the mere sound of it. He pushed his tongue through her warm and soft parted lips, drinking from the sweet taste of her mouth. Reggie's arms snaked around his neck and allowed him to lift her feet from the floor as he pulled himself up into an erect position.

He squeezed from between them the space that separated their bodies. The instant closure sparked an uncontrollable need within them both. They ate hungrily from each other's mouths. Soulful cries and more low, husky, audible moans escaped their lips. Their souls merged with each second that their lips locked. Soon it was hard to tell where her body ended and Trae's began.

Reggie lost herself the moment she felt the warm air flaming from Trae's nostrils. His soft lips melted away every thought and feeling she ever had. With eyes shut, she surrendered to him totally. She didn't have to see him to know that he was feeling everything she was. She allowed him to take control, and he did – pulling her into the fog of his passionate desires. Air, although needed to sustain life, was disregarded. All that mattered at the moment was the hold he had on her lips.

She held tight to his neck, praying he wouldn't let her go. When he moved his mouth from hers it was only for a quick second before he recaptured her swollen lips. His body trembled, and not sure he could hold them both up on his own legs, he released Reggie and placed her on her feet while moving his body slightly away from hers. Her arms were still locked around his neck.

He spoke breathlessly through clenched teeth into her open mouth, "Baby, please. I don't want to drop you." He gently urged her away.

His shaky hands held onto the sides of her narrow waist. Reggie reluctantly loosened her grip as her head fell back. Her swollen lips remained parted, and it took her a moment to open her passion-filled eyes. Her chest heaved and her heart rammed against her ribs.

Trae watched Reggie fight to lift herself from the fog that had consumed them both. He fought his need to pull her down to the floor and fill her with the hard erection screaming against his gray, cotton briefs. Holding her at bay, he placed his forehead on top of her head. He fought to regain some control.

"Hi," he whispered.

"Hi," she returned.

One of Trae's hands left her waist and eased up behind her until his large thick fingers clasped the back of her head and then gently continued to move until they cupped the bottom of her face.

"I thought I'd missed you." She wasn't sure the strange voice she heard was her own.

"Sorry, I was late. I got a major butt-chewing from the coach this morning."

Reggie's glance met his heavily lashed eyes. The concern in her eyes moved him to yet another level. She cared about him. It was evident in everything she said and everything she did.

"What happened?" she asked.

"Well, for starters, I left campus last night and didn't return by curfew." He moved away slightly. "Secondly, I didn't make it back in time for practice. I was about 15 minutes late."

"Oh," she said. She wanted to ask why he left and where he'd been, but Trae beat her to her question.

"I went to Uncle Ted's last night."

"Is everything okay? Hopefully the butt-chewing wasn't too bad."

"Well, there's a possibility that I'll be benched the first game. Not to worry, everything is okay." He smiled down into her pretty face. He kissed her softly on her already swollen kissed lips.

"I'm not worried about it." He regarded her for a few minutes before his expression turned extremely serious. "We need to talk," he said.

Small creases gathered at Reggie's forehead as she gazed in to the serious mask that had then taken over his otherwise handsome face.

"Okay," she replied. His expression and tone of voice concerned her a little.

"Can we turn off the music?" he asked.

"Sure," Reggie responded, leaving the warmth of this embrace. She looked over her shoulders once she reached the wall unit. She retrieved the CD and returned it to its case sitting on top of her bag. Trae held out his hand, and she took it. He led her to a bench bolted to the sidewall opposite the wall of mirrors. Slowly they both lowered themselves to the bench.

Trae turned to face Reggie. It had taken him all night to decide that he *had* to tell her his news today. His heart-to-heart talk with his uncle reassured him that it was better to do it sooner than later. When he finally did fall asleep, he didn't wake up in enough time to beat the rush hour traffic. He ended up spending an extra thirty minutes on the field, which made him late for his first class.

Trae dreaded having to fess up to Reggie and almost changed his mind on his way to meet her this morning. He had second thoughts and turned around originally, but once he was halfway back to his dorm, he turned around and headed back toward the gym.

The sight of her swaying back and forth in the middle of the dance floor intensified his anxiety because he knew he was about to shatter her world. Reggie's eyes were closed as she faced the wall of mirrors; otherwise, he was certain she would have seen him watching her. He couldn't help himself as he guiltily moved behind her and pulled her into him. She affected him in ways he couldn't explain.

Trae's heart ached fiercely. It pounded within his ribcage as he watched her. What a jerk he'd been. He was sure he didn't deserve her. She certainly didn't deserve to have her heart broken, especially by him. Trae held firmly to her hand. He was angry with himself for agreeing to the bet and for what he was forced to do now. He took a long, cleansing breath before speaking.

"Reggie, I would never intentionally hurt you, I promise." He paused momentarily, encouraging himself to continue.

Reggie sat almost completely still. She had no idea what he was about to say. His statement alarmed her. The emotions etched in the sharp lines of his face and eyes were signs of the stress she knew was attributed to what he was about to tell her. Her eyes lowered until they were completely closed, hoping it would remove the distress. Her heart rammed loudly against her chest. Her hands turned clammy as they often did whenever she got nervous or antsy. She wanted to pull her hand away from him, but found it more comforting enclosed between Trae's.

"I need to tell you something about me before you hear it from anyone else. And you'll have to *pleeeease* understand this wasn't about you...not really," he stammered.

She slowly opened her eyes and sought his. The compassion in the depths of her eyes tempted Trae to halt what he was about to say, but he dug deep within himself for the courage to continue. He cared for her more than words could explain.

"Reggie, you may have heard a lot of things about me. I don't know if that's bad or what." He watched her face as he paused.

The anxiety in her eyes grew as she waited for him to continue. How could he explain his actions? How could he be so careless about another person's feelings? The fact that he'd toyed with people's feelings for his own gain never bothered him before. Now, as he stared down into her concerned eyes, he came face to face with who he was, or had been, before he met her. It hit him hard, and he didn't like it one bit.

"Reggie, hear me out, okay?" he pleaded. "On the day of the try outs, at the gym when you and the other girls were warming up, me and a few of my teammates watched from the top bleachers."

Reggie recalled seeing the group clustered on the very top.

"Well, I made this bet, with Rykard," he held onto her hand, his eyes too ashamed to meet hers, he gazed at her hands as though he was examining them for some good reason. He could feel the moisture gathering in the center of her palms and on the fingertips. He pulled them to his lips, kissing the inside of each tip before he continued his dreadful duty.

"We, we were joking about my reputation, in particular, my reputation with the ladies. I was boasting about my ability to have any woman I wanted." He met the immediate alarm he saw in her eyes.

Reggie jerked her hands from his as if he'd shocked her.

"Please, Reggie, hear me out," he begged. "I bet Rykard that I could get you even though word on campus is that you're hard to get," he regretfully sputtered out.

Reggie's sharp breath couldn't be mistaken. The sting of his words cut off her air supply. The heaving of her chest was evident as she attempted to control an outburst certain to explode. The room began to spin out of control as she attempted to focus on something, something other than his face.

The water in the corners of her eyes sat at the very edges, threatening to spill over any minute. Trae's hands balled into tight fists. He bit down hard on his bottom lip.

"Reggie," he begged her to look at him.

Her eyes strayed from his face to a space on the right side of his head. She couldn't, no she wouldn't let him see the hurt he'd caused. At that instant she remembered Val's warning. She seemed to always have to learn things the hard way. She had to get out, now. Reggie stood and began to back away. She wouldn't dare turn her back to him. Like a tiger, she was sure he would have lashed out at her. She could only move a couple of short steps before he was on her and had his hands on her shoulders.

"Reggie, please, give me a chance to explain."

"No, don't touch me," she demanded and tried to pull away from his grip.

Trae held her firmly, adding slight pressure with his fingers.

"Please listen."

"Take your hands off of me, Traekin," she sneered between clenched teeth and angry eyes.

The usual dimpled smile did not greet him this time. What he would give at this very moment for a peek of her earth-shattering smile. He would do anything for her. Anything she asked him to do, but in his heart he didn't want to release her. He feared that if he released her he would lose her forever. More than anything in the world, he wanted to respect her wishes. He had never forced himself on a woman, or believed any man should. "Okay, Reggie, I will let go, but please you have to hear me out. Please."

"Why should I, Trae? Why do I owe you that much respect when it's apparent it wasn't reciprocated?" Her voice was filled with hurt. "The truth is we both know you don't care about anybody except Trae."

"That's not true. I care about you, Reggie. I don't deserve a chance, but I'm asking just the same," he explained and at the same time he released the grip he had on her shoulders.

Reggie whirled around and headed toward her bag and sweat pants. Trae was on her heels every step of the way.

"It was stupid, Reggie, I know," his voice sounded more desperate than before. "It was the stupidest thing I've ever done in my life." Every word was given emphasis. "That's why I had to tell you. I couldn't let you find out from anyone else."

Reggie snapped around to face him. "Just to save face right, Trae?"

"No! I care about you, Reggie. More than I care to say. I don't want to lose our friendship. I value that more than anything."

"The only thing you give a damn about is your precious ego, Traekin. You're such a lowlife bastard, you know that, don't you?" she said through her quivering voice.

Her glassy eyes finally met his.

"I know. I know. I'm so sorry, Reggie. I never meant to hurt you."

"Go to hell, Trae," she turned again. His hands went for her, but she fought him with balled fists. The actual blows were hardly enough to squash a mosquito. Nevertheless, the blows they made to his emotional state were like sticks of dynamite.

"Please, Reggie."

"No! Let go of me," she cried out. The tears finally spilling over as she attempted to get away. Unwillingly, Trae released her.

"Stay the hell away from me," she barked as she leapt backward, placing much-needed space between them. Reggie scooped up her belongings with some items spilling over her arms as she hurriedly approached the door. Tears streamed down her face and a wail threatened to escape. *I've got to get out of here*, she coached herself. She dropped a dance shoe yet refused to stop and pick it up. Lord knows they were too expensive to just throw away, as she was about to do.

"Reggie" was all she heard when she fled through the door. Not looking back, she hastily made it through the exit.

"Whooooa! Where are you going in such a hur..." Val attempted to ask her friend as they met face to face at the base of the steps. "Reggie, what's wrong?"

"Not now, Val, please. I'll talk to you when I get back to the room."

Reggie didn't give Val a chance to reply or stop her before she was on her way. Val watched her friend's retreating back for a second before she turned and entered the gym. Halfway down the hallway she saw Trae and immediately knew he was the cause for Reggie's distress. She wasted no time stepping toward him, entering his personal space. Her eyes narrowed as she appraised the emotional turmoil on his face. As she neared she spotted the black dance shoe in his hand.

"What did you do to Reggie, Traekin Brooks?" she demanded to know.

"Look, Val, I'm not in the mood," he attempted to move around her, but she wasn't having it. She stepped into his direct path.

"I'll ask you again, Traekin. What's wrong with Reggie?"

She snatched the dance shoe from his hand. Annoyed, he glared down at the little pit of fire, her eyes dark and daring him for a smart-mouthed answer.

"This is between Reggie and me. Butt out," he warned.

"You're a dog, Traekin. And you better stay the hell away from my friend. I'm warning you." She challenged him with a killer glare.

Trae watched her for an instant, and then moved past her. He was in no mood for a showdown with Valerie. He was angry enough with himself.

Trae threw the basketball as hard as his strength would allow. Throwing the ball with such force and unguided aim guaranteed that it wouldn't make it through the hoop. The hot air fusing from his nostrils was only a slight indication of his frustration. He knew his news wouldn't go over well, still he thought that he would at least have the opportunity to explain his case.

Nothing had prepared him for the total devastation he observed this morning. She hadn't allowed him to touch her, let alone console her. She hadn't allowed him to say all the things he'd practice in his head over and over again. He wished he hadn't told her, and even wished he'd never met her.

This kind of turmoil was new to Trae. He'd never experienced anything close to it in his life. When things didn't work out between him and a woman, it was usually she who was unhappy with the situation, not the other way around. He neither knew what to do with his frustration, nor did he like having to deal with such emotional turmoil. *So this is what it's like,* he wondered. He was getting a dose of his own medicine. The misery of a broken heart was new to him.

Trae threw the basketball so hard that it crashed against the glass backboard of the hoop and hit the steel rim. His anger was so thick it robbed his sense of awareness. Growing up in the Crescent City required that your keen senses to be alert at all times. Depending on where you lived, you could lose your life if your mind wasn't on your surroundings. He'd mindlessly wandered to the basketball gym. Playing ball always seemed to help him release his frustration. Somehow he'd made it there, stripped down to just his gym shorts, and chased the ball up and down the court. He relentlessly took his frustrations out on the ball and Plexi backboard.

Trae had been so engrossed in his efforts to crucify the ball that he'd not seen his basketball coach observing his every move. He slowly approached while taking in the young man's posture and the sure signs that something serious was happening with him. The sound of the coach's deep, resounding voice broke the reverie, but not before Trae bashed the orange and black rubber ball against the backboard, totally missing the rim of the basket. The shrilling echo of the ball against the board echoed through the gym several times before it halted.

"Are you trying to break something?" the commanding voice picked up where the crashing sounds left off.

Trae stopped dead in his tracks. His pursue of the rolling ball temporarily halted. He didn't turn at first. There was no need to. He knew exactly who it was. Instead, Trae took a moment to check his rage. He couldn't afford to lose control with his coach. He could be benched for both his first football game, and either a portion of, or the entire basketball season.

He closed his eyes, inhaled a few long breaths, then slowly turned in the direction of the deep voice, and met the coach's concerned stare.

Trae took a bit longer to respond than the coach expected and barked, "Didn't you hear what I said, boy? What's wrong with ya?" his voice rang in the space between them.

Trae's posture lost its defiance and slumped until his eyes met those of his sports mentor. The emotions from the heated exchanged with Reggie were still strong, and Trae was unable to speak with his mouth, only with his defeated stance. For a quick instant, he allowed his eyes to stray past the coach, then quickly returned them to the face that, besides his father and uncles, garnered great respect.

The coach knew something wasn't right with Traekin. He'd known this boy since he was a freshman at Grambling. Traekin was a bit of a womanizer, something he didn't particularly care for, however, he was very respectful to the staff, was bright, and well-liked. There weren't many occasions when he'd seen him upset about anything. This behavior was uncharacteristic of the young man he'd come to know.

Coach remembered the conversation this morning with the head football coach, who warned that he'd given Trae a butt-chewing. Was it possible that he'd carried this over from this morning? Surly Trae had to know he was the best all-around player they had. Such a small mess up wouldn't warrant being benched, even though that's what he'd been told. Nonetheless, Trae loved playing sports and played with all of his heart and ability. It was understandable how this remarkable athlete could be upset about not being able to play for whatever reason.

Coach could tell Trae was trying to keep his emotions in check. And so he waited for the young man's response.

"Hi, Coach," he finally broke.

Coach stood with arms akimbo and feet slightly apart as he observed his star player. "You know you can talk to me about anything, Traekin."

"Yes, sir," Trae replied.

A few awkward seconds of silence ticked away before the coach turned and walked away. "I'll be in my office if you need me," he advised, and slowly moved across the smooth shiny floor.

Trae watched him for a moment until he disappeared through the door leading to the bank of offices designated for the coaches. Once he was out of sight, Trae allowed his head to drop down to his chest in total defeat. Never in his life had he experienced such raw frustrations before. Slowly inhaling the hot air trapped between him and the tension he'd produced in the gym, he followed his coach's trail until he was in the suite of offices at the rear of the gym.

Understanding that Reggie needed time and space to deal with the hurt hadn't made things any easier for him. In fact, they made it worst. He'd been advised to stay back if he had any hope of mending any type of relationship with Reggie. He would have to respect her wishes and give her the space she wanted and needed. As hard as it would be for him to honor her request, he promised to try.

Trae walked across the gym floor and retrieved the ball he'd left earlier. With purpose and grace, he moved from one end of the court to the other, dropping lay-up after lay-up into the netted rim, causing it to make swishing sounds. He did this until he was exhausted. He then retrieved his bag and headed back to his dorm. Every step was heavy with dread. He scanned the campus as he walked, hoping for a glance of her. When he neared her dorm, he contemplated stopping just to check on her and make certain she was okay. He then remembered his pledge to give her space. Besides, he knew her better than anything. She wasn't okay.

When he reached the outer living area of his dorm room, Rykard was waiting for him. Trae's grim appearance was reflective of his entire being. Rykard met his roommate and long time friend's weary face. His eyes filled with worry. He'd already heard about the incident between Trae and Reggie, as well as the confrontation with

Val. He somehow thought it had ties to the incident at this morning's practice as well. He would soon find out that the two incidents, although separate, would require that he watch his friend extra closely.

CHAPTER 10

Reggie practically ran the entire way back to her dorm. The heavy pounding of her heels against the paved bike path and her rapid breathing kept her from totally falling apart on the journey to her safe haven. It wasn't until her feet crossed the threshold of her bedroom did she allow herself to fall into her bed and weep uncontrollably. She'd not heard Val enter into the room, but felt her pull her into her embrace.

"Hush," she consoled. "He's not worth it, Reggie. Whatever he did isn't worth you crying over."

It took a few minutes before Reggie was able to gain some control of her emotions. She proceeded to tell Val about Trae and the stupid bet he made with Rykard. It made everything she'd felt about him seem so cheap and meaningless. Val was livid. In her mind, she considered the beat-down she was going to give Rykard Wiggins because she got the feeling he'd used her in this little scheme.

Their time together at breakfast in the main cafeteria was a little awkward. She didn't quite understand why until now. He told her that he had something to tell her, that it would wait until they met later today. What she couldn't erase from her mind was how gullible she was to believe he was genuine about his feelings for her, and all along he had planned her into this mess.

If he did, she couldn't guarantee that Rykard would walk away with as much luck as his friend did. He would be lucky to be able to use both feet by the time she finished stomping on them. His shins would have permanent nicks and cuts once she was done kicking him. Her grip became firm around Reggie's shoulders at the mere thought. If she had her way, they'd think twice about pulling this kind of crap again.

The trauma from the events of the day drained Reggie. She couldn't cry anymore. She hadn't a single tear left in her entire body. Val had fussed over her, and she wasn't sure she could stand her friend's nagging much longer. It started with making her crawl under the comforter and propping the pillows beneath her head, then making her herbal tea and forcing her to drink it. Now she was back with a sandwich and fruit, demanding she eat it because she needed something in her stomach, like that would make the sharp piercing of her heart or the throbbing ache in her head go away. Val was adamant and stood over her until Reggie made some attempt to eat.

Reggie picked at the food, nibbling at small bits of tasteless matter until she felt herself drifting off into the slumber. No longer having the strength to think of the horror she'd experience earlier, no longer caring about anyone or anything around, she allowed the humming sound of sleep to take over, leaving behind all the lies and heartaches. Reggie didn't dream. She didn't toss or turn. She just slept.

Hours later, Reggie woke up feeling the weight of her body glued to a surface. Still caught in the fog of sleep, she wasn't sure where she was or how she'd gotten there. It took a few minutes to fully open her heavy, swollen lids, and then it all came rushing back. She was wrapped beneath the plush comforter on her bed. Reggie took a sharp breath when she thought about what had occurred today. It hadn't been a bad dream. Her head throbbed like ten horses had just trampled on her temples. She opened her eyes completely and as wide as she could, but the limited vision proved that they were only opened slightly. The swollen lids were heavy as her red eyes scanned what she knew to be her room. The area was strangely familiar, although she couldn't tell how long she'd been in the soft cushion of her bed.

She pushed her body from beneath the covers, sat up slowly on the edge of the bed before standing on one, then both feet and padded to the bathroom, all without turning on a single light. She resisted turning on any light for fear it would shock her already throbbing head.

Opening the shower door, she turned the knobs until the steamy spray oozed from the silver dome hanging at the top of the tiled wall. Slowly, she peeled away the tank, shorts, and underwear, then slipped beneath the warm mist.

The soothing sensation of the water eased away the throbbing inside of her head. She stood there for minutes, doing nothing except allowing the water to wash away the misery of the day. She lathered her body with the fragrant body wash she kept in the shower caddy. When she was done, she stepped out of the shower and groped in the dark for the towel she kept on the front rack of the shower door.

Once she completed drying off, she wrapped the towel around her and tucked the end just under her arm. When she opened the door, sharp piercing light from the outer living area nearly blinded her. She squinted a few seconds before her face masked into an instant frown. One hand covered her forehead just above her eyebrows in an attempt to shield her eyes from the intrusion while the other hand groped at the towel snug around her until her eyes adjusted to the light.

Val was seated in the chair closest to her bedroom door. She sat waiting on the edge of the chair until she saw the long, terrycloth-wrapped figure emerge from the bathroom. Val stood the moment Reggie's feet crossed the threshold, and immediately she reached for the hand that covered her eyes.

"Are you okay? I've been worried sick about you," she said as she pulled Reggie into her bedroom.

Not so fast, she groaned inwardly. A headache threatened to return. Ashamed, Reggie couldn't look her friend in the eye for being such a fool when it came to Trae. She casually allowed the towel to fall to the floor and reached into her drawer for underwear. "I'm okay, Val. Thanks; I don't want you to worry. I'll be fine." She attempted to smile at her friend. She saw concern etched in her face and in her posture. "Really," she attempted again. "I'll be okay. I'm going to go back to bed. I have an early class tomorrow, I mean this morning," she said as she glanced at the digital clock next to her bed. It was past 2:00 a.m.

"You need to go to bed, too," she said as she slipped into jersey pajamas and leaned over and hugged Val's neck. "Come on. We've got a long day ahead of us."

Reggie mechanically moved throughout the entire dance routine. She didn't feel anything, not the foot stomping, booty shaking rhythm of the song she'd picked weeks ago for her routine. By now, the instructor's worried expression gazed at the young woman who, in her opinion, was by far the best dancer in the state. Reggie's attitude and concentration was even worst than it had been earlier.

She walked over and hit the stop button on the CD player, killing the sounds of the backbreaking drumbeats. Reggie's rigid movements ceased almost as immediately as the music did. She knew that she would soon have to explain her behavior. She just wasn't sure she was up to telling her instructor the real reason for her funk.

Instead of pressing her for an explanation, the instructor said, "I think we should stop now." Removing the CD from the player, she placed it in the cover and extended the case between loose fingers in Reggie's direction. Reggie slowly approached her to retrieve the CD. As she took it, her instructor embraced her with a brief hug.

"See you tomorrow," she looked up into Reggie's puffy eyes.

The ice packs had reduced most of the swelling but not all of it. Reggie bowed her head slightly. "Thanks," she whispered, gripping tightly the plastic case. She slowly turned and headed for the dressing rooms.

Why am I doing this? she wondered silently. *I don't want to be a part of this anymore*, she concluded. Her reference to "this" included the dance team, the school, and the other students and faculty.

Her next thought was to leave Grambling and transfer to another school. Then she realized that the thought was crazy. She wouldn't be pushed off like she'd committed some crime, or hide because her feelings were hurt. She was stronger than that. Besides, she was already a year ahead here. One more semester and she would graduate. She wouldn't give that up, not for Trae or anyone else for that matter.

Being on this dance team had always been a dream, and only until recently had she found the courage to tryout. She deserved to be on this team. She was a better dancer than any of them, including the coach. Even if she didn't make the team, Reggie knew she would survive. She'd competed in state championships and world championships that made this dance group pale in comparison to the level of dance she was accustomed to.

To hell with all of you, she snarled. *I'm doing this for me. And I'm going to make this team,* she reassured herself.

Reggie walked back to the dance room and went to work. By the time she was done, she was whipped. She quickly showered and prepared herself for class. It dawned on her that Philosophy class was next. She didn't want to face Trae just yet. The feelings were still too fresh. Though she didn't want to, she decided to go to class. She knew he would attempt to approach her yet she was determined to get beyond him.

Reggie waited until class was in session before making her approach. She eased through the doors, proceeded down the center aisle, and slipped into the nearest available seat. Her intent was to avoid Trae, hoping he sat near the front as he'd began to practice over the past several weeks. Instead, there he sat, in the last row of seats, in the chair at the very end of the row. She caught a glimpse of his large figure in her peripheral vision as she made her way through the door.

Reggie knew without turning that he watched her. She fidgeted in the seat for a few seconds before she opened her book and journal and began scribbling notes. The scribbles she made on the pages had nothing to do with class. She couldn't concentrate, not with Trae's burning eyes on her back. She sensed his every move as though he had been seated right next to her. How was she going to make it through this class? she wondered inwardly.

You have to, she reminded herself. *Just forget Traekin.*

Traekin's beacon went up the instant she stepped through the door. His eyes took in every inch of her body in one quick glance as she moved up the aisle before slipping into a seat a few rows ahead of him. He thought that she would proceed to the front of the auditorium as she'd always done. The fact that she hadn't indicated she was avoiding him. That deflated any hope he had that she might give him a chance to tell her what he wanted to tell her yesterday.

The seat next to her was vacant. Trae considered moving to the seat, then exercised control he didn't think he had. He wanted desperately to be near her, to rake his fingers across her smooth silky face and to taste the sweetness of her kissed, swollen lips. Of course, his heart won and he remembered that she asked him to stay away. He wanted all those things, but more importantly, he wanted back her trust. What she asked him to do seemed unrealistic; on the contrary, his heart said he had to protect her. Here and now wasn't the place.

Trae watched her body language. It spoke volumes, a hurt, broken, and unforgiving form. Never before had he been able to tune himself into a person as he'd done on so many occasions with Reggie. He didn't like what he saw. He caused this and knowing so didn't set well with him. He kept watching, hoping to make eye contact with her. Long ago he'd disregarded the voice of the instructor and all of the advice that came with it. Reggie wouldn't so much as acknowledge anything around her.

Reggie had closed herself off from the world around her. With all his might he attempted to communicate with her, not with words, but with his soul and his heart. *Please baby, look at me. I need you.* Even if she heard him she wouldn't acknowledge him.

About forty minutes into the class, she suddenly stood, gathered her books, and proceeded out of the row and into the aisle. Trae's heart raced frantically. He sat up from his slumped position and watched her every move. Where was she going? What's wrong? His eyes searched her, begging her to make eye contact if only for a second. She didn't. Instead, she moved hastily down the aisle toward him and the door to his right. As she neared him, he stuck out his hand to touch her. Without looking at him, she quickly sidestepped his outstretched hand, then slipped quietly through the door.

The sting of her rejection caused him to swiftly pull his hand back to his lap before moving it to his face to cover the hurt in his eyes. Seconds ticked away before he gradually pulled his hand down his face, stopping momentarily over his mouth as he inhaled deeply. He allowed his heavy lids to shield what he felt. The pain seeped into the core of his spirit. *Where is this coming from*, he wondered. His hurt was as deep as hers.

After class, Trae sat in the chair he'd occupied for the last hour and a half. It was long after the last student and the instructor had left the room that he even attempted to lift his face. With his eyes still closed, he sat there and allowed his mind to wander. It wasn't until he felt the soft warm touch of a female's hand on the back of his hand did he lift his head completely. Could it be her, coming back to grant him the chance he desperately needed? He stared at his friend and former lover. Hope seeped into the crevice of his soul. His heart raced, and then faltered. The disappointment in his eyes was as clear as day. His heart was heavy once more.

Veronica stood above him in a skimpy top and skin-tight shorts, the usual ware for her on a warm day like today. The concerned eyes and pouting lips slowly erased some of the hurt he knew was evident in his eyes. Someone cared about his feelings. She'd always been his friend. In some ways, Roni always cared about him even when he didn't quite treat her the way he should have. He attempted a weak smile.

"Hi, Roni. What's up?"

Veronica had never, in all of the days she'd known Trae, seen him in a broken state as he was at this very moment. It had been a couple of days since she'd seen him and sought him out because she feared he'd been avoiding her. Her effort to get him back would be futile if he was-n't around to be seduced. She knew his class schedule. She originally thought he had stayed behind in the auditorium with Reggie when they didn't show up in the cafeteria as they'd done the last few days. She had every intention to win him back. After all, this was a free country and she wasn't about to lay down and die, not even for little-miss-good-ie-two-shoes.

What she saw was a far cry from what she'd expected. Veronica was speechless for a moment, not certain what to say. She hadn't missed the disappointed look in his eyes when he looked up and found it was her in his personal space. It wasn't her presence he'd anticipated. But she let it slide. It was the warm, seductive way his eyes spoke, that brought the smile to her curvy lips.

"Hi yourself. I'm just checking on you. I was a little worried about you. I haven't seen you in a couple of days," she confessed.

Trae turned over his hand and gently caressed Veronica's soft long fingers. He'd almost forgotten how they felt. The manicured extensions at the tip of her nails were painted a bright red. He looked at her, real-ly looked at her, as if he'd not seen her in a very long time.

Veronica saw and felt something very different about Trae. She'd been moved by the tenderness in his touch. It was almost shocking.

"I'm okay," he finally offered.

He stood up and the nearness and the power of his sheer height and strength seemed to take her breath away. This moment reminded her of the time she first met him. The smooth, sweet words flowing from his mouth made her head spin. Her mind had been cluttered by the anticipation of being his. She wasn't a virgin, still, he'd made her feel as though she was.

"Thanks for checking on me," he continued sincerely.

Afraid she would lose this moment, she quickly asked, "Have you eaten yet?" Her excitement rose at the thought of gaining on this opportunity. She might have him back sooner than she'd anticipated.

Even if she had to use her body to weaken his resolve she would. Emotions were peaked. She could tell. This was just the break she needed to get back what was hers.

"No. In fact I haven't eaten all day."

"Okay, what do you say we go and get a bite to eat? Maybe we can talk. I'm good at listening, you know," she reminded him.

That she was. Until Reggie, he hadn't known just how hollow his conversations with Veronica had been. Reggie challenged every word he uttered. Not in defiance or to discredit, but to get more details. She wasn't satisfied with just a statement left hanging without proof or substance. Their conversations were sharing experiences. Each giving and taking something from it.

Veronica, on the other hand, hung on his every word as gospel. She didn't know much about football or basketball or anything else he liked, still she seemed always delighted to hear what he had to say. Nodding approval even when she didn't understand what he was talking about. She enthusiastically primped and stroked his ego. Somehow, that wasn't enough anymore. Trae doubted anyone could fulfill his needs, except Reggie. Right now that piece of his life was missing. Yet, at this very moment, he needed someone to listen to him. He wasn't sure where else to turn.

"Okay," he'd finally agreed.

He wasn't up to a public place, yet he didn't want to go someplace exclusive with Veronica, either. He could tell by the smothering glare in her eyes that she would give him anything he wanted to make him feel better. She would go through great lengths to seduce him, and he also knew he couldn't let that happen. He had to think with the head on his shoulders and not the one in his pants. It had been weeks since he had sexual release, and it had been knocking at the front door each time he folded Reggie into his embrace. As bad as he needed to burn off the frustration, the need for Reggie was greater.

Trae reached down and retrieved his book bag. "Let's go," he instructed as he reached for and held Veronica's hand as they left the auditorium. The gesture was such a natural tendency for them. He was grateful for the temporary distraction. Veronica seemed happy, too, and was more talkative than ever. She chatted about an upcoming event, asking him if he would accompany her. Trae made no promises, however, the idea of keeping busy was exactly what he needed to do until he could work things out with Reggie.

When they strolled into the cafeteria, Veronica hooked her arm into Trae's and showcased a smile plastered from ear to ear. Trae couldn't help but feel some of the life radiating from Roni, and he smiled down at her tooth-filled grin. Arm-in-arm, they seemed to glide across the shiny black and white floor. Trae absorbed the pulsating energy Veronica discharged. It felt good for the moment.

"Thanks, Roni." His eyes recovered some brilliance of light. "I needed a lift," he confessed and leaned down and kissed her on the cheek.

Veronica glowed brighter than the sun. *Oh yeah baby. Soon you will feel the cushion of my body and cry the relief only you and I know*, she promised herself. The moment Trae's lips touched Veronica's soft cheek seemed calculated and deliberate. Her head fell back and the small laughter that roared from the depths of her throat drew attention to them. Her eyes were shiny as though he'd just made her the happiest person in the whole world. She could only hope little-miss-thing was in the room. Trae was her man and she would dictate control of where he found his pleasure. She would see to it, or else.

It was too late when Trae realized that Reggie was in the cafeteria as they'd entered. Her books and bag were scattered around a tray of food that hardly seemed touched. On the back of the chair was a gray sweatshirt. From a distance, he wasn't sure the sweatshirt and other items belonged to her. It wasn't until he moved in closer, pulling his arm from Veronica's as he made his immediate retreat to the vacant table, that he became certain that the stuff indeed belonged to Reggie.

His movement caught Veronica by total surprise. Stunned at his sudden retreat, she sensed she was no longer the center of his attention and walked in the same direction.

As Trae drew closer to the table, he could smell the fragrance of Reggie's cologne lingering in the immediate area. His eyes scanned the small eating nook for her. In haste, he turned and bumped into Veronica who had followed him to the table. His heavily lashed-lids expanded to give the brown eyes full view as he scanned the area. His breathing quickened and panic was close to setting in. *Where is she? She can't be far away.* Then he saw her through the section of the opened windows. She was advancing toward the fountain.

"Trae," Veronica called out uselessly because he didn't hear her or see her, even though he'd just bumped into her. "What's wrong?" she attempted to get his attention.

At the moment his focus was singular. His awareness of and for Reggie was heightened and had been that way once he'd realized his true feelings for her. Why hadn't he considered that she would be here? He quickly realized that he just might have messed up again, big time. He didn't want Reggie to get the impression that he had moved past '*them.*' There was no getting past '*them.*' That very thought stimulated his next move. He began to gather Reggie's belongings before acknowledging Veronica.

"These are Reggie's things. She must have left them," he explained as if it should have been obvious to her that Reggie went absolutely nowhere on this campus without the bag lying on the table. It had everything in it, her music, her planner, and her dance shoes. She had to be awfully upset to leave it.

Veronica's beautiful face formed a confused frown mixed with unbelievable anger. Did he really expect her to understand where he was coming from? She'd been so shocked by his explanation that she was momentarily speechless. Trae's interest in providing a believable explanation was short-lived. After he'd completely gathered Reggie's belongings, he turned and walked away, then turned back around. "Sorry, Roni. I'll have to give you a rain check on lunch." He left through the exact same door Reggie had previously exited.

He left a gaping Veronica standing in the middle of the cafeteria. By now she was furious. She couldn't quite figure out Trae's fascination with Reggie. Not once had he shown this much interest in her. And she surly wouldn't treat him the way Reggie has obviously treated him over the past couple of days. She would do anything for him. He wouldn't have to ask her to. *Has Trae slept with Reggie,* she wondered? He was a hard man to please. He'd said so himself. Veronica refused to give up so easily. This fight wasn't over by a long shot. Tomorrow was destined to come.

The timing of this little fiasco was so exact that it caught Reggie off guard. As she sat alone at a table far off in the corner of the cafeteria she watched the little love fest brewing between Trae and Veronica. She sat far enough out of Trae's eyesight, but not far enough to miss yet another stab at her heart. It hadn't taken him very long to revert to his old ways, his old women. The sting of seeing Veronica on his arm and to hear the laughter pouring from her was just a little too much to stomach. Reggie nearly lost the little control she had.

Without thought, Reggie swiftly stood and exited through the lone side door of the cafeteria, leaving behind everything, her food she'd been picking at, her keys, book bag, and sweatshirt. She had to get out of there fast. She stalked into the courtyard and was almost near the fountain, which was in the courtyard's center, before she slowed her pace. Taking deep breaths to calm herself, her long narrow fingers cupped the sides of her waist and her back stood board-straight in defiance. Tears threatened but she forced them back. She had no intention of crying anymore.

The numbness slowly dissipated and was replaced with pangs of hurt and humiliation. Her hands slipped from her waist and fell into knotted rigid fists down along the sides of her thighs. Squeezing her eyes shut tightly, she willed the pain to go away. *Pleeeaassee just leave me alone. I don't want to feel this anymore*, she begged from deep within. Never in her life had she felt so helpless and lost.

Reggie would eventually go back for her stuff. At the moment she wasn't prepared to watch Trae throw in her face the fact that he'd wasted no time moving from courting her to being back with Veronica. This was by far the biggest mistake she'd ever made in her entire life. This lesson was far more painful than anything she'd ever gone through before. In the midst of grief, a shadow stole behind her, watching her deal with her rage. It wasn't until Trae was a few inches away that she noticed him approach her. Had she seen him sooner, she would have certainly fled. It was too late. She jumped when he called her name. She didn't stare him directly in the face. Instead she caught a glance of her book bag dangling from his hand.

"Reggie," his voice was thick with emotion.

Reggie turned away attempting to escape, but she would have to walk through the water fountain to make her retreat. Her body language was closed and on guard. Trae didn't like it one bit. He was a big man, however, never before had he felt threatening to any woman.

"Reggie, we need to talk."

She didn't respond. She didn't turn to acknowledge him, even after she knew he closed the distance between them. Her body was turned slightly and had tensed at the thought of him touching her. Trae knew, had the water fountain not blocked the path between them, she would have hurried away. Not attempting to make a big scene, he chose not to challenge her to do what he knew she would feel she had to if he'd pressed her.

"Is this yours?" he asked knowing very well that it was.

He held the bag out to her. Initially, she made no attempt to retrieve it. She hadn't seen her sweatshirt draped over his shoulder, only a peripheral view of the black canvas bag dangling from his hands. Reggie's defeated postured turned slightly, her muffled thinking began contemplating how to retrieve the bag without having to touch him or look him in the face. She stood for a few seconds, after folding her arms beneath her breasts. Her eyes scanned the cement pavement beneath her feet, and she pulled her bottom lip between her teeth. Seconds ticked away as she calculated her options. Without warning or a second thought, she quickly stepped around him, grabbing the bag from his hand.

"Thanks," she said off-handedly and kept walking.

As swiftly as her legs would carry her without the appearance that she was sprinting, Reggie cut through a crowd of students before retreating to the bike path that led to her dormitory. She refused to let Trae see her this way, near a breakdown. No, he hadn't earned the right, even though he was the cause of her misery and pain. She looked forward to the day all of this would be behind her.

Trae watched Reggie's swaying hips hidden beneath the gray sweats as she hastily retreated from the garden. Her back straight and eyes focused out in front of her, she quickly and intentionally closed him from any further consideration. Her bobbing ponytail swished from side to side, mocking him sternly as if to say 'see ya sucka!' Before long she disappeared into the sea of people busily moving about the campus grounds.

As soon as she disappeared, he raised his hand and covered his eyes before brushing it down his face until it lightly brushed the gray sweat-shirt still hanging over his shoulder. He immediately grabbed it and held it up as if to beckon its owner, but she had already disappeared. He'd considered going after her, then thought better of the idea. He would get nowhere with her, at least not now.

Trae lowered his hand and stared at the sweatshirt gripped between his long thick fingers. Without hesitation, he brought the garment to his face and swiftly inhaled the scent of Reggie's fragrance. He held it close to his nostrils and closed his eyes. The familiarity of her unique scent stirred a need deep within him.

Beneath the closed lids, smoky passion slowly crept through every fiber of his body. He'd nearly forgotten where he was, and soon those feelings were webbed with frustration and helplessness; his body swayed slightly from side to side. *Just how long will I have to endure this,* he wondered? He speculated that it wouldn't be long before he lost the small edge of control he'd managed to maintain.

Opening the heavy lids, his glassy eyes stared into the world he'd left momentarily and saw things differently. He loved Reggie, and in order to win her back he needed to get control of his feelings. He had to set aside his hurt temporarily and plan how he would get her back. Determined, he glanced at his surroundings and took a deep breath before he, too, left the garden.

CHAPTER 11

Three days had passed since the exchange with Trae in class and at the cafeteria courtyard. Reggie did her very best to avoid him, even going to the extent of moving to a different Philosophy class on a different day. She couldn't officially change classes. It was too late and the classes were already close. Professor Gaines offered to let her join the other classes on the days she needed, on a short-term basis, with the agreement that she would test with her regularly scheduled class.

She maintained her sanity by throwing herself into her studies and preparation for the tryouts. She'd spent all week perfecting her routine. She could do the thing in her sleep without thought or effort. Every move was precise and smooth. She'd practiced everyday for at least two to three hours straight. Monday was only a few days away. She would be glad to get all the stumbling blocks in her life behind her once and for all.

With no dance lesson at the community center today, Reggie stood outside of the aerobics classroom chatting with a fellow classmate. She tried with effort to focus on their conversation. She just didn't know how to tell Gina she wasn't interested in her plans. Reggie was anxious to get to aerobics class to relieve some of her nagging frustrations. Just as Gina began a great production about her next few weeks, Reggie caught sight of Justin and was relieved to see him. The moment he walked up to her, she eagerly stepped into his embrace.

"Hi," she greeted him. Her voice was a tone higher than normal.

Justin was elated. He'd been admiring Reggie from a distance. He'd even tried, several times, to ask her out. She turned him down each time. Deciding on an alternate approach, he settled on becoming a good friend. He prided himself on his patience. It seemed to be paying off. Had she finally given way to the idea that they would be perfect together?

Justin quickly took advantage of this good fortune and pulled Reggie into his embrace. She seemed eager and willingly surrendered into his arms. Gina watched the exchange, horrified that she was being ignored. She shook her head and quickly retreated, leaving the two locked in what could be perceived as a lovers' embrace.

Feeling awfully good, Justin lowered his head until his lips crushed against the inner side of Reggie's cheek. She didn't resist, so he boldly took it a step farther and moved his mouth to rest on top of her very soft lips.

At first, Justin ignored her muffled refusal and attempted to push his tongue between the closed lips. Reggie pushed with the flat surface of her free hand against his face and attempted to break free, her hand now at his chest, she moved her head to one side. His advances had completely taken her off guard, but she quickly recovered.

"No, turn me loose, Justin," she pleaded, her voice just above a whisper, and her head shook from side to side, indicating a 'no' response.

Trae watched Reggie from a distance as she chatted with a woman, who could easily be mistaken for a man. The desire to approach her almost got the better of him. She'd demanded he stay away if he truly cared. He would keep his distance because he did care. He cared too much. Not being able to touch her or witness the dimples in her cheeks weighed heavily on his heart. He had yet to recover from the knowledge that she did everything she could to avoid him; even switching classes to make sure they weren't in the same place. Her actions pierced his heart like a thousand daggers.

He couldn't stand himself or the situation that he'd placed them both in. If only he could get her to listen to him for just a few minutes. He would explain the magnitude of his remorse, and tell her how this had changed him for the better. He had to try once more to convince her of this. The pain he saw in her face and the slump of her body told Trae she was hurting. It didn't have to be this way. He had to try.

Just as he'd convinced himself that he should approach her, his feet moved then suddenly halted. His eyes almost turned black with anger when Justin Cater walked up to her and immediately pulled her into his embrace. She seemed to go willingly. One arm was still wrapped around the books she carried, her body seemed to lean into Justin's and rested at his torso.

Trae's hands balled into tight fists. Had he been closer they would have made contact with Justin's face. The raw jealousy crept through his entire body. Never had the possession of something or someone hit him so hard. His next thought was to act out what he felt on Justin's face, then he remembered, Reggie wasn't his and she'd asked him to stay away. He thought perhaps this was her way of getting back at him for the scene in the cafeteria with Veronica.

He turned and headed out of the building but something urged him to look back. When he did, he saw Reggie attempting to push Justin away from her. One arm snuggled the books against her chest and the other aimed at his face. Justin attempted to pull her back into his body. His head lowered almost inches from her mouth. Reggie was saying something; her head bobbed from side to side. Before Trae knew it, he was standing almost on top of Justin.

"Take your freakin' hands off of her before I break your neck." His hand went immediately around the back of Justin's neck.

"Trae, take it easy, man." His hands dropped to his sides. Several seconds ticked away as Trae tightened the grip on Justin's neck. "Okay, already," he choked out.

Trae's strong jaw-grip around his neck intensified. Finally, after what seemed like eternity to Justin, Trae released him. Justin never turned to acknowledge Trae. Instead he looked down remorsefully into Reggie's face. He'd gotten carried away. He adored Reggie and wouldn't intentionally hurt her. He certainly had misread her. Her reaction to him, the vibes over the last couple of days seemed to indicate that she'd felt-the same way he had. He thought she'd finally come around and seen the potential of a relationship with him. He'd certainly been wrong.

"I'm sorry. I really didn't mean any harm. You know I care about you, Reggie." Reggie didn't respond. Instead, she looked him in the face.

She knew Justin was a good guy. She knew how he felt about her and should have kept her distance. She'd gotten carried away. Her desire to be comforted was, at best, bad timing and with the wrong person. Her expression softened at his pleading glare. Even though she didn't utter the words, Justin knew he was forgiven.

He regarded her briefly before departing. "See you later," he promised.

Trae waited the few seconds it took Justin to leave before placing his complete attention on Reggie. "Are you okay?" his voice was so surprisingly soft he wasn't sure she'd heard him. The stir of emotions by being so close to her was evident in his expression. His body ached to touch her. Fighting the urge to reach for her was stronger than tackling an outfielder on game night. The storm of emotions slowly began the move to frustration, a familiarity that was becoming a part of him lately.

Reggie looked him in the eyes. What she saw there was as disturbing for her as it had been for Trae. She didn't want to feel his pain. Her own was more than enough. It was high time the shoe was on the other foot. She fought the inclination to retreat. He needed a dose of medicine. He had been dishing it out for a long time now. Reggie pledged herself not to be drawn into his charm or the need she saw in his eyes, nor would she react to his plea for forgiveness. No. She wouldn't retreat. Grateful that he had came to her rescue; she lifted her chin and thanked him out of common courtesy. "Thanks, Traekin. I'm okay," she answered. "I have to get to class," she said and moved away.

Trae didn't move, his eyes followed her until she disappeared through an open door. He did nothing to stop her from leaving. His hands, his arms, nor feet would cooperate. Each time she left him, the stabbing wound to his heart intensified. Trae glanced around him looking for a witness or a sympathizer; however, no one seemed to care about what had just occurred between him and Reggie. Reassured that he would have another chance, Trae took a long cleansing breath before turning and leaving the building.

Reggie hurriedly moved through the classroom door and to the opposite side of the room. The searing glare on her back kept her aware just how vulnerable they both were. Had she looked back, she knew she would have bolted into Trae's embrace. The pleading in his eyes was branded in her mind. A small part of her wanted to believe the remorse she saw there was genuine. It was impossible to mistake what she saw and felt. Then again, she'd made a mistake already. Despite his reputation, in her heart Reggie wanted him to be something he wasn't.

Reggie's dance practices went smoothly, as did the next two days. She made certain to avoid Trae, spending most of Saturday evening reading and preparing for the week. After church on Sunday, she packed her bag for the tryouts Monday afternoon. Although her nervousness had subsided, it wasn't completely gone, so she packed just to keep busy. Her last morning class ends at eleven. She could do it then, but she wanted to be prepared early. Val must have sensed her mood, and suggested that they spend Sunday evening watching movies. They decided on a comedy to make sure the mood remained light.

By Monday morning, Reggie was a ball of nerves again. Food was the farthest thing from her mind; still, she forced herself to eat a piece of fruit. By the time she'd gotten to the gym, all of the well-wishes from fellow classmates and friends put her at ease again. Reggie hurriedly dressed and stretched, long before others started piddling into the gym. With the Walkman strapped to her hip and earphones glued to her lobes, she allowed the music to keep her concentrated on the task to come. The volume of the music was high in order to block out the chatter around her.

As they filed into the gym, Reggie glanced around, not really seeing anything or anyone. She and the others pulled numbers to determine who would go first. During the initial try-outs, she'd picked number one. Today she would be fourth. Reggie filed into the gym along with ten other women. She eased her long body down onto the cool wooden bench to wait her turn. Although the routine lasted two-and-a-half minutes, it seemed an eternity as the three women before her waltzed through the short version of one of the dance group's most noted routines. None had perfected the kicks, turns, or swerves.

Reggie, on the other hand, had mastered the routine as though she'd choreographed it herself. Only a small trickle of sweat appeared on the upper sides of her temple when she finished the last eight counts. Her breathing was normal as she executed the last kick that slid into a full split. With a smile pasted on her face and her arms extended above her head, she waited a full thirty seconds before gracefully standing and posing at parade rest. Unlike the initial try-outs, no cheers met the conclusion of her dynamic performance. Onlookers had been told applause would be appropriate only after everyone was done. That didn't stop Val and crew from silently cheering as they watched their friend complete the flawless routine.

Trae watched from the far side of the gym as Reggie took front center on the gym floor. He caught sight of her the instant she stood and eased the gray sweats over her hips and down her long lean legs. She did an abbreviated stretch before she took her position. From looking at her, he was more nervous than she was, or so one would have thought. Her cool smile, revealing the dimples in her checks, gave no indication that she was the least bit nervous. Still, only he knew that the smile on her face didn't agree with the turmoil raging through her body.

The instant music blared through from the speakers, Reggie began the first movement of the piece. Trae held his breath as she breezed through the session. He was on edge. The tightness in his chest steadily increased until she'd finally ended the routine and walked off the gym floor. There was no doubt in his mind that she'd made the team. He was awed by her abilities to move so freely with the music. Happiness eased through his pores. Something good would happen to her today. She deserved it more than anyone.

The coaches busily scored and tallied each performance. After the last performance was completed, they huddled. The discussion apparently was very serious because it took fifteen minutes to select six of the eleven girls. All had been summoned to stand in a straight line for the results. Four names had been called when Reggie began fidgeting with the insides of her palm with her thumb. She worked hard to listen to the names, as each was sounded out followed by jumping and cheering of the selected individuals. One name left to call. The air was thick with anticipation and nervous energy.

"Jerica Williams."

The bottom of Reggie's heart fell through the floor. The rapid movement of her throat, the sudden halting of her pulse, and the stinging tears in her eyes nearly caused her to pass out. She refused the urge. She refused to allow them to see her disappointment, the shattering of her hopes, her dream, her heart. Afraid to look anyplace but in front of her, she glared emptily into the space in front of her until she felt movement around her. She never heard the coach's 'Thank you ladies, you were all wonderful.'

Absently, she stepped away from the crowd. Her feet hammered on the glossy gym floor until they stepped through a single door and met the carpeted floor in the hallway. She had no destination. She just needed to get as far away as possible.

Trae stood up straight from his seat, as did a few other onlookers after the last name was called. It couldn't have been true. He was sure he was hearing things wrong. Immediately his eyes honed onto the spot where Reggie stood, his eyes focused on the horror clearly etched in her eyes. He began to descend the bleachers and before long he found himself almost in the center of the gym floor. Many of the girls and their family and friends had already begun congratulating the winners. Trae's eyes were honed on Reggie's blank face. The thunderous pounding of his heart rammed in his ears as he moved in her direction, and as long as his strides were, they had failed to get him there before she fled the gym.

His mouth became dry and the tight clip in his throat made it hard to form the words loud enough to be heard. *Reggie*. He sidestepped a number of people trying desperately to reach her. No "excuse me" was given to those he intentionally shoved aside. Not even a sideward glance was provided from audibly loud protests. After easing through the door, he spotted Val and a few of their friends bounding in the same direction, toward Reggie. Trae rushed past them. Val caught the corner of his T-shirt, which only slowed him down for half second.

"Leave her along, Traekin Brooks," she ordered.

Trae glanced back in her direction, the hard cold mask on his face and the clipped anger in his eyes kept her from challenging him farther. Val slowed her pace, both arms extended blocking passage of the others who followed the same route. They stopped and watched Trae move down the hallway and enter the women's dressing room. Their worried eyes assessed each other. Trae wasn't the least bit concerned about the dark, bold letters "WOMEN" and the outline of a female on the center of the cold gray metal door. He didn't exactly fit the description that provided access to that part of the gym, but his mission was urgent and getting to Reggie was more important than anything else. Very quickly a few women came scurrying out of the dressing room, surprised by his presence.

Oblivious to where he was headed, Trae waltzed freely into the dressing room, not caring who was there or that many of the occupants were half naked. He moved in and out of the rows of lockers. Some of the women actually screamed at the sight of him being in there. The loud shrills did not deter him from his mission. He thought about calling out to her but knew she would evade him. She would resist him at first, but he knew she needed the support. He would move mountains to change the outcome, if he could. However, that wasn't bound to happen. Yet being there for her would equal, if not surpass, the gesture of moving mountains.

He'd covered half of the dressing room when finally he saw her. Her back was slumped into a trounced arch. Her hands shakily shoved articles of clothing into a partially opened bag. Trae moved behind her before extending his arms, and wrapping them around the center of her body. The hot air from his nostrils raked the back of her neck. Reggie knew he was there even before he'd moved in close to her. She didn't want him here. She didn't want anyone here. She attempted to free herself from his embrace. He, in turn, closed his hold tighter on her now trembling body.

"No! Let me go Trae. Leave me alone!" she pleaded.

"It's okay, baby."

Reggie was beside herself. She turned in his embrace and tried to push away. When the futile attempts were unsuccessful, she began to pound her tightly clenched fist into his chest. Some of the stray punches met his face and neck. He did little to stop her. Instead he allowed her to place angry blow after blow to his body.

"Baby, it's okay. It's okay," he consoled.

A few of the women who'd occupied the dressing room when Trae entered, made their way around to peek at the two, but didn't stay. Instead, they all left the dressing room giving them privacy. Val stood guard outside of the dressing room door, not allowing anyone to enter. She spotted Veronica from a distance. However Veronica wasn't brave enough to approach to find out what was going on. She watched Trae leave the gym; knowing full well he'd gone after Reggie. The defiance in Valerie's stare dared her to come anywhere near her post. In some small way, she felt Veronica was responsible for Reggie not making the team.

It hadn't taken long for Reggie to give in to Trae's comforting arms. She coiled herself into his chest and allowed the stream of hot wet tears to dampen the black and gold T-shirt and the shaking tremors to overtake her body. Trae pulled her in close to him. One of his large hands caressed her back while the other held her head close to his heart. He placed small warm kisses on the crown of her head and consoled her with loving and encouraging words.

When the tremors subsided and the tears slowed, Trae bent his head down until his lips touched the lobe of her ear. "Come. I want to take you out of here," he instructed.

Reggie nodded. She wiped the back of her hands down the front of her face. Trae reached over and pulled the sage-colored towel from her bag and helped wipe away the tears from her face. Her eyes were reddening and the puffy lids were shimmered by wet sticky lashes. He gently placed his hand under her chin, his long fingers lifting her head until their eyes met. No words were needed.

Without hesitation, he lowered his head. The air between his lips and hers was charged with heated anticipation. Heated blood instantly filled the swell of her lips and the heaviness of the air drew her eyelids shut as she eagerly awaited the fall of his soft lips. A pang of disappointment ebbed her heart when his lips didn't capture hers. Instead, they caressed the side of her face. The affect was nonetheless the same as if he'd kissed her mouth. A moan from the back of her throat escaped once his lips touch her soft and slightly damp cheek. She leaned further into his body, hoping that it would encourage him to continue the quest. She moved her head slightly, seizing the opportunity to smell his minty fresh breath. Her opened mouth touched the smooth edge of his chin before gathering small amounts of flesh between her teeth. Instead of taking her mouth as she'd urged him to, he severed the contact.

The sound of her sweet response to his calling was more than Trae had anticipated. He couldn't take advantage of this weak moment. Though tempted, Trae wanted their reunion to be sincere and on more solid terms. In order to make certain that when the fog cleared and they would regret nothing, he halted what could have been a heated exchange. Her feelings and protecting her meant more to him than anything else in the world.

Trae knew he would see disappointment in her eyes when they finally met his. More than anything he wanted to get her out of the dressing room and away from roaming eyes and ears. There would be another time to savor her swollen lips. One hand fell from her shoulder and picked up her gym bag with items still spilling over the top. His other went to the small of her back.

"Are you ready?" he asked.

Reggie nodded her response. The passion was still thick and unrelentingly close to exposure. She allowed Trae to guide her to the exit. As if he'd anticipated Valerie's presence at the door, he slowly opened it to find her posted there like a hired bodyguard. To make certain she knew where he stood without being disrespectful to her, he prompted a question that could have easily backfired.

"Is it okay?" he asked.

Regardless of her response, Trae was hell-bent on getting by her and her army of friends. Val didn't resist. A whole new respect emerged and instantly they were both on the same side, protecting someone they cared dearly about. Val stepped aside and nodded. Her eyes instantly searched Reggie's. Had she seen anything other than approval in Reggie's face, Traekin would have been in serious trouble.

They moved past the group who had been waiting on them. No one said anything. They watched Trae and Reggie move down the short hallway to the side exit. Unsure of how they'd just helped their friends, they cuddled and took solitude in one another's embraces. Val felt helpless. She only hoped she'd done the right thing. Watching Trae and Reggie leave the building, Trae's arm now snuggly wrapped around Reggie's frame, made her feel somewhat confident that she'd placed her friend in good hands. She could only hope so.

By the time Trae got Reggie to his SUV, they had crossed the path of a number of students who had attended the tryouts huddled together around the grounds of the gym. Some stopped their conversing and observed them as they passed. Reggie didn't meet any of their curious or sneering glares. Her eyes remained straight in front of her aware of nothing and silently allowed Trae to escort her from the gym.

On the other hand, Trae met their glares straight on and dared any of them to cross the line. He was madder than a chastised bull and would have pounced anyone who dared tempt him to. Reggie and Trae made it to his parked car in no time. She managed to keep up with his long strides as they crossed several intersections before reaching the SUV parallel parked on the street. He opened the passenger door and waited until Reggie was in and buckled before he closed it again.

He moved swiftly behind the vehicle, stopping only a moment to place her gym bag in the back. When he slid into the driver's seat, he glanced over at Reggie. Her head laid snug in the smooth leather headrest. Her eyes were closed and her breathing was long and labored. He reached over and touched her face lightly with the back of his hand. The gesture was enough to undo what little control she had left on her emotions. The steady flow of tears spilled from beneath the tightly closed lids.

Trae unfastened her seatbelt and pulled her into his embrace. It tore at his heart to know she hurt so badly. The soothing motion of his hands down the center of her back helped to bring Reggie back to control. He held her snugly in his embrace until she pulled away. The warmth shared between them chilled quickly.

"Please, take me to my dorm," she demanded in an almost cool, unyielding tone.

Reggie wouldn't make direct eye contact with Trae. She was happy that he'd been there for her when she needed him the most. She had no intentions of leading him to believe that things were okay between them. Being in his arms a second time was definitely weakening her resolve as far as she was concerned. The memory of how good it felt and her desire to be kissed earlier alarmed her. Getting back with Trae was the last thing on her mind at this point. She couldn't risk getting hurt again. Mostly, she knew deep in her heart she was madly in love with him and could easily be persuaded to give their relationship another try. She would rather risk misery than chance having her soul ripped from her again. Had he seen what was hidden in her eyes, Reggie knew that Trae would have responded differently.

Trae gazed down at the face that wouldn't meet his. Her posture was defeated and lacked the eloquence that was so naturally hers. Was she shamed by what had happened earlier today? Surly she couldn't blame herself. Even a blind person knew she'd been the best dancer of all those who'd tried out. Hell, she was better than the girls already on the team.

As he more closely observed her, the truth came sailing along like a lightning bolt. It wasn't shame he saw in her posture. Fear. Maybe. How? Why? What could she possibly be afraid of? He pondered the thought for a moment. Before it could fully register, it occurred to him that it was all the things she'd said before, all that she believed. It was definitely fear he saw. He could feel it because he had sensed everything she did.

She feared that he was too close. Feared that she melted in his embrace because in her heart she wanted to. It wasn't at all strange to Trae that their chemistry was so right, that it was automatic. No words were ever needed to know how they felt. Did she think so little of him to believe he would take advantage of a weak moment? The thought sickened him.

His lead-filled arms unwound from around her slightly damp body, and he forced himself back into the driver's seat. Reggie crawled back into her seat, her eyes focused in front of her. He jerked the black strap a little too swiftly across his waist and slapped the metal into the silver casing, the shrill of it caused Reggie to jump.

Her eyes immediately flew to the iron mask that only moments ago, was filled with tender understanding. Reggie leaned further back into the warm, soft leather and attempted to fasten her seatbelt. She fumbled with the clasp as Trae slammed the gear into drive and sped into the street without checking the traffic behind him. Luckily, there was no one behind them. The eight minutes it took to pull up to the parking lot of her dorm had been done in complete silence. Neither looked in the others' direction.

Trae pulled up near the curb closest to the rear door entrance. He didn't shift the gear into park or even make any effort to acknowledge that he'd stopped for any good reason. His right temple jumped in response to the tightening of his jaw, which drew a straight line across his face where plump, full lips were usually in a crooked smile.

Reggie's eyes were drawn to the masculine outline of his taut face, absorbing every detail as she waited for the cold hard stare to turn on her. He wouldn't oblige her.

It was never her intention to hurt him. Trying to hurt him would serve no purpose to either of them. She had no words at the moment to express what she was feeling. Confused seemed to be the appropriate description. Reggie really did care for Trae. More than she cared to expose. She didn't want to appear ungrateful for his gesture.

Still, she had no intention of leading him to believe there was any chance for them to renew their relationship. He had more than his share of things to divert his attention to. She, on the other hand, feared she would shatter if she exposed herself to him, only to toss her aside like he'd done others so many times.

Sensing that he wasn't going to say anything or look at her, she unfastened her seatbelt and clasped the handle on the door. In a twisted position, hands still nervously gripping the door, her eyes drew in again the taut expressionless face. Without hesitation she opened the handle, released the door and slid from the leather seat.

"Thank you Trae. I'm really grateful." The shaky voice was only loud enough to hear within personal space.

What the hell was that? she thought as she closed the door. *I'm truly grateful? What an idiot? Now he should really be pissed off at you,* Reggie agonized over her words.

She practically sprinted across the short distance to the rear entrance before easing through the metal doors. It wasn't until she'd made it halfway to the third floor when her steps faltered. Her backpack was still in the back of Trae's car. Had she stopped for a moment to consider her last words before dashing off like a scared cat, she may have remember to retrieve her bag. Reggie turned to descend the painted cement stairs until she was once again at the rear entrance to the dorm.

She pushed the doors open thinking that Trae wouldn't be there. To her surprise he was. He hadn't moved one inch from the spot she'd left him in. His rigid straight body was misplaced in the smooth leathered driver's seat. Reggie approached with caution, even though she knew Trae wouldn't do anything to hurt her. As she neared the car, she decided to go around to the driver's side, passing directly in front of the vehicle, into his line of sight. With her mind made up, she decided she would apologize, and she would remain stern on her decision about them. There could be no relationship between them.

It would be better that way.

Trae didn't blink when he saw the lean figure pass in front of him. He forced his resentment to a space in front of him in order to remain in control. He wanted to shake her senseless. Instead, he decided not to force the issue. It wouldn't have gotten him anywhere with Reggie. When she got out of the car, his first thought was to go after her; to hold her and let her know he was willing to wait things out until she was ready to be a permanent part of his life.

After she'd entered the building, he didn't have the heart to move. He tried to figure out what he planned to do next. His head fell into the palm of both hands the moment Reggie tapped on the window. The overwhelming need to have her in his arms again dissolved the anger he first felt when she asked him to bring her here. Heat flared through his nostrils into his sweaty palms. Dark red circles flashed behind his closed lids. It wasn't until she tapped the pane a second time did his head slowly rise and turn in the directions of the dull thumping.

Trae stared out at her not really seeing her tear-stained face; her bottom lashes were glued to the delicate surface beneath her cinnamon eyes. Reggie shifting from one foot to the other, pulled him back from the place he'd lost himself. It took several more seconds before regaining full awareness of where he was. Instead of lowering the window, he opened the door and attempted to exit the car but not before it rolled forward. Instantly he depressed the brakes, moved the gear into park, and released the tab of his seatbelt before towering over her.

Reggie jumped backwards a few steps, not certain what Trae was doing. Surely he wasn't trying to hit her with his car. She realized that the car had been still in drive gear. She felt small as he rose like a mountain from the SUV. The SUV lifted when all of his 220 pounds eased entirely from the driver's seat. She didn't want a confrontation or a discussion. Just wanted to get her bag and leave. Her eyes danced nervously over his impassive stoic expression. Reggie readied herself for a confrontation. Time stood still as they eyed one another, neither knowing exactly where they stood.

"I forgot my bag," she stammered, her right index finger pointed to the rear of the vehicle.

Eyes trained on her face, Trae moved slowly to the tail of his slick black SUV and depressed the small indicator just below the handle causing the top lid to pop open. He reached into the center of the compartment, his hand steadied until it touched the canvas handle.

Reggie moved closer, her hand slightly extended in the anticipation that he would give her the bag freely and without a fight.

Trae pulled the bag from the trunk with little effort, and, instead of handing it to Reggie, allowed it to fall to the side of his taut muscular thigh, ignoring Reggie's extended hand. The stoic glare turned to passion as he groped for control. Everything he felt for her came to the surface at once and he was certain he would fall apart if she refused him. Trae caught a glimpse of the outreached hand, knowing it was there to retrieve her bag. Instead of handing it to her, he reached out with his free hand and grasped it firmly in his large warm palm and pulled her toward him until they were only inches apart.

Reggie could feel the pulse in his hand vibrate through her. Trae's thumb pressed firmly against the inside of her hand. Reggie's eyes fluttered closed. Trae leaned down and tenderly feasted on the partially open lips. Tender and silky, they baited him into a fog that not even he could resist.

Dropping her hand, Trae snaked his large hand around her waist and pulled her body into his until she was flushed against his midsection. A small moan escaped, and it was hard to tell from where it originated because they both released a soulful yearn at the same instant. Trae tighten his hold. Her soft, full breasts were crushed against the hard lines of his chest. Just when he was ready to take things to another level, Reggie's piercing fingers drummed into the wall of his chest.

Reluctantly, Trae released her. His passion-filled gazed sought hers. Mixed with sheer lines of passion was fear. The sign gripped him so fiercely that he had to take in a sharp breath. The pleading was so obvious. What was she really saying? Her head swung from side to side. Tears gathered at the corners threatened to spill over. When they did, his blunt fingers rose to erase them. The floodgate opened as trickles of salty tears steadily flowed down her cheeks.

"No. No, Trae," she whispered. "I don't want this. Please. Just leave me alone," she pleaded as her head still nodded the words "no" and slowly stepped out of his reach.

"Reggie, p-l-e-a-s-e listen to me."

"No," she hissed very insistently. "Please, could I have my bag? I need to go."

Trae glared at her. What in the hell was wrong with this girl? He couldn't ignore the passion or the surrender of her body to him. How did she expect him to do anything except pull her back into his embrace? Trae looked for a long hard moment attempting to assess if he'd miss something. In his peripheral view, he saw her extended hand for the bag that was gripped so tightly between his already pale knuckles that they turned white. Not knowing what else to do, he placed the canvas bag in her hand, but didn't release it.

Staring at one another in what looked like a standoff, Reggie tugged lightly on the bag. "Please, Trae."

"What about us?" Trae asked in a tight husky tone.

"There is no us, Trae," her wavering voice cracked.

At that instant his heart fell. Once he was able to overcome the initial shock of her words, anger soared through his entire body. No woman had refused him anything. He saw no satisfaction in chasing a woman who didn't want to be chased. Hell, he'd never had to chase a woman before in his life. He damned sure didn't need to start.

Releasing the bag, it fell heavily and collided into the side of

Reggie's thigh. She groped at the bag to keep it clutched between her fingers. Trae's hand floated in the air where it had been when the bag was still in it. Cool, hard eyes bore into hers, and for the first time ever, Reggie felt afraid of him. Trae took several steps backwards to put space between them.

"Okay, Regina. You don't want this, fine. I won't pursue you anymore." He'd addressed her by her given name. A sure sign that he was very upset.

The heavy brows rose in a questioning gesture. His expression asked the unspoken question, *are you sure?* She didn't respond. Instead, she stood calculating his next move. When Reggie hadn't said anything or responded at all, Trae turned his back to her and wiped one of his large hands down his face and blew out a frustrating sigh before turning back to face her. When he did, she'd already begun to move away from him. She didn't turn her back until her feet had hit the grassy area between the parking lot and the sidewalk along the side of the building.

For the second time Trae watched her leave. Like the first time, he made no attempt to stop her. He'd lost her and would stick to his promise not to pursue her again. Damn her! It was better this way, he finally convince himself. He could do a lot better, he lied. There would never be another woman who would come close to Reggie. Still there were a lot of women on this campus, in this state, hell, in this world. Women come and go and it wouldn't be long before Reggie became just another encounter. The thought was final.

Trae took the few steps needed to push his long frame back into the driver's seat. Shifting the vehicle in gear, he left the campus and headed to the one place he knew was his sole refuge. In the distance it took him to leave the campus and pull up behind the Cadillac parked in the driveway, he'd resolved that it would take him a while to get over Reggie. For now, football and his studies would fill the void until, that is, some young thing tempted him again. Trae got out of his vehicle and scratched his head. He didn't pay much attention to his uncle's car when he pulled up because his mind was truly someplace else, until now.

CHAPTER 12

Reggie hadn't been mistaken about the bone-chilling stare Trae had given her. The glare and the fact that he'd called her Regina assured her he would keep his word. That much she could count on. The truth was, somewhere deep in her soul she didn't want him to. At the moment, she couldn't see herself with Traekin Brooks. Reggie had loved him from the instant she laid eyes on him. Her dreams over the years had been the desire to be in his arms. The first time he held her and kissed her was a dream come true. She loved him, even now; however, she was too afraid to trust her heart to him again.

Drained from the events of the day. Reggie's brooding figure continued to ascend the stairs until she reached her floor. She dragged the bag alongside her as it bounced back and forth into her leg. Hoping to retreat to her room and close the world out around her, Reggie hadn't anticipated Val's greeting when she stepped into their dorm room. Apparently Val was as surprised to see Reggie as much as Reggie was to find her roommate pacing the floor of their common living area. The moment Reggie stepped into the room, the pacing ceased. The worry lines covered her friend's face. A sigh of relief crossed her expression the moment their eyes met.

"Reggie," Val broke almost into a sprint as she darted forward and embraced Reggie in to a tight hug.

Reggie returned the hug and a sea of emotions returned, rearing its head in true form. She thought she'd already dealt with the emotions of betrayal and rejection. Clearly the last few weeks her life had been filled with turmoil. Two weeks of misery came tumbling down like Niagara Falls. It started with being talked into trying out for the dance team. She had been convinced. To think she'd fooled herself in believing she could become a member of the pretentious dancing floozies.

Fully assessing her decision, Reggie seriously questioned whether she even wanted to be a part of them. She'd always considered them superficial and vain, yet she wanted to be a part of this team. Reggie had to take her thoughts back for a few minutes. Truth be known, the dance team was highly respected and extremely popular. She would have been honored to be a member of the team. The sting of rejection tainted her view. Maybe the coaches were intimidated by her abilities. That thought brought her some consolation for a second or two. Still it hadn't erased the hurt she'd experienced today.

Soon the hurt will be over, she thought *and my life and routine will continue as it did before. Soon I'll resume dance instruction and competitions I've been a part of almost my entire life.*

Reggie wasn't as certain about her love life, losing a love destined only for soul mates wasn't so easy. The bond between her and Trae had been special. The beauty of that bond had been tarnished by deceit and egotism. She was determined to fully blame Trae for what happened and ignored her part. Trae's reputation alone could have deterred her from cutting loose. His actions, not his reputation, opened her heart to him. What they shared couldn't be faked. She was convinced. Never!

Val gently squeezed Reggie's back, consoling her friend… her girl. Her own heart ached. The day's tryouts were clearly an injustice. Many of the students who filed out of the gym stopped and expressed their astonished outrage. No one expected Reggie to not make the team. Val felt helpless. At the moment, she could only offer her friend the comfort of her embrace. She had been certain Reggie would have rather been in Trae's arms. She soon realized how much he cared about her. More importantly, she knew how wacko Reggie was about him. At one time the bond seemed unbreakable, even after Trae came clean about his original motive for seeing her. When she and Val talked the night he broke the news to her, Reggie defended him, even though she'd called him a low-down, dirty dog.

So where was he and why was Reggie here with her and not Trae? Why were her arms and not his stroking away the hurt? The thought didn't go very far. Instead, she pushed them to the back of her mind for later. Her first priority was to comfort Reggie. Val guided her to the loveseat in the center of the room and slowly pushed her down onto it. Reggie still gripped the bag in her hand. Val extracted her fingers from it and allowed the black canvas to fall to the floor by their feet.

"Come on, girl. Talk to me," her arms draped around Reggie's shuttering shoulder.

Finally tears refused to fall. The only thing left was a dark hollow feeling. Spent from the crying and hiccupping while she bared her soul to Valerie, all Reggie wanted to do was what she'd first intended to do when she at last reached her room. She dragged herself to the bathroom and turned the knob until steam fogged and covered the tile walls with sweaty dew. Reggie allowed the hot spray to slowly erase away the frustrations of the day. Slipping into her favorite PJs, she crawled between the cool sheets and pulled the covers up until it covered her head.

One week into September and the numbness was still in place. Reggie severed any conversations about the tryouts. Eventually, most people got the hint that it was still too hard to talk about and gave her the space she needed. This week was particularly hard because the coming weekend was the Tigers' first game. And although it was away, most of the students had planned to travel to cheer for their team. The campus was buzzing in preparation for the weekend festivities. Reggie had no part in any celebration whether it was on campus, during the evening events leading up to the weekend, nor would she travel to attend the game. She planned to engross herself in something that would keep her mind off how miserable she really was. Besides, she was still preparing her Saturday class for recital in November.

Trae stayed true to his word and didn't seek her out. In most cases, he avoided the places they would likely bump into each other. He'd even taken to eating his meals in the smaller cafeteria on the other side of campus. The hairs on the back of his neck stood at attention the entire time during Philosophy class and he couldn't figure out why until he'd finally turned and caught a glimpse of Reggie at the back of the auditorium. She had managed to switch class days and times with Professor Gaines, however Trae wasn't aware that it was a temporary arrangement.

Seeing her today for the first time in weeks, stirred uncontrollable emotions within him. The light that once shone brightly in her eyes, was dim and distant. He watched her for a few moments as she fidgeted with a stack of papers. He could tell by the flustered look on her face that she was uncomfortable being there. By the time class ended and he'd gathered his books to leave, she'd already left the room.

The week after he left her at her dorm, he found her sweatband tucked in between the passenger seat of his car while cleaning it. He knew it was only a sweatband; still he wanted to make certain he returned it. He caught Val in the hallway one morning and asked her to return the black band to Reggie. For the first time since dealing with Reggie, Val had openly smiled and acknowledged him. And thereafter, Val and Rykard resumed their friendship as well. He heard their muffled giggles when she came over to visit. At times, it was hard to hear their happiness because it reminded him of what he and Reggie once shared, and most of the time he left them to their privacy.

By the time Thursday rolled around, most of the campus was jammed into the student union in preparation for the upcoming game. That is, everyone except Reggie. She stayed clear of all the festivities. Trae hunkered down at a table with some of his teammates who sang, off-key, the words to the song spewing from the speakers.

A few of the cheerleaders passed and sang in unison, "Hi, Trae!"

His crooked smile spread and revealed his straight, white teeth. He nodded, acknowledging their greetings. Casey elbowed him in the side and with a wide grin nodded his head.

"Dang man! Trae's back in business, y'all."

Trae didn't say anything. He did nothing to acknowledge or debate his friend's claim. Instead, he bobbed his head to the music. His eyes scanned the crowded room. They searched for one person, but her face wasn't among the crowd. He'd only caught a glimpse of her here and there. Each time her face was masked by a sad, far away glare. The sweet, deep dimples had vanished. It had been a long time since he'd seen her smile, since anyone had seen her really smile. He knew exactly where to find her if he really wanted to see her. All he had to do was go there. Control kept him in his chair; doing what he did before every game, hanging out with the boys. Besides, he'd given his word. His word was his bond.

The courtyard was empty. On a usual Thursday evening the benches were cluttered with students, some engrossed in small debates, while others were clung together by limbs and lips. Tonight it was deserted. The evening's air was muggy and stuffy. Music blared from the earphones and Reggie's ponytail gathered at the top of her head bobbed from side to side as she hasten across the courtyard. She was headed back to the dorm. She'd spent the last two hours in the dance room. Val's offer to attend Tiger's Night hadn't been her idea of fun. Besides, the Student Union would be crowded. She'd opted, instead, to workout. Dancing relaxed her, plus she had some studying to do for an early-morning exam. Feeling a bit more relaxed, Reggie headed back to the room to put in a few hours of studying before turning in for the evening. She slowed her pace as she rounded the corner from the student union. The loud voices and music could be heard, even over the music from her CD player. Her heart accelerated at the prospect of seeing Trae hanging out there. In the last few weeks she'd only caught a glimpse of his slouching figure during class. Everyone thought she'd changed classes, although she hadn't. After her initial arrangement with the professor, he told her that if anyone dropped from the class he would let her change. It didn't happen, so she returned to her original class, only she made it a point to come to class after it had already begun. During the last class, her eyes had been so intently honed on the back of Trae's head that when he turned and caught sight of her, she pretended to busy herself with the stack of notes she'd not looked at in days. A small part of her wanted him to seek her out. She really missed him and yearned for his touch, the silly, crooked smile and the deep voice that always overpowered her from inside out.

Sighing, Reggie increased her pace and continued on. She wouldn't get a glimpse of him tonight or the rest of the weekend. The team was pulling out first thing in the morning and wouldn't likely return until Sunday evening. Once behind the closed doors of her room, Reggie dug into the books until her eyes were heavy and the words ran together. Placing her head down for what she thought would be a moment turned into hours until she was awakened by a fitful dream. She sat straight up just as Trae was about to lock lips with some raving beauty from the dance team.

"Get a grip, girl. You either want the man or you don't."

Reggie crawled into bed fully clothed. Her fretful, sleepless night had only begun.

The bus pulled away from the sportsplex bright and early. Even though the drive to Baton Rouge was only a few hours away, the team wanted an early start in order to get some practice time in for the afternoon. Reggie had just exited her dorm when she saw the rear of one of the buses turn off of the main street. Val filled her ears this morning with the news of how much fun it had been at Tigers' Night.

"You don't even like that kind of stuff., said Reggie. "Now, all of sudden, you're hanging out. What's up with that?"

"Don't be hating, Reggie. You should have been there. It was really fun."

"Yeah, right. Really fun!" Reggie mocked her.

"Trae was there."

The three words hung in suspension for a moment. The brush gliding through the full brown mane ceased. Val continued. "He looked kind of lost without you there, girl. I think the man's really sweet on you."

Uh-ooh! Reggie thought.

Her eyes turned slightly in the mirror to catch a glimpse at her friend's smiling face. She hoped Val wasn't trying to patch them up. Just because things were progressing between her and Rykard didn't mean she wanted Val pushing her into Trae's arms because the two guys were best friends. She eyed her friend cautiously.

"What?' Val yipped. "It was just my observation. Okay?"

"The answer is no! N-O." Reggie turned to face her. "Don't, okay?'

Giving in to her friend's wishes, only because she had a great amount of respect for her, Val agreed. "I hear you, hussy!"

Reggie picked up the dried washcloth on the counter and threw it at her, which landed smack in the middle of her face.

"See, that's why I called you a hussy," and she ran from the bathroom before Reggie could find something else to throw at her.

The ear-piercing roar in the Tiger's locker room was beyond belief. The growling and banging of lockers and benches was deafening to say the least. The players, coaches, managers, and team physicians all crowded around in a huddle fully engrossed in the intense pre-game ritual. The sweaty smell of testosterone fueled the air. Players banged against each other's chest and the clashing of pads mingled with explicit promises to smash their opponents echoed against the large concrete walls. Trae chimed in and was propelled by his teammates' aggressive boosting.

Charged up and ready to kick tail, the Tigers charged from the locker room and headed out to the field. Trae meditated profusely on the plays they'd practiced for the last several weeks. With no time to wallow in his misery, he pushed to the back of his mind any distraction that might affect his game. He had a job to do, and, at the moment, it was the priority in his life. He was in tune to each player and knew their positions without actually looking to make sure they were where they were supposed to be. The fact that every man gave as equally as he, the team was able to execute each play with perfection. Victory was sweet because the pain and suffering was well worth the conquest. And for now, something was going right in Trae's life.

The after-party wasn't as celebratory as he'd hope. Trae eased from the crowded club and headed back to the hotel where they would spend another night before returning to Ruston. Just as he reached the door, he ran into Veronica whom he hadn't spoken to since the day after Reggie left the gym devastated. He was sure she'd been one of the reasons why Reggie hadn't made the team. He confronted her when he left Reggie at her dorm, and Veronica defended herself by telling Trae she had voted Reggie in.

Each time they met in the weeks following, he wouldn't meet Veronica's eyes nor would he stop when her hand gently touched his arm. So, when Veronica saw Trae at the entrance she expected nothing more than the cold greeting she'd gotten before. To her surprise he greeted her in the familiar tone of the pre-Reggie days.

"Hi, Roni." He half-smiled.

Totally shocked, Veronica was certain she was seeing and hearing things. Her eyes grew as wide as saucers. Trae chuckled at her surprised expression. Had he really been that hard on her? Being pissed with Veronica wasn't going to help the situation with Reggie, and he wasn't ready to alienate her. She'd always been there when he'd needed her. He extended his hand to touch the soft spot just below the edge of her chin. He knew she liked it when he'd touch her there. The response was almost tearful. Veronica covered his hand with hers and held it for a short moment.

"Do you want to talk?" her words were filled with emotions.

"No. Maybe later," he responded softly. "I'm pooped."

Not wanting to push her luck, Veronica nodded. "Okay."

At least he was talking to her now. She knew there would be tomorrow and the day after. When he was ready, he would come to her. She stood in the entryway until she saw his wide back disappear in the dark.

CHAPTER 13

Reggie could account for practically every detail of the Tigers' victory. The seventeen-inch television blared throughout the common living area the entire game. BET was the only station broadcasting the game, and Val was practically glued to the set in hopes of seeing her beau. Each and every time she saw his number she screamed at the top of her lungs. After the tenth episode of watching her perform the funkiest little dance back and forth across the entrance to her bedroom, followed by her fitful screaming, Reggie leaned over from her desk and slammed the door shut so loud the pictures on her wall shook.

"H-a-t-e-r," Val yelled through the closed door. "Don't hate me cause I'm having a good time." She giggled and continued her funky cheer before plopping down on the sofa, eagerly awaiting the next opportunity to see her man.

She'd planned to accompany the team and others students to Baton Rouge, but decided at the last minute not to because Reggie wouldn't go with her. Val felt obligated to keep an eye on her friend. A pouting Rykard was very understanding. He, too, had been concerned about Reggie and Trae. Trae hid his misery a little better. He knew his friend struggled. Rykard and Val talked about how to get the two back together. Val warned him that Reggie wasn't interested in reconciliation and had made her promise not to try. So they agreed that, for now, they would back off.

Shortly after the game ended, Val tapped on the Reggie's door and asked her to join her at the pizza bash down in the lobby. Reggie hastily agreed to Val's invitation. For the first time in several weeks she didn't want to be alone. Many of the students attending actually lived in their dorm. Happy for the distraction, Reggie laughed and talked with friends in the lobby. Even conversation with Justin seemed to be a breath of fresh air.

He gave her a hug and engaged her in light conversation. The small crow's feet that gathered at the corners of his eyes when he smiled made him look older that his twenty-one years. He looked very distinguished. Reggie examined the fine lines of his smooth, rugged face. He was truly a handsome man. She wondered why she hadn't fallen heads over heels with this man instead of Trae. The lean muscles bulged beneath the snug black T-shirt. He wasn't as built as Trae, yet he was as muscular. The closer she inspected the gorgeous man who had incredibly delicate hands and danced with such intense grace, his touch didn't burn through her soul nor did his eyes make her heart flutter.

Pizza boxes were scattered around tables, chairs, and the floor. Music from the lobby stereo hummed, stroking the rhythm in every warm-blooded body and enticing every head in the place to bob. In the wee hours in the morning, students finally dispersed to their rooms. By the time the morning sunlight streamed through the partially opened blinds, Reggie had just closed the cover of a book she'd begun to read the day before. Once she got back to her room, she couldn't sleep. Stretching her arms above her head, she moved to close the blinds completely shut and crawled into bed.

Sunday was a blur. Reggie had opened her eyes long enough to meet Val's happy gaze.

"Are you planning on sleeping the day away?" she cheerfully asked.

"Yes. Now go away," Reggie threw a pillow at the door.

"Dang. You need a life. I'll make sure I work on that while I'm out," Val teased.

Soon another pillow landed in the same spot as the previous one she'd thrown.

"Okay. Fine!" Val said, dodging the second pillow. "You know you really need to work on your people skills. You would make a terrible consultant you know."

"Urrgg!" Reggie groaned. She pulled the comforter up over her head.

"Alright. I'm gone!"

Val slipped behind the door and closed it quietly. Rykard had called earlier to let her know the team would be returning early Sunday afternoon. By the time she'd gotten to the sportsplex, many of the students were already lined up at the entrance waiting to greet the infamous Tigers. So far, the team was off to a good start for the season. As each player and coach filed out of the Tigers' travel bus, the crowd cheered at the top of their lungs. Rykard, standing on the bottom step, looked out over the crowd before taking his last step. His eyes moved to the far right when he heard Valerie screaming his name. *Yeah*, he applauded inwardly. There were lots of girls waiting around the bus, yet his eyes were honed on only one. Who would have thought he would be so snared by one little fireball.

It hadn't taken the Grambling Tigers long to understand what consequences they would have to pay if they lost the upcoming game. For two weeks they glowed in the glory of their first two victories. This weekend the stakes were higher. Being defeated on your own turf wasn't an option. Excitement and school spirit were high. Trae and Veronica were once again on speaking terms. From the outer appearance it would have seemed that things had picked up from where they'd left off, on the contrary, their relationship was in no way the same. After a long, emotionally-fueled talk, Veronica and Trae had agreed to remain friends but would sever any romantic relations. Veronica wasn't happy with the suggestion and knew she wouldn't be able to change his mind. If he'd decided to sever their relationship altogether, she would lose him with certainty. So she decided she would play the game cautiously, until all the trump cards were in her hand. Little did he know she was playing to win. Knowing Trae as she did, she knew it wouldn't be long before his head would be clear of Regina Miles.

On one particular instance, Veronica made it a point to lean in closer than necessary to Trae's body while they talked between class, once she saw Reggie flopping up the hallway. As soon as she was within ear range, Veronica seductively tossed her head back as though the words Trae had spoken elicited the erotic mirth to escape her lips.

Reggie could have handled Veronica's put-ons because she'd been certain she was making every effort necessary to draw attention to her and Trae. Even knowing that, Reggie's body went rigid the instant she heard his low raspy voice reply, "Ah, you like that, don't ya?"

A pang of jealousy crept up her spine. She'd spent a lot of energy moving past Trae and her spirits had begun to lift a little, especially after the pizza party on Saturday night. The once-propelled shoulders slowly deflated the moment she spotted them in her direct path and sank even lower upon hearing Trae's comment. She'd refused to skirt, hide, or turn around whenever she'd see him or Veronica. What she'd discovered, however, was that her bravery was appearance only. It bothered her to see the two together, and hurt even more that he was so quick to return to Veronica, as though nothing had occurred between them.

Veronica celebrated each time she was able to break Reggie's spirit. This was going to be easier than she expected. Bobbing her head up and down and fixing her doe-eyes directly on Trae's handsome face, she pouted as she responded, just as Reggie was passing directly in front of them, "Yeah. You know how I like it."

Trae's eyes strayed from her face only for a few seconds, long enough to watch Reggie's sagging figure pass them. When he looked back into Veronica's perfectly painted face, he reprimanded her but only mildly. After looking into those breathtaking eyes, he knew she had been aware that Reggie was within hearing distance and probably mistook their conversation for something other than what it was. She grinned sheepishly at him and rubbed his right cheek with the butter soft tips of her fingers. She had a way of making a man forget sometimes and this was one of those times.

Yet Trae had the ability to maintain control when and where he wanted to. He could, if he wanted to, be immune to her seducement. He'd known Veronica a long time. Regret etched its way into his soul because he knew that one day he would have to hurt her and she didn't deserve it. He also knew she wouldn't accept the terms they'd agreed upon without attempting to prove to him that she knew him better than he knows himself. She was so eager to prove that she was all the woman he needed. Regardless of how he treated her, she was there for him. He could never settle for anything less than a woman who stood with him toe-to-toe. He could respect her when she did.

No. Not even Reggie knew what affect she had on him. He was a changed man and every woman after her would pay for it. He would never be satisfied, and no other woman would ever win his heart or move his soul as she had. Until now, he'd never cared one way or the other. Today, his heart still ached and he wanted so badly to have Reggie nestled in his arms, not Veronica. Somehow, he had to get her out of his system. Just how, he didn't know. What he did know with certainty was that he'd be damned if he went sniffing after her like a sick puppy. If she didn't want him, so be it!

His foul mood followed him in everything he did. His teammate was kicking his tail at the pool table and talking smack to boot it. Finally having had enough, Trae slammed the stick down on the table and left the building, not sure where he was headed. He ended up on the track field, running until he was totally exhausted. When he got to his room, the phone rang. He snatched up the handle and bellowed into the receiver.

"Yeah!"

"I certainly hope that's not the way you always answer the phone, young man," came the firm, yet sweet voice.

"Mama," Trae chimed into the phone.

"Now that's more like it. How's my baby doing?" she sang.

"Mama, I'm not a baby."

"Look here, boy, you'll never be too old for a smacking. And smacking I'll do to any child of mine who sasses me, yeah!"

"Yes, Ma'am," He closed his eyes.

Trae could picture his mom, all five-feet nothing, pointing her finger up to his face, almost touching his nose. He wouldn't dare move one way or the other because she would take his movement as defiance. She commanded respect from everyone, including his dad. For a little woman, she held a lot of power in the Brooks' house. Uncle Ted said she'd been the only one to keep his father in place. In his day, it would seem Alvin Brooks had been worse than Trae when it came to womanizing. It had taken the little spitfire, Diane, to cease his wayward behavior. She wasn't having any of it and told him she would separate his head from his body if she'd even thought he was stepping out on her.

Needless to say, Diane wasn't the least bit happy to know her youngest son had similar tendencies as his father. She tried to make sure he knew how to at least treat women. She couldn't bear the thought of her son's outward disrespect for women. Worse than that, she didn't want some woman, or man, gunning down her youngest. In this day and age, women were more aggressive and didn't care the least bit about whom, if anyone, got hurt.

Like all the Brooks men, Trae was devastatingly handsome, skin the color of light caramel and eyes that would melt the skin off of your body. The one attribute that set him apart from his father and brothers was his mesmerizing charm. Trae had a knack for words, spoken and unspoken. Diane believed his charm was the sole reason why most women flocked around her youngest child. Even at twelve, as a lanky pre-teen, Trae had women fawning over him.

When his older brother Michael introduced him to weightlifting, and he managed to add bulk to his bony frame, things became worst. He would bring things home that women had given him because they liked him. She had threatened to call the authorities on one woman who called and cursed her out because she thought she was 'another woman.' She thanked God profusely when he never bothered to bring any of his strays home, more importantly, that he was focused on building a life and future for himself and the women hadn't been a negative distraction. She had hoped he would find a nice young lady, someone to bring to family gatherings occasionally. It never happened.

After awhile she didn't bother asking or wondering if he would. As a mother, she wanted her son to find some stability in his life, which entailed a family. She could only hope it would happen with time. Although she was content with him being in college, doing well academically, and excelling in sports, she worried that he might never find a woman who would do for him what she'd done for his father.

"It's good to hear you, Mom. How's everybody?" He usually called home on weekends, a ritual he'd started since coming to Grambling. During the week, he usually got calls from his brothers. Realizing that his mother was calling him in the middle of the week, he became a little concerned. He had just talked to her a couple of days ago. *Could something be wrong?* he wondered. It didn't take long to find out.

"Your Daddy and I are coming up to Ted's house this weekend. We figured we would come to your game on Saturday," she informed him.

Elation quickly filled Trae bones, until the realization that he couldn't hide his misery from his mother dug into his consciousness. She could read through him like a book. Most men would deny that they were "Mommy's boys." Well, Trae never denied being a "Mommy's boy." It was easy for him to charm his number one girl, until she got angry with him. Nobody messed with Diane Brooks when her feathers were ruffled. For the most part, she was fluff when it came to Trae. His family attended most of his games during both football and basketball seasons. He shouldn't have been surprise that they'd plan to attend this game.

The Saturday game would hit a lot of milestones. It was the first home game of the season. It was also Trae's last "first" home game as a

Grambling Tiger. Seniors would be recognized for their achievements. Also, this year the team moved up in its conference and this game was the determining factor for where they would be ranked in their division. Trae also knew there would be scouts at most of his games, this one in particular because they would have a chance to talk to his coaches. A few had already approached him as a potential NFL draft candidate. The thought of playing professional football hadn't been appealing to him, although he hadn't closed the door on the opportunity, as yet. After all, his family had a number of businesses across the state and it was hoped that he, like his older brothers, would step into the family business. Uncertain of his future, he pondered his options.

"Trae," his mother's soft voice intruded his thoughts. "Did you hear me, son?"

"Yes, Ma'am. That would be great, Momma. When will you be up?"

"Well, we plan on leaving Friday morning. Now I know you can't get away on Saturday night, you young people like to go partying after the game, so I want you to come to Uncle Ted's on Sunday. Ted is promising to cook up a storm. I want you at your uncle's house. You hear me, son?"

"Yes, Ma'am. I guess I'll see you right after the game."

"Okay, sugah. Momma loves you. See you on Saturday."

"Love you too, Momma," he said before hanging up.

If his friends could hear how he turned mushy with his mother, he would never hear the end of it. Trae showered and pulled out the homework he'd pushed aside for the last three days. The work was easy to do. He just wasn't in the mood to do it. Now propelled to study, he whisked through the reading and a pre-test for his economics class.

Trae hadn't been home to New Orleans since he got to Ruston in late July for summer training. With Uncle Ted so close, he didn't miss home cooked meals or a bed. He was thankful for someplace to sleep other than the extra long twin bed, shoved up against the wall in the middle of his room. Even with family so close by, it still wasn't home or his mom's cooking. He knew his mother would make sure Uncle Ted had all of his favorite dishes on Sunday. With that thought in mind, Trae scooted into his bed, placed his cuffed hands behind his head, and smiled up at the ceiling. The comfort of knowing he would be with his family this weekend soothed Trae's worried soul.

The streets were lined with students headed to the stadium. The sun was still high as it usually was in Louisiana on a late September day. Bellies, boobs, and booties peeked from beneath short skimpy clothing on practically every female on campus. As usual, Reggie's three "Bs" were covered with t-shirt and sweatpants and she seemed to be the only student walking in the opposite direction on the crowded campus. She headed to the studio armed with her bag containing shoes, towel, water bottle, and music. She fought with Val about her decision not to go to the game.

"You can run, Regina," Val scowled.

She knew Val, like her mother and, as of late, Trae, was upset with her anytime her given name was used.

"I'm not running. I just don't want to go. And even if I wanted to run, Valerie, its my prerogative," she fumed before stomping off. She snatched up her bag and slammed the door as she left the room.

How could she expect Val to understand what she was feeling? She'd lost everything she dreamed of. This had been her last chance. She didn't want to be reminded that she wasn't good enough for the precious dance team performing tonight. She'd be damned if she would sit in that stadium and watch those girls dance, knowing full well she should have been among them. Also, there to stimulate her failure was a man she'd longed to be with since the first time she saw him. She wanted so desperately to not feel for him. She couldn't help it. Yet she couldn't trust enough to forgive him. Determined steps willed her further away from the misery and closer to the one thing that always found a way to soothe her struggling soul.

Long after the game was over, Reggie pushed herself through another sequence of repetitive leaps and jumps. It wasn't until the tempo of the music changed did she feel the pulse in her temples racing. She began to stretch, cooling down and bringing her racing heart back to normal. Reggie sat in the middle of the dance floor surrounded by three mirrored walls, listening to Brian McKnight's song "Anytime." The soft melody pulled her into a trance. Soon the words were hers. The realization of how some people never find their soul mates hit close to home.

Remembering the strong embrace of Trae's arms around her and his comforting words provoked a calm she'd not felt until then. Within her soul he'd been the one she cried out to, even though unconsciously she hadn't realized that she had. She remembered begging for strength. Unselfishly he was there. His hard, wide chest absorbed her during her unspeakable heartbreak.

Reggie wrapped her arms around her shoulders and allowed her head to drop in the pocket between the flesh of her arms and chest as she remembered the feel of his hand stroking her back and the soft gentle words caressing her ears. She knew Trae wasn't a perfect man. He knew nothing about her when he'd made the bet and although he started out with the bet in mind, she knew he cared about her. Everything he did said so.

He'd said so in the note she'd found wrapped within her personal belongings he'd asked Val to return to her. She hadn't wanted to read it. She'd even contemplated ripping it into shreds without reading the red ink scribbled across the lines. Yes, he'd use red ink. He'd said it signified the bleeding of both of their hearts. His promise to never hurt her again was a pledge he'd never vowed any woman before. His pledge to not pursue her extended itself to avoiding her because he couldn't stand the thought of not being able to touch her again.

After reading his letter, she folded it and placed in her keepsake box. She didn't know why she'd kept it. At the time, she didn't believe a word of what he'd said. With her arms still around her body, the song switched from one sad melody to the next, keeping Reggie lost in her thoughts. Nothing was worth having without some risk. She had to seriously question whether or not she would ever experience a love like the love she felt for Trae. Would she regret for the rest of her life her cowardly attempt to keep her heart safe? The only person keeping them apart was her. In her heart she wanted this man. The last few lines of his letter resounded from the back of her mind as she recalled them, *I won't come to you again, Reggie. I love you enough to let you go. My heart will always be with you.*

CHAPTER 14

Reggie bounded from the floor, grabbing and shoving her things into her bag. She looked up at the clock on the wall. It was still an early night. Once she got to her room, she rummaged through her closet, coming out with a slim mid-thigh skirt and silk tank. It took longer than she wanted to blow-dry her hair. In order to keep it from frizzing she had to use a lower temperature setting, which meant it would take twice the time. Reggie went through the painstaking care of lathering her body in her signature fragrance lotion, got dressed, and slipped her feet into three-inch leather sandals. By the time she made it through the door of the crowded club, she wasn't sure what to expect. What if Trae was with someone else? What if that someone was Veronica?

Squeezing pass a huddle of people, Reggie paused a moment to allow her eyes to adjust to the lighting. She scanned the room looking for any sign of Trae or Valerie. The music was so loud, she felt it vibrate through her body. The tingling thought of Trae's hand on her caused her body temperature to rise in anticipation. Reggie moved in closer, yet cautiously, into the club. People were packed into what would be considered a fairly large club. Before long she was able to spot Candice and Linda at a small table. They exchanged hugs before Reggie asked if they'd seen Val.

"Yeah," Linda was practically yelling to be heard over the music. "She and Rykard are few tables over that way." She pointed to her right.

"Thanks, guys. Catch you later." Reggie nodded and headed in the direction given.

Reggie pushed past people before she was able to spot the table with the couple seated. Before she reached the table, Val was already standing and heading in her directions. She watched as Val touched Rykard's arm, and he looked across the table and saw Reggie approaching. Val leaned down to his ear before leaving. She hadn't given Rykard time to acknowledge what she'd said. She met Reggie with her hand extended and led her towards the ladies' room. When they got close to the entrance, the line extended along the narrow hallway. Pulling Reggie along, Val headed for a door that said "Staff Only." The room was dimly lit. Val didn't stop until they entered yet another door that said "Private." The two friends hugged briefly. The harsh words spoken earlier were easily erased with the brief embrace.

"Whose office is this?" Reggie asked in surprise as her eyes roamed the confines of the small office.

"Let's just say I know the club owner, okay," Val joked. "You changed your mind?" she said without preempt and instantly changing the subject.

Reggie looked admiringly into her friend's face. The warm smile reached her eyes and instantly the dimples in her cheeks smiled with her as well. Nodding her head, the long silky strands of hair flanking about her face and shoulders, Reggie's words came forth as a confession. "Yes. I came to my senses, Val. I want to see Trae. Have you seen him?"

"He's here," she admitted.

The words caused her heart to flicker. What she wasn't sure of and what Val's simple reply made no indication of, was whether or not he was here with someone. She squeezed her friend's hand before posing the next question. "Is he here with someone, Val?" the hope clearly showed on her face.

Again, her heart did a flip when she saw Val shake her head and said, "No. He's with some of his teammates."

Reggie closed her eyes and sighed before opening them again to a smiling Val. They embraced again. Happiness emitted from one to the other.

"Come on. I'll help you find him," Val offered.

"No." Reggie hesitated. "I'll do it. You go back to your m-a-n," she placed emphasis on the word man. Val had fallen as bad as she had.

"Okay."

It hadn't taken her long to find Trae engaged in serious conversation with one of his teammates. She stood back for a moment to assess his mood. Moisture gathered in the center of her back and in the palms of hands. Reggie contemplated how she would approach him. His promise to not approach her had been honored up to this point. If she made herself visible she doubted seriously if he would approach her. Just when she was pondering what she would do, one of Boys II Men's slow jams filled the room. *Ask him to dance*, a voice said from within.

Before Reggie had a chance to second-guess what she was doing, she was standing closely behind him. His back was to her as he held a drink she knew was ginger ale in his right hand. Her hand softly grazed the back of his arm. The scorching touch sailed through her entire body. Her mouth became extremely dry. Her eyes were glued to the back of his head, ready to confront the eyes that had haunted her night after night. Her breath caught in her throat and suddenly the thought that her choice of wardrobe may not have been such a good idea.

As if in slow motion, Trae turned his gaze on the figure he knew, without even turning around, was Reggie. His eyes traveled up her long lean legs, momentarily pausing at the hem of her mid-calf skirt and then again at the lush soft flesh peeking over the top of her salmon colored tank top. He allowed his eyes to finish its tour until they rose to meet her beautiful passion-filled eyes. He'd longed to see this face every waking moment. Her eyes were filled with the same yearning that dwelled in the pit of his stomach every time he thought of her.

His heart rate quickened. His blood stirred; sending the same quickening effect to his groin. Trae, just as quickly, rose to control the urge that made him want to damn any consequences and take her into his arms. His eyes scanned her beautiful face in the dimly lit club.

When her lips moved, Trae had to clear the cobwebs from his brain. Not only did he not hear what she had said, he was also oblivious to the ballad playing in the background. He lowered his head, offering her an apology for not hearing what she'd said.

When his ear was within inches of her berry-covered lips, tingling goose bumps crawled up his spine. The warm, minted air flowed from her lips, and the words, softly spoken, were loud enough to know she'd asked him to dance. Turning to look into her face once again, the seconds ticked away as he watched her, assessing whether what he was about to do was the right thing. The warm tongue slipped through and traveled along his lusciously ripe lips before he spoke, at the same time he extended his right hand backwards and placed the drink in his hand on the bar. "Yes," he gazed down into her waiting face. Trae only turned long enough to excuse himself from his friend.

Reggie thought she was going to pass out in the time it took Trae to first assess her. His bold appraisal was erotic. His eyes left hers for only a brief moment. The chill of that instance left her void. Her heart sang the moment his dark eyes embraced her again. Trae grabbed her hand and led her to the dance floor. His thumb rubbed the backside of her hand, a comforting move to let her know they were on the same wave link. He pushed their way through the crowded dance floor until they were in the center of the crowd.

Trae's arms circled her waist, brushing her snuggly against his hard lean frame. Reggie followed by wrapping her arm around his neck. The space between was enough to feel the heat of one another's body, without the onset of an earthquake erupting while they were on the dance floor. The swaying of their bodies took root with the rhythm of the music. Both Trae and Reggie drank the essence of each other. Caught in the rapture of being his arms again, Reggie allowed her head to fall into the wall of shoulder. Her body yielded and Trae fought with all the control he had to not respond. One song led to the next and they hadn't missed a beat. Neither was ready to let go.

Midway through the second song Reggie raised her head, no longer able to hide what she was feeling. She extended her head up the side of Trae's neck until her lips grazed his chin.

"I've missed you," her shaky voice whispered up to his face.

She closed the grip she had around his neck and pulled herself up until her face was buried into his neck. Trae at that point had lost the battle he'd been fighting. Squeezing her into the contours of his body, he pulled her up to his full height, her feet dangled beneath her. When he placed her on her wobbly legs, his grip didn't waver. His head lowered until his lips covered hers. The sparks that ran through them both kept their lips tight and hungry. The swaying had ceased. Instead they stood in the center of the dance floor in an arm and lip lock.

Trae couldn't get enough of her or the access he wanted. Tearing his lips from hers he whispered down into her ear. "Lets get out of here."

Reggie's head was tilted up, and her eyes remained closed. She nodded her response. He held her for a little while before asking, "Ready?"

Reggie nodded.

Reluctantly, he loosened his hold on her but didn't release her entirely. He pushed their way through the sea of bodies in the opposite direction they'd originally come. Once they were off the floor, he pulled her by the arm behind him through a maze of people standing around watching couples on the dance floor.

Trae had managed to get about halfway to the door before being stopped. A fellow student offered his congratulations for a well-played game. The guy extended his right hand for a handshake. Trae's right hand held onto Reggie, so he quickly made the switch and extended his comrade a brief handshake and shoulder bump. The guy seemed to want to talk longer than Trae had patience for. He was antsy to get Reggie out of the crowd and into his arms in a much more secluded setting.

Pulling her closer into him, he moved her around to his side so the guy would get the hint that he was on a mission. As soon as Reggie's passion-lit face moved around his large frame, it became easier to excuse himself from a conversation he had no interest in at the time. Relieved to be on his way again, he kept Reggie in front of him as they made their way to the exit. Val and Rykard had been on the dance floor at the time and saw the two locked in a passionate embrace. Val smiled and reached up to give her man a passionate kiss.

The sticky night air was much cooler than the stale air in the club. No words spoken, Trae led Reggie to his car parked at the far end of the parking lot. Disengaging the locks with the remote clasped in his left hand, the lights flickered brightly indicating that it was safe to open the passenger doors. He helped Reggie into the passenger side, even though the skirt she was wearing only gave a little when she extended her legs to slide into the seat. Trae's eyes caressed every inch of the long lean pillars. The dark desire glazed in the depths of his eyes.

He held Reggie's gaze until he heard the crisp sound of the seatbelt lock into position. His hand stroked the side of her face when what he really wanted to do was devour her whole. Reggie's eager response moved him to the bizarre state of rage. He bent down and lightly brushed his lips against hers. Control kept him from taking what he wanted. There would be time to get what he wanted. Now was the time to concentrate on what he needed. He needed this woman badly, mind, body and soul. He would never be able to get enough of her.

Like the walk to the car, they drove in complete silence. Only the sounds of soft jazz filled the car's interior. Electrical sparks fueled the air between them. Each time he'd glance over at her, she would be watching him. Finally, Trae turned into the parking lot of one of the few exclusive restaurants in Ruston. It was late and Reggie was certain the place was closed. There were a few cars in the parking lot scattered about, and she assumed they belonged to the employees closing the place up. When they walked up to the door, she found her assumption to be correct.

Trae lightly tapped on the door, and a tall, dark man approached and yelled through the pane glass. "Sorry, we're closed."

"Tank, it's Trae."

It only took a few minutes before the locks clicked and the door opened. A smiling face greeted them.

"Hey, Red man. Whose the pretty lady?"

"This is Reggie. Babe, this is Tank. He's worked for my uncle ever since I could remember."

Reggie smiled brightly at the rugged darkly tanned face. She hadn't missed Trae's words. *Babe this...* Already, she liked the sound of it.

"It's a pleasure to meet you, Tank." She extended her hand.

Tank looked at it a moment before completely ignoring it and pulling her into a loose hug. He patted her back a few times before releasing her.

"Any friend of Red man's is a friend of mine," he cheered. "Come on in. Can't say there's anything to eat around here. We're almost done putting everything away," he informed Trae.

"It's okay, Tank. We just need a quiet place to talk for a little while."

"Well, help ya selves. The room over there is all cleaned out if you want."

"Thanks." Trae hugged the old guy's neck and led Reggie to the room Tank had pointed to.

Once behind the closed door, Trae pulled Reggie into his arms. The fire ignited in his kiss reminded him of the day he had decided to come clean and tell her about his bet. He brought her here to talk. He knew they would need to clear the air before they would be able to move on. He was determined to have his say. He couldn't be certain what prompted her to come to him. He'd promised to stay clear of her, as she'd requested. And he had. Had she read his letter? She had to know that the letter came nowhere close to explaining all the things he wanted to say. So much had happen between them. So many things had changed him since they'd been apart.

For the moment, he was satisfied with tasting her sweet, soft lips, and feeling the soft curves of her body. He drank from her mouth like a drunk on a liquor binge. He squeezed out any space that separated their bodies. Loud moans escaped between them. Only when his body began to throb did he lift his head. His hands were locked in her long hair. Panting and visibly shaken, Trae pushed her away. Reggie held on for dear life. She didn't have the strength or will to stand on her own. She used Trae's hold on her body as support to keep her upright.

He picked her up and carried her to the corner booth. There they sat across from one another, their eyes still ablaze with passion. Trae folded her long fingers into his hands. He placed her on the opposite side of the table because he knew it was the only way they would talk and not kiss, and holding her hands would keep them connected.

"We need to talk," he began.

"Yes."

Reggie and Trae talked for almost two hours. Only close to the end of their discussion did the conversation turn playful. Tank and the other workers had long gone, leaving them in the dimly lit room. Pulling her up from the booth, Trae held Reggie in a tender embrace. She'd forgiven him. The weight of a thousand tons lifted from his shoulders and elation ruptured his soul. Their new start began with a promise of no secrets. She'd even agreed to go with him to Uncle Ted's house. Trae knew his mother would be beside herself with pleasure. What she had done to his father, Reggie was slowly but surly doing to him. And he liked it, liked it a lot.

"I guess I better get you home," he smiled down into her upturned face before covering her lips.

Trae sampled the insides of her mouth for several minutes before he nibbled his way down the sides of her neck until his mouth covered the hard tips of breasts beneath the salmon colored tank. Reggie's body lifted in response. His relentless teasing sent warm liquid to the core of her being. His mouth moved back up to feast on her kiss-swollen lips. By the time Trae released her mouth, they both were close to erupting. The thought of taking her on the large buffet table or the burgundy and gold carpeted-floor wasn't his idea of a first time to make love to the woman who'd upset his world. The first time was destined to be more than physical gratification. With so many promises ahead of them, he knew he could wait until the time was right. With that thought in mind, he eased her away for a second time. He gave them a few minutes to catch their breaths.

"Let's go."

Trae took Reggie back to her car in the club parking lot. He followed her to her dorm and waited until she was headed up the elevator before he got back into his car and headed to his own room. He looked at the digital clock on the nightstand. Two-thirty. After the beating he'd taken on the field last night, he should have been knocked out the moment his head hit the pillow but he was too wired to sleep. Only after a short while did he slip off into a dreamy sleep. Reggie was everywhere. The scent of her cologne hung in the air. Sleep came nice and easy.

More cars than she'd remembered from the last time filled the long driveway and parts of the grassy area alongside the detached garage. Trae plastered a hard, passionate kiss on Reggie's lips before opening his door and swinging his legs outside of the car. He turned and glanced over at Reggie.

"You might want to redo your lipstick," he said, sporting a grin from ear to ear.

"And you might want to take yours off," she teased.

By the time he'd moved around to the passenger door, he heard greetings from family members already headed toward the car. He used the towel tucked in the back pocket of his shorts to wipe away Reggie's berry lipgloss. He opened her door and extended his hand to help her out. Reggie clasped tightly to Trae's outstretched hand after she tucked the tube of lipgloss back into her pouch. Trae's eyes were centered on the freshly coated lips. He licked his own and considered kissing her until she became putty in his arms. The smoky passion in his eyes caused the tips of Reggie's breast to rouse. In the heat of the afternoon, goose bumps crawled up and down her skin. If Trae kept this up, she wasn't sure she would be able to last through an afternoon with his family. It had to be evident that she'd lost her mind every time he looked at her that way.

"Trae, please!" she begged. "Behave!" she hissed.

The sensuous smile that graced his handsome face made his eyes shine and lit his entire face. He had to be the most beautiful man she'd ever known.

"I promise I'll be on my best behavior." He kissed her on her left brow.

They turned at the wisecrack of a tall, stocky man with the same skin color and eyes as Trae. She'd imagined he had to be one of his brothers. He was taller and had about fifty pounds on Trae. His body was wide enough to block the sun from behind, then tapered off to a slim waist and lean muscular thighs and legs. He and Trae embraced, the entire time he talked trash as he held a man-hold on his younger brother. When he let go, his attentions fell onto Reggie. She squint-ed as she looked up into his handsome face. The sun was to his back, and she hadn't pulled down the shades cradled on top of her head.

"My, my… you can't possibly be with this old ugly dog," he smirked down into the most gorgeous face he'd seen in a long time. This wasn't the first time someone called Trae an ugly dog. She imme-diately thought they derided one another because all of these men were drop-dead gorgeous.

"This is Reggie. Babe, this is the ugliest of all my brothers, Travis." He shoved his brother backwards. Travis had stepped into Reggie's personal space. He certainly wasn't shy in the least bit. Travis recovered quickly and moved back in front of Reggie. He grabbed her fingers, his surprisingly soft, and brought it to his lips.

"My… you are a beautiful woman. It's my pleasure to meet you." He grinned from ear to ear.

Trae watched the exchange and rolled his eyes before snatching Reggie's hand from his brother's claws. "Don't touch." He pushed his brother once again.

All Reggie could do was laugh. Travis was bigger and apparently stronger than Trae. He could easily bring him down. She wondered if they'd always acted this way. She got the impression that they fought over everything. Trae, with Reggie close in his embrace, moved around his brother before she had the opportunity to return his greeting. She turned as Trae pulled her along.

"It's nice meeting you, Travis." She grinned. The dimples in her cheeks sparkled.

Travis playfully stumbled backwards and held one hand to his heart, the other waving above his head, as though he was having a heart attack. "Oh my goodness. What loveliness!"

Reggie glanced up at Trae who was shaking his head profusely. "Stay away from her," he yelled back at his brother. As they neared the house, more people met and greeted them.

"Where's Momma?" he asked one of his cousins.

"She's in the kitchen with Auntie," one of the youngest kids announced.

"Thanks." Trae rubbed his head before heading for the house.

When they entered the kitchen, everyone cheered his name, "Trae!"

A beautiful woman who had been standing at the stove turned her eyes on Trae. She stood about five feet, maybe. She quickly wiped her hands on the nearby dishcloth and went into her son's opened arms. The petite frame was lean and curvy. Trae leaned down to allow his mother to take hold of his neck. He picked her up as though it was a ritual he often did.

"Hey, baby. You made it," she crooned.

"I wouldn't miss my momma's cooking for anything in the world," he patronized his mother.

"Well I'm glad you came. And who do we have here, Traekin?" Small crow's feet gathered at the edges of her eyes as she smiled up at Reggie.

"Momma, this is Regina Miles. We call her Reggie. Reggie, this is my mother, Diane." he beamed with pride. She imagined he'd never done this before because she could feel his nervousness. It amazed her how she could pick up on his vibes so easily. Reggie went all out and took the risk of leaning down to hug Diane. It would seem that most of his family preferred a hug than a handshake.

"It's a pleasure to meet you, Mrs. Brooks." She hugged the older woman's shoulders.

It was no surprise that Diane quickly returned the embrace. When Reggie released her, the smile was still in place, and she knew she'd done the correct thing.

"Well, Reggie, it is pleasure to meet you too, sweetheart. Welcome," Diane greeted her, still holding on to Reggie's hands. Her glance went from Trae back to Reggie. "Well everyone, this is Trae's friend Reggie. Honey, there's so many of us it'll take awhile to learn all these names. I sometimes have trouble remembering them myself."

Just then an older version of Trae and Travis came through the doors to check out what all the commotion was about. His eyes immediately fell on his son and the beautiful young woman whose hands were clasped in his wife's hands.

"Well I say, it's good to see you again, boy," he said breaking through the crowd until he had his son in a bear hug. "Great game last night, sonny."

"Al, this is Regina. Trae says everyone calls her Reggie," Diane made the introductions.

Alvin leaned down and embraced Reggie. Diane didn't watch the interchange between her husband and Reggie, but the one of her son watching. She recognized instantly his feelings for Reggie. Her son was in love. She couldn't have hoped for anything better. Her first impression of Reggie was that she was a sweet and respectful young woman. She appeared to be a good girl, one who could be easily misled. She was fragile.

From the look in her son's eyes, he cared for this girl. And she saw a difference in him, from last night. When she saw him last night, she saw signs of worry and a hint of sadness in his eyes. What had changed since they'd talked last night? She was certain Reggie and Trae hadn't just met last night. Her gut feeling was that they'd known each other for a little while, at least.

Besides, Trae wouldn't just bring anyone around his family. He cherished family far more than a sweet little thing he could have his way with. Diane wondered if there had been some strife between them before last night. Had it been the reason for his sadness. Oh, he guessed she hadn't notice. She'd not said anything but had planned to talk to him today. It wouldn't be necessary. She liked the change she saw and became anxious to learn more about this Reggie.

Reggie exchanged greetings with Alvin. Just as he loosened his embrace, Ted entered the kitchen.

"What's all the fuss…" the words died in his throat. "Well, well, Little Ms. Reggie. It's good to see you, again. You know, I didn't think I'd ever see you again. Come on over here and give Uncle Ted a hug, girlie," Ted roared.

Ted's comment confirmed Diane's suspicions. Reggie and Trae had history. Traekin Brooks had a lot of explaining to do. Reggie hugged Ted and a group of others she'd met from her first visit. Michael was last to enter the kitchen and, when introduced to Reggie, was just as playful with her as Travis had been. "Ah, the ugly duckling has brought home a princess," he teased. Trae only rolled his eyes at his brother.

The Brooks men all took center on the basketball court while the ladies retreated to the family room. With Reggie in tow, Diane dragged the young woman from Trae's side. When she looked back, he offered a sympathetic shrug. Their gathering didn't turn out as bad as Reggie had thought it would be. No one probed about her and Trae. They were all just interested in her, where she was from, what her favorite music was, who was her favorite hunk. And before she could answer, Trae's cousin yelped, "And you better not say Trae or you'll get the beat down!" Everyone burst into laughter. She told them that Denzel Washington was the man of the century. They all agreed.

After everyone ate until their bellies ached, they listened to and danced to some of Uncle Ted's old blues hits. Trae managed to get her on a dirt bike, which turned out to be a lot of fun to ride. She sat on the back of a bike with him the first time. When he jumped a small ditch, Reggie screamed at the top of lungs. When he zig-zagged along the trail, she giggled until her side hurt. He finally convinced her she should try riding one of the bikes on her own. She promised to skin him alive if she fell and hurt herself, but she didn't. In fact, she got into a racing match with Trae and his cousins and she won. She somehow thought they'd let her win. Reggie couldn't remember when she'd had so much fun.

When it was time to leave, Reggie walked down the long trail of people and gave each and every person a hug. When she hugged Diane, she whispered into Reggie's ear, "Thank you, sweetheart."

Reggie looked into her smiling eyes and whispered, "Thank you, Mrs. Brooks." She wasn't sure what she was being thanked for. She felt at home with Trae's family and was grateful that they made her feel like she was apart of their family. With foil-wrapped trays in tow, Trae pulled out of the driveway and headed back to campus. They were quiet for a few minutes. They had spent a little over five hours with his family, and Reggie didn't seem to mind at all. His eyes moved toward the passenger side and stole a quick glance at her.

"Tired?" he asked.

She smiled broadly, nodding her head up and down. "Yeah! I had a wonderful time though," she smiled, turning her attention to him. He glanced her way again.

"Thank you." She placed her hand over his. He moved her long fingers between his and squeezed them.

"You're very welcome. I'm glad you had such a good time."

Reggie closed her eyes and drifted off to sleep as Trae cruised up the interstate. Her head had slipped off to her right shoulder and her hand laid open in her lap. When he pulled into the front of her dorm he parked along the curb. Placing the car in park and unfastening his seatbelt, Trae reached over for Reggie's sleeping form.

"Hey, sleepyhead," he whispered, pulling her body toward him.

She woke up, sleep still heavy in her eyes.

"You're home." He kissed her forehead.

Reggie stretched. "I fell asleep on you, didn't I?" She grinned sheepishly.

"Yeah. You're definitely a bad driving companion," he teased.

"I'm sorry. I'll try to do better next time." She leaned in and kissed his lips.

Trae moved her in closer, savoring the feel and taste of her lips. When he was done tasting, he moved around the car to open her door.

"You want to come up for a little while?" she asked

Trae pulled her into his embrace and sunk his head into the crook of her neck. The salty scent of her perspiration mixed the scent of her cologne was drugging. He could devour her whole.

"I wish I could, baby, but I have a curfew tonight." His eyes were dark and smoky with passion.

Reggie nodded. "Okay. Call me later?"

"Yes. I'll call you later." He kissed her one last time and left before he changed his mind.

CHAPTER 15

The hour-long conversation on the phone just wasn't enough for Reggie. She was antsy. She felt like a caged animal in heat. She longed for Trae's hands and lips on her body. The center of her body was on fire. The peaks of her breasts ached. It hadn't help that he'd promised to make her body ache all over for him. The words were raw and erotic. She couldn't reply after he'd told her what he would do to her. Reggie knew nothing about loving a man. She just knew she wanted to. Trae had enough experience for them both. All he had to do was kiss her the way he did. Every time she thought of him, her breathing became labored. She paced the space between her bed and desk like a wild cat. Trae had a curfew—she didn't. She stole a peek at the digital clock. It was ten-thirty.

Reggie walked over and picked up her cordless phone. She plugged in the seven numbers and continued her pacing until she heard the line click on the other end.

"Rykard," she whispered as if someone was listening.

She knew that if she called Trae he would have discouraged her from coming. Lord knows she needed to be with him right now. The constant throbbing between her legs wouldn't go away.

"Yeah… Reggie? Is something wrong?"

Reggie stopped pacing and shook her head, forgetting Rykard couldn't see her.

"No. No, nothing's wrong. Listen. I want to come over to see Trae, only I don't want him to know I'm coming." She waited a few seconds for Rykard's reply.

"Okay, Reggie. I'll unlock the door. What time will you be here?"

"In about ten minutes."

"Okay."

What was she doing? Had she completely lost her mind? Rykard hadn't indicated that it wasn't okay or that she couldn't come. So she had every intention of doing what she'd put her mind to do. She stripped from her PJs and slipped into a pair of jersey shorts and a tank top without bra or panties beneath. When had she become so brazen, she would never know. Trae seemed to have a profoundly addictive affect on her senses. She scurried about her room before slipping her feet into suede leather sandals. Reggie raked the wide-tooth brush through her freshly shampooed hair and applied a small amount of petroleum jelly on her lips before tipping through the door. Val would have a cardiac arrest if she knew she was slipping out to Trae's room.

Val wasn't the only person who would have a fit knowing she was off in the middle of the night to bone some man. Her mother came to mind fairly quickly. She knew both objected, yet, she'd made up her mind to do this anyway. By the time she bounded the last set of stairs, she slowed as her heart rate ran rapid. When her hand turned the knob of the door, Reggie could feel the perspiration gather down the side of her temple. On wobbly legs she stepped into the dimly-lit room that separated Trae's and Rykard's bedrooms. When she was completely in the room, Rykard stood and nearly sent her already fragile nerves sailing.

"Hey, Reggie." He walked up to her and kissed her on the forehead. "He's in there. 'Night."

Without waiting for a response, he shuffled back into his room on the far right. Reggie's hand was still over her heart as she recovered from her initial fright. Rykard hadn't questioned her motives or made her feel the least bit uncomfortable. Moving hastily toward the closed door, Reggie took a sighing breath. Although she was nervous, the fire within her hadn't chilled. She pushed opened the door and allowed her eyes to adjust to the dark surroundings. The only light in the room glowed from his alarm clock next to his bed. Trae's large frame was stretched across the bed positioned in the center of the room. She moved cautiously toward his bed and prayed she didn't trip over anything that might be between the door and Trae's bed.

Once she was near, her hand reached down touching the fabric on the bed. Her hands lightly grazed a muscular leg hanging from beneath the covers. Midway up the side of the bed she climbed onto a space that hadn't been taken up by Trae's large frame. His body shifted and Reggie's hand went to the partially covered but bared chest.

"Trae," she whispered.

Trae bolted straight up. It only took a few seconds to recognize where he was, and that there was a soft body in his lap and butter soft fingers pushed up against his unclad chest. The familiar scent, which assaulted his nostrils, was recognizable but not possible. Was he dreaming that Reggie was in his bed? His hands wrapped around the uncovered flesh of her waist. Instantly, he drew her close as his eyes struggled to focus on the figure in front of him. His nostrils flared and a piqued arousal took over his body.

If he was dreaming, it was a damned good substitute for having her in his arms. She felt and smelled so good. Tightening his hold on the warm luscious body in his hands confirmed that he wasn't asleep nor was he dreaming. The woman in his lap was real. The quickening of his groin verified that the soft smooth rump in his lap was real.

"Reggie," he groaned. Sleep still drugged him.

Reggie's hands slid up his hairy chest and circled around his neck until her body was flushed against his. She covered his lips with trembling wet kisses. The smell of her hair as it swept across his face and the feel of her body against him assaulted every male fiber in his body. Hungrily, Trae crushed her into the wall of his chest and took lead to the song and dance she attempted with her tongue. Reggie amorously rolled her hips into his groan, eroding what little control Trae had left. A loud moan escaped from his lips as he suckled the insides of her mouth. One of his large hands moved around and cradled her ripe firm butt, intensifying the rolling pressure of her body against the rail hard-rod strangled beneath the cotton briefs.

Reggie lost the battle. Her trembling body melted into his. The pressure of Trae's arousal against the lava-soaked core between her legs throbbed, and she couldn't seem to find the release she so desperately needed. Trae began a series of slow, deliberate kisses down the sides of her neck and throat. He loosened his hold on her just enough to allow Reggie's head and upper body to fall back to give him the access he needed to suckle the hard pointed tips of her breasts. A burst of fire coursed through her, and she became drunk by the relentless onslaught. She was certain she would die any minute.

Trae pulled up on the tank top until it released the two mounds. Reggie was putty in his arms. She responded by arching her body. Trae's fingers roamed her burning flesh. He tugged at the elastic band of her shorts until his hands slid down the hairy patch before making contact with the wet, hard tip of her core. Reggie bucked and rocked, forcing his fingers to search for and find the opening slit to the molten volcano waiting for release. She cried out his name. Trae quickly covered her mouth with his to subdue the shrill of his name escalating from her parted lips. He knew Rykard was on the other side of the wall, yet he enjoyed the sweet sound of his name vibrating throughout the dark spaces of the room.

When the tidal wave passed, he slowly pulled his hands from between her legs, but didn't release the hold he had on her mouth. He caressed the firm muscles of her behind and the slow grinding of her hips began again. When the agony of passion escalated again, this time they both were near the end, Trae jerked his mouth from hers and pushed her pulsating body away. The fog of passion hung between them as Reggie attempted to release the glue that kept her eyes closed. The lids were too heavy to keep opened. She tried to make out his face. Desire etched in the crevice of her soul prevented the use of any coherent thought or use of senses.

"Trae, please," was all she could manage to get out.

"No, Reggie." The words were tight and came out as though they pained him.

He pulled her down next to him as best as he could without her falling over the edge of the bed. He then reached over and turned on the lamp, which sent in a blinding glare across the room. Reggie's arm came up to protect her eyes from the blitz of radiating light. Her tank was still pulled up above her chest and the scantly snug shorts clung to her hips. The sight of her ignited the flame to yet another level. Trae sucked in a breath and moved his eyes away long enough to calm down the rage within. The dark tips of pointed breast stood at attention. Small goose bumps were visible on her flesh. Her chest still heaved up and down noticeably.

A pang of regret filled Reggie as she came down from the lewd high. She began to wonder if her coming here had been a mistake. Trae seemed angry with her. Fighting the tears threatening to gather in the corners of her eyes, she held her arms up to her face to hide her feelings from him. Tears were close to spilling over. What had she been thinking coming to this man's room and shamelessly throwing herself at him? She could only imagine the disappointment she would find in his dark penetrating gaze. How many women had done this very thing? And how had she thought she was different from all the rest?

Reggie agonized over the thought that Trae may think less of her. She clearly acted like so many of the women who had come and gone through this room with their minds clearly on making Trae theirs forever. Not even she could resist his overpowering magnetism. She would admit any day that she was under his spell. She tugged at the tank top and tried to pull it down over her breasts with her other hand. It was a long moment before she felt him move. He broke the silence by scooting back down next to her and gently tugging at the arm over her face.

Trae watched her and knew the instant she attempted to pull down her top that she thought he was rejecting her. He hadn't realized how delicate the situation was until now. It probably had taken a lot for her to get up the nerves to come to him this way. Quickly he pulled at both arms so that he might see her face.

"Reggie."

When he finally got her to meet his gaze, he responded so tenderly that the words even melted his insides. "I love you, Reggie," he confessed with every fiber of his body.

He'd said those words once before. Hearing them now comforted her, easing the awkwardness of being in his bed half-naked. His eyes brushed the length of her face lovingly. His hand cupped one of hers, which he slowly brushed down the contours of his hairy chest, and didn't stop until it rested on the hard, hot, throbbing beneath the cotton briefs. When the soft flesh of her hands made contact with the shaft aching for release, Trae took a quick breath as though her touch had been a pleasant surprise. He hadn't anticipated the shock it would cause. He had done so to prove to her that he wanted her more than words could ever say.

"I want you, Reggie," he was able to grind out in a low husky voice.

With her hand still draped in his own, it traveled back up their bodies and stopped just beneath her left breastbone.

"I want what's here," he continued, as did their hands.

"And, I want what's here," her hand now rested on the side of her temple.

Their eyes met for several seconds, each searching the other's soul. Reggie's eyes fluttered closed before Trae's lips covered hers. The soft yielding of lips and tongues succumbed to a hungry feasting that could not be fulfilled.

It hadn't helped either, that the sweet welcome and soft surrender of Reggie's body in his embrace had erased his ability to stay in control. He buried his head in the tender nook between her head and shoulders to release an audible groan and to regain some control before his mouth moved along the sides of her face and then recaptured her deliciously ripe lips. Reggie gave in freely to Trae's appraisal of her body. She opened her mouth and accepted the urgency of his tongue as it searched for the familiar spot in her mouth that made them both soar.

Flipping Reggie beneath his body, Trae shifted most of his weight on his elbows and knees. Reggie wrapped her long legs around his trim waist edging out any space between them. Slowly and unmercifully their bodies rolled into one another. Reggie's fingers dug into Trae's bare back until her body lost the battle to uncontrollable shakes. The soft, muffled cry released between breathing caught his attention. His body stilled. Thinking he may have hurt her in some way, his eyes opened and he pulled away from her swollen full lips.

He cradled her like a mother would a newborn baby. Tears slipped from beneath the closed lids and the rapid rise and fall of her chest alarmed him.

"Reggie. Baby, did I hurt you?" he asked.

Desire quickly put into check, Trae lifted her chin with the tips of his fingers. His first and foremost concern was her well-being. Reggie shook her head. Her voice was drowned somewhere beneath her uncontrollable emotions. She couldn't verbalize, even if it was to save her life, how good it felt to be in his embrace. It felt so right. Her arm slipped beneath his. When she opened her eyes, she ran the trembling fingers along the rigid angles of his face. All the love she felt for him glistened in the unshed tears, and he didn't have to ask her again what the tears were for.

"I love you, too," Trae declared. He kissed each lid and then gently touched the swell of her lips.

Trae moved off of the bed. His manhood still at attention, there would be no release for him tonight. He pulled Reggie to her feet, and helped right her clothes.

"We have plenty of time," he whispered into her ear. He stepped away from her and leaned over until he was able to pull open a drawer and retrieve a pair of running shorts and a T-shirt. He slipped both on as Reggie watched. She could see the physical evidence that Trae wanted her as much as she wanted him and knew neither of them would get relief from the fury raging through their bodies.

"How did you get here?" he asked.

"My bike," she responded like a reprimanded child. She hadn't missed Trae's silent chide.

"Come on. Let's get you back to your room." He reached for her hand and led her through the darkness of the common area.

"I thought you had a curfew," Reggie scorned.

"I do. There's no way I'm letting you track across this campus by yourself at this late hour, Reggie."

Reggie knew it wouldn't have mattered if she had explained that she'd taken self-defense classes and was capable of holding her own. Lord knows how many nights she'd walked from the studio to her dorm at all hours of the night. Not once had she been afraid to come and go as she pleased. She wouldn't share that small secret with Trae. Before she knew it, he would be demanding that she didn't go anywhere. She had no intentions of allowing Trae to dictate when, where, or what time she could go places. So she allowed him to lead her down the stairwell, through the lobby, and into the dark humid night.

Once they retrieved her bike and secured it in the back of his vehicle, Trae helped her into the passenger seat. When they reached the circular drive to her dorm, he helped her secure the bike in the empty space on the bike rack. He walked her to the lobby and pulled her into a tight embrace.

"Sweet dreams, baby," he crooned.

"Honestly, I don't know how either of us will be able to sleep, Trae," she stood on tiptoes and kissed the bottom of chin. Passion blazed in the depths of his eyes. A crooked smile lit his face as he stepped away from her.

"I don't know about you, but I'll be dreaming about how it will feel to be buried deep inside your body." The thought cause liquid to stir within her.

"Goodnight, sweetheart," he said and waltzed through the lobby doors before she was able to respond to him.

Trae knew coach would have his hide if he got caught outside the dorm. It was a chance he was willing to take to make sure Reggie was safe. He eased back up the semi-dark stairway and slipped through his dorm room door. He flopped his aching body down into his bed, Reggie's scent still mingled in the folds of his sheets and comforter. He rolled over onto his stomach and planted his face into his pillow, willing his mind and body to stop yearning her. Some time after one o'clock, Trae slipped into a stubborn sleep.

CHAPTER 16

The week had been filled with intense moments in which Trae and Reggie played on the edge of their unruly passion. It was hard to keep the desire in check. The profound ache Trae endured the entire week urged him to plan making Reggie his before the week ended. The weekend game at Pine Bluff only strengthened his plan to have her to himself. All he had to do was to make their first time special.

Reggie climbed into the back seat of the crowded Hyundai Elantra. The five women made a late morning start to join the crew of students and family members in Pine Bluff, Arkansas. Reggie's dance class hadn't ended until ten-thirty. When her friends offered her a ride to the game, she had originally turned them down because of the weekend dance class. Recital was fairly close and getting the girls ready was very important to her.

A second reason she turned down the offer was because Reggie wasn't quite ready to attend a game. The half-time show was certain to stir up emotions she'd worked hard to forget. When Trae asked her to come to the game, she hadn't promised that she would, only that she would think about it. She'd hoped for a good excuse to not attend. Her badgering friends hadn't conceded until she agreed to tag along. They agreed to wait until her dance class was done before heading up north.

The rowdy chatter the entire trip made the drive seem shorter than it actually was. They pulled into the hotel's entrance, and Val jumped out to check them into the room they'd reserved earlier in the week. With a couple of hours to kill, they decided to go on campus and scout the place out. The fivesome giggled like kindergarteners as they flirted with every good-looking man on campus. The cat and mouse game was funny until one guy attempted to pull Candice into his embrace. However, he hadn't expected to get the beat-down. All five of the girls pulled, pinched and punched the poor guy.

"Whoa! You ladies are vicious," he complained. He quickly left them without a backwards glance.

They didn't want to stir up anything and risk another episode or replay of what happened, so they decided to go back to the hotel, shower and return to campus for the pre-game festivities. Reggie wore a pair of hip-hugger khaki capri pants with a red tank T-shirt and red slip-on mules. The T-shirt was tied and knotted in the center of her back, which provided a seductive peek at her rippled abs and belly button. The long mane was pinched between a large red clip, with tendrils trailing down the sides of her face and large silver hoop earrings dangled from her ears.

The game was a tight match as half time drew near. Reggie and Val positioned themselves just above the exit on the visiting side of the field. When the team approached, Val yelled Rykard's name. It was hard to hear over the loud entrance of the band onto the football field, yet some how Rykard's eyes went skyward and caught a glance of Val vigorously waving her hands. His smile was seductive and sure. He touched Trae on the sleeve and pointed in their direction.

Trae stopped just above them. His eyes honed on the beautiful face he'd come to be intimate with even in his sleep. The dimpled smile greeted him lovingly. He mouthed the words, "I love you." Reggie blew him a kiss and mouthed the same words to him. He was then pushed through the entryway by a cluster of his teammates.

The victory party was bound to be noisy. Tigers bolted from the locker room and headed for the bus that would take them back to the hotel. Reggie and Val stood a short distance from the bus, waiting on Trae and Rykard to emerge with the clangorous crowd of football players. Rykard emerged first and Val bolted forward until she was wrapped into his arms. Reggie lingered back and patiently waited on Trae. When his large frame moved through the door, his eyes moved toward her like he knew where she would be waiting for him. He sauntered across the distance until he stood directly in front of her.

The connection between them was sparked with electricity. One arm curved slowly around her waist and pulled her into him. Their lips married instantly. Reggie snaked her arms around Trae's neck and allowed him to explore the warm insides of her mouth. When his lips released her mouth, he smothered her with small hot kisses from he cheek to her ear.

"I want to make love to you tonight," he whispered into her ear.

The heat from his peppermint breath grazed her neck and evoked a wave of goose bumps that flooded across her flesh. Reggie pulled away slightly to look into his waiting gaze. The smothering passion in his eyes was enough to send her hiding. She'd never in her life seen such raw desire in a man's glare before. The racing pulse in her neck and the quickening of heart drown the words caught in her throat. With eyes locked with his, she nodded her reply. Yes, she would make love to him right here in the streets in front of everyone with eyes to see if he'd asked her to.

He leaned in and captured her lips again. This time the kiss was brief and promised all the wonders he'd planned to share with her later tonight.

"Who's driving?" he asked.

"Candice," she replied, her gaze still locked with his.

"Here, this is where I'm staying. Can you get over?" he asked. "If not, I'll get a car and come and get you," he offered.

Reggie shook her head. "No. I'm sure Candice will drop me off," she assured him.

"Okay. I'll wait for you in the lobby," he kissed her once more before moving toward the rowdy bunch in the bus.

"Trae, man bring your black tail on, man. We're missing the fun," one of his teammates yelled.

Trae walked backwards with eyes still glue to Reggie's beautiful face until he reached the opened doors of the bus. Butterflies swarmed in the pit of Reggie's stomach. Tonight would mark a change in her relationship with Trae. It felt right. She was nervous, but she was ready.

Trae's long legs stretched across the paisley pattern of the lobby's carpeted floor as he slouched down in a low leather armchair off to the right of the busy lobby. He was antsy. He'd planned this night for the last couple of days. Everything was ready. All he needed at this point was the woman he'd fallen madly in love with. It was exactly an hour and fifteen minutes since he'd left her standing in front of the stadium. His body ached badly. Some of his pain was the result of the banging his body had taken on the football field tonight. All in all he ached for Reggie's body. He needed to feel the soft flesh beneath his. He needed to be lost in the folds of her virgin body. The pain he endured on the field dulled in comparison to the ache throbbing between his legs.

He straightened the moment he saw the Hyundai pull into the circular drive. He eased from his sitting position and moved to the entrance of the lobby. A smile a mile wide lit his handsome face and a pang of relief rushed through his long frame. She hadn't changed her mind as he had begun to suspect as the minutes ticked away. When Reggie exited the car and slammed the door behind her, her movement seemed to go into slow motion.

Reggie wore a slim fitting jersey dress that clung to every curve of her body and stopped midway down her thighs. The muscles in her long powerful legs flexed with each step she took in the high-heeled sandals. Her hips swayed seductively beneath the delicate fabric. Trae's mouth fell opened and his body instantly responded to her bold appearance. He would have an extremely tough time carrying out his plan as intended, to love Reggie slow and thoroughly.

Trae shuffled from one foot to the other and he sucked in a breath to maintain control. The passion raging through his veins went into overdrive. He stood rooted at the post he'd taken until she walked through the automatic doors. The air blew the long lock of hair away from her face. It had originally draped her cheek and partially covered one of her almond shaped eyes. The remaining long locks were knotted at the top of her head with an exquisite tortoise barrette. She looked like a runway model. The long measured steps were graceful and provocative.

Reggie could only hope the fear raging within her wasn't evident as she set her eyes on the man she'd long for since the first time she saw him three years ago. He stood tall and confident. Everything around him demanded his authority. The smoldering torrid desire set in his dark gaze frazzled her already berated nerves. Beneath the flame she saw love and that alone made her feel that what they were about to do was right. All the doubt and the fear soon dissipated and the eagerness to be his soon took root.

Trae opened his arms as soon as Reggie was within arms distance and she walked right into his waiting embrace. He closed his arms around her soft curvy body, pulling her into his and with great ease lowered his mouth to ear. The heat fused between their bodies sparked goose bumps to rise on Reggie's exposed flesh, and she relented without a single thought.

"I've missed you," he whispered into her ear, which was slightly turned into in his face.

His soft full lips grazed the side of her face and tenderly kissed each of her closed lids. Reggie's hands rested in the center of his chest. His gray silk shirt felt soft against her skin. She allowed his embrace to drown her into a sultry haze. The movement around them was forgotten and the world, for those few seconds, belonged only to the two of them. Dropping one of his hands around her waist and using the other to urge her forward, Trae led her through the lobby.

"Are you hungry?" he asked as he looked down at her from partially close lids.

Reggie looked up into his face, her eyes searching his. She couldn't eat anything even if she wanted to. Her hunger for him was much stronger, and from what she saw in his smoky gaze, he felt the same way. She slipped her arms around Trae's waist until their bodies once again united. With her face turned skyward, she pulled up and met Trae's lips with eagerness. Her trembling body melted into his, and her tongue flickered in and out of Trae's open mouth.

Managing some control, Trae allowed her to take what she wanted without interference on his part. He opened his lips to allow her entry into his soul. A deep moan roared from the back of his throat. Had he given in and added what he wanted to the brief encounter, they would have been escorted out by the hotel's security. When he lifted his head from hers, no words were needed to answer his question. He led her to a bank of elevators, boarded the first doors to open, and got off on the tenth floor.

They walked silently to the room as they'd done during their elevator ride. Reggie stood close with Trae's arm snuggly around her body. When he slipped the plastic card into the slot of the door and the green indicator flashed, Trae pushed opened the door and allowed Reggie to enter the semi-dark room. She entered the room casually. What took her breath away was when she entered, there were thirty or so candles illuminating the spacious suite. Soft music echoed from somewhere, she wasn't quite sure from where. A bouquet of roses laid in the center of a king size bed with the covers pulled down and the pillows set up against the chrome headboard.

Reggie was pleasantly surprised by what she saw. Her eyes turned to his, begging for an explanation. Doubt eased through her consciousness. A week ago she was ready. She had practically thrown herself at him in his room, and they'd been at each other like canines in heat the last few days. She had given him permission long before tonight, still she questioned herself. Sighing briefly and putting all of her doubts aside, Reggie decided she was indeed ready for tonight. She was more to Trae. He loved her. He'd said so himself.

She liked what he'd done to the room. Tonight, Trae revealed a softer side she knew lurked somewhere beneath his macho exterior. He had gone to this extreme to show his romantic and considerate side. A sweet smile winked at the corners of her mouth. Relief raced across Trae's expression when he saw the surprise and approval from Reggie. Having her approval was important. He wanted this evening to be one they would both remember forever.

His promise to make sure their first time together was special had been a priority the moment he decided he would make her his lover. He wanted the place and the mood to be right with no concern about whom they would disturb. The night Reggie came to his room, they both had had a great need for one another. Waiting was worth the smile on her face and the desire banked in the recess of her eyes. It heightened his desire for her. Tonight he would pleasure her with the sweet loving he's held at bay from the moment he'd met her. Here, they could take as much time as they needed to get their fill of one another. They wouldn't have had that option in his cramped dorm room.

Reggie didn't wait for his approach. She retraced her steps and draped her arms around his neck. The kiss was heady with need and urgency. Trae let down his guard and took what he wanted, what he needed. His hand slid down the contours of her body, caressing every inch of flesh, stroking and urging them both into an impetuous fog. He eased the tail of the jersey dress up and then over her firm behind. His fingers flexed the ample and firm muscles between his wandering hands. Reggie moved her body into Trae's groin, and the hard shaft could be felt against her aching body.

It hadn't taken Trae long before he lifted her from the floor. Reggie wrapped her legs around his waist. When he finally pulled away, he was ready to burst. Beneath the loose fitting slacks, he throbbed with agony. He eased her across the bed and climbed in next to her. The dress still draped around her waist, Trae's eyes feasted on the black see-through panties and the dark v-patch they refuse to hide.

With tender lips, he caressed every inch of her face with warm kisses. Reggie urged his lips downward with the arching of her body as his hand cupped and massaged her swollen breasts. Even through the fabric, his touch scorched her flesh. His lips soon followed his roaming hands. They grazed down the smooth, tender flesh between her legs and returned until he captured her mouth again. When he pulled away, Trae eased from the bed and reached for Reggie, dragging her body down the silky insides of the comforter.

Pulling her to her feet, Trae took great care in removing every stitch of clothing including the see-through panties. Without preempt, Reggie began the same painstaking task. Her hands brushed against the soft, thick hair that trailed down his chest, into the recess of his black briefs. Trembling fingers struggled with the button and zipper of his slacks. Trae's hands went to help, then stopped and hung suspended in air out to the sides of his body. He had plenty of time. He willed his body to wait and enjoy the agony.

Reggie concentrated on the task of undressing Trae. She struggled with the button at his waist, her shaky fingers fumbled with it until it slid through the buttonhole. When she looked up into his face, the alluring and seductive sight of his labored breathing and closed eyes ravished whatever fear she had. She eased her hand into the fabric and slid it down the length of his long muscular legs. The bulge trapped beneath the dark cloth partially betrayed his desire for her. Only when the leather softness of the insides of her hands cupped him did they both jump. Neither had been prepared for the startling electrical shock.

Trae quickly covered her hands and pulled her into him. He kissed the insides of her hands and wrist. Stepping away, he removed the roses from the bed, picking from the bunch one red bud. He used the red fragrant stem to trace a line from her head, down the front of her face, stopping momentarily at her lips, then down to tips of her chest. Reggie withstood the sweet torture like a champ. Her head fell back, and goose pimples saturated her skin.

Finally, her will caved in. Trembling fingers dug into the flesh of his bare shoulders. "Trae please."

Trae discarded the rose, and with the ease of a giant, picked her up. Her satin skin felt like smooth powder. In one quick step, he placed Reggie on top of the cool sheets. Reaching for the foil package on the nightstand, Trae eagerly shielded himself.

Reggie watched through partially opened lids. The sight of Trae in his magnificence accelerated her breathing. She watched him roll the latex over his manhood. Eyes filled with anticipation met and held until he covered her body with his.

Trae captured her mouth, evoking a cry from somewhere deep within Reggie's soul. His hand slithered down her body and eased her legs apart. His fingers massaged the tip of her womanhood until he felt moisture seeping from her. He eased the fat tip of his manhood into her, bracing the majority of his weight on his elbows.

"Just relax, baby," he crooned into her open mouth. "I love you," he whispered, his words meant to distract her from the pain his entry would make.

He entered slowly. His lips continued the assault on her mouth. The nails penetrating the flesh on his back and her sharp intake of breath signaled he'd pushed past the boundaries of her virginity. Trae used all the skills he'd learned over the years to moved her from pain to pleasure.

"We're almost there, baby." He intimately kissed her and protectively held her within his embrace.

Reggie screamed into Trae's mouth the instant he pushed his way into her body. Tears trickled down her face and into her hairline as she withstood the sharp pain of his entry. Finally, her body opened and the pain was replaced by desire. The fierce heat eased up her spine, and she rolled her hips, meeting him stroke for stroke. She wanted more of him, but Trae's hands moved down to her rolling hips to steady her movement.

"Slow down, baby. I don't want to injure you," he whispered in her ear.

Reggie could only respond with a loud groan.

Soon their bodies sang in unison. Each thrust was urgent and yielded by another until Reggie fell off the face of the earth. Trae's control to hold his release at bay erupted shortly after Reggie's climax. The descent from the volcanic spew was heady, making it difficult for either to regain control of emotions gone wild. Both were taken by how deeply their passion ran.

Reggie clung to him with weak arms and legs. Perspiration seeping through her pores mingled with the salty liquids from Trae's body. Trae lost all control. His energy had been spent giving her everything he had. Soon his heavy body crushed Reggie beneath him. After a few seconds, he used what little strength he had left to move off of her. With arms snaked around her damp body, he pulled her with him when he landed on the opposite side of the bed. He kissed her damp brow.

"Are you okay?" he asked, looking down into her beautiful face.

Reggie nodded. "Yes."

Her kissed-swollen lips curved into a smile. Trae couldn't resist the swell of her mouth. Capturing them again, he kissed her passionately.

"I love you." His eyes sought hers.

"I love you." Her fingers trailed across his lips.

They snuggled and fell into a lover's slumber.

CHAPTER 17

It hadn't taken long before Trae and Reggie rekindled the fire between them. He loved her until the wee hours of the morning. When they finally came up for air, both were ravished. Trae picked up the phone next to the bed and ordered room service. He then led Reggie to the huge, marbled bathroom.

"Shower or bath?" he asked.

"Bath"

He drew the warm water and added the bath salts from the basket of bathing condiments provided by the hotel. Trae stood in the sudsy brew and helped Reggie before pulling her into his lap. Her head rested against the wide wall of his chest. They soaked in the comfort of each other's embrace until they heard the knock at the door.

"Sit tight." Trae moved from behind her. "That must be our breakfast."

He eased into one of the hotel terrycloth robes and left her prying eyes on his body.

Reggie gloated in the aftermath of unbelievable lovemaking. Trae had been gentle and considerate each time he loved her. Her appetite for him grew from one episode to the next. He gave himself totally and she greedily accepted every thing he gave. She hadn't imagined the chemistry between them could be so connected. She wondered how long it would be before she got her fill of this magnificent man. Her thoughts manifested solely on the gentle giant. Reggie's lids slithered downward as she withdrew from the world around her. It wasn't until she felt Trae's moist lips on her closed eyes did she make the unwanted return to the world.

"You'll turn into an alligator if you stay in there any longer." He tenderly caressed her face. "Come on. Breakfast is ready." He leaned down into her upturned face.

Reggie crooked a saucy smile on her face. Her passion-filled eyes slowly peeked from beneath the thick dark lashes. The dimples were pronounced in her cheeks. The combination of both sent a jolt of lightning through his veins.

"Are you on the menu?" she teased.

"You're an impossible woman, you know that?" He used her arms to pull her upright.

The want in his eyes bore through her core. Reggie wrapped her wet arms around his neck, and her lips moved within inches of Trae's.

"You haven't answered my question," she challenged. The warm air fused between them was thick and suffocating.

"No. If I were, it's a guarantee that neither of us will make our rides back to Ruston," he countered. "And you'll be walking bow-legged for a week."

His deliberate assault on her mouth evoked a moan from them both. Pulling away, Trae eased her from the tub before reaching for a plush bath towel hanging on the rail next to the tub. He was afraid that if he attempted to dry her off it would lead to another heated interlude. His bus was scheduled to pull off at noon, and he had to be on it when it left Pine Bluff. The coach made no exceptions.

"I would," he offered, pointing to the towel. "It would get us both into trouble if I did."

Reggie smiled, knowing full well that what Trae said was true. She lightly patted the plush towel over her skin to absorb the moisture. She slipped into the other robe left hanging on the wooden hanger and tied the belt around her waist before following Trae into the opened suite. Candles were lit in the center of a white tablecloth-covered table surrounded by several silver lids, goblets of juice and water, and silverware wrapped in burgundy napkins.

191

They ate in a lovers-sated ease, chatting about what their plans were for the coming week. Trae hadn't been home since the summer. He asked Reggie to go home with him. She agreed. Homecoming was in three weeks and the Bayou Classics was in November, leaving them little time to get away. Because Saturdays were off-limits for them both, they finally settled on a Sunday drive there and back. New Orleans was at least a four-hour drive.

Reggie and Trae waited in the lobby, arm-in-arm, until Candice pulled into the circular drive. He walked her to the car. Four pairs of prying eyes observed their every move. Trae pulled Reggie into his embrace and soulfully kissed her before releasing her again.

"I'll see you tonight," he promised.

"Okay," she replied.

He acknowledged Reggie's friends with his award-winning smile.

"Hello, ladies," he hummed. The dark eyes sparkled beneath his long dark lashes. Trae leaned into the car with his arm against the opened window.

"Ladies, have a safe trip. See you back on the block."

He locked eyes with Reggie one last time and eased away from the car. When they pulled away from the hotel, Reggie kept her eyes on him until the car moved out of sight.

There was no chatter on the way back. Everyone was exhausted from the party-weekend. Reggie was so keyed up from her night of delicious loving that she couldn't sleep. The other three passengers had no problem and passed out the moment the car hit the highway. She kept Candice company for the duration of the drive. Reggie had been grateful that Candice hadn't pried for details about her night with Trae. Reggie knew Val would pry until she told her something. And the minute their feet crossed the threshold to their rooms, her prying started and didn't end until she had all the facts she wanted.

Val had accepted Reggie's decision to sleep with Trae without question or condemnation. She and Rykard had already crossed that bridge.

Their union had been consummated in Rykard's room the Sunday following the Tiger's first game. Last night, the two spent the better part of the night in the room he and Trae had been assigned. Only Rykard had taken her back to her hotel in the wee hours of the morning. Exhausted, Val slept with her head tossed back against the gray textured headrest. Reggie smiled when she glanced at the peaceful look on her friend's face.

No sooner than Val and Reggie were into the common area of their room, the outside door had not yet hit the jam before Val's question erupted from her mouth. The knowing smile on Reggie's face flustered her friend.

"What?" she asked. "You know full well you're not getting away without telling me all about last night."

"You know we don't kiss and tell." Reggie smiled teasingly.

"I don't want your black tail to tell me all your business. I just want to know how it went and whether or not you felt it was worth it, girl!"

Reggie's smile grew, and without answering Val's question, entered her sleeping quarters and closed the door.

"Good night, Val. I'll talk to you in a couple of hours," she called from behind the closed door.

Reggie's hand groped for the ringing phone.

"Hello," she moaned into the receiver.

"So... I wore you out, huh?" the smothering voice penetrated from the other end of the phone.

Like a gallant feline, Reggie stretched her arms and legs out, and allowed the tremor of his voice to wash over her entire body. Her sense of awareness quickly peaked. The remembrances of his hard body over hers heighten a need that, as of late, had become familiar and uncontrollable. She was out-of-her-mind crazy about this man.

"A girl has got to get her beauty rest you know," she teased.

"Nothing could mar your beauty, sweetheart. How's my, baby?"

"Wishing I was with you."

"That could be arranged." His own desire had been checked. Reggie consumed his every thought the entire ride back.

The week had passed like a thunderstorm. On her way to dance class, Reggie noticed a group forming by the entrance to the dance room. As she neared, she could hear her fellow classmates' whispers. They began to part like the Red Sea as she neared. Cautiously, she moved through the entrance. In the center of the room were her dance instructor, the two coaches from the Dance Team, and three of the dancers. Veronica was among the group and caught Reggie's glance the moment she stepped through the doors. A faint smile crossed her face before she diverted her attention back to the group.

What the heck is going on? Reggie wondered. She stopped at the edge of the crowd of students now standing in the room. Her dance instructor glanced over and summoned Reggie to approach.

"Reggie," her hand pulling forward in gesture. "Coach Murray and her team want to have a word with you."

What now? her mind screamed.

She'd already gone through the grieving process from the last try-outs. Under no circumstance had she planned to be humiliated again. With her feet rooted to the same spot, she watched as the instructor's hand once again gestured her to approach. Reggie's gaze went directly to Coach Murray. Her nose seemed so poised in the air that the sagging beneath her chin showed. It wasn't until the third time the instructor called her did Reggie's feet moved. She approached slowly, her eyes captured and held each of their gazes.

"Hello, Regina." The nasal greeting was almost a snarl. "We were just discussing with Eleanor the possibility of featuring you in our homecoming show."

The bottom of Reggie's face nearly fell off of her body. Had she heard her correctly? They wanted to feature her in their half-time show? With her mouth still agape, Eleanor urged her further into the group. Reggie rigidly allowed the dance instructor to pull her forward. Arms still draped round Reggie's sweatshirt clad arm, Eleanor used one of her hands to coax Reggie for a response.

"Well, Reggie," she chirped. "What do you think? It'll be the first year for a spotlight performance during the half-time show."

Lost for words, Reggie stared at her mentor. Eleanor smiled and gently squeezed Reggie's hand. She would never knowingly put her in harm's way. It only took a few seconds to consult her knowing advice to make her decision. Yes! This offer was an opportunity to showcase her talent. She would do it.

"Yes," she answered, her eyes still hone on the instructor, before they slowly moved to the coach.

"Great," Eleanor beamed. "When Coach asked me if I thought you would do this, I told her I was certain you wouldn't turn down a chance like this. I think you are perfect for the show she has in mind," she rattled on.

Reggie's eagerness dwindled when she heard Eleanor's comment. So her dance instructor begged the coach for a spot for her. Unconsciously, Reggie began to back away from Eleanor. The last thing she needed was their pity. She could feel the sting of rejections creeping back over her. Eleanor's had caught Reggie's arm.

"What's the matter, Reggie?"

"I, uh, think this might not be such a good idea after all." She wouldn't meet any of their eyes.

"Actually, you're exactly what we need Regina," Coach Murray intervened. "We were afraid you would turn us down, considering you tried out for the dance team and all. To tell the truth, Regina, you fit more as a showcase dancer. We would really be honored if you'll do the feature spot for the homecoming half-time show."

Reggie looked even more surprised by her comment. She had to give her credit. It took a lot of nerve to ask her to spotlight their performance after turning her away several months ago. Her talent hadn't been overlooked. Or was there another motive the small voice cried from within her. Once again, she sought approval from Eleanor. The dance instructor lightly squeezed her hand. In turn, she turned back to Coach Murray and accepted her offer.

"Okay. Yes."

"Whew," the coach finally consoled. "I'm relieved." Her long slender hand extended out to Reggie. "Thank you and congratulations, dear. We have a lot of work to do in the next few weeks." She explained to Reggie what she had in mind and why they thought she would be right for the show.

Reggie watched with peaked interest as the words slid off of the coach's tongue. When she sought her eyes for their true meaning, she saw sincerity. Her eyes finally moved to the extended hand.

Reggie reached for and closed her long fingers around her hand.

"Thank you. The pleasure will certainly be mine."

CHAPTER 18

Reggie hadn't expected the week-and-a-half to pass so quickly. Between preparing for the homecoming show and the recital at the center, her time with Trae had been limited. Every chance they got, the two locked lips, arms, and legs. Their desire grew each time they were together. It took longer to come down from the high after climaxing and neither wanted to part after they made love. They talked on the phone when they weren't together. They studied together. Ate together. They made love as often as they could between eating, sleeping and studying.

Reggie stretched her flexible limbs in preparation for a show rehearsal, and she smiled when she remembered their interlude in this same dance room two days ago. Trae hadn't seen her all day. The hunger for her had been more than he could stand. She had practiced her routine for two hours. Her frustration had peaked after she couldn't nail the no-hand flip. She couldn't get up high enough to roll into the cylinder wrap. Her body was too worn and fatigued to master the routine, yet she kept trying.

Trae moved silently behind her, causing her heart to somersault. His kiss was hard and fierce. His arms crushed her body into his lean, hard torso. No formal greetings were given. His hands unmercifully ravaged the weakest points of her body, evoking totally surrender. Before long she was on her back on the hardwood floor with no bottoms on, Trae's full erection pumped in and out of her hot wet body. His movement was coarse and his hands clung to her hips in a penetrating grip.

Something drove him today. She couldn't put her finger on it;

nevertheless she could feel in his touch and kiss that he yearned for something. It wasn't until he cried his release did the tenderness return, his touch and his velvety lips soothed her. He flipped her over until she lay on top of him.

"I'm sorry, baby. Did I hurt you?" he worried.

"No," she whispered. "What's wrong, Trae?"

"I'm sorry. I've missed you like crazy! You've been on my mind all day. I needed you so badly I hurt. Everything else has been a distraction," he attempted to excuse the roughness.

"Are you okay?" She laid half sprawled on top of him.

"I will be in a little while."

Pulling her up and helping her with her things, Trae took her back to her room. There he made up for all of his shortcomings earlier. He moved Reggie through sensuous and tender loving. Reggie's arms draped around his neck the moment he closed the door.

His fingers slipped through and eased down the shorts, tank, and panties from her sweaty body. Under other circumstances, Reggie would have resisted his advances until she had a chance to wash away the perspiration from her body, but not today. The urgent need to feel him inside her pulsating body relinquished the formalities or rituals. Trae wasn't affected by the haste of Reggie's fingers, or her low, hoarse pleas to love her now. He exacted deliberate slow and flesh-tingling kisses to her salty skin. Her body arched and rolled into his touches.

The storm brewed for a while. Reggie squirmed within his fingers, and whimpered each time he teased a delicate part of her body. By the time he was ready to enter her, the agony was so fierce that they both screamed into each other's mouth. Their bodies bucked and rocked in unison, until Reggie, then Trae, fell off the edges of the earth. Trae had an extremely hard time coming down from the rush. Unexplainable emotions washed through his entire being. He gave himself totally to her tender kisses and gentle stroking. He squeezed Reggie between his heavy frame and the twin mattress. The poor bed bowed beneath the weight of the sated lovers. Trae moved, even though he didn't want to, so he wouldn't crush her beneath his weight.

He sat on the side of the bed, pulled Reggie into lap, and cradled her like she was a newborn. She fell fast asleep within his embrace. When he left her room, her love soaked body laid sprawled beneath her comforter. Her hair was tousled around her pillow and a peaceful satisfaction conquered her beautiful face. He paused at her door just before easing behind it and smiled at the woman he loved more than life.

Finally, she'd mastered that dang flip. Reggie breezed through the segment of the dance several times before she moved through the entire routine from beginning to end. Homecoming was in two days and the campus buzzed with excitement, but Reggie grew nervous. Not only was she the featured performer for the evening, she was also a contender on the homecoming court. Veronica had been cordial in her presence, still she knew the woman hated her guts. Weeding out her chance for a spot on the court was the straw that broke the camel's back.

Reggie felt that given the right opportunity, Veronica planned revenge because that was the type of person she seemed to be. It was just a matter of time. Gliding through the last sequence of the routine, Reggie moved smoothly and swiftly across the dance floor. She took her time stuffing her things back into her backpack before heading out to the final rehearsal. When she got to the stadium, most of the band and dancers were already on the field.

The first song erupted across the field and the marching tigers strutted across the field to one of the latest R&B hits. Heels stomped. Arms, legs, instruments, flags, and rifles swung in a funky rhythm to the beat. The dancers entered from the opposite side of the field shaking their greatest asset, their rumps. Arms were suspended above their heads, and then popped on the six, seven, eight count.

The three drum majors rocked on the backs of their legs. Their long gold batons swung up and down the sides of their bodies. Reggie hung in the backfield until the music signaled her entrance. Her thoughts hung and concentrated on her routine. She mentally walked through the routine as the music blared from the field. She kept saying inwardly,

Once I enter the field, I'll climb the three steps and leap onto a platform; there spotlights in gold and purple will swing from side to side, and I should stay stage center. She listened to the cadence of the drums.

It was her turn. She counted inwardly… five, six, seven, eight. Smile in place, her hips popped from side to side as she made her sultry entrance on to the field, her arms swung out in poised waves. Like clockwork everything fell into place. The band rolled from the first song to the second. At the conclusion of the second song, Reggie strutted off to field left and crossed the white sideline. She continued until she met the spot marked for her.

"Yeah, Yeah," the director roared. His hands waved frantically out in front of him, giving directions with his swinging arms and hands.

Once Reggie made it to her spot, he glance over at her and nodded his approval. Reggie was winded, yet it felt wonderful. Her smile never faltered. She was amazed by how remarkable the show looked. This was the first complete walk-through, and the entire show looked great. The dance coaches were pleased with her performance and told her so.

She waltzed over to retrieve her bag and saw Trae standing near, waiting on her. Their eyes met. Would she ever be able to look at him without feeling this volcanic rush? The passion-filled gaze warmed her insides. A smile crooked his handsome face as she neared and his arms opened awaiting her retreat. Reggie walked straight into his opened arms. Trae closed his long limbs around her body and pulled her into the wall of his massive chest.

"Well… what do you think?" she smiled up to his handsome face. The faint scent of his shower gel mingled with the aroma of his musk cologne. The heady exchange lit a fire that never seemed to extinguish whenever she was near him.

"Wow!" his eyes sparkled. "That was unbelievable. You look absolutely gorgeous." He kissed her briefly.

"You're just saying that to get a whopping kiss."

"What would it take to get more than a kiss?" His face leaned down into hers until their noses touched.

"Not a whole lot," she said breathlessly.

Veronica watched the exchange with churning hatred. A mass of icicles marred her otherwise gorgeous face. Her red-coated lips pouted in an unbecoming gesture. Her plans to win back Trae's affections were slowly dying. She'd tried just about everything to get his attention. She'd even shown up several times to his room in the middle of the night. On one such occasion, Rykard had told her Trae wasn't in. She pushed passed him at the door because she hadn't believed him. She sauntered over to the closed door of his sleeping quarters. When she pressed the door opened, she turned and huffed passed Rykard without a backwards glance. It didn't take a rocket scientist to figure out where he was.

Now here they stood in front of God and everyone else displaying the affections she'd always wanted Trae to share with her. Not once had he touched her in that manner. If they kissed in public, it was because she'd initiated it; most times leaving red smears along the sides of his mouth. And he always used the back of his hands to wipe it and the kiss away.

Not once had he caressed her face or stroked her hair as he did now. Veronica remembered the smothering and fierce stroking of his body inside hers behind closed doors. Trae had an enormous appetite, and she doubted seriously that little Miss-Thang could handle what it took to keep Trae satisfied. In reality, she was banking on the very fact that she couldn't. Soon he would be tired of her little bony ass and come back to where he belonged. She would be waiting with opened arms and opened legs.

Veronica decided to go in the opposite direction of the two. She couldn't chance Trae ignoring her while the others watched had she past directly by them. Some of her teammates scrutinized her as she observed the situation, attempting to gauge her reactions. She'd be dammed if she would give them something to talk about. She wasn't about to give them, or Reggie, ammunition to use against her. Swinging her hips beneath the snug shorts, she moved from the field and the stadium. She had to figure out what she would do to get her man back. Her patience was running thin. Something had to give.

Trae and Reggie were oblivious to the world around them. Enjoying the sweet taste of each other's lips, he tightened his hold on Reggie's soft body.

"I'm starved. Let's go eat," he urged.

"And I thought you were going to suggest something a little more stimulating than filling your stomach with dead stuff," she challenged

Trae looked down in to her face and shook his head as if in defeat. "What am I going to do with you, Reggie? You're an animal." His hands pinched her chin between his fingers.

She only smiled.

Reggie hadn't been named homecoming queen, but she would be a part of the royal court. She and Val spent hours at the mall in Shreveport looking for a dress to wear for the opening ceremony. She had to change for the half-time show after the first quarter. Once she selected a dress, they spent just as much time searching for matching shoes. Her parents had arrived in Ruston a few hours ago. It would be Cheri and David Miles' first time meeting Trae, and Reggie was a little antsy about the whole thing. Yet, dinner with her parents went better than expected. They loved Trae, and he seemed to have them eating out of his hands, and that didn't surprise Reggie the least.

She struggled with the cosmetic case packed with all of her accessories in it. She grabbed the garment bag with her dress and dance outfit from the hanger on the door as she left the room. She peeked over into Val's room and called out to her.

"Hey, Val, I'm out of here." She moved toward the door.

"Wait one minute, speedy," Val rushed toward her. "Do you have everything you need?" she fussed.

"Yes," Reggie grumbled impatiently.

"I'll be there in an hour to help you dress." She fidgeted with one of the stray curls on Reggie's head.

Reggie lightly slapped her hand away. "Yes, Mother."

Val rounded her eyes. "Whatever, Missy."

When Reggie arrived at the stadium, she was given directions on where to go to dress. The room they'd been assigned was a makeshift area spaced between two iron beams. Tables were lined against the concrete wall, and women were already seated and applying the finishing touches on their makeup. Reggie found a place for her things and went off to find a place to stretch and to practice her routine. She retrieved the hair net and secured it over her hair. She leaned against a cold concrete wall near an exit, stretching her legs against it. Small goose pumps crept up her spine, and her sense of awareness peaked.

She turned and only saw the shadow of a figure move past the opening. She stood and watched up the hallway before shrugging her shoulders, then continued her stretching routine. She leaned, squatted, and stretched until she felt her muscle loosen. Careful not to over do it, she practice only certain moves. Fifteen minutes later, she went back to the dressing room.

Justin watched from a distance as Reggie retreated to the dressing room. He'd followed her in and would have called out to her had he not been stopped by one of his many female friends. He had no interest in anyone except Reggie. Sure, he'd use them to satisfy his huge sexual appetite. Even Veronica's blazingly wild and satisfying sexual favors didn't warm his heart. Although she was an attentive lover, Veronica's habits kept him from seeking an intimate relationship with her. When they first met, she had the potential to be a steady girl, until he accidentally bumped into her in Monroe. He was totally surprised. They mutually agreed to keep each other's secret. Sometimes he used it to get her into his bed when he got an urge for something special.

For the most part, he sought the women on campus and of all the women he knew, none made his heart throb every time he saw them. Only Reggie made him feel like he wasn't yet complete. With Traekin back into the picture, it was hard to get any of her attention. Still he tried every chance he got.

By the time he'd gotten rid of the woman, Justin watched Reggie move to an empty hallway to stretch. He approached but lost his nerve at the last minute. All he needed was Trae Brooks' looming figure to walk up and catch him with her. He wasn't afraid of the guy, even though he out-weighed him by fifty pounds. He wasn't the kind who knowingly sought trouble. Over the last several weeks he'd noticed the drastic change in the relationship budding between Reggie and Trae, and he didn't like it one bit. Things would have been fine had she stuck to her guns and left that creep alone. He started toward her then stopped. When she turned, he quickly retreated behind the wall before sneaking past and eventually leaving the building. There would be another time to approach her.

After the court was presented and escorted from the field, Trae escorted Reggie to the court platform. He kissed her tenderly on the brow and wished her well on her performance. His family stood in the wings smiling and snapping pictures to capture the moment. Minutes later the Tigers came roaring from the home gates. By the end of the first quarter, Reggie made her way back to the dressing room. Val waited for her by the entrance. They briefly embraced one another.

"Come on, your highness. Let's get you into that skimpy little get-up!"

With hair and make-up in place and the skimpy sequenced purple and gold one-piece snaked onto her body, Reggie eased her hands through the fingerless gloves. When she got out to the meeting area, most of the band had proceeded from the stands. The dance team stretched and then tidied their hair and re-glossed their lips. A few of the girls were friendly toward her the past couple of weeks. One of those was Jerica. Their conversations were always easy and light-hearted. They chatted for a few minutes before they all moved out to their designated starting points.

The entire student body and guests got into the half-time festivities. Reggie stood on the sidelines awaiting her cue. Her hips bounced from side to side until, on the eighth count, her feet crossed the white line and she stepped onto the field. Over the music the announcer announced her entrance. The crowd went completely mad! A smile on her face, Reggie made her entrance with all the sway and funk she could muster as she sauntered across the green meadow and climbed the three steps. Her no-hand flips brought even greater roars from the crowd. By the time she left the platform and eventually the field, everyone was on their feet.

Pride beamed in Reggie's parents and friends. A new admiration for her talent struck many who knew very little about her. When the band marched off the field and to the sidelines, many of the students stormed her. Hugs and pats on the back made Reggie feel like she'd just won the lottery. Her smile was broader and brighter than a hundred-watt light bulb. When Val was finally able to get through the crowd, they both squealed with delight. They hugged one another and jumped up and down. The other members of their crew made it through, as well.

"We're gonna p-a-r-t-y tonight," they yipped.

Reggie remained on her high throughout the rest of the game. She sported a satin wrap over her costume. The gold satin clung loosely around her hips and stopped mid-thigh. She sought out her parents in the stands, seated near the band. Lord knows why they choose to sit so close to the noisy crew. The music and cheers were nonstop. They left a few minutes before the game ended, as did others trying to avoid the crowd.

"So, what are you young people planning on doing tonight?" her father asked.

"There are several parties planned. I think we're just going to hang out. You guys want to come?" she asked.

"My dear! You have to be kidding. I doubt seriously you want your parents tagging along behind you," her mother exasperated. "You go right ahead and have fun. We'll see you before we leave tomorrow." They kissed her on the brow and left.

Reggie received praises everywhere she turned. An overwhelming number of people approached and commended her on her performance. She met with Trae's family following the game. They all greeted her with hugs and kisses.

"My, my, what a talented girl you are," Uncle Ted teased. He swung his hips from side to side to mock Reggie.

His wife punched him on the shoulders.

"Ted, you best behave yourself or else," she admonished.

Reggie's fame had extended beyond the campus as well. There

was even a bunch of brave souls who had approached her while she was on the dance floor with Trae.

"Excuse me, man, mind if I have this dance?" one guy cocky enough to impose asked. Of course Trae shot daggers straight through him, and without a word, the poor guy turned and left them swaying to the slow jam. Of course he wasn't having any of it. Reggie was dancing with one man tonight: him.

He held her close as they swayed from side to side while a slow jam roared from the speakers on either sides of the dance floor. Trae knew this would be the closest he would get to her tonight. Since her parents arrived, their passion had been put on hold. However, tomorrow night would be a different story.

Trae had been given rave reviews about Reggie's performance. It made his heart swell. She'd been given a chance to prove that she indeed should have been a member of the dance group from the start. A small amount of satisfaction filled his heart knowing this night would erase the doubt he knew was still in her very soul. Maybe the saying "everything happens for a reason" was true. The half-time show was by far a more significant moment than any he could imagine.

By the time he left Reggie at the door of her room, they both were exhausted. She had to get up early to have breakfast with her parents before they returned home. Later that afternoon, she and Trae planned to go to his uncle's house for their family gathering. He kissed her briefly, and held her close. Tired and broken down, his aching body responded when she leaned into him.

He savored the softness of her body before he eventually pulled away. Passion stared back at him.

"I love you," he whispered.

"I love you." She stood on her toes and kissed his partially open mouth.

"Good night, sweetheart. I'll see you in a little bit."

Reggie nodded before stepping back and closing the door.

CHAPTER 19

Reggie waved as her parents pulled the rental car from the curb, heading back to Shreveport. Tears welled in her own eyes when she caught a glimpse of her mother's teary stare. Cheri Miles was known to cry whenever she parted from her children and other family members. Only after the car disappeared did Reggie turn and head back to her room. She picked up the cordless phone from its bay and hit the fast dial key for Trae's room. When the ringing ceased, his voice floated across the lines and settled in the nest of her heart.

"Hi, baby. How did it go?"

"Good," she choked.

Trae sat up from his reclining posture, alarmed by the emotions he heard in her voice. "What's wrong?"

"Nothing. I'm fine. It's just…" her voice trailed off.

"I'm on my way," he moved as he spoke.

"No, Trae," urgency rang in her voice. "Really, I'm fine. It's always hard to part from my parents, that's all."

"Are you sure?"

"Yes," she reassured him. "What time are we leaving for Uncle Ted's?"

Trae had just pulled the jersey shorts up his hairy muscular legs. The phone was tucked into the curve between his head and shoulders. He stopped to assess the sincerity in her voice. Had he thought for a second something wasn't right, he would have been out the door. He sunk his tall frame back onto the bed and pushed his body back onto the mattress before replying. "In a couple of hours, say eleven."

"Okay. I'll be ready."

The kiss they shared when Trae met her at the door was spicy enough to delay their trip to Uncle Ted's house. Trae allowed his hands to run under the back of her white T-shirt, touching the silky-soft skin on her back. Reggie caved at each stroke. He moaned at the sweet surrender of her body in his arms. As quickly as the interlude started, Trae pushed her away, panting and throbbing all over.

"Ah, I think we better move sweetheart, otherwise…" He looked around them. "Otherwise, we'll cause a scene."

A saucy smile lit Reggie's oval face. Her eyes sparkled with the glitter of a happy and cherished woman. She snaked her arms up his chest and around his neck, gaining back some of the heat from his body. The world never mattered when she was with him. She wondered if she would ever tire of his electrifying presence. The magnetism between them was fierce, even when they were apart. Reggie's long fingers massaged the taut muscles in his neck. In response, Trae's eyelids slipped, the long dark lashes resting momentarily on his cheeks.

"My room's vacant," she challenged.

Slowly his dark eyes peeked from beneath the shadows of his lashes. The passion etched in them told Reggie even before he spoke the words, that if they retreated to her room, his family wouldn't see them at all today.

"Then, I'll have to answer to my mother, Reggie, because there's no way we'll come out of that room until I'm done. And right now, that won't be for awhile," his lustful voice was serious and filled with promises.

He released her and pulled Reggie along by the hand until they reached his vehicle. The ride to Monroe was quiet except for the smooth thumping of Missy Elliott's latest CD. Trae held her hand in his, which rested on his right thigh. Reggie's head reclined in the headrest as she took in the large, sagging thicket along the interstate. When they finally pulled into the long driveway, he glanced over at her and smiled. The smile lines in his face softened his handsomely rugged features. Her heart sang with joy.

Trae pulled up behind a gray truck. Before getting out, he pulled Reggie into him and melted her insides with a soulful kiss before pulling away and going around to open her door. Trae barely got Reggie's door opened before they were stormed by a swarm of siblings and cousins.

"Hey, ugly," Trae's oldest brother quipped. "Hi, beautiful." The eldest Brooks brother turned his award-winning smile on Reggie.

Trae rolled his eyes and at the same time elbowed his brother in the side. "Keep your claws off, old mangy dog," he teased.

Reggie marveled at the sibling rivalry that seemingly always occurred between the brothers. They playfully dogged one another; still, she could tell the love was deep and sincere.

"When you're tired of looking at this alley cat, darling, don't hesitate to give me a call." Travis gracefully pulled her hand to his lips.

He then winked at her; showcasing the gorgeous and seductively handsome Brooks' features prominent in all the Brooks men. Traekin, Michael, and Travis, were all younger versions of their father Alvin Brooks. Looking into Travis' handsome face, all Reggie could manage was a bashful smile. It hadn't taken long before the other relatives pushed him aside.

"Move it! Give the girl some room, will ya?" Shelly shoved her way into the crowd and pulled Reggie's hand from her cousin's claws. "All the ladies are inside," she announced as she prodded her way through the small crowd.

Trae could only watch and wonder when he'd lost control of the situation. His hurt expression hadn't gone undetected by his brothers and his cousins.

"Dang, man!" they sympathized in unison.

Reggie briefly looked back at him and smiled, two of Trae's cousins dragged her towards the house. Throughout the afternoon, it would seem his family kept him and Reggie apart purposely. When he finally managed to be in the same room with her, she would be dragged off to the kitchen or parlor. Every chance he got, Trae spied on her from a distance. On one occasion, when she'd slipped off to go to the bathroom, Trae lurked in the dark doorways down the narrow hallway waiting for her to return.

When she was about to pass him, he reached out and grabbed her, instantly covering her mouth to suppress the guaranteed scream after being pulled into the dark room. Once she realized it was Trae, she wrapped her arms around his neck and met his hungry kiss. Trae held her tightly.

"Hmmm, I've missed you," he whispered hoarsely in her ear.

Reggie smiled. They were in the same house. How could he possibly miss her? She knew what he'd meant. In the two hours since they'd arrived, they had only been close enough to catch a glimpse of one another. She'd longed for his touch. Somehow they hadn't been allowed in the same room for very long. His mother, aunts, and cousins kept the girl-chatter going, which turned out to be a lot of fun. Every now and then, she would drift from the conversation, seeking him out. And as always, she would catch him staring in the same direction as if expectantly answering his silent call.

"You nearly gave me a heart attack a moment ago," she fussed.

"I'm sorry, baby. I just needed to taste you. I was dying there for a minute."

He kissed her again before releasing her and pushing her back down the hallway.

"You better go before someone comes looking for you," he warned.

Reggie smiled devilishly. "You big chicken!"

"I'll show you who's chicken later, my fair lady!"

"Promises. Promises." Reggie sashayed down the hallway, quickly dismissing her seductive sway once she was out into the opening of the hallway. She looked back briefly to see if Trae had been watching her. He had. He only shook his head. He waited a few minutes before he himself emerged up the hall and casually strolled out the side patio door.

The cat and mouse game of him watching her and she watching him continued most of the afternoon. Trae watched Reggie laughing with his sister and cousins. He'd been so engrossed in her beauty that he'd failed to hear Travis and Michael quietly move in behind him.

"You got it bad, man." They shook their heads solemnly.

Without taking his eyes away from Reggie, Trae shook his head acknowledging that he'd long fallen for the slender beauty. "I love her, big brothers." His eyes left his intended long enough to meet each of his brothers eye to eye. "You know, I've never in my life said anything remotely close about any woman I've been involved with. Someway, somehow she's changed me, and I can't explain it. None of it."

"Well, I would say, from a big brother's perspective, that it's for the better." Travis patted his younger sibling on the back. "I like the change I see in you little brother. She's what you need in your life."

Travis and Michael walked away and left their little brother to his musing. Trae had to admit silently that he too liked the change. Being with Reggie was so much easier than dodging women he didn't want to be bothered with. Not that any of them had stopped trying to win his favor. Women still congregated wherever he went, smiling and prancing like prized felines. He didn't worry about offending any of them. His eyes were set on Reggie. He wasn't interested in anyone else. Strangely enough, he'd pledged his loyalty and love to one woman.

Trae spied Reggie closely. She was the most beautiful creature he'd ever encountered. Her skin glowed as the sun kissed her from head to toe. She sat on the grass with both legs folded beneath her in a yoga-type wrap, facing his young cousin, Rain, who sat in a similar position. The bright colored tank complimented her smooth skin. Reggie's almond shaped eyes twinkled delightfully, giving Rain her undivided attention.

The two sat as if they'd been longtime friends. Reggie and Rain's hands were clasped together. Rain chattered as if whatever she was saying was the most enchanting story ever told. The bright aurora surrounding Reggie emitted love and tenderness, no matter the person, time, or place. Slowly, she untangled one of her hands from Rain and moved her long fingers slowly and deliberately upward to tuck a long curly strain that had escaped from the twisted knot held by a decorative clamp. The delicate movement evoked a raw sensation through Trae that he could barely control.

Again, lost in his rapture of watching Reggie, Trae was caught off-guard. His mother strolled up to him and wrapped her arms around his waist.

"Hey, Sweetie," she crooned.

She'd watched him intently watching the breathtaking-young woman several yards away. She instantly recognized the look, which was even more pronounced than the last time they were all together. She sensed a change in her son that could only warm a mother's heart.

Trae looked down at his pint-size mother. She looked ageless and as beautiful as he'd always remembered.

"Hi, Ma'Dere." He closed the loop of the embrace by wrapping his arms around his mother. He kissed her lightly on the brow.

"Are you enjoying yourself?" she asked.

Trae met her hazel eyes and smiled. "As a matter of fact, I am having a great time." He squeezed his arms tightly around her, causing a squeal to erupt from her lips.

"Quit it, boy, before I swat your tail," she attempted a reprimanding glare, knowing full well her licks wouldn't harm a fly.

The fear of having to be reprimanded by the little ball of fire had always been enough to keep him and his siblings in line. Before Trae could form a rebuttal to her futile threat, his father appeared like a giant cat from the foliage of the jungle.

"Unhand my woman, boy, before I kick your butt," he barked. "She's already spoken for. Find your own girl." He pried Trae's arms from around his wife and pointed in Reggie's direction. "In fact, that one over there seems to be available."

Trae's eyes followed his father's finger, knowing full well he was pointing in Reggie's direction. He slowly backed away with both hands up in the air as a sign of surrender.

"You're right, sir." He continued to move away from the two. "Please forgive me. I do like my women a little older than this little young thing here," he teased his mother with a flirting smile.

"Get." His mother swatted at him with an open hand. She smiled brighter than the sun shown in the sky.

Blowing her a kiss before he turned away, Trae made his way over to where Reggie sat.

Reggie watched the exchange between Trae and his parents. She smiled when the elder Brooks wrapped his arms around his wife and kissed her passionately. She wanted that kind of love with Trae. Her smile ceased when her eyes shifted to the moving figure headed in her direction. His presence consumed everything around him. The sun hid behind him just as he neared. Reggie still held one of Rain's hands in her own, but the bubbly pre-teen seemed to vanish from the face of the earth when he finally knelt by them. Trae leaned forward and kissed her on her parted lips.

"Hi, baby," he whispered, his eyes locked with hers.

"Hi," she barely whispered.

Trae drew his attention for a quick moment to his little cousin who sat near and watched their heated exchange. He leaned over and kissed Rain's cheek.

"Hi, Sunshine," he teased.

Rain rolled her eyes skyward, trying extremely hard not to snicker. "It's Rain, cousin Traekin. Not Sunshine."

"You're a beautiful sunshine. I don't care what your name is." He lightly pinched her chin. Rain's smile confirmed Trae's assessment. "Mind if I steal my girl for a minute?"

"Okay," Rain replied, her head bobbing up and down.

Trae pulled Reggie to her feet and led her to a set of abandoned swings beneath a giant oak tree. Reggie slipped into the nearest swing. Trae moved behind her and began pushing her forward.

"Ahhh!" Trae sighed inwardly. "Alone at last." He was relieved to finally have some time alone with her.

The two chatted comfortably until Uncle Ted rang the huge black bell on the back porch signaling that the food was ready to eat. The entire clan congregated near the opened area between the long buffet tables stacked with every mouth-watering Cajun dish imaginable and another long table lined with chairs. The blessings were given and two lines were formed, one along each side of the table.

Laughter and chatter filled the entire yard. Once dinner was finished, many of the older kin scattered to find cool lodging places to lay and rest their overly-stuff bellies. The young folk gathered at the makeshift softball diamond ready for a game of softball. The sun had just begun to descend and provided an orange glow in the background. Trae and Reggie played on opposing teams just to spice things up a bit. It was clear that Trae's team had the better players, however, with the help of Uncle Ted and Alvin Brooks, who were officiating the game, Reggie's team came out on top.

"The umpires are cheating," the losers protested.

"Suck it up and be good losers," Uncle Ted warned. "One more outburst and you're outta here," he yelled.

It was the bottom of the ninth inning, with one man on second base and one out; Trae was up for the bat. When he swung, he hit a base run, which scurried down the field between second and third base. By the time the ball was caught, Trae was on his way to second base, and Reggie, two of his female cousins, and his sister, all jumped him. With his arm snuggled around his sister's waist, Reggie's arms wrapped around his neck, and his cousins yanking on both sides, Trae dragged the four of them with him as he attempt to get safely to second base.

His teammates on the sidelines ran to his aid. By the time he made it to second, his father yelled, "You're OUT!" "OUT!"

"No way!" they all protested.

They all looked outdone. The third base runner and Trae had both been called out. Before long everyone was on the field, yelling and pointing fingers. Uncle Ted slipped off of the field and was now snuggled up with his wife, gloating at the commotion he helped cause. In the middle of the spew, Trae and Reggie locked by arms and lips, as though no one else was around and ignored the noise around them. Everything and everyone around them disappeared.

At dusk, Trae and Reggie gathered their foiled cover platters and headed to his SUV. As the family had done with other departing family members, they all gathered near, hugging and waving goodbye. When Trae pulled away, he took one last glance at his parents. His mother was encased in his father's arm. Alvin's chin rested on the top of her head. She blew him a kiss and smiled.

"I had a blast," Reggie confessed.

"Great. I did too." His eyes shifted to catch the sparkling dimples winking at him.

CHAPTER 20

They were both exhausted by the time they reached the campus. The ride was mostly quiet. A few times the car filled with laughter as they recalled certain events of the day. And even though Trae's body was running on fumes, it hadn't extinguished the furious fire raging from within. His mind was still intent on loving Reggie. When they stopped in her dorm parking lot, Reggie invited him up to her room.

"I don't think so, sweetheart. If I do, I'm going to love you until you can't stand me any more." He remembered the condoms still lying at the foot of his bed. He'd intended to put them in his wallet, but rushed off and forgot them. Making love to Reggie without protection was out of the question.

"I'm not ready to go in just yet," she confessed.

Lust and longing hung between them. Trae, contemplating their dilemma, finally suggested that they go back to his dorm. Reggie readily agreed. She was eager to be in his embrace.

Trae pulled into his dorm parking lot by the side exit. He and Reggie walked silently, hand-in-hand through the corridors. Their passion grew thick and intense with each step. Neither spoke, even after Trae slipped the key into the lock. He hesitated before he entered the common living area to make sure Rykard wasn't running around in his underwear as he often did when he was in their room.

Once it was deemed safe to enter, Trae pulled Reggie into the room, closed the door quietly, and pulled her into his aching body. He throbbed from head to toe with want and need. Hungrily he suckled from her parted lips, feasting on the sweetness of her mouth until a loud audible groan escaped them both. He trailed long heat kisses down the sides of her neck, only stopping at the peak of her tank top. The soft flesh peeking above the top of the bright tank fluttered with goose bumps the instant his tongue caressed them. Reggie's skin reeked of salt from perspiring throughout the day. He could only imagine that his body was as salty as hers.

Reggie yielded, willingly to Trae. A slight tremor raced through her when his heated lips and hands snaked down the contours of her body. She trailed small kisses up his throat and lower jaw. His after-five-shadow prickled her face in sweet agony. Her fingers slipped beneath his T-shirt, grazing the hard outline of his muscular body. Her fingers, soft and warm, shroud his body with a sheer layer of spiky goose bumps from head to toe. Together they exacted the same induced torture on one another.

Trae pulled away from her, almost too quickly. He stared into her upturned face.

"Do you want your shower cap?" he asked. So many of their long escapes either started or ended in the small shower stall he shared with Rykard.

"No," she managed.

"How about the shampo?" He was already moving away from her and heading toward his closet to retrieve two plush towels from the top shelf.

Again she declined. He leaned over, scooped up a foil package from the bed, and jammed it into the pocket of his shorts. With the formalities out of the way, Trae led her through the narrow bathroom door. Once the door jammed into place, he turned the silver level just above the handle that locked them in the small blue-tiled room.

Gracefully, Reggie eased out of the sticky, and soiled clothes. With his back against the door, Trae watched her while she teased him with the provocative movement of her hips as the last thread of clothing slipped down the contours of her long legs. His shaft thickened against the snug briefs. His tongue slid across his lower lip before catching between his teeth. Eyes lurking with passion, he could feel the blood rushing from other parts of his body to fill the throbbing need between his legs.

Reggie's soft flesh burned with anticipation. *How long is he going to keep me waiting?* she agonized. They had played the cat and mouse game all day long. Their little necking episode at his uncle's house only fueled the desire raging between them. Tired of the wait, she made the first move. She sauntered toward him until she could feel the heated air from his nostrils comb her face. She reached for the towels in his hand and allowed them to fall to the floor. Her long fingers then went to the hem of his T-shirt. She dragged it up the contours of his muscular chest, her fingers lightly grazing the firm knots of his upper body.

The heavy rise and fall of his chest matched her heated gaze. With prompting, he raised his arms up to allow her to remove the musty shirt. It, too, fell to the floor, and she moved to her next target, his now snug shorts and briefs. Her warm finger slid between flesh and cotton and slowly eased the fabric down his hairy legs. The buttery touch evoked tremors up his spine. When she'd completely undressed him, she stepped back and appraised the solid centurion standing before her. The throbbing shaft danced up and down in crazed anticipation. She reached for it and his body jumped violently when her fingers closed around the silken-hard beam. He closed his eyes to calm his enraged passion. His hands eased around hers and gently removed them from her intended target.

He closed the gap between them bringing her body into his. He moved his hands down the sides of her body until they were filled with her firm, apple behind. Groaning, he pulled her up until their hips met. Reggie's body went limp. The heat fusing her to him released a raging volcano from the pit of her core. Her body shuddered. Her arms snaked around his neck, and she held on for dear life.

Somehow Trae managed to get close enough to the shower stall to turn the water on. The steam quickly engulfed the room. With his back to the heavy spray, the warm water encased them both, fueling the passion to yet another level. It was hard to hold onto her wet body, yet he managed to keep flesh against flesh. They teased one another with wet hot kisses to erotic parts of their bodies.

When Trae felt he could no longer restrain his release, he yanked the shower knobs downward, and with more force than he'd planned, he scooped Reggie up into arms. He'd totally ignored the towels he brought in with him. He fumbled with the door lock while holding firmly to Reggie's wet body. He didn't look or stop until he was behind the door to his bedroom.

He placed Reggie on top of the comforter and reached over and grabbed another foiled package and impatiently tore it opened. Once in place, he moved Reggie's legs apart and entered with an overly-anxious thrust. Reggie's fingers dug into his flesh. Her body rocked in concert, matching Trae's stroke for stroke. When their worlds collided, neither could hear above the screams of release. It was only moments yet it felt like an eternity before they were able to come down from the explosive rush. Not having had enough of her yet, Trae began his second bout of sweet loving.

By early morning, squeezed together in the small bed, Trae woke Reggie from a groggy sleep. "Come on, sweetheart. I need to get you back to your room."

Reggie's arm, which had been lounged beneath Trae massive body, had fallen sleep. She shook it to get the blood flowing back through her arm.

Trae sat on the side of the bed and helped by rubbing his hand up and down her arm. "Sorry, babe."

She gave him a sleepy smile. "It's too early, Trae."

"No, it's not. Come on, sleepyhead, let's go. I have to be at the fitness center in thirty minutes. Up." He patted her on the behind.

Trae moved from the bed to the closed door heading back to bathroom he knew they'd left in a shambles the night before. When he got there, apparently Rykard hadn't been in there or just chose to leave things as they were. He collected the towels and the discarded clothes and padded back to the bedroom. Reggie sat on the edge of the bed with her knees up to her chest, her arms loosely draped around them. She waited until Trae cleared the path to the bathroom. Her bladder was screaming. He handed her his bathrobe, and she slipped her arms into the oversized garment and followed him to the bathroom. She dressed in a pair of spare shorts and shirt that had been left in Trae's room from previous escapades.

No sooner had Trae and Reggie closed the door behind them, did they run smack into Veronica's surprised glare. Trae's arm hung loosely around Reggie's neck. His head rested in the small of her neck and shoulder. Reggie's giggles ceased the moment her eyes locked with Veronica's now stony scowl. Wondering why Reggie had suddenly stopped, his head came up, and, to his surprise, he met the same stony scowl.

Trae was no longer affected by Veronica's feminine charms. Nothing she did these days lured him from the claws of Reggie's heady grasp. It was like she'd place a voodoo spell on him, a hex, a charm more potent than anything he could control. It was overpowering and hard to dispel, not that he wanted to anyway. So her anger didn't move him the least. In a way, he was somewhat amused. He'd long since asked her not to come by his room without calling first. He had done so specifically for this very reason. There were no issues with them and he never wanted Reggie to feel threatened by her presence.

"Roni. What are you doing up here?" he questioned. His anger reared its ugly head. His eyes narrowed and his lips formed into a thin line. His embrace unconsciously tightened around Reggie's neck. Fuming air seeped through his nostrils. Reggie attempted to ease out of his now painful grip, but he arm remain firm around her neck.

Unable to mask her anger, and now matching Trae's rage, Veronica hissed, "Did you forget, you promised to work out with me this morning. I've waited more than a half-hour for you." Her eyes strayed back to Reggie.

"Roni, we haven't worked out together for over three weeks, and I never told you that I would be at the center this morning, at no time."

"What the hell is wrong with you, Traekin? Ever since you've been hanging out with this little bitch, you've been acting like a complete asshole. Have you forgotten that I'm the one who has always been there for you?"

Hearing the verbal attack on her, Reggie, with angry ease slipped from Trae's grip and moved toward Veronica. Just who in the hell did she think she was? She wasn't about to take crap from Veronica. Before she could get in her face to tell "Ms-Too-Much-Make-up" what she thought, Trae pulled her back and behind him. Veronica hadn't expected Reggie's move and was somewhat taken back by her advance.

"No, Reggie," he pleaded. The stone that masked his face should have forewarned Veronica of the slaughter to come. It took Trae a few seconds to contain himself. He knew this was a trap and he was about to get caught in it if he wasn't careful. He had to play this cool. Feigning indifference, Trae took a sighing breath before speaking. His tone was hard and just above a whisper.

"Look, Roni… I'm going to ignore this little incident for a number of reasons. I know you're upset. If you are angry with me that's one thing, and I won't hold that against you. Understand this, under no circumstances will I allow you to attack Reggie. She's not your problem. I am. Now I'm being clear when I say this Roni, there's nothing but friendship between us. I suggest you move on," he spewed between clenched teeth as he bore down into her face.

Reggie stood on the sidelines as she watched the exchange between Trae and Veronica. She didn't miss the physical flinch when Trae placed emphasis on the words "there's nothing but friendship between us." She couldn't mask the damage his words caused. The hurt clearly masked her face. Reggie suddenly felt sorrow for her. By this time, residents had begun to stir after hearing the commotion in the hallway. Reggie touched the rigid muscles in Trae's arm, hoping to move this confrontation outside before they caused a scene. His right temple jumped and the tense line of his face would melt stone.

Trae saw red for a moment. Reggie's touch pulled him from a fury he'd hope to avoid. This was the first time Veronica had pulled a stunt like this. In past incidents it hadn't mattered much. The women he dealt with at the time meant nothing to him. They most often fled to avoid a knock down, drag-out with Veronica. She had a way of intimidating her rivals. He knew Reggie would never back down to Veronica or anyone else. And he didn't want her involved in a catfight. He had more respect for her than that. Trae knew he had to set things straight here and now.

"Stay away," he said before moving around her, Reggie's hand now locked in a tight grip between his fingers.

They left a fuming Veronica staring at their backs, and Trae didn't give a rat's ass what she thought or what she felt. She'd ruined his mood, but not for long. He knew eventually he and Reggie would have to discuss what happened this morning. For now, he had to get her back to her dorm then go to the center to release his frustration. He planned to hit the weight room first to throw around some iron in hopes that it worked off the steam.

Veronica was so angry she could barely make out Trae and Reggie's retreating figure. Every nerve in her body was energized. The flesh visible just above the skimpy tank top blushed from embarrassment. Her heart thumped loudly in her chest and ears. Humiliation filled every fiber of her soul. Oh hell, both Traekin and Regina would pay, and pay dearly! She would see to it. With that promise in her heart, she left Trae's dorm as quickly as she'd come.

CHAPTER 21

Valerie's wide-eyed look matched her concern for her friend when Reggie told her about the incident with Veronica.

"Reggie, you need to watch your back, girl. Veronica is a snake hidden behind all of that Fashion Fair makeup."

Reggie fanned off Val's warning. "I'm not about to be bullied by Veronica. I'm not looking for trouble, but I'm not about to run and hide."

The following Sunday, Trae and Reggie spent the day in his hometown, the Crescent City. In the weeks that followed, she continued to prepare for the dance recital. On the day of the performance, the event's turnout had been overwhelmingly positive. The girls did extremely well. Reggie beamed with pride as she and Trae watched their performance.

Reggie went home for Thanksgiving, and then met Trae in New Orleans for the Bayou Classic. Diane Brooks played hostess for the group. She was an excellent host, providing eats and waiting on them hand and foot. However, she didn't allow any hanky-panky under her roof. The guys all slept downstairs and all the girls slept upstairs just past her bedroom suite. The festivities from the Battle of the Bands parade, where scores of people came to watch the two university bands and some of the local high schools, strut their stuff, to the late-night partying at various clubs around the city, the college crew enjoyed themselves to the fullest.

Trae had to be at the Superdome early on game day. Reggie was again featured during the half-time show, but she felt a certain uneasiness when she arrived at the dome. The nagging feeling loomed over

Reggie the moment she stepped through the assigned dressing room. The hairs on the back of her neck stood at attention. Not able to shake the feeling, her eyes roamed the dressing room. Band members, flags, and dancers were all busy readying themselves for the game. Small groups gathered. They chatted about the previous night's excitement and what post-game festivities they planned to attend.

Reggie's eyes continued across the room and froze the moment they rested on a hatred-filled face. Veronica's brute expression ran cold through Reggie's veins. It appeared she was wearing two coats more than usual of make up on her face. Her eyes were void of human feelings. A sneer lurked just beneath the thickly coated red lips. The sinister appearance reminded her of Valerie's previous warning. Inhaling deeply, Reggie eyed Veronica for a short while longer, ensuring she knew she wasn't moved by her obvious threat.

Finally shaking what hold Veronica had on her, Reggie unzipped the garment bag and began to extract her costume. Just as she pulled the boots from the bottom of the bag, something wet and cold slithered up her arm. Reggie quickly pulled her arm back. A piercing scream sliced through the entire room. The noisy chatter ceased. Every eye in the dressing room now focused on her. She continued to shake her arm, and at the same time feverishly slap at it with her other hand. The long multicolor reptile wormed past her feet and was making it's way toward booted-feet now scrambling to move out of its path. More screams erupted. Many of the girls climbed into chairs to avoid contact with the creature that was obviously as scared as they were. He slid faster across the floor until some brave soul picked it up by the neck with one hand.

"I've got it!" she exclaimed. "It's just a snake!"

Reggie was deathly afraid of snakes, and the mere thought that one was in her personal belonging sent her nerves into overdrive. Physically shaken, tears streamed down her face. Questions of how the snake got into her bag, and when, plagued her thoughts. She attempted to mentally recall where and if she had left her bags unattended. Who would want to play such a cruel joke? It was obvious whoever planted the snake in her bag knew her fear of reptiles.

The excitement was soon contained, yet Reggie's physical and mental state was still shaken. It took a couple of the girls, including Jerica to calm her down. With only ten minutes before they were to report to the stadium, Reggie had the task of pulling herself together before the start of the game. She would have the painstaking task of reapplying her makeup. She'd worked hard to perfect the details of her show-face. Many of the girls came to support her. Most, except Veronica and a few of her cronies.

When she looked around the dressing room again, Veronica was nowhere to be found. Suspicions filled her being. She somehow got the feeling that Veronica was behind the snake fiasco. She would have a tough time proving it, but she was almost certain Veronica's name was written all over this. The coaches hadn't thought the trick was at all funny. They reported the incident to the band director.

Upon Veronica's sudden disappearance, Reggie became angry. She wasn't about to allow her to ruin this day for her. With only a few minutes to squeeze into her costume after reapplying her makeup, Reggie picked up her gloves and cape and followed the others to the staging area. Once they were settled into the stand, she looked over to the area where Val and her other friends were seated. Val knew instantly that something had happened. Normally she would have been in the dressing room to help Reggie dress and to lend her moral support, but today only band members were allowed passed the staging area.

Reggie didn't want to alarm her friend, so silently mouthed that all was okay, even though it wasn't. She would get through this. Veronica had made certain she was on the far end of the line up, away from Reggie's prying eyes. Taking several deep breaths, she looked to her friend once again and smiled. The corners of her mouth never really reached the fullness of her smile. It was the best she could do. Val nodded her support and returned a smile. Reggie knew she could always count on her friend to get her through the rockiest of storms.

Her mind and eyes wandered back down in the direction where Veronica now sat. Two, could play her game, if she really insisted on it, she fumed. Reggie didn't want a catfight with Veronica. She would have to carefully plan how to give Veronica a taste of her own medicine. A smile, a real smile graced her face at the possibilities as they clicked through her mind. She visibly relaxed and got into the spirit of the football game. Three minutes into the second quarter, they descended from the stands in preparations for the half time show. The Tigers were up by six points. Grambling students and fans were in high spirits.

Once the teams departed the field, the Grambling Marching Tigers were on the sidelines. They were to perform first. Nothing moved and only the sounds of the announcer's voice blared through the high ceilings of the Superdome.

"Ladies and Gentleman, welcome to the Bayou Classic's, Battle of the Bands. For all eyes to see, the funkiest, the magnificent, the electrifying, and foot stomping, MAR…CH… ING… TI…GERS!!!!!

A funky drum roll belted out as the two drum majors strolled to the center of the field and took their normal back rolling bow. Before long, the thunderous entrance of the Marching Tiger erupted on to the field. The routine choreographed specifically for this show, every band member, flag, and dancer, popped and locked the shake to Jennifer Lopez and Ja Rule's "I'm Real." When the music changed, the formation changed into the traditional 'GSU' and then the initial's "BC" for Bayou Classics.

Upon the third transition, Reggie anxiously awaited her cue. The classic 'Miles lecture' infiltrated her thoughts, "You can do anything you set your mind to, Regina Miles. Physical boundaries are only stepping stones." Assured and confident, she pasted her smile in place and waited. The announcers boomed, "Ladies and Gentleman, presenting the Dancing Orchesis, featuring Ms. Reggie Miles, under the directions of Merriam Murray!"

First, Veronica and her crew took center stage, rocking to "Money Ain't a Thang." Hips swayed and pumped from side to side. Reggie's feet crossed the sidelines and took center on the fifty-yard line in front. Arms above her head, she moved her shoulders and hips, then swirled her body to the funky brass of the horn section. Effortlessly, she entered several no-hand flips and more funky rolling of the hips and rump. By the time the song ended, she was slightly winded, and her chest heaved, but her smile remained in place until she exited the field. The band transitioned again, this time blasting the school's fight song, flanking into a march routine before exiting the field.

Word traveled fast. Reggie's incident in the dressing room had reached some of the students and, eventually, the locker room during half-time break. Trae was livid when he heard and was ready to bolt from the locker room to check on her. Only reassurance from the coach and the proper restraint from his teammates kept him steady. His concentration no longer on the second half of the game, he paced the long side of the locker room along the row of metal lockers. The coach's instructions were lost on him.

When they entered the field, Trae glanced directly toward the stands where the band had reassembled. Without breaking a step, his eyes roamed the rows until they settled on her slender frame. She was standing and cheering as the team entered the field. She appeared fine, but he couldn't be sure because he was unable to make eye contact. She was too far away to make out the details of her face. He had to accept for now that everything was okay.

Reggie watched Trae look up into the stands. She knew he was searching for her. She could only hope he saw her. A dimple smile lit her face as she watched him reach and eventually turn to the huddle of ball players. She knew that he would be ten times madder than Val had been after learning about the incident. Val was ready to gang up on Veronica and whip her tail, Reggie assured her that she had another plan.

During the break, she'd noticed something odd. Veronica and Justin were in deep conversation. What could the two of them have to talk about? Justin was a knockout as far as looks were concerned, but definitely not Veronica's type. She went for the stud or macho type. If she and Justin were an item, it definitely had to be because she was using him. Shaking loose of the thought, Reggie quickly banished the idea that Justin would be lured into Veronica's claws. Knowing Veronica, anything was possible. The distinctively good looks won Justin a lot of attention. His looks paled in comparison to the infamous Traekin Brooks. He avoided eye contact with her when he passed her and Candice. Candice touched her arm when her eyes followed his lean frame as he ignored them both.

"Wasn't that Justin," Candice probed.

Eyes still glued to his back, she eventually turned her attention to her friend. "Yeah. I don't know what's up with him."

They both hunched their shoulders and returned to stand with drinks they'd just purchased.

Justin made up his mind to stay clear of Veronica after today. When he found out she used the snake he helped her catch to get back at Reggie, he was enraged. Veronica knew he was crazy about Reggie and he readily agreed to help her win back Trae.

Although he knew she walked the streets to supplement her income, she threatened to tell Reggie it was he who put the snake in her bag. After all, he knew she was afraid of snakes. Veronica convinced him that Reggie would never forgive him for his role in her scheme. No matter what the situation was, Justin would never deliberately hurt Reggie. He couldn't even look her in the face knowing he had something to do with what happened today. He walked straight out of the dorm and hailed the first cab he saw.

As she watched the team move out to the field for the start of the third quarter, Reggie's thoughts slipped, musing about how it felt to be in Trae's embrace. She watched as he kneeled into position for the play, the steel muscles in his leg flexed to support his domed position, most of his weight supported partially on the hand touching the artificial grass on the field. Within seconds, the ball snapped and his body went forward and was instantly lost in the sea of bodies piled on top of one another with the brown and white ball just beneath the poor soul pinned on the bottom of the stack of helmets and shoulder pads.

Tonight was their last night in the city. She hadn't sampled his loving for more than a week. They spent the day before Thanksgiving together before both departed to go home. His touch was slow and deliberate. He caressed every inch of her body as though it was to last a lifetime, or in their case, until after the holidays ended. When they finally found the strength to let go, he promised to make up for the lost time. She would have an agonizing three and a half hours drive back to Ruston. Would his promises start the moment they left the Crescent City? Would they last the trip or would they wait until they got back to campus to make love?

Whenever it would be, the thought of loving him caused her insides to warm. Small flesh bumps crawled up her skin. Sweet anticipation lurked from the core of her being. Only the cheering crowd broke her from her reverie. Fans were on their feet, jumping and shouting. Reggie eyes went to the figure racing down the field with the ball tucked under his arms. Trae carried the ball for sixty-seven yards for the first touchdown of the quarter. When it finally registered that it was he who carried the ball, she bolted to her feet and cheered him on.

By the end of the game, the band did a repeat performance of the halftime show, as it was customary to do. After the final show and after everyone had gathered in the dressing room to retrieve their belongings, Reggie decided she would confront Veronica there, in front of everyone. Veronica was busily shoving her belongings into a train case and didn't hear or see Reggie's approach. Apparently everyone else did because their eyes followed her until she stood toe-to-toe with Veronica. Her voice was just above a whisper so that what she said was heard by Veronica's ears only.

Caught off guard, all Veronica could do was stare and gasp when Reggie took several steps back before turning and walking away. Veronica's face paled with shock. All eyes watched in wonder about what had just transpired. When a few of her cronies came to her side, she took her frustrations out on them. She flung the half-full train case against the wall. Reggie quietly picked up her bag and headed for the door. The threat to reveal a secret that Veronica thought only she and Justin knew before today would certainly keep her away from Reggie and from Trae. Reggie was so confident that she was correct that she didn't bother to look back at Veronica for a response.

Trae anxiously waited for Reggie, and when she finally emerged from the dressing room with her things in hand, his heart sang with relief. He could see the storm in her face. He wasn't sure if something else had occurred since the earlier incident. He knew she was deadly afraid of snakes. He recalled an evening in the park when a little gardener slid up next to where they were stretched out on a blanket. It had taken him almost an hour to calm her down.

Her eyes met his the moment she cleared the door. Standing with him was the rest of the gang, and Val was encased in Rykard's embrace. The serious faces foretold what kind of greeting she would get. Still pissed at Veronica, she tried to push her feeling to the back of her mind. The fact that they were all waiting for her and ready to embrace her made her feel much better.

When she was within arms reach, Trae retrieved her bag and pulled her into his embrace. The hug was so snug she thought he would squeeze all the life from her. Their friends stood back and watched the encounter. Trae loosened his hold enough to lower his mouth until he captured her lips. Once he got his fill, he looked down into her upturned face.

"Are you okay?" he asked.

Just being in his arms and feeling the love and security within them, Reggie's voice betrayed her. She couldn't get a word pass the knot in her throat. She shook her head in reply.

He searched her face for any trace of doubt. He smiled and pecked on her lips once more. "Let's get out of here. We have a party to go to." His dark eyes gleamed like sunshine.

Reggie didn't really want to go to a party. She was still consumed with thoughts of being in his arms, in his bed. Desire ached beneath the dimpled smile. Not wanting to be a party-pooper, she perked up and said, "Then let's go!"

Trae hadn't missed the passion in her eyes. He wanted more than anything to take her someplace and love her until she cried his name. The timing somehow didn't seem right. He thought back to the snake. He had every intention of finding out the truth behind the snake in her bag. Somebody was going to talk, and when he found out who it was, they would have hell to pay. For now, all he wanted was to see the dimples peeking from each side of her cheeks and to keep her thoughts off of what happened today. Everyone took turns hugging and reassuring her that they were there for her no matter what.

Travis and some of his buddies boiled crawfish and crabs at their parent's house. Every so often, they dumped buckets of steamy hot shellfish loaded with potatoes and corn on the cob onto the lined wooden tables under the covered gazebo. Music blared from the stereo. Good food, music, and company kept the growing crowd happy. By nightfall, they moved the party inside to the walkout basement. Trae was never more than a few inches away from Reggie. When most of the guest left, the two hung back and cuddled together on the sectional sofa.

Reggie fell asleep first. To not disturb her, Trae remained still and he, too, fell asleep. No one bother either of them. When Diane came through to assess the damage the kids had left behind, she found the couple sound asleep. She pulled a blanket from the hall closet and draped it over them. Neither moved an inch. She then proceeded to pick up remnants of leftovers the kids had forgotten to put away. She took one last look at Trae and Reggie, climbed the two flights of stairs, and retreated to her bedroom suite.

Trae could feel Reggie stir in his embrace. He closed his arms around her, pulling her closer to his body. Not fully awake, he had to think of where they were. He'd remembered her falling asleep in his arms in their family's downstairs basement. With her soft body pressed against his manhood, and in the mist of a fog between being awake and asleep, he reprimanded his body into control. He ached for her, yet he had managed to keep things in check. Taking Reggie here would compromise her and anger his mother in the same instant.

He looked through half-closed lids at the light illuminating on the face of his digital watch. It was 5:30 a.m. In a few hours they would be on the road headed north back to Ruston. In the meantime, he would enjoy the feel of her soft warm body. He savored how her rump tucked into his groin. The slow, even rise and fall of her chest indicated that she was resting easily. He nuzzled his face into her thick brown mane. The scent of her favorite cologne lingered on the soft flesh just below her hairline.

His hand moved down the length of her hips and then traveled in front, up the lines of her flat stomach. They didn't rest until he cupped one of her ripe breasts. A low groan escaped from his throat. He could feel his manhood's refusal to cooperate with his intent to remain unmoved. Reggie's body automatically yielded to Trae's busy hands. Her hips rolled in response to the throbbing against her backside. She could feel his warm breath at her nape and the points of her breasts peaked in the palm of his hand.

She turned into his embrace. She too had forgotten where they were. It hadn't mattered. She was in Trae's arms. She met his lips with eagerness. He growled as he greedily took what she offered. It didn't take long to escalate their need for release. Desire was laced in the moans escaping their lips. Trying to get beyond their clothes is what slowed the pace long enough to snap Trae back to the reality. Swollen and beyond himself, he pulled Reggie away, kissing her on her closed lids.

"We can't, baby," he managed in a tight whisper. "Damn," he spat. He stood quickly leaving Reggie trapped in the folds of the blanket that at one time covered them both. He willed his body to still, but it wouldn't listen. Instead it throbbed with unchecked need.

Reggie looked up through the darkness. She could hear his heavy breathing. At first she thought he might be angry with her, but she knew better. She groped into the darkness until she touched his arm. "Trae."

"Just a minute, baby. Give me a minute, okay," he begged. He held her hand tightly. Not until he met her had he ever had to exercise such control. He never suffered the torture of an unsatisfied erection. He got his release when he needed it, no matter the time or place. Reggie stood, now that she knew where he was. She attempted to adjust her eyes to the darkness. Only the green indicator on the stereo beamed any light.

"I can take care of that, sweetie," she crooned. "Let me take care you, Trae."

Somewhat back in control, he turned in her direction. He cupped the bottom of her chin. He traced tiny kisses along her jawline. "I'm okay," he whispered. "Come here." He held her close to him for a few minutes. "Go back to sleep. We'll need to be up in a few hours. I want to get on the road early."

"Where are you going?" she asked.

"Upstairs. I'll take a quick shower and then pick up some of the stuff we left out back last night," he told her.

"I'll help."

"No."

"Yes," she countered. "I'm coming up whether you want me to or not."

There was silence at first. Trae finally agreed. "Okay, but you're going to be tired. I'm not letting you sleep on the way back to Ruston," he teased.

"Okay. Deal." She stuck her hand to seal the deal.

"Stay put," he ordered. "Let me turn on the lights before you break your beautiful little neck."

Trae and Reggie worked well together. They were able to clear the Gazebo in almost no time with the two of them working side by side. The sun had just begun to peek into the sky when they walked across the damp lawn. The morning air was chilly but not bad for November. The cool air and the cold shower helped extinguish some of the fire that hung between them earlier. When they were done outside, they moved to the kitchen and began breakfast. Before long the house wafted the distinctive odor of freshly brewed chicory coffee, bacon, sausage, eggs, and biscuits. Reggie was pleasantly surprise by Trae's culinary skills. She seemed to learn something about him daily.

"My momma made certain we all knew how to cook. Look at us. Does it look like we lack for food?" Trae teased.

Slowly, one by one, the Brooks and their houseguests moseyed into the large breakfast room. The room was filled with laughter and jovial conversation. By the time everyone loaded up their cars for the return trip back to campus, Diane had packed lunches for each group of drivers. They all exchanged hugs and good-byes. Trae and Reggie led the way.

Four hours after leaving his house, Trae pulled up to Reggie's dorm. Rykard and Candace's car pulled in behind his. Worn out beyond description, he hugged Reggie snuggly and kissed her firmly.

"I'm whipped, baby. I'll come by later, okay?" His tired eyes looked down into hers.

"Okay." She leaned up and kissed his chin.

Trae showed up at Reggie's door with a pizza box and two bottles of lemonade. A smile a mile wide graced his handsome face.

"Hey, pretty little lady. Wanna share some bread with an ole ugly dog?" He winked at her.

"Hmmm. I'm not sure I'm suppose to talk to strangers."

"Well, I'm no stranger, Miss. Just ask any of your neighbors."

Reggie threw a punch that landed in the center of his chest. "My neighbors better not know you as nothing other than a stranger."

Trae fell back several steps as if her little blow to his chest had struck him hard. He coughed profusely. Faking injury. He bent forward, continuing to pretend he was harmed. He held tightly to the pizza box and plastic bottles, but continued to cough.

Reggie couldn't imagine that her pint-sized blow did anything to injure Trae, still his actions seemed real. Concerned she moved toward him. "Trae, are you okay?" she asked.

When her hand landed on his shoulders, Trae quickly straightened and threw the arm with the two cold drinks in them around her waist. He pulled her into him tightly. His mouth covered hers, and he suckled her until her surprised fight melted into surrender.

"You're a bad boy, Traekin Brooks," she whispered.

"I can show just how bad I can be, little miss. We can do it here if you like." He looked up and down the hall for a quick second. "I'm sure we would attract a lot of attention if we did it out here, don't you think?"

Reggie eased out of his embrace, took the two drinks, and pulled him into her room before closing the door.

"I don't want to shock these poor girls. They don't realize what an animal you really are."

"Oh! And I guess they don't know what a little freak you are, right?"

Reggie feigned innocence. "I have no idea what you're talking about."

Placing the pizza and the drinks from her hands on her desk, he picked her up and laid her across the bed. Food was forgotten. He fed his need to fill her body first.

CHAPTER 22

Word got around campus that Trae had been looking for the snake bandit. Nothing materialized, not even Veronica. She stayed clear of Reggie and Trae. She couldn't afford to have her secret leaked. *How in the hell did Reggie find out?* she wondered. She'd been careful in harboring her secret. Only a few people for certain knew about her extra curricular activities. Justin. She approached him first. "What the hell did you tell Reggie about me?" she demanded. "You've been sniffing around her for the past several weeks."

"What is it to you? I don't answer to you," he fumed. His eyes bore through her like hot daggers. "Even if I did, ain't a damn thing you can do about it." His imposing stance caused her to retreat.

She knew Justin wouldn't sell her out. Besides, he was the one who provided the reptile for the Bayou Classic incident. Trae would break him into a million pieces if he found out. Who? She continued to ponder. If anyone found out about her, not only would she be kicked off the Dance Team, but could be kicked out of school and possibly serve time in jail. Veronica celebrated the fact that she only had one more semester left to graduate. Once that happened, she planned to leave Ruston forever.

How she managed to keep her secret all this time was a wonder. It was no real secret, though, that she was provocative in more ways than defined in the dictionary. She used her body to get what she wanted, when she wanted it, and where she wanted it. There was no shame. Hell, she was good at what she did.

Her parents hadn't cared, as long as she kept money coming to help feed their nasty habit. Her mother first introduced her to the trade of selling her body for money when she was a young girl. Flat broke, she needed a fix and her precious little daughter was the only valuable thing she had at the time. Looking to her mother for an explanation as to why and how she could do something so horrible to a child. Her mother berated her, "Just be glad that's all you've got to do." She spat in idle disgust, "You're getting off easy." Veronica cried for three days afterwards.

Now, none of the horrible, childhood experiences mattered to her. Over time she learned to use the situation to her advantage. In the end, she always had money in her pocket. Veronica was determined to not follow in her parents' footsteps. She had dreamed of one day making it big. She was hell bent on not becoming a drugged out whore. She looked at what she did as temporary, at least for now. If anything, it would lead her to a life of luxury and she wouldn't have to do it any-more.

Fortunately for her, she had book-sense and took it upon herself to get an education. It could only help, she'd rationalized. Almost four years later, she was closer to completing what she'd started. There were times when she didn't think she would. It had gotten harder to turn her tricks and maintain the double life as a popular campus beauty. Veronica had become innovative with her habit, leaving far enough away from the campus to not be recognized. She opted for group jobs so she didn't have to be out for any extended period. One time, one of her regulars, Mitchell, brought six of his buddies she had to take care of in one night. She didn't care. Out of habit, she numbed to it all. It never mattered.

The only man she ever cared about, the one man who ever meant anything to her was Traekin. And now, like all the rest of them, he'd tossed her aside like a used rag. She'd been used before, so why did it hurt now? Even when they were together, he was with other women, but it hadn't mattered. He always came back to her. She knew they meant nothing to him.

She often traveled to Ouachita Parish to make her deals. She even took the precaution of not driving her own car. Justin had been more than willing to let her use his. She gave him what he wanted, even a portion of her bounty. Veronica practically bolted in terror the one Saturday she thought she saw Trae's SUV go by.

Apparently she'd been mistaken because he never said anything to her about it. Deep down inside she knew his car couldn't be mistaken for any other. It was the only one in the state. It had been custom designed for him. He never loaned his vehicle to any one. At least not that she knew of. She knew he would have approached her had he seen her on the streets. After Reggie's little revelation, she knew why. Trae hadn't seen her because he'd been distracted by Reggie. Reggie had seen Veronica and now she used it against her.

It had gotten harder and harder to hide her desperation. She felt she was losing Trae fast. The hectic practice and school schedule and her evenings on the street had become harder to manage. With her world spinning out of control, she'd found herself slipping, especially on this particular Saturday afternoon she worked the streets. She wasn't supposed to be out there during the day, but at the last minute decided she wanted to spend some time with Trae that evening. In order to do that and keep her purse full, she had to go out that day. Unbeknownst to her at the time, Trae was in Monroe when she went looking for him on Saturday evening.

She'd inwardly reprimanded herself for such sloppy work and now it was costing her. She fumed, unable to hide her desperation. She didn't know what she was going to do. When she remembered Reggie's threat, "I saw you walking the streets of Monroe," she was shocked beyond words, but deep inside she was livid. She could have easily denied her claim; however, she didn't want to take that chance. What if Reggie had challenged her? Even to deny her claim would place doubt and cause suspicions. She couldn't afford to have that happen. So now what?

The pleasure of seeing Reggie miserable when she found the snake in her bag had been rewarding, but short-lived. It had been simpler than she expected to have the snake dropped into her bag. Pure elation flooded her soul when she saw the horror painted on Reggie's little smug face. Veronica, in a small way, regretted her actions only because it pushed Reggie to the end. Now Reggie called her bluff and with the threat to expose her, she wouldn't be able to carry out her other plans to punish Reggie for Trae's betrayal. It didn't matter anymore. She didn't need him. Sooner or later he would grow tired of her bony ass. He would be back. *Patience*, she consoled.

Veronica lounged across her bed in a skimpy, lace teddy. She slid the red nail polish across the hard acrylic nails until they were fully coated. She raised them above her head to inspect them. Finding them perfect, she blew warm air from her puckered lips to speed up the drying process. When she heard the knock on the door, she didn't bother to cover up. She sashayed to the door and released the lock. Justin caught a glimpse of Veronica's firm ripe behind. He ripened beneath the already snug jeans. His promise to stay away from her was long forgotten.

During the finals week, torrential rains fell nonstop for three days. Valerie left the building to get her car while Reggie stood at the lobby door. There was no sense in them both getting drenched. The effort proved hopeless. When Valerie pulled the car up to the entrance, Reggie dashed to the passenger door. Her lightweight coat was soaked by the time she made it inside the car. Umbrellas didn't stand a chance in this storm. The winds were high and forceful. Valerie could barely see the road in front of her as she inched farther off the campus.

"Maybe we should pull over," Reggie suggested.

Valerie leaned into the steering wheel in hopes that the effort would help her see the road clearer, but to no avail. Her concentration was totally on the task at hand. Reggie's coaching did little except irritate her. She gripped the steering wheel so tightly that her knuckles paled. She turned toward Reggie to ask her what she'd said. Valerie unknowingly crossed the medium in the process. The last thing she heard was Reggie's piercing scream. It was too late. The high-beamed headlights were the last things either of them saw.

Reggie fell off into a darkness that felt strangely familiar, almost like diving into the gym's indoor pool. Unlike the pool when you dove in, you eventually hit the bottom. She didn't reach a bottom nor could she stop the fall. She groped out in front and to the sides of her body, but continued to tumble downward at an alarming rate. Because she could not stop or touch anything, she panicked. Another piercing scream left her lungs; no one heard it except her. Her heart raced and she suddenly couldn't breath. A burst of energy bolted through her.

And then she let go. She didn't feel anything; not the twisted bones in her chest or the opened gash on her head. Her body didn't feel the bloody and sticky clothes on her flesh, or the heavy spray washing it away. Trae. She saw Trae's crooked smile gazing at her. She called him. But he didn't answer. The more she called him, the farther away his face moved from her line of vision. She was tired.

"Maybe if I rest a minute, I'll be okay," she rationalized. Her darkness then turned into nothing.

Sirens blared from both directions. The rain let up slightly as the crew worked desperately to free the passengers of the car. The car had been hit so hard that the driver's side had been crushed almost completely into a ball. The shrilling roar of the battery powered saw moved meticulously slow to make certain the blades didn't accidentally penetrate the driver's body. When firemen were finally able to remove enough rubbish to extract the body, the fireman checked for a pulse or any other sign of life. When there wasn't any, he helped the paramedic place the driver's body into a black bag. The sound of the zipper rolling over her remains could be heard several feet away.

The remaining crewmembers were still working on the passenger side when the fireman returned his attention back to the car. The little, four-door sedan had been dragged several yards from the impact. The passenger was slowly extracted from beneath the inflated air bag. She, too, was placed on a stretcher as the paramedics checked for injuries and for any sign of life. The pulse, slow and faint, was nonetheless a sure sign that she had survived this tragic accident. He couldn't be sure she would make it. Her upper body showed signs of extensive damage. The gash on her head was bad, but not life threatening.

A chopper had already been called to the scene. Traffic had been halted in both directions. When the gurney rolled up to the door, two medics met them and quickly pushed it into place, locking it down before signaling a thumbs up to the pilot. They disappeared within minutes.

The crash hadn't been far from the campus, so word that a tragic accident had occurred close to the university spread like wildfire. Several small fender-benders had occurred over the last several days. The blaring of sirens got the attention of many students and faculty. Many ventured by foot once their vehicles were not able to go out any farther. Someone recognized Valerie's car. This news sent Rykard in a world-spin. He, Trae, and a couple of other teammates stood outside the men's gym. Both Trae and Rykard broke into a sprint at the same time. Val and Reggie were together. After running an errand, they were to meet them at Favort.

Fear sliced through them like a spear. Neither was in any condition to drive. A teammate pulled up next to them and they jumped in. No one said a word. Trae's heart raced. His hands shook when he attempted to clasp the seatbelt closed.

By the time they got close enough to the scene they were detained by law enforcement officers. They explained who they were and that they knew the passengers in the car. Needing personal information to notify next of kin, one of the officers escorted them to another officer who had begun compiling a report.

When Trae caught a glimpse of the mutilated car he ran toward it screaming Reggie's name. Rykard was in total shock when he saw the car and was unable to move or say a word. The driver's side of the car was gone. Whoever was driving, he knew without a doubt, hadn't survived the crashed. God, he hated himself for thinking so, but he'd prayed it wasn't Valerie. Tears welled up and rolled down his cheek without a sound from his lips. Trae was beside himself. It took every man standing to keep him from the car. It took awhile before any information could be exchanged.

The rescue crew retrieved a purse with Valerie's license and student ID card in it. No identification was found for the passenger. They figured it was on her, perhaps in clothing pockets. When Rykard and Trae were told the fate of their beloved, they clung to one another for support. Tears and screams of agony hung in the air leaving not a dry eye in the crowd. No words could describe the pain echoing from their very souls. Reggie had been airlifted to Dallas Regional Hospital. Trae knew he had to go, yet he was torn between finding the woman who meant everything in the world to him and consoling his best friend who had lost the woman he loved.

Butterflies fluttered in Trae's stomach as he impatiently waited for the seatbelt sign to extinguish. His brother Travis had already boarded the first plane leaving New Orleans and would beat him there. He had driven to Shreveport to catch the first flight to Dallas. He could barely contain himself the moment he stepped off of the plane and saw his brother waiting for him.

Reggie was still lost in a fog she was unable to break. She moaned. Something hurt and hurt really badly. She couldn't tell what or where.

She attempted to move, but couldn't. She heard beeping noises. It was so loud it made her head hurt. She tried without success to open her eyes. They were glued shut. She attempted to raise her hand to discover what covered them. She couldn't because they felt like lead. Her brows creased into a scornful frown. *What's wrong with me,* she whined inwardly. The exertion soon became too much, so she gave up and fell back into blackness again.

After three hours in the operating room, the nurses rolled Reggie's bed into the Intensive Care Unit. Hearing the young woman's moans signaled that the anesthesia was wearing off. One nurse added a small vial to the top of the IV connected to her left arm. She tapped it a few times until the liquid that would help ease the pain began to seep into tube.

Trae paced the waiting area for what seemed like a lifetime. He refused every offer of food or drink. Because he wasn't a family member, he wasn't allowed to see her or be given any information about Reggie's condition. Her parents had been contacted, but hadn't yet arrived. They couldn't make the earlier flight. When they finally reached the hospital, Trae rushed to greet them.

"They won't tell me anything about her condition," he explained.

"What happened, Traekin?" Cheri Miles pleaded.

"I'm not sure. She and Val were out running an errand. The police say Val's car crossed the median."

He attempted to provide them with as much information as he could. What little he had to offer didn't console her grieving parents. They were thankful however that her life had been spared. Still no one had been sure that she would pull through it. They waited another hour or so before the attending doctor came out and asked to speak to family members.

Reggie's parents followed the man who looked too young to be an emergency doctor down the hallway. The three moved until they stood close to the reception desk. Trae watched them huddled together as the doctor relayed the extent of Reggie's condition. He could see a visible sigh of relief wash over her mother's face. That only meant one thing—that she was going to be okay. He released a breath he hadn't known he held until he saw them hug one another. Mr. Miles placed a tender kiss on his wife's forehead.

The doctor would only allow the Miles to see Reggie, at first. When the Miles finally allowed him into her room, Trae didn't recognize the small, fully bandaged body as the woman he loved more than life. He broke. The fact that she still held on to life was the only hope that kept him from wanting to curl up and die.

Two days had passed and Trae barely ate or slept. Travis worried, telling him he would be no good to Reggie if he got sick. He didn't need or want food nor sleep. Trae spent the majority of his time in the small chapel, praying profusely that Reggie would recover. By the end of the fourth day, her mother reported that Reggie was awake. Tears of relief ran down his face.

"Can I see her?" he begged.

Cheri touched his arm lightly and shook her head.

"She doesn't want to see you, Trae."

The words hadn't totally registered, causing Trae to asked her to repeat what she'd just said.

"She doesn't want to see you right now, Trae. I'm sorry, sweetie. Maybe she'll feel up to it in a couple of days." Her hand still rested on Trae's arm. He jerked it back as though she'd slapped him with a brick.

"Why? Why not?" he stammered.

"I don't know, but she's awfully upset right now. We had to tell her about Valerie."

Trae's legs gave out, and his brother was there to catch him. Travis attempted to console his younger brother. A sense of hopelessness and abandonment washed over Trae. He had to see Reggie. He had to tell her he almost died when he thought that he had lost her. He had to tell her how much he loved her and that nothing else in the world mattered… to tell her he'd prayed and made promises to God if he spared her life.

"Give her some time," Travis soothed. "She's been through a lot, Trae."

As the days passed, Reggie still refused to see him. He'd already missed taking his finals. He'd been excused and would have to make them up when he returned at the beginning of the spring semester. His mother begged him to come home.

"There's nothing you can do for her right now, son," she appealed.

Finally, he gave in and returned to New Orleans. He called the hospital every day. Her mother would speak to him and provide him a report of her progress. He accompanied Rykard to the memorial services for Valerie. Her death had left him a broken man. The bags beneath his bloodshot eyes foretold his misery. He hardly slept. He woke up in the middle of the night screaming for Valerie, a nightmare he knew would continue for a while. He spent some time with her parents who shared pictures of her when she was a little girl. She was a beautiful child. He didn't think he had a tear left, but found himself wiping away the salted tears that streamed down his face like a raging river. He knew she would be a part of his life forever.

On Christmas Eve, Trae sent several dozen red roses to Reggie's room. He knew they were her favorite. Still, she wouldn't take his call. Trae spent New Year's Eve locked behind his bedroom door. He was sporting a week's worth of hair on his chin. His face was drawn from a lack of food and sleep. Earlier in the day, he stepped into the shower long enough to wipe away some of his gloom. The hot spray had refused to refresh his heart with hope of seeing his love before the year ended. Reggie's refusal to see or talk to him drained the desire for anything. His family attempted to get him away from the house, but he wouldn't budge.

By the first week in January, still not able to talk to Reggie, and against his parents' wishes, Trae took the first flight back to Dallas. When he reached the front desk and asked about visitation, he was told that Reggie had been transferred. The deflated look in his eyes tugged at the nurse's heart, but under no circumstance was she allowed to release information to anyone outside of the immediate family about her condition or where she was. Crushed, Trae checked into a hotel and for the first time in his life drank until he passed out across the king-size bed.

Unable to comprehend why she'd decided to shut him out; violent rage crept through his bones, piercing straight through his soul. The need to pound his fist into something or someone increased with each shot he threw to the back of his throat. *Doesn't she know I hurt as much as she does; maybe not physically, but certainly with the same intensity mentally.* He cursed her, wishing the unthinkable, that she had been the one who perished in that car crash. Valerie, had she lived, wouldn't have treated Rykard with such inconsiderate contempt. Blurred visions of her marred face answered every explicit word spewing from his lips.

"Damn you!" he cried.

Reggie, filled with unbelievable guilt, cried each day until she fell asleep again. Her parents feared she would have a nervous breakdown. She had been medicated constantly to keep her calm. Every waking moment seemed to be filled with uncontrollable bouts of crying. Reggie blamed herself for Valerie's death, claiming had she not been trying to talk to her, she would have been able to concentrate on the road in front of them. Nothing her parents said consoled her.

Her parents and the attending physician at the hospital thought it would be better if she was moved to smaller and more private facility to recover. It would be months before she would be able to leave her bed and even more months before she would enter an extensive reha-bilitation program. It was a miracle she'd survived the crash. The physical scars would heal soon enough. No one was sure whether or not the mental hurt would vanish anytime soon.

By spring, Reggie had begun to heal physically. The scar across her forehead was tiny in comparison to the scar she wore in her chest. She couldn't find the strength to forgive herself. Not only had she lost her friend, she also left behind, what seemed like eons ago, a love that had been sweeter than a bowl of her mother's homemade ice cream. Every time she thought about him, her eyes welled with tears. How could she ever face him again? she wondered. Shame convinced her that she didn't deserve him or anything else for that matter. Valerie didn't deserve to die. It should have been her.

Sitting in the swing, on her grandmother's back porch, tears streamed down Reggie's face. Her chest ached, not just from the shattered ribs, but the loss of love she would have willingly died for. She and Valerie had become as thick as thieves. She fluctuated between hurt and anger whenever she thought about her death. Question after question about why all this happened nagged her constantly. Why hadn't they waited to go out? Why didn't she die instead of Valerie? Was it to punish her? She pounded her fist into her thighs, hoping the blows would distract or take away the pain.

Losing Trae was equally painful. He would never forgive her. How could he? She couldn't forgive herself. He would soon forget her, and that thought pained her. Her body was broken and bruised. Her marred features would surely send him running. Vain, she didn't want to chance him rejecting her. Besides, she needed time to deal with Valerie's death. She attempted to convince herself that soon her ache for him will fade. Lord knows she didn't want it to, but she knew it would. Reggie wrapped her arms around her body, as snuggly as she could. She was still bruised on the inside.

When her Nana stepped out on the porch, she moved to Reggie's side and eased her into her embrace. For a woman in her eighties, Margaret Miles moved with great ease. She'd convince Cheri to send

251

Reggie to her for a while hoping somehow to help her heal. To see her precious little granddaughter in such misery tore at her heart.

"Hush, child," she consoled. "God done give you another chance. He didn't leave you here for no reason." She ran the aged, long hand down the sides of Reggie's face.

"Now your friend Val wouldn't want you carrying on like this, Regina Miles. And you know that. That girl had more life in her than anybody I know. The Good Man upstairs got her fussing at other folks now," she taunted.

The thought of Valerie up in heaven bossing God and his angels around caused Reggie to smile between the tears.

"There," her Nana smiled. "Now, what's with this boy whose been trying to find you? Do you love him?"

Reggie nodded.

"Then what's wrong with calling him?" she asked. When Reggie didn't reply, her grandmother patted her on the leg. "Come on. I've got the biggest and fattest banana split in the kitchen, and it has your name on it."

CHAPTER 23

December should have been a great month. The holidays were near. Reggie was now twenty-one. Less than two days ago, she took her last final. Making up the semester she missed at Grambling was no easy feat. It had taken her awhile to make it up. She started with a few of her elective classes at the local junior college. The university had given her special permission to finish her last two core classes via satellite courses.

Going back to school on campus was out of the question. The pain, still new, kept her away from anywhere remotely close to Ruston, LA. Her diploma would arrive in the mail in about four to six weeks. With time and a tyrant for a therapist, she'd regain practically all the strength in her legs and arms. "You should consider dancing to help strengthen your legs and arms," he suggested.

At first she balked at the idea because her heart just wasn't in it any-more. But dancing was etched into her soul and she slowly began a reg-imen as a part of her therapy. Like riding a bike, dancing was hard to forget. She easily returned to her flawless pirouette combinations. By the time Lance visited for a third time since the accident, she was phys-ically strong again.

"You look wonderful, little sis," he cooed.

"Enough to beat your rump in some pool brother-man," she joked.

"Bring it on."

While some parts of her life returned, other more profound parts of her life still remained empty. Not a day went by that she didn't think of Trae or remember the sweet agony of his strong embrace. Especially after she began to recover, her body failed her whenever his face came to mind. The memory of his hot sweaty body riding atop of hers penetrated her dreams and robbed her of many restful nights. Even though a year had passed since laying eyes on him, the thought of him melted her to the core. She couldn't seem to get him out of her system.

Yet, she couldn't go to him and beg forgiveness. Somehow, she believed that whole ordeal happened for a reason. No one believed that the two would ever survive the entire year together. He'd been known to stray from one woman to the next. What made her think that she could tame the infamous Traekin Brooks. Every time that thought entered her mind she was sure that staying away from him was best for them both.

The anniversary of the accident rolled by, but not without painful memories. The tragedy had changed her life forever. She and her parents spent the holiday with her grandmother. "Merry Christmas sweetheart," her father cheered when he handed her a small box. She smiled openly as she unwrapped the velvet box and found a pair of diamond stud earrings.

"Thank you, Daddy." She squeezed his neck tightly. They were both a Christmas and graduation present.

Although all three were relieved that Reggie had begun to pick up the pieces of her life, they worried that she'd not fully recovered mentally from the accident. Whenever they tried to talk to her about it, she would change the subject, assuring them that she was fine. She really wasn't.

Lance took several months off to spend with his younger sister. He and Reggie had always been close. Even though he'd been away for years, it was easy to fall back into the easy comfort they'd always shared. He'd become her sounding board and the strength and encouragement, on top of the support she got from her parents, to get back on her feet and make the best of life.

"Aside from Mom and Grandma, Reggie, you're the strongest woman I know. No one can take that away," he promised. "Don't give up. Never!"

Taking her brother's advice hadn't been that simple. She soon learned that everything came with a price. Her time on this earth was valuable. With that in mind she decided she didn't have a lot to give, nor was there a lot she wanted in return. She didn't want to hurt the way she had over the last year and wrapped herself in self-loneliness.

Reggie, at all cost steered, away from relationships, both male and female. She couldn't trust her heart enough to share herself with anyone, which made her world lonely. Committed to her dancing once again, she spent a lot of time getting back into shape. Reggie worked day and night to polish her skills. The discipline of dance also gave her an outlet to work off her frustrations. By early February she felt like new.

She received word that her old friend, Joe Lanteri, was now the director of the New City Dance Alliance, and needed dancers to tour. Her reputation alone gave her a shoe in, if she wanted the job. Joe called Reggie the minute he got her portfolio. "The job is yours, Reggie, just say the word," he offered.

Reggie and Joe, in the earlier days, had formed an unconditional bond. She was talented. He had an eye for talent and knew how to mold it until it blossomed to its fullest. He valued her discipline and her true commitment to the art. He was also very interested in her. When they first met, she was far too young to pursue. She was no longer a little girl. She'd matured into a very interesting young woman. If nothing else, he hired her just to have her near him.

Moving to New York in the middle of winter wasn't as enticing as the opportunity to perform again. Yet, the cold air was a refreshing change. Reggie fell into an easy regimen with the group. She was in awe with the dance company's talent in general. They were scheduled to open the first show in San Francisco, in March and by the end of May, they would have toured twenty major cities.

The busy work kept her from thinking much about her woes. They practiced for ten, sometimes twelve hours a day. She would get up early and not return home until late in the evenings. By the time she got back to her apartment, she was exhausted beyond description. Her body ached in more ways than one. She hadn't been physically attracted to any man since Trae. She concentrated on school and getting well enough to return to dance. Every now and then her body would betray her whenever she thought about Traekin. His musky scent assaulted her senses even though she hadn't been within miles of him since the last time she saw his handsome face.

Reggie knew Joe was interested in her, still it was too soon for her. She didn't want to be involved with anyone. Joe's good looks and maturity intimidated her. She was also concerned about mixing work with pleasure. Afraid things might get too serious, Reggie refused his request to wine and dine her. Joe didn't give up so easily. He backed up a little, giving her some room and time to consider their great possibilities as a couple.

Reggie, on the other hand, knew her heart had belonged only to one man. Now that he was no longer in the picture, she had no plans to give it to another, at least not for a long while. She had made certain that Joe knew and understood that. "Please, Joe. I'm just not ready for anything serious," she confessed. Reggie valued his friendship, and his commitment to the craft. She pledged not to ruin it. A relationship was absolutely out of the question. They finally agreed to that fact.

Joe kissed her on the brow and asked, "Are you sure?"

"Yes." She nodded.

Still, in Joe's mind, time brought with it a lot of things, including change, and only time would tell whether or not they kept their word.

Trae slid from behind the large mahogany desk and stood at the large window. Sighing, he ran his hand down the front of his face. He closed his eyes for a brief moment, allowing the sunrays to kiss his clean-shaven face. He stared out of the window, not really seeing anything from beneath the heavily coated lashes.

He stuck one hand into the pocket of the gray pleated pants and clutched the trinket he carried every single day since sharing the other half of the charm with Reggie. The trinket was the one reminder he refused to let go of. The other half of the locket he'd given to Reggie shortly after meeting her. The small gold metal between his fingers was the one crutch he often used to help him through hard times, especially when he became restless as he was today.

Over the past months, his restlessness seemingly grew with each passing day he walked through the lobby of his downtown office. Maybe it had been a bad idea to come into the family business. Perhaps his decision to forgo professional sports was a mistake, too. At the time, when scouts hounded him, he didn't think so. His love for football and basketball took a back seat. He had been consumed with the tragic events that turned his world inside out. The events of that one day shifted many things his life. He'd lost both his friend and the love of his life. Rykard transferred to another school in the spring semester. He couldn't deal with the constant reminders of Valerie.

Although he was popular, Trae didn't have a lot of close friends, people he connected with, someone he told his secrets to. Yeah, he hung out with the boys. Most of the time all they did was talk trash. Trae had few options for venting his frustrations and getting meaningful advise when he needed. Rykard had been more than a roommate and sounding board. Now, with no one he really trusted with his secrets, he bottled up a lot of his frustrations. The one night he got drunk was more than enough drinking for a lifetime for Trae. So now to hide from his pain he ran, often and sometimes ten to fifteen miles each time. He also spent a lot of time lifting weights. When he wasn't doing one or the other, he was off someplace studying. Women continued to pursue him, however, he kept them at arms length.

Once he decided to let go of Reggie, he closed himself off into his own world. Somehow the accident had changed him completely. His sexual frustrations never eased. No woman measured up to Reggie's hidden passion. He got release but never got the satisfaction he yearned for. Perhaps it was because he never gave up a part of himself to them. He kept a tight rein on his feelings. His interactions were strictly physical. Veronica attempted to console him, but she, too, was too close a reminder of what he had with Reggie, and he avoided her at all costs.

Rykard and Trae managed to stay in touch after he left Ruston. Rykard moved to Atlanta and went into business for himself. In all the years they'd known each other, neither thought they would run a business. Although both majored in business, only Trae, because of the family business, was in a position that would remotely associate him with entrepreneurship.

He fingered the gold charm he had removed from his key ring when he returned from his last trip to Dallas. He intended to throw it away, just as Reggie had obviously done with their love. He couldn't discard it, even after trying several times. He would always return to reclaim it. Had he truthfully wanted to get rid of the thing, he wouldn't have left it in places he knew he could go back for it. Deep in his soul he knew he would see her again. The charm held hope that it would indeed happen.

The small, half-heart with a jagged edge in the center, fit perfectly into the charm on Reggie's bracelet. The piece in his hand was slightly worn on the face from his constant rubbing. It seemed to lose more than the wear as the black engraved letters slowly began to vanish. It also began to lose the luster that had always kept him going. With each passing day, his hopes dimmed.

The ringing phone temporarily pulled him from his funk. He turned to his desk and snatched it from its base. "Brooks," he belted into the phone.

"Who crawled up your butt?" Michael asked.

Trae sighed heavily into the phone. "What's up, brother?"

"Just thought I'll let you know, I'll be by later to pick up the reports you've been working on after lunch."

"They'll be ready," he replied.

"Sure. You want to talk about it?" Michael offered.

"No, man. I'm cool. I'll see you for lunch."

"Okay." Michael hesitated but decided not to push the issue. "Later."

"Later," Trae responded. "Thanks man."

"Anything for you, Trae."

Trae hung up the phone and returned to the window, his thoughts still on Reggie. He tried finding her again, even when he said he wouldn't. Shortly after she left Dallas, her parents moved from Shreveport. His mail was returned with the notice "No Forwarding Address" stamped on the front of it. Trae tried finding them and Reggie using the Internet but wasn't successful. He remembered meeting her brother only once, and because he moved around so much it was hard to track him down as well. In the short while they got to know each other, he learned that Reggie's family moved around often. Several leads led him to different places, however, he always came up empty-handed.

Sighing heavily, he moved from the large bay window back to his desk. From the bottom left-hand drawer, he pulled out a small leather album and flipped through the few pages with pictures of a happier time. He brushed his finger over the plastic film that covered the smiling faces of Reggie and him in his Uncle Ted's backyard. The dimples winked at him and pulled at his heart as it had always done. A yearning seeped through his soul. It had been well over a year and he still couldn't get over her. Lord knows he tried. He quickly realized that he didn't want to.

Trae moved on with his life out of sheer necessity. With a future pretty much planned out for him, he was fortunate to have options. He chose not to pursue sports, even at the constant pleading and large contract offers. His father had hoped to have all of his sons involved in the family business. Alvin took advantage of the situation and lured his son in, claiming he needed to stay close to home and family to help him through his tragedy. When he finished school, he moved back home into his old room and lived there for six months before finding his own place.

As he gazed down at the picture, he remembered the sound of her voice as though he'd heard a few moments ago. "Reggie," he whispered. Her eyes had always sparkled when she smiled or laughed. He knew she loved life. She told him often. He also knew she took her commitments seriously. She would crash and burn before backing out of something she had pledged to do. That knowledge alone helped fuel the prospect that he would see her again.

Shaking himself from his musing, Trae placed the album back into the drawer and closed it along with the thoughts of Reggie for the time being. He shoved his long stocky frame into his leather chair and pulled out the keyboard tray tucked away in a small compartment of his desk. His fingers furiously stroked the letter and number keys on the black panel; words quickly filled the screen until he was done. Ordinarily his secretary took care of typing reports, but the substantive and critical impact of this report was strictly confidential. Only a few key people knew the details, purpose, and possible impact to the company. His eyes scanned the screen for several minutes before he sent it to the printer.

Trae's father wanted him in the company for more reasons than keeping the business in the family. His youngest son wasn't only smart; he was keen and business savvy. In the short time he'd been in the downtown office, he'd completely transformed the company. In the first phase of his three-phased strategic plan, he trimmed various departments, added new and updated equipment and computer networks, sent all employees to on-site training, and relatively boosted productivity and revenues in eight months.

He drowned himself in his work, dragging many of his employees with him. He was on a mission, and it had to do with more than cleaning up his father's downtown office. Industriously working late into the wee hours at night, mostly to keep his mind occupied and away from Reggie, Trae restructured the office, fired people, especially the dead weight, and hired new ones.

"I hate seeing a fine young man like yourself married to his job," his administrative assistant, Mavis, often chastised him.

Trae was out to prove himself. Many in the management chain were skeptical of his decisions. After all, he was only twenty-one and fresh out of college. What could he possibly know about running a business? Trae had a business savvy that belied his young life. Months later, when the fruits of his labor materialized, the skeptics, soon learned to respect his judgment.

"Job well done," his father commended. Trae took his father's recognition in stride. He worshipped his father and welcomed his praise, but it was the work that kept him from drowning in an empty soul.

This report outlined his next phase of bringing the family-owned business into the twenty-first century. He understood the importance of engaging key people in the planning process; however, the decision would be totally and unconditionally his. He didn't want his final decision to leak out until he got final approval from the board of directors. Mavis was a great administrative assistant, but she had a problem keeping her mouth closed. Trae, on several occasions, threatened to fire her, knowing full well, he wouldn't. She worked hard and was a key asset to the continue growth of the company.

Trae stuck several copies of the printed report into folders and locked them in his desk drawer. He glanced down at his digital watch. He was meeting his brothers at twelve o'clock. Whenever the two older siblings got together and ordered him to meet them for lunch, he knew he was in trouble. The only subject that dominated their conversations these days was Trae's lack of female companionship. He'd refused, he couldn't remember, how many blind dates Travis and Michael tried to fix him up with. He loved his brothers, but he didn't need them babysitting him.

Reggie paced the auditorium stage contemplating how to handle the bit of news she'd received only hours ago. The tour scheduled to go through St. Louis was diverted to another city because the Fox Theater, where the show was scheduled, had closed its doors for late structural repairs. Contract delays and striking workings pushed the repairs out to a later date, therefore making the theater unavailable for the scheduled show.

The tour director could have decided on any one of the major cities not planned for this tour. Chicago, Dallas, or even Atlanta, were all good choices. The one city Reggie had dreaded to return to was the very city for which a last minute change had included. New Orleans, the "Big Easy," was added to the schedule. Now, as she made one long streak along the high gloss floor, she pondered her dilemma. She thought about asking Joe to send her back to New York, and she would meet them in the next city. She knew her dance company depended on her. There were several dancers who would have loved the opportunity to be on stage, no matter the circumstances. However, for Reggie, to bail on them was the unthinkable, even more than the possibility of running into Trae again. *Why is this happening?* she agonized. *Especially now.*

After a few more moments of considering her crisis, Reggie relented in the confidence that New Orleans was a big enough city to avoid running into Traekin there. He'd never expressed an interest in ballets. He attended the recital at the youth center only because she'd asked him to. She contemplated the odds of running into him at one of the shows. She was almost certain that the odds were in her favor and that Trae didn't go anywhere remotely close to a ballet performance.

Besides, she wasn't even sure he was in New Orleans. Traekin was destined to do great things in sports. Although she hadn't heard any news about his stardom, she was sure he was somewhere in the sports limelight. Reggie halted her pacing long enough to consider the thought that Trae wasn't even in his hometown.

The next thought that came to her mind was his family. What about them? They must have thought poorly of her. After all, they had taken her in as though she was family. What would she do if she ran into one of his family members? Would they tell him where she was? She knew he had on several occasions tried to find her. Avoiding him hadn't been easy or encouraged. Her grandmother pleaded with her to contact him and at least let him know that she was okay. Reggie unconditionally refused her grandmother's request.

Joe caught her deep in thought as he strolled through the front aisles of the auditorium.

"Something wrong, sunshine?" he queried.

Joe's inquiry broke her from her reverie. Her thoughts instantly went back to the one sunny afternoon at Uncle Ted's house when Trae embraced his little cousin Rain with the same sweet coddling. Loneliness crept up her spine like a spider would his intricately spun web. Joe became concerned by Reggie's distraught expression. Thinking something seriously wrong, he climbed the stairs and rushed to her side. He pulled her into his slow embrace.

"Are you okay, Reggie?" the concern masked in his deep hazel eyes.

Reggie physically shook herself and stared up into Joe's concerned face.

"Yeah, Joe. I'm fine, just fine."

"Maybe you should sit out of the next couple of shows. We have more than enough understudies to give you a break."

"No," Reggie quickly responded. Even though Joe had given her the perfect out to her dilemma, she recalled her earlier statement. She had a job to do, and she couldn't let small setbacks keep her from doing her job. "I'm okay. I just needed a short break, is all," she easily lied. She eased out of his embrace.

CHAPTER 24

Trae strolled through the doors of the crowded Praline Connection, the hostess Chelsea greeted him and pointed to the table where his two oversize siblings seemed to take up all the space in that corner of the restaurant. They sat there doing the one thing they loved the most, eating. Their mother Cheri never complained when the boys were always in the kitchen looking for something to eat. They drank milk by the gallon and ate cereal by the box when they were growing up. The two appetizers they ordered were almost gone. Travis licked the spicy buffalo-wings sauce from his thick fingers as he watched Trae near the table.

"Hey, ugly." Travis didn't even give him a chance to get close to the table. A sneer was laced on both Travis and Michael's faces.

"Lil' Bro." Michael stood first and hugged his brother. Travis repeated the same gesture.

Traekin returned his brothers hearty greeting.

"We've ordered already. Food should be here in awhile," Michael explained.

They patronized this eatery a lot and were well known by the cook. Whenever they came in as a group, they ordered enough food for a small army. The first time they came as a group, Peewee, the cook's nickname, couldn't believe the order was for one table. The place couldn't really accommodate large groups. The small restaurant had two sides, one for sit-down meals and the other side had some seating to accommodate customers who ordered take-out or wanted to sample their creamy sweet pralines. So he strolled from the kitchen to get a look at the three. After introducing himself and he was reassured that they had indeed ordered the food, he shook his head and returned to the kitchen.

The three shared their meals and jovial conversation as they'd always done. Talking trash was another of their other favorite past-times, and the threesome talked enough trash to warrant a garbage pickup. Michael was the comedian of the three. Because he was the middle child of the boys, he often joked with his brothers about how Travis always got him into trouble and dared him to tell their parents and how Trae was the pampered brat.

"Remember the time we hid Papa's dentures?" he recalled.

"Yeah. I couldn't sit down for a week when Daddy was done with my behind." Travis punched Michael in the shoulder. "And all because you went and blabbered afterwards, you chicken head."

"Nah, man, I wasn't about to catch one of Dad's infamous whip-pings. Besides, you were the oldest."

When the plates and platters were emptied, their conversation turned a little more seriously. Both brothers turned their solemn glares at Trae. Trae shifted in his chair. He eased rearward into it until his back was flushed against the wooden base. *This was a setup*, he confirmed his earlier conviction. The warning lights in his head were on high beam. Trae folded his hands into his lap and waited for the mêlée. He wasn't surprised when Travis spoke first.

"Listen Trae, we know you've had a rough time getting over this thing with Reggie, man, but it's time for you to move on. You're young and there are a lot of women out here. Fine women!" His hands moved in a rounded outline to denote the robustness of a woman's behind, and his mouth sauced into a crooked grin.

Trae watched the animations of his brother's face and gesture with interest. He planned not to get upset with them today like he did most of the time when this subject came up. He knew they had his best interest at heart.

Michael chipped in the conversation. "Darlene and I have this friend we want you to meet, and before you say anything Trae hear me out." He leaned over and touched his brother's arm.

"In couple of weeks, we're planning supper, and afterwards we will go to this ballet performance she's been all worked up about. It would seem the performance is making a last minute stop in the city," he spoke rapidly trying to ward off any refusal before he gave Traekin all the facts.

"She's a nice girl, Trae, and it's not like you have to be with her by yourself. Travis and Lynette will be with us as well," he rushed on.

Michael's expression turned into a question after several minutes ticked by and Trae hadn't spoken a word. He gazed at Trae, then Travis, and then to Trae once more. Travis watched in amusement. He knew his youngest brother was playing it cool. He admired how calm and collected he always seemed to be. The only time he'd ever seen him lose that cool was in Dallas. He'd never seen his younger brother cry before that day. Now, as he looked across the table at him it seemed like a lifetime ago, yet the rawness of the tragedy was fresh and still haunted him with great intensity.

Trae gathered his thoughts. Because his brothers had tried so hard, he wanted to give in to them this one time. They had been his sounding board and strong pole to lean on over the last year and a half. He couldn't resist the temptation to mess with them by making them wait for his answer. He eyed both Travis and Michael. Only size separated the siblings. In all else, they were very similar. When he decided he'd kept them waiting long enough, he took a sighing breath before speaking.

"Okay, Mike. I'll do this for you." He smiled. "But don't go fixing me up with an old, ugly rag, or else," he warned.

"Look at Darlene," Michael teased. "Now, does she look like she hangs out with ugly rags?"

"Well, Elaine is hitting pretty close to old and ugly," Travis interjected. He couldn't help himself and burst into a laughing fit.

Michael rolled his eyes at his oldest brother. Elaine was a sweet girl and, even though she wasn't beautiful, she wasn't ugly, just sort of plain-looking. Michael had some one else in mind for Trae.

"Don't worry little brother. It isn't Elaine. Destiny is new to the city. I'm sure you'll like her," he explained and gave both brothers the scoop on the woman he promised would knock Trae off of his feet.

When Reggie stepped through the gates at Louis Armstrong International Airport, nervous energy, like prickly needles jetted through her entire body. The warm greetings by the airport personnel and then the hotel staff put her at ease. She'd almost forgotten what it was like to be in her home state where everyone spoke to you even though they didn't know you. She quickly unpacked and grabbed her bag with shoes and towel in it. When she got to the lobby she and the other dancers boarded a shuttle that took them to the theater.

Reggie's fears were calmed by the rushed preparations for the first show opening. By mid-week they'd done six shows. The opening performance got rave reviews, and Reggie seemed to ease into her surroundings, worrying very little about the possibility of running into Trae. So far, the encounter hadn't happened, and as she moved about the city her confidence soared. Reggie planned, at the end of her last show in the city, that she would go and visit her grandmother. She only had a few hours to visit, but couldn't image coming this close to her grandmother's house and not see her.

Reggie hadn't seen her grandmother, Margaret, since leaving for New Year's; and Convent, Louisiana was only an hour and ten minutes drive away. She spent the better part of her recovery in the large white frame house that sat across from the high levee and the Mississippi River. The small town was quiet, with the exception of the hustle and bustle of loading cargo onto barges that would take goods up the Mississippi River. She spent quiet moments laid out on a blanket in the late evening watching nature do its thing. Her dance company wasn't scheduled to fly out until mid-day following the final performance.

Reggie strolled swiftly with the swarm of people on the streets, easing in and out of the crowd. She'd opted to spend a couple of hours in the French Quarters. Lost in her thoughts, she almost crossed the street directly in the path of an oncoming car. Her reflexes kicked in the moment the car came into her peripheral view. Trembling hands moved to her heart. A flash of a time 'before' crossed her mind. She dreamt about it often for months following the accident. The dreams rarely occurred now, but every now and then something triggered a reminder, and she remembered the events as though it happened days before.

Reggie stood on the corner, still slightly shaken, and as soon as the people around began to move again, she fell into step with them crossing the intersections at Chartres and St Peter. She was headed to the St. Louis Cathedral. Casually dressed in jeans and T-shirt, the warm sunshine was a welcoming change in the weather. It had been cloudy and rainy earlier in the week. Her eyes gazed skyward and took in the massive structure of the building that now served as the Roman Catholic Archdiocese of New Orleans. In awe, she followed other visitors through the doors.

Trae stepped out into the sunshine once he left the Gumbo Shop. He'd just left the little quaint restaurant after having lunch with several out-of-town clients. Both men were at the Hotel St. Marie, a half block from Bourbon Street and only a short walk from the Gumbo Shop. Clearly pleased with the outcome of the meeting, Trae walked the short distance to his parked car. Just as he neared the corner, he caught a glimpse of a ponytail flopping from side to side. It looked so strangely familiar, as though it mocked him in its knowing.

The streets were crowded and the tall slender body sporting the ponytail was lost in the sea of people when they crossed the street. Uneasiness, without description, angrily crawled up his spine and seeped into his soul. The woman seemed familiar to him, although he only caught a glimpse of her retreating figure. It took a few minutes to register in his mind to whom that familiarity was connected; by that time it was useless to retrace his steps and follow the crowd.

"No," he shook his head. He refused to believe Reggie could be here right under his nose and he not know it.

Still, the uneasiness nagged him long after he returned to his office, which made for an extremely long day. On top of this strange feeling was the knowledge that he would have to keep his promise to his brothers. Dinner and theater tonight as promised would start out at Michael's house. Trae groaned inwardly at the thought. How had he allowed his brothers to sucker him into this? He regretted the decision the moment he left the restaurant several weeks ago.

Destiny was indeed a beautiful woman. She was a few years older that he was, but age never mattered when he was involved with a woman. She was quiet, and from his initiated conversations with her, he could tell she was an intelligent woman. He hated more than anything a flighty woman, gorgeous or not.

He'd had his share of both. He soon found himself looking for brainy chicks whenever he pursued a woman. He remembered his last semester after returning to Grambling. He couldn't stand to be around Veronica, not just because she reminded him of the relationship between him and Reggie, but also because she was just another pretty face. She had no substance.

Trae learned that his date was originally from Detroit, Michigan and was an associate working for the same company as Darlene. Dinner was surprisingly nice and Trae was able to relax throughout the evening. Michael had gone all out for this evening. He'd even ordered a limo to take the three couples to the theater. After dinner, they all piled into the back of the limo and exchanged pleasantries. The New York Dance Academy was the featured performance, however, when Trae looked through the program, he paid very little attention to the names of the cast members. Instead, he and Destiny talked quietly. She was an interesting woman and Trae felt comfortable enough to open up to her, attempt to get to know her.

Only after the lights dimmed, the curtains opened, and the introductions began, did Traekin's entire being rivet into a storm cloud large
enough to flood the entire state. His eyes opened and closed a few
times as though it would clear his hearing because he certainly thought
he'd heard incorrectly. One of the performers was Regina Miles, a
native of Louisiana. It couldn't be his Regina Miles. It couldn't be true.
He unconsciously stood, winning the gaze of the people near him. A
concerned Destiny looked up at his taut frame, she then looked to her
friend for an explanation.

Travis also heard and knew instantly that his brother would soon
have a panic attack. He wasn't sure what to expect, so he stood and
pushed Trae from the aisles where they stood. Michael followed. Trae
allowed his brother to push his numb body through the door and into
the lobby. His shocked expression was more a question than anything.
They shuffled through the pages of the program he got when he first
entered the theater. When he found and frantically read the bio for
Regina Miles, the pages he held in his hands fell to the floor.

"Trae." Michael shook his brother's shoulders.

Travis bent over and retrieved the fallen pages, and he too anxiously read the contents. It was Reggie. The same woman Trae had desperately searched for. Months of endless and sleepless nights, Trae looked
and called everyone he could think of. And here she was in the flesh.
His eyes combed Trae's cold, tortured feature.

"We should leave, Trae," Travis suggested.

Trae's eyes strayed to his brothers. An understanding only these
brothers shared danced in the air between them. Trae shook his head.
They stood close by ready and waiting to do whatever it took to protect their own.

"No," he barely whispered. "I want to stay," his eyes iced with
anger. "I need to find out why."

When the trio moved back into the theater, the performance had already begun. Destiny's soft, soothing touch to his arm forced him to look in her direction. Even in the dim lights he could make out her face. It bore support and understanding. He placed his hand on top of hers and pulled the small delicate fingers into his lap. His eyes returned to the stage and he watched in awe.

She was even more beautiful than he'd remembered. She moved with graceful ease. The tempo of the music was slow and hypnotic as she and ten other dancers waltzed, leaped, and besieged the audience with magnificent seasoned and elegant dance movements. When the music and tempo changed, Reggie executed a demanding series of leaps and turns while her arms and legs created fleeting angles and shapes like the lines of a Picasso painting. Her body moved into positions no one thought possible. Her stage presence embodied a professional confidence. Trae couldn't take his eyes off of her.

Her slim muscular frame was encased in a black leotard with sections of the front cut out in blocks revealing the tight ripples of her flat rib cage and stomach. The bodysuit was no more than three strings across the top of her body. The neck was high, but between each strip that hid flesh, including her high firm breasts, the costume did nothing to hide the provocative and seducing affect of her exposed flesh. Trae released Destiny's hand, and wiped both of his hands down the front of his face. His blood boiled as he watched and remembered what Reggie's body felt like in his embrace. He released a deep sigh, demanding that his body cooperate, but it had a mind of its own.

With eyes still glued to the stage thirty minutes later, he watched the precision, strength, and sheer stamina in which Reggie performed. He hadn't noticed many of the other dancers, except on the occasions when one of them interacted with her physically. She captivated the audience with her extreme torso manipulation and control, powerhouse muscles and sensual artistry. No one would ever believe that nearly every rib in her body had been injured.

Reggie moved with ease and deliberate purpose. She hid the uneasiness beneath the layers of confidence. She knew this show and the routine she'd practice a thousand times. So why was she getting this weird feeling? She pushed it to the back of her mind. She'd always known dancing was enlightening and challenging, but it still had to entertain. It was her job to make certain she entertained the audience beyond their expectation. She had great faith in her talent and tonight she used it to woo every eye and soul watching her tonight.

For the finale, the director of the show, Joe, accompanied the dancers, which included a very seductive exchange with Reggie. A pang of jealous seeped through Trae. His eyes narrowed and his body tensed until the interaction between the two ended. Trae wondered if it was he who kept Reggie from seeking him. He would soon find out everything he wanted to know. He intended to wait for her and an explanation backstage at the end of the show.

CHAPTER 25

Trae decided he would stay after the show to talk to Reggie. He apologized to Destiny for not accompanying her back, and was honest when he explained why he had to stay behind. Disappointment filled her eyes. He placed a small kiss on her cheeks, careful not to make any promises to her. His brothers asked for the third time if he knew what he was doing. Raw nerves prickled his skin and his heart blared into his ear. Yes. He knew he had to in order to close this chapter of his life.

"Yes." He shook his head to confirm his spoken word.

They each hugged him and made him promise to call later to report in. He assured them that he would. Trae sweet-talked one of the guards into letting him backstage, assuring her that he was a close, and personal friend of the lead dancer. She escorted him to an area just beyond the dressing room. He asked one of the female dancers to point out Reggie's dressing room.

"In there, sugah. But that's where all the girls dress. You'll have to wait out here. I'll tell her you're waiting." She smiled openly up at him. "By the way, who should I tell her is waiting, handsome." She looked over his dark features and thought *damn he's fine!*

Traekin was always aware of how females acted toward him. He could charm a woman with little or no effort. Since his relationship with Reggie, he refrained from his old habits. Tonight was an exception. He needed to get to Reggie, and he would use his charms if he had to. His mouth eased into a crooked smile, the white teeth gleamed with sparkled.

"Just tell her an old college friend is waiting for her." His long dark lashes slowly lowered and concealed his dark and seductive eyes.

Flustered by the enigma of this tall, handsome stranger, she made one parting comment. "If things don't work out with you and Regina, give me a holler. I'm at the Maison St. Charles. Room 245." She then sashayed through the dressing room door.

It always took Reggie a little time to cool down after a show. The water trickling down the back of her throat, not only quenched her thirst; it also helped cool her off. Her slow gait across the crowded dressing room didn't cease until Rosetta yelled across the dressing room.

"Regina. If you don't claim the man standing outside the dressing room, I have a mind to grab him for myself."

All eyes instantly traveled towards the door. Mumbles and grins soon filled the room. Reggie stilled. The water bottle hung in suspension and her skin turned almost white. Without another spoken word she knew who her caller was. The unexplained jitters were suddenly cleared. She and Traekin had this bizarre ability to feel one another's presence. Slowly, she lowered the water bottle. Her mind desperately searched for a way to get out of this crisis. She didn't know what to do.

She closed her eyes and took a sighing breath. Heat fused through her blood and unmanageable tremors caused her to stumble backward.

A fellow dancer saw the distress in her face and movement and reached over to help her to her station. "Dang, girl. This must be some man," she attempted to be discriminate with her comment. Reggie glanced at her briefly. "Do you want me to go and tell him to leave?" she offered. She could feel every nerve in her body spike.

Thankful it was Colleen and not one of the others, Reggie shook her head. "No. Thanks, Colleen." She half smiled and pulled her arm from Colleen's grasp.

Colleen didn't move until she was sure Reggie was okay. The second nod was a little more reassuring and so she left Reggie to the grueling task of removing the layers of no-drip make-up.

Reggie's fingers shook as she dipped the five-inch square cotton swabs into a bowl filled with facial cleanser. She removed layer by layer of make-up until she saw what used to be unblemished skin. The permanent, three-inch scar above her right eye was the constant reminder of a gloomier day. She felt remorseful every time she looked in the mirror.

Trae paced the small area waiting for Reggie to emerge from the dressing room. He was approached by the director, Joe something or the other. He wasn't at all interested in what the guy's name was. He somehow had the feeling he was attracted to Reggie and that fact didn't sit well with him. Joe could have had him kicked from the backstage area if he wanted to, so Trae decided to play it cool. He told him he was an old college buddy and just wanted to say hello to her. He seemed to buy that story.

However, Trae had no intention of telling him or anyone else. He planned to demand Reggie explain her actions and was prepared to not leave until he got the explanation he wanted. About ten minutes after Trae talked to Joe, a few of the women casually strolled from the dressing room. Each time the door opened, his heart leaped until he saw it wasn't Reggie. Every passing woman eyed him with piqued curiosity. He could only imagine what the woman he'd met earlier told them. When the woman walked from the dressing room, he moved anxiously toward her.

"Is Reggie still in there?" he asked. Worry lines drew curves into his forehead.

She stuck her hand out. "Rosetta Jarrett."

He tried not to show his frustration and accepted her proffered hand. "Traekin Brooks." His gaze strayed to the closed door. "It's a pleasure to meet you," he lied.

If it was the only way to find out if Reggie was behind those doors, so be it. His gaze came down and kissed the pale freckled face free of make-up. Her red hair draped around her thin shoulders. She had a pretty face, but she wasn't his type. At that thought he huffed to himself. He had said the same thing about Reggie. He had learned not to look totally at a person's outward appearance.

He smiled again. This time genuinely. Rosetta blushed and for the first time he remembered what it was like to steal the heart of a woman so similar to the one who, in turn, stole his.

"Reggie, as you called her, is still in the dressing room. She should be out in a minute."

"Thank you."

"You're welcome." She moved around Trae and looked back at him. "It was nice meeting you," she said before walking away.

"The pleasure was mine," he said to her retreating back.

When Reggie finally emerged from the dressing room, Trae's heart stopped, as did his pacing. His eyes strolled over her several times before resting on her eyes. His hands were cold. His heart pounded in his chest like a thousand drums. All the hurt, anger, disappointments, and questions lurked from beneath the long black lashes. She moved toward him until she was only several feet away. Seconds ticked away and neither could move or speak.

Reggie waited five minutes after she'd taken off her make-up and packed her things before leaving the dressing room. Almost everyone had left by the time she was done. She contemplated how to handle Trae's stormy greeting. She knew he had to be upset with her and didn't know what to expect. Nervous fingers gripped the door handle for a while before she was brave enough to pull it open. When she finally caught a glimpse of his overpowering presence, she couldn't stop herself until she was within arms length of him.

The moment she stepped into his personal space, the overwhelming urge to touch his taut face was drowned by the danger she saw in his eyes. The musty cologne assaulted her senses. She was breathless and overcome by his towering stature. It was the identical feeling the first time they'd met. The only change from now and then was the questions glaring at her from beneath the sensual lashes. She held onto the black backpack gripped between her fingers. Her bottled-up emotions slipped as his eyes slowly assessed her. Tears welled into the corner of her eyes. And then…

The anger Trae felt slowly slipped from his heart. Love and passion from God knows where filled him from head to toe. Then he lost control, a storm of emotions overwhelmed him. He loved this woman with every fiber in his trembling body. That feeling hadn't changed one bit. Time did nothing but harbor his feelings for her. The scent of her fragrance hadn't changed and it drugged him as it had always done. His nostrils flared, warning all of his senses that he was close to the edge. Control ceased to exist. He devoured every detail of her upturned face as though he was looking at her for the first time.

Upon a closer assessment of her features, his eyes were drawn to the visible scar just above her right eye. Without warning or explanation, he extended his hand until his finger softly ran across the long, marred line on her forehead. Electrical bolts speared between flesh and flesh. The charge shocked them both. Reggie jumped, and he drew his fingers back as though he'd been slapped. His fingers returned to their intended target. This time Reggie's eyes closed at his touch.

Trae savored her buttery soft skin. He trailed a line down her cheek and then across her trembling lips before his entire hand cupped the right side of her face. Tears streamed from the closed lids. He eased them away with the blunt tips of his fingers. His gesture seemed to increase the flow of salty tears, coupled by the rise and fall of her chest beneath the red T-shirt. Unable to resist, his other hand closed the cup and now her entire face was encased in his hands pulling it closer to his waiting lips. He shattered the space between them and placed warm tender kisses on each lid.

Reggie caved. Trae's hands healed months of agony and pain she'd harbored for the last year and a half. She leaned into his body and allowed him to take possession of her senses. The tears were soon accompanied by low sobs from the back of her throat. She dropped the backpack to the floor and clutched onto the front of Trae's dinner jacket.

He eased one of his arms around her waist. His lips moved to the side of her face until it was flushed against her ear. "It's okay, baby. I'm here," he soothed.

His body responded to the healing they both needed and obviously wanted. He wrapped both arms completely around her until their bodies were one. It felt so right to have her in his arms again. Nothing else mattered. None of the questions mattered anymore. All he wanted to do for the time being was hold her close to his heart.

Reggie squeezed her arms around Trae's large frame with all the strength she could muster. Nothing in the world could have prepared her for this feeling. The soothing words he whispered in her ears were the balm she needed to release the demons that haunted her all this time. Had he forgiven her so easily? She wanted desperately to tell him that she didn't think he would. The words were buried behind the agony in her cries.

Trae moved his mouth until he covered Reggie's soft lips, drowning out her heart-piercing cries. He drank from her opened mouth like a crazed maniac. He stood up to his full height bringing Reggie up with him. Her feet hung beneath her, and she held on with a serious grip. Fiery passion ebbed through her entire body. Air wasn't an option. Only the desire needed to quench their thirsts for one another.

When Trae did release her, he slowly placed her on her feet again. He loosened his hold just enough to look down into her tear-stained face.

"Reggie," he whispered. It took her blood-shot eyes a second or two to meet his gaze. "I want to take you someplace so we can talk. Is that okay?"

"Yes," she managed.

Trae reached into his pocket and extracted a neatly folded handkerchief and handed it to her. She used it to wipe her eyes and runny nose. When she was done she looked up at Trae through sticky wet lashes. She half-smiled at him.

"Thank you," she offered.

"Are you ready?" He leaned down and picked up her discarded backpack.

She nodded her head and allowed him to lead her from the building.

CHAPTER 26

Trae wrapped his arm snuggly around Reggie's waist as they left the stage area. He had called his car service before going backstage. Charlie waited in front of the theater door, and when he saw Traekin and his guest approach the revolving doors, he got out and opened the rear passenger side door for them.

"Thank you, Charlie, for coming on such short notice." He patted the older guy on the shoulder. He handed the driver Reggie's backpack.

"No problem at all, Mr. Brooks. Just glad I was available." He nodded as Trae eased his long frame into the leather seat next to Reggie.

Her eyes met his. They spoke volumes, and he slipped his arm over the top of the seat behind her and pulled her into his embrace. Reggie's head slipped and rested into his chest. Neither spoke as the car pulled away from the curb. She closed her eyes and ten minutes into the drive was fast asleep. When the car pulled into the circle driveway at Trae's house, his lips touched her brow.

"Reggie. We're here sweetheart."

It didn't take him very long to fall back into his old practice of pampering her. She stirred but didn't come fully awake at first. When he called her again, she peered at him through groggy-eyes.

"Hmm," she answered.

"Just sit tight for a minute. I'll be back for you, okay?"

Reggie bobbed her head and answered in sleepy voice. When Charlie released the door, Trae got out and took several long strides until he was in front of the covered panel. He keyed in a sequence of numbers, which shut down the alarm. He stuck the key into the door. Charlie was steps behind him and handed Trae Reggie's bag. He pulled his wallet from his coat pocket and pulled out several bills and shoved them into Charlie's hand.

"The ride, add to my invoice," he instructed. "This is a little something for your time."

"You don't…" Charlie's words died as Trae held up his hand halting any further discussion.

Charlie had been driving for the Brooks family for the last twenty years. When the Brooks' youngest son moved back to the city, he used the car services for practically everything in the business; to transport employees, shuttle visiting clients, and to deliver products. Charlie went out of his way to accommodate Trae whenever he needed something.

Trae strolled back to the opened car door. He eased Reggie into his arms and thanked Charlie again before moving through the door and closing it with his foot.

Reggie protested. "I'm awake, Trae. You can put me down."

However, Trae didn't stop or put her down until they were in a room with a large fireplace in the center of it. He placed Reggie onto the cool leather couch. She brushed her hand across her face to erase some of the sleep. Sheer exhaustion claimed her tired and worn body. She'd been up since five this morning. Her tired eyes looked up in to his expectant face.

"Can I get you anything?" he offered.

"Water." She half-smiled.

"I'll be back in a few. Make yourself comfortable."

Reggie watched him as he left the room. He slipped his arms from the dinner jacket and dropped it over the back of the wing chair. Her eyes scanned the room, taking in the elegant décor. Most of the furnishing and pictures were muted browns and olive greens. Her hands glided across the brown leather sofa. *How long has he lived here?* She wondered. *What has he done with his life since the last time I saw him?*

By the time Trae moved through the large kitchen, he'd rolled up his sleeves. He dropped the gold cuff links on the counter top and pulled two bottles of spring water from the refrigerator door. He handed a bottle to Reggie and took a seat next to her. He waited until she took several sips from the bottle before speaking.

"I was so scared, Reggie. When I got to the scene of the accident, I…" the remaining words lodged in his throat.

A well of uncontrollable emotions filled him that instant. His eyes bore through her, pleading with her to understand what he felt. It was like he'd never talked about this before, but he had. He'd told his story to his brothers and to his parents. Each time he did so his eyes welled with a sea of tears. The truth of it all was that it hadn't mattered when he told his family. Telling it to Reggie was the only way to move past the helplessness he felt that rainy day.

Reggie felt the wave of emotions creeping through her body, too. She reached over and cupped his hands into hers. She'd considered many times what the tragic accident had done to her family and friends, but never understood how they dealt with it. The mask that covered his face broke into despair. He pulled her into his embrace, squeezing her body as tight as he could. They spent a few minutes crying and holding one another.

When they were in better control of their feelings, they began to talk. Reggie explained why she refused to see him in the beginning, how and why she couldn't forgive herself. She truly believed the accident was her fault.

"Val would be here today, Traekin, had I not tried talking to her while she was driving," she explained.

"Reggie, you can't blame yourself for what happened. No one else is blaming you." He stroked her face. "Val wouldn't want you to do this to yourself."

"Would you forgive me?" she pleaded with Trae.

He pulled her into his lap and cuddled her close to his heart.

"There's nothing to forgive, sweetheart. But if you really need to hear the words, I forgive you." He pulled her face in so that they were eye-to-eye. "Now will you forgive me as well?"

Reggie frowned as she shifted in his lap.

"I was really angry with you Reggie for shutting me out of your life. As time passed I struggled to live from day to day. I just wanted to know that you were okay and doing well." His hand rubbed the small of her back as he talked.

"I've never stopped loving you, Trae. And there wasn't a day that went by that I didn't think about you, about us. I didn't think I deserved what we'd shared," she confessed. "I was also afraid that what we had wouldn't last."

It was Trae's turn to frown. His eyes searched hers again for an explanation. It took a few minutes, but with a sighing breath and another sea of tears streaming down her face, she finally told him, "I didn't trust you enough to believe that you wouldn't get tired of me sooner or later. I didn't trust myself enough to be able to get over it if you did."

Trae looked at her for a long moment. He wondered what mixed signals he'd sent that made her think that he would have left her for anything. Because he couldn't remember, didn't necessarily mean that he hadn't. Their love was new and they spent a lot of time trying to discover who they were. His eyes strayed away for a few seconds. His reputation at the time hadn't help. She had to know that she'd changed him completely. He was totally satisfied with being with her and her alone.

"I'd changed, Reggie. After I met you, I wasn't the same man anymore. There was no else for me. There's no one else for me now, Reggie. Only you, if you're willing to give me another chance."

"I want that more than anything in the world."

Trae leaned in and covered Reggie's mouth. He nibbled on her lower lip, then the upper lip, before tasting the sweet tender insides of her mouth. Reggie drowned willingly into the passion-filled fog. Trae's hands danced down her curvy spine until they reached the firm muscle in her backside. Coaching her body to squirm in his hands, Trae pressed her swaying hips into his groin. His passion accelerated. He couldn't get enough of her.

"I love you, Reggie, more than life," he whispered hoarsely.

"I love you, Trae, more than life."

"Then promise me, sweetheart, that we never, ever let anything else come between us." His eyes bore through her soul. "Promise me, Reggie," he commanded.

"I promise."

He kissed her again and said, "Tell me about you, Reggie. What's your life like these days?"

They spent another hour catching up on each other. Reggie used the back of her hand to hide the yawn. Trae kissed her forehead.

"Where are you staying?" he asked. "It's time to get you back to your hotel."

Reggie slipped her arms around his neck. Her mouth covered his, savoring his sweet full lips. She eased her tongue in and out of his mouth. Trae allowed her to reacquaint herself with his body. A groan erupted from his lips when her fingers wandered dangerously down the front of his body until they rested on the bulge he had no way of concealing. Throbbing with need, his mouth pulled away.

"You're not going to make it back to your hotel, Reggie, if you keep this up."

"I don't want to go back just now." She attempted to recapture his lips, but Trae kissed her briefly then pulled away again.

A serious line creased his face because he didn't want to rush things. He wanted her so badly he could taste it. It had been months since he'd been with a woman. However, he wanted more than one night or one week. A lifetime, at this point wasn't enough, and this time, everything was at stake. He planned to play for keeps this time. A cold shower would take care of the hard-on temporarily, but he didn't know of any cures for another broken heart if she walked out of his life again. Just thinking about the pain made him sick inside. He wanted her just as much, if not more, than he did when he pledged to love her and no one else.

"Are you sure about us?" he asked.

Reggie nodded. "Yes. Very sure, Trae. I love you," she responded sincerely.

"What time to do you have to be at practice tomorrow?" he asked. He knew that dancers, even when they were on tour, were responsible for honing and learning new skills. This was something they did on their own, at their own expense, in addition to the rigorous rehearsal scheduled. He remembered Reggie telling him about the life of a dancer on tour. He could never quite understand why she loved it so much. He guessed it was the same as any sport.

"My class isn't until nine and show-practice is from three to five. The first curtain is at seven." She smiled at him. "You remembered."

"There aren't a whole lot of things about you that I can forget, Reggie."

"Ditto." She kissed he lips. "Now, where did we leave off?" She wound her arms around his neck again.

Trae smiled. From what they'd shared about each other earlier, Reggie had grown a lot in the last year and a half. What hadn't changed, and what he liked a lot, was her sauciness. His shaft stirred and he changed their position, pushing her from his lap until she was flat on the soft leather couch.

CHAPTER 27

Trae teased Reggie into total submission. It hadn't taken much. She was as hungry for him as he'd been for her. The only difference was that Reggie hadn't been with anyone since they'd last made love. It was almost like the very first time for her again. In the midst of their teasing, Trae paused, his mouth and hands slowed. He tried to remember if he had condoms in the house. He never brought women to his house. Most of his interludes had been planned and he generally had time to get what he needed on his way.

Damn, he spewed inwardly.

Reggie, even under the heat-filled passion could sense a change in Trae. Had he changed his mind? She slowly opened her eyes to his. Trae shifted his body and moved off of Reggie's. Worry in her eyes and face quickly won his attention.

"Something wrong?" her concerned voice reached his heart.

He kissed her briefly. "Honey, I don't think I have condoms in the house," he attempted to explain to ease the doubt in her eyes.

"Oh," she said, relieved. She would have been totally crushed had he said something else, like you don't warm my blood anymore.

"I don't do this, Reggie. I've never brought a woman to my house before," he explained.

Reggie was somewhat comforted by the thought although he hadn't said that he hadn't been with anyone since her. She knew better than to expect that he hadn't. After all, he was a man. They somehow attended to their needs a lot differently than women did. Women mostly ignored it, gone without, or filled their lives with clutter and busyness so that they didn't have time to consider that they lacked physical attention.

"Come on." He pulled her up by the arms.

He led her up the stairs. When they reached the top, they made a left and entered a large master bedroom suite. Reggie's attention was immediately pulled to the large bed snuggled against the far wall. It had four, high, column-like bedposts and was covered with an African print comforter. Tall green planters were positioned around the room along with African art, lamps, and stands, giving the room a safari look.

Trae pulled her through the room and didn't stop or let go of her hand until they stood in front of an exquisite rattan armoire. He pulled open the doors and lifted the top of a small box tucked away in the corner of one of the shelves.

Reggie eyes scanned the contents of the ornate storage compartments. The gold charm winked at her and instantly she knew what it was. Her fingers outlined it before she picked it up for closer inspection. Trae, still busy looking through the trays, hadn't seen her pick up the half-heart charm. She fingered it between her thumb and index finger. Her other hand went to the base of her throat. Hidden beneath the red T-shirt was the other half of the charm she held in her fingers.

Trae picked up a box and flipped it over to see the expiration date. He sighed with relief and it was then that he looked down at Reggie's hand at the base of her neck. He moved to the charm she fingered. The condoms forgotten momentarily, he pulled her hand down and fished beneath her shirt collar until his finger pulled out the charm dangling from a thin gold chain. Their eyes caught and held. Neither had truly given up the love they'd shared. No words were needed.

With the charm cupped in her hand, Reggie moved into Trae's arms. Unable to suppress his desire any longer, Trae made the first move by devouring her mouth until they both moaned. Without looking, he extended his hand across the armoire until he felt the small box of condoms, and without missing a beat he picked Reggie up and carried her to his bed.

His lips trailed down the front side of her body, stopping a second or two to savor the swells of her chest. He enjoyed rediscovering hidden spots that made her cry out his name. Reggie, with the charm still cupped in her hand, arched her body each time Trae's teeth nibbled a sensual spot. Her passion soared closer to a guaranteed eruption.

With a small measure of control, he worked her out of her clothes. His eyes ran down her body, drinking in the erotic dimensions of her fitted form and remembering what spots pushed her over the edge. His erection throbbed against the snug briefs. He watched her from beneath his heavy lashes, his focus set on the erotic patch between her legs. Her body sang with need. A light coat of perspiration covered her skin. Trae left the bed for a few seconds to strip away his clothes, and before he climbed back into it, he removed a silver foil packet from the box and laid it next to the platinum digital clock.

Reggie's heart raced and her entire body felt like it was on fire under Trae's intense gaze. The throb between her legs ached in the anticipation of having his body in hers. When he moved back onto the bed, his progression was slow and deliberate as though he moved in slow motion. He eased next to her; the hard taut muscles in his arms and chest bulged as he balanced his weight on the bed. His eyes were smoky and fiery all at once, speaking clearly his desires. They continued to sear her skin from head to toe. Slow tremors moved until they covered her entire body.

Trae moved closer to her. He strained to hold onto his composure. He had to take this nice and slow. He didn't want to hurt her. Just how he planned to get enough of her in one night and not hurt her was beyond his thinking abilities at this point. He knew she had to perform tomorrow, and he wanted to make certain she would be in a condition that wouldn't hamper her performance. His hand touched the half-heart charm flushed against her chest. He kissed it, then made his way down her trembling body.

He placed wet kisses along the insides of her thigh; the scent of her womanhood filled his nostrils. Using his hands, he slowly moved her legs apart, his tongue flickered side to side on the ripened flesh protruding from her core.

Reggie lost her mind the moment his kisses landed between her legs. The charm she'd held in her hand fell onto the soft cotton sheets. She rocked from side to side, her hips rising and falling with each gentle stroke. When she couldn't hold on any longer, she rode the wave that assaulted her body and mind. She cried Trae's name from the depths of her soul.

While Reggie was still caught up in the rapture of her orgasm, he trailed his kisses up her body again until his mouth covered her lips. His hand reached over to the nightstand for the condom. He took a moment to shield it over his hard shaft. Reggie's trembling hands helped roll it down the length of him, sending electrical shocks up his spine. He gently moved her legs apart and guided the ramrod-straight erection into her waiting body.

Both Reggie and Trae screamed when he entered her. Trae tried to coach himself, remembering it had been awhile for Reggie. Reggie's nails dug into his back, but Trae only felt the agony of his throbbing erection, which was about to explode. He covered her mouth and bit down on Reggie's lower lip, then the bottom of her chin. He continued to fight for composure; his large hands held firmly to her swaying hips to still her movement.

"Not yet, baby," he managed to grind out. Perspiration shielded his body. It was too late, Reggie had pushed him over the edge and he wasn't able to hold it back. Only the knowledge that she was coming over with him allowed him to let go entirely. Their screams pierced the sound of what ordinarily had been a silent room. Trae's body rocked in unison with Reggie's. The ride was long and hard. He grunted with each push into the tender flesh. Only when the last essence of his passion was released did he regain some control of his body.

When the ride down was completed, they held tightly to one

another. The rapid heartthrobs resounded in both of their chests and seemed to beat in unison. Trae supported the majority of his weight on his arm and legs. He held up as long as he could before he rolled over and pulled Reggie's sweat soaked body on top of his. Her head fell into the croak of his neck. Her hair sprawled across his chest.

Reggie was exhausted. Her body lay atop Trae, and she couldn't move one muscle. Trae held her firmly, not wanting her to move an inch. He needed and savored the warmth of her body on his. If it were left up to him, they would stay in this bed for a month. He knew that would never happen, at least not just yet. He kissed the top of her head. She didn't move. She'd fallen asleep. Trae allowed his guard down and he, too, entered the slumber world.

Trae's eyes opened at five like clockwork. He glanced at the digital clock on the nightstand. The body sprawled on top of him brought a crooked smile to his mouth. He closed his embrace tighter. Reggie's head came up, and sleepy eyes and a smile met him.

"Hi, sweetheart," he crooned.

His whole body was alive. His heart soared like a raging river. Eighteen months of misery vanished. Nothing between the time they'd been apart mattered. His loving eyes touched her completely.

"Hi, yourself." The dimples winked at him.

"Do you want to soak?" he asked.

Reggie shook her hand no. Surprisingly, her body openly yielded to Trae last night. She wasn't sore. In fact, she yearned to make love to him again.

"No. It's too early," she pouted. "I want you to love me again."

Trae rolled her over, and his large frame laid partially on top of her.

"If I love you again Reggie, you won't be performing tonight."

" I don't think you can handle it," she bluffed.

The unruly passion erected its head. It lurked in the recess of his dark penetrating gaze.

"Don't bite off more than you can chew," he warned.

"I want you, Traekin," her hand ran down the hair-stubbed face. "I need you, baby."

Trae needed no further coaching. He would be lucky if he got to the office by mid-morning.

CHAPTER 28

Three days just wasn't enough time when they only got to see each other between and after Reggie's performances. Following the first night they spent together, Reggie was antsy. The show and the dance, for the first time in awhile, was a nuisance. Unlike the previous evening, taking off make-up and gathering her belongings hadn't taken any time. She rushed out of the dressing room and into Trae's waiting arms. It wasn't until the third night that she and Trae visited his family. Reggie changed her reservations to return to New York several days later. It gave her time to see her grandmother, and at the same time, allowed her more time with Trae. She didn't expect the visit to his parent's house to be overly welcoming.

Cheri was the most concerned. She remembered the tough time Trae had the first few months after the accident. Reggie understood Cheri's apprehension and felt like a defense lawyer, trying to state and justify her case. There had been no doubt that the two loved each other even now. As parents, they wanted to make sure that the duo didn't rush into anything that would do more damage in the end.

The trip to her grandmother's house was the most rewarding and promising for the couple. Trae's car turned off of I-10 at the Donaldsonville exit. Just before crossing the Mississippi River on the Sunshine Bridge, Trae followed the two-lane roads in to the small community, Convent. Time seemed to stand still in the sleepy river town. When they pulled into the graveled driveway, Margaret was waiting for them on the front porch. She knew right away that she liked Reggie's young man. She helped them sort out the puzzle that destined them for a long life together. She told animated stories about her and Reggie's grandfather, Richard Miles. In the swing out on the screen porch was where they had a chance to talk, dream, and plan out their lives together.

Even though he would be willing to relocate, Reggie knew she could dance in any city and thought the idea of Trae settled into his family's business was stable and full of possibilities to restore and advance the company. Besides, he'd already told her he hated the cold weather and wanted to stay someplace where it was warm. She just didn't care where they lived, as long as they were together.

"Can we live on Mars?" she joked.

"I think we would get an eviction notice within two weeks," Trae teased.

Reggie jabbed him in the side for his snide remark. She leaned back into Trae's side and looked up into his partially closed lids. He was totally and ultimately more relaxed than he'd ever remembered being.

"Do you want children, Trae?" she asked.

"Yes," he remarked without opening his eyes.

"How many?"

"Six." He opened his eyes this time to gauge her response.

Of course Reggie's mouth flew opened. No one she knew had more than two, maybe three kids. This man wanted six.

"Six?" she exasperated.

"Six. How many did you want?" he asked.

"Two," she answered confidently.

"Well, let's see, your two and my six, that means we can have eight." He smiled.

Reggie's eyes grew the size of saucers. "Certainly you're kidding, Traekin Brooks."

Trae's face lit into a crooked grin. He loved poking fun at his now-intended. He closed his arms around her and kissed her on the cheek.

"I tell you what… how about a compromise. You want two, I want six, down the middle of my six is three. How about three?" he offered.

Reggie smiled into his handsome face. She loved this man. Her days and nights were certainly going to be eventful, to say the least. "It's a deal. Three children." She grinned.

"You better hope we have three girls, because if you have three boys like my brothers and me, you're going to be in big trouble," he sneered.

Her grin vanished She'd seen Trae and his brothers in action. As she continued to think about that possibility, a smile returned to her beautiful oval face.

"I don't care, as long as they are healthy," she reassured. "I can handle Brooks' boys."

They swung for several minutes in the aged swing before Reggie posed her next question.

"When we celebrate our fiftieth anniversary, will you promise me one thing?" she asked.

"What's that?"

"That you look into my eyes the way your father looks at your mother." She smiled happily into his face. "I want the way you touch me to still send chills down my spine and make me feel complete." The thought of being with him for fifty years and sharing the same kind of love their parents' have, warmed her heart.

Trae considered her request for a short moment. "Yes," he answered without reservation. "More than anything in the world, I want that kind of love and more."

They snuggled for a long moment, quietly thinking about what love meant to them. Trae rested his face on top of Reggie's head. His hands lovingly caressed her back.

"I never thought I would be lucky enough to find a love like the one my parents share, Reggie," he admitted. "Until I met you, I'm not sure I wanted that at all. Believe me, when I made that bet with Rykard, finding my soulmate was the farthest thing from my mind."

He paused and pulled away so that he could see her face. He never once considered that a twenty-dollar ante would change his entire life, let alone promise him fifty years of cherished love.

"I remember the first time I touched you. I knew nothing would ever be the same again." His eyes moved across her face, remembering every detail. She smiled, and her dimples winked at him.

"I didn't know what I was doing, Trae. I just followed my heart," she confessed.

"I'm thankful I made that bet. It wasn't the smartest thing to do at the time, but my life is so much better because I did. I promise never to betray you or your love ever again," he whispered.

Tears glistened in Reggie's eyes. Yes, he'd gotten more than a bargain, but so had she. He leaned down and savored her lips until the world around them disappeared.

AUTHOR BIOGRAPHY

Ann Clay and her family reside in Southern Illinois. She enjoys reading, writing, crafts, and family time. She earned a Bachelors of Science Degree in Industrial Technology from Southern Illinois University at Carbondale and a Masters of Arts Degree in Computer Resources and Information Management from Webster University in St Louis Missouri.

Ann began writing in 1999. ***More than a Bargain*** is her debut novel. She has published several short stories with various on-line magazines and is a member of Romance Writers of America and Missouri Chapter of Romance Writers of America.

Thanks to the support of family and friends, Ann shares her heartwarming stories with readers of the heart.

EXCERPT FROM
CAUGHT UP IN THE RAPTURE
BY
LISA G. RILEY
Publication Date August 2004

Thirteen years earlier

Jack Winthrop stared hard at Julie Emery. There she stood in the middle of her parents' richly appointed parlor looking like the ultimate high society debutante. But she was using again; he could tell. His trained eye spotted the signs. Her eyes darted about the room, never landing in one place, her skin had the cast of an addict and her too-thin body practically vibrated as she paced jerkily from one end of the room to the other.

Jack gently grasped her shoulders to hold her still. "Julie, you're doing cocaine again, aren't you? Why, honey, after all the work we did to get you clean and back to your parents?"

Julie swallowed and looked down. Refusing to look at him, because she never could and lie, she broke away from his grasp and stumbled back. "It's r-r-really none of your business what I do, Jack Winthrop. I-I-I don't need your help. I'm doing fine on my own. So why don't you go back to Chicago and do what you do best—be a cop. You're not my social worker!"

Jack looked cautiously into her green eyes. He'd first run across her two years ago when she'd been a 19-year-old University of Chicago dropout selling her body to get the drugs she so desperately craved.

He'd been a rookie cop who'd thought he could save the world. Because she'd really seemed to want to get help, he'd taken an interest in her. He'd gotten her into a shelter and into a drug treatment program. He'd even helped her find a job so that she could make the money to go back home to Boston.

She'd been afraid to ask her wealthy parents for help, saying that they wouldn't take her back until she showed them that she'd made the effort to turn her life around.

With a lot of hard work, she'd done it and six months ago, he'd put her on a plane to Boston, promising her that he'd keep in touch and come visit whenever he had a chance.

Well, here he was and there she was, looking as if a good, stiff wind would blow her over. "Julie, what happened?"

Julie swiped at the mucous that was perpetually dripping from her raw nostrils. She wished Jack would just leave her alone. Why couldn't he and her parents understand that she was fine? "Nothing happened, okay?" She avoided his eyes. "Just go away, Jack and don't ever come back! I don't need you or your self-righteous help. Go find some other cause to get behind, because I'm getting married and I don't need your help anymore. Everything is fine." She swiped at the mucous again in agitation.

Jack pulled his handkerchief out of his pocket and gently wiped the blood from her nose. Blood that he was sure she didn't even know was oozing from her nostrils. "You're bleeding, Julie. Here, hold your head back."

Julie snatched the handkerchief and moved away from him. "I don't need your help, Jack!" she repeated in a muffled voice as she held the handkerchief in place over her nose. "This doesn't mean anything. Everyone has nosebleeds. It's perfectly normal." God, she wanted a fix so bad, she could almost taste it.

"Do your parents know that you're using? Your fiancé—does he know?"

"Leave my parents out of this. As for my fiancé, I've known him since we were children and he understands me. He's a very generous man because he loves me. He gets whatever I need from his cousin."

Suddenly, she desperately wanted him to understand and she tossed the handkerchief aside to grab his hands. "You don't have to worry, Jack. It's not like it was in Chicago. I'm safe. Kevin's cousin Alex has the finest powder on the eastern seaboard. He supplies all of my friends. We don't have to go out looking for it, it comes to us."

Jack sighed. "What have you gotten yourself into, Julie? Is that why you're marrying this guy? For the drugs he can get you? Come with me. I can get you into another treatment program."

Julie's face twisted in anger and she threw his hands away from her. "Screw you, Jack! I love Kevin Brickman and he loves me. My parents like him as well. He's from one of the finest families in the state and I'm not going to let you screw this up for me! Get out before I have you thrown out!"

Jack turned away to leave, but said over his shoulder. "You know how to reach me if you need me. Call me at any time, day or night." He left.

Four months later, Jack came across an article in a news magazine. The title read, *From Debutante to Strung-Out Prostitute: How a Child of One of Massachusetts' Most Prominent Families Ended Up Dead in Back Alley Boston.* Underneath the title was a picture of a smiling, healthy Julie, blonde hair shining, green eyes sparkling. Jack hurled the magazine across the room. The bastards had killed her. He knew that Julie's fiancé and his cousin were responsible for her death as sure as he knew his own name.

CHAPTER ONE

Jack opened the door to his Parisian flat and dropped his carryall on the floor. He was disgusted, exhausted and supremely pissed off. He sighed and walked over to slouch on his sofa. That Brickman bastard was just too slippery. He'd been chasing Alexander Brickman for eight months now. This time around, anyway. In the grand scheme of things, he'd actually been after Brickman for 13 years. This last round, he'd started in Chicago, then on to the Bahamas, where a rookie mistake had made him lose him. Then it was on to the Cayman Islands and now, here he was in Paris.

Brickman's trail was getting harder and harder to follow. The man was a criminal genius and the time Jack had to catch him was fast running out. As it was, the money for this trip to Paris had come out of his own pocket. After he'd lost Brickman in the Cayman Islands, his "boss" at the agency had said he was on his own. She'd given him two weeks to "find the slug and get your pretty-boy ass back to Chicago, or else you'll be out of a job! I don't care if you are only free-lance!"

She'd hung up before he could point out that as an independent, his time was his own and he could take two months or two years if he wanted. He'd turned in his resignation with the department all those months ago specifically so he could go free-lance and not worry about the bureaucratic red tape that came hand in hand with a "government job."

Jack rose and went to look out the window of his flat. The view was magnificent, but he barely took notice of the Seine or Notre Dame. Catching Brickman and putting him behind bars were the only things on his mind. No one understood his obsession because he'd never told them about Julie and what Brickman had done to her. No one needed to know; it was enough that he did. The fiancé was already taken care of. He'd died of an overdose several years before. Jack went up the stairs to his bedroom. Brickman was long gone for the day. He'd track him again tomorrow, but for now, he'd just go down to the café, let his uncle know he was back in town and enjoy an early dinner.

2004 Publication Schedule

January	Cautious Heart Cheris F. Hodges $8.95 1-58571-106-3	Bodyguard Andrea Jackson $8.95 1-58571-114-4
February	Wedding Gown Dyanne Davis $8.95 1-58571-120-9	Erotic Anthology Simone Harlow & Caroline Stone $14.95 1-58571-113-6
March	Crossing Paths, Tempting Memories Dorothy Elizabeth Love $9.95 1-58571-116-0	Office Policy A.C. Arthur $9.95 1-58571-119-5
April-July	No Titles	
August	More Than a Bargain Ann Clay $9.95 1-58571-137-3	Code Name: Diva J. M. Jeffries $9.95 1-58571-144-6
September	Vows of Passion Bella McFarland $9.95 1-58571-118-7	Time Is of the Essence Angie Daniels $9.95 1-58571-132-2
	Stories to Excite You Anna Forrest & Ken Divine $14.95 1-58571-103-9	
October	Hard to Love Kimberley White $9.95 1-58571-128-4	A Happy Life Charlotte Harris $9.95 1-58571-133-0
November	Caught Up in the Rapture Lisa G. Riley $9.95 1-58571-127-6	Lace Giselle Carmichael $9.95 1-58571-134-9
December	A Heart's Awakening Veronica Parker $9.95 1-58571-143-9	Path of Thorns Annetta P. Lee $9.95 1-58571-145-4

After February, the size of the titles will increase to 5 3/16 x 8 1/2, as will the price to $9.95.

2005 Publication Schedule

January

Echoes of Yesterday
Beverly Clark
$9.95
1-58571-131-4

A Love of Her Own
Cheris F. Hodges
$9.95
1-58571-136-5

Higher Ground
Leah Latimer
$19.95
1-58571-157-8

February

Timeless Devotion
Bella McFarland
$9.95
1-58571-148-9

I'll Paint the Sun
Al Garotto
$9.95
1-58571-165-9

Peace Be Still
Colette Haywood
$12.95
1-58571-129-2

March

Intentional Mistakes
Michele Sudler
$9.95
1-58571-152-7

Conquering Dr. Wexler's Heart
Kimberley White
$9.95
1-58571-126-8

Song in the Park
Martin Brant
$15.95
1-58571-125-X

April

The Color Line
Lizette Carter
$9.95
1-58571-163-2

Unconditional
A.C. Arthur
$9.95
1-58571-142-X

Last Train to Memphis
Elsa Cook
$12.95
1-58571-146-2

May

Angel's Paradise
Janice Angelique
$9.95
1-58571-107-1

Suddenly You
Crystal Hubbard
$9.95
1-58571-158-6

Matters of Life and Death
Lesego Malepe, Ph.D.
$15.95
1-58571-124-1

June

Pleasures All Mine
Belinda O. Steward
$9.95
1-58571-112-8

Wild Ravens
Altonya Washington
$9.95
1-58571-164-0

Class Reunion
Irma Jenkins/John Brown
$12.95
1-58571-123-3

July

Falling
Natalie Dunbar
$9.95
1-58571-121-7

Misconceptions
Pamela Leigh Starr
$9.95
1-58571-117-9

Life Is Never As It Seems
June Michael
$12.95
1-58571-153-5

August

Beyond the Rapture
Beverly Clark
$9.95
1-58571-131-4

Taken By You
Dorothy Elizabeth Love
$9.95
1-58571-162-4

Rough on Rats and Tough
 on Cats
Chris Parker
$12.95
1-58571-154-3

2005 Publication Schedule (continued)

September

A Will to Love
Angie Daniels
$9.95
1-58571-141-1

Blood Lust
J.M. Jeffries
$9.95
1-58571-138-1

Soul Eyes
Wayne L. Wilson
$12.95
1-58571-147-0

October

Blaze
Barbara Keaton
$9.95

Untitled
Kimberley White
$9.95
1-58571-159-4

Red Polka Dot in a World
  of Plaid
Varian Johnson
$12.95
1-58571-140-3

November

Hand in Glove
Andrea Jackson
$9.95
1-58571-166-7

Untitled
A.C. Arthur
$9.95

Across
Carol Payne
$12.95
1-58571-149-7

December

Bound for Mt. Zion
Chris Parker
$12.95
1-58571-155-1

Other Genesis Press, Inc. Titles

Acquisitions	Kimberley White	$8.95
A Dangerous Deception	J.M. Jeffries	$8.95
A Dangerous Love	J.M. Jeffries	$8.95
A Dangerous Obsession	J.M. Jeffries	$8.95
After the Vows	Leslie Esdaile	$10.95
(Summer Anthology)	T.T. Henderson	
	Jacqueline Thomas	
Again My Love	Kayla Perrin	$10.95
Against the Wind	Gwynne Forster	$8.95
A Lark on the Wing	Phyliss Hamilton	$8.95
A Lighter Shade of Brown	Vicki Andrews	$8.95
All I Ask	Barbara Keaton	$8.95
A Love to Cherish	Beverly Clark	$8.95
Ambrosia	T.T. Henderson	$8.95
And Then Came You	Dorothy Elizabeth Love	$8.95
Angel's Paradise	Janice Angelique	$8.95
A Risk of Rain	Dar Tomlinson	$8.95
At Last	Lisa G. Riley	$8.95
Best of Friends	Natalie Dunbar	$8.95
Bound by Love	Beverly Clark	$8.95
Breeze	Robin Hampton Allen	$10.95
Brown Sugar Diaries &	Delores Bundy &	$10.95
Other Sexy Tales	Cole Riley	
By Design	Barbara Keaton	$8.95
Cajun Heat	Charlene Berry	$8.95
Careless Whispers	Rochelle Alers	$8.95
Caught in a Trap	Andre Michelle	$8.95
Chances	Pamela Leigh Starr	$8.95
Dark Embrace	Crystal Wilson Harris	$8.95
Dark Storm Rising	Chinelu Moore	$10.95
Designer Passion	Dar Tomlinson	$8.95
Ebony Butterfly II	Delilah Dawson	$14.95
Erotic Anthology	Assorted	$8.95
Eve's Prescription	Edwina Martin Arnold	$8.95
Everlastin' Love	Gay G. Gunn	$8.95

Fate	Pamela Leigh Starr	$8.95
Forbidden Quest	Dar Tomlinson	$10.95
Fragment in the Sand	Annetta P. Lee	$8.95
From the Ashes	Kathleen Suzanne	$8.95
	Jeanne Sumerix	
Gentle Yearning	Rochelle Alers	$10.95
Glory of Love	Sinclair LeBeau	$10.95
Hart & Soul	Angie Daniels	$8.95
Heartbeat	Stephanie Bedwell-Grime	$8.95
I'll Be Your Shelter	Giselle Carmichael	$8.95
Illusions	Pamela Leigh Starr	$8.95
Indiscretions	Donna Hill	$8.95
Interlude	Donna Hill	$8.95
Intimate Intentions	Angie Daniels	$8.95
Just an Affair	Eugenia O'Neal	$8.95
Kiss or Keep	Debra Phillips	$8.95
Love Always	Mildred E. Riley	$10.95
Love Unveiled	Gloria Greene	$10.95
Love's Deception	Charlene Berry	$10.95
Mae's Promise	Melody Walcott	$8.95
Meant to Be	Jeanne Sumerix	$8.95
Midnight Clear	Leslie Esdaile	$10.95
(Anthology)	Gwynne Forster	
	Carmen Green	
	Monica Jackson	
Midnight Magic	Gwynne Forster	$8.95
Midnight Peril	Vicki Andrews	$10.95
My Buffalo Soldier	Barbara B. K. Reeves	$8.95
Naked Soul	Gwynne Forster	$8.95
No Regrets	Mildred E. Riley	$8.95
Nowhere to Run	Gay G. Gunn	$10.95
Object of His Desire	A. C. Arthur	$8.95
One Day at a Time	Bella McFarland	$8.95
Passion	T.T. Henderson	$10.95
Past Promises	Jahmel West	$8.95
Path of Fire	T.T. Henderson	$8.95
Picture Perfect	Reon Carter	$8.95

Pride & Joi	Gay G. Gunn	$8.95
Quiet Storm	Donna Hill	$8.95
Reckless Surrender	Rochelle Alers	$8.95
Rendezvous with Fate	Jeanne Sumerix	$8.95
Revelations	Cheris F. Hodges	$8.95
Rivers of the Soul	Leslie Esdaile	$8.95
Rooms of the Heart	Donna Hill	$8.95
Shades of Brown	Denise Becker	$8.95
Shades of Desire	Monica White	$8.95
Sin	Crystal Rhodes	$8.95
So Amazing	Sinclair LeBeau	$8.95
Somebody's Someone	Sinclair LeBeau	$8.95
Someone to Love	Alicia Wiggins	$8.95
Soul to Soul	Donna Hill	$8.95
Still Waters Run Deep	Leslie Esdaile	$8.95
Subtle Secrets	Wanda Y. Thomas	$8.95
Sweet Tomorrows	Kimberly White	$8.95
The Color of Trouble	Dyanne Davis	$8.95
The Price of Love	Sinclair LeBeau	$8.95
The Reluctant Captive	Joyce Jackson	$8.95
The Missing Link	Charlyne Dickerson	$8.95
Three Wishes	Seressia Glass	$8.95
Tomorrow's Promise	Leslie Esdaile	$8.95
Truly Inseperable	Wanda Y. Thomas	$8.95
Twist of Fate	Beverly Clark	$8.95
Unbreak My Heart	Dar Tomlinson	$8.95
Unconditional Love	Alicia Wiggins	$8.95
When Dreams A Float	Dorothy Elizabeth Love	$8.95
Whispers in the Night	Dorothy Elizabeth Love	$8.95
Whispers in the Sand	LaFlorya Gauthier	$10.95
Yesterday is Gone	Beverly Clark	$8.95
Yesterday's Dreams, Tomorrow's Promises	Reon Laudat	$8.95
Your Precious Love	Sinclair LeBeau	$8.95

Order Form

Mail to: Genesis Press, Inc.

P.O. Box 101
Columbus, MS 39701

Name _____
Address _____
City/State _____ Zip _____
Telephone _____

Ship to (if different from above)
Name _____
Address _____
City/State _____ Zip _____
Telephone _____

Credit Card Information
Credit Card # _____ ☐ Visa ☐ Mastercard
Expiration Date (mm/yy) _____ ☐ AmEx ☐ Discover

Qty.	Author	Title	Price	Total

Use this order

form, or call

1-888-INDIGO-1

Total for books _____
Shipping and handling:
  $5 first two books,
  $1 each additional book _____
Total S & H
Total amount enclosed _____
Mississippi residents add 7% sales tax

Visit www.genesis-press.com for latest releases and excerpts.